# Praise for *Sea of Red*

"Sea or Red is one of the year's best military thrillers."
-*BestThrillers.com*

"This is a book for true military buffs. A military thriller
with…high stakes." -*Kirkus Reviews*

"High Stakes and well plotted, the military thriller Sea of Red
reflects how real soldiers think and act…a gripping military thriller.
-*Foreword Clarion*

Award Finalist 2023 -American Fiction Awards
Award Finalist 2023 -BestThrillers.com
Award Winner 2024 -Independent Press Award

"An adrenaline-fueled military thriller...with fast-paced action and a
gripping narrative...a thrilling ride from start to finish...5 out 5
stars." -*OnlineBookClub*

"Right from the first page, Bultema makes it clear to audiences that
this is no ordinary thriller...In this sweeping saga...Strong-willed
characters and nonstop action...makes for a battle royale that
exhilarates all the way to the end."
-*US Review of Books*

"A thriller that becomes increasingly frenetic with each passing
moment...Bultema's military thriller hums with hyperactivity while
offering a deep dive into the perilous realm of geopolitics, from
grand strategies to ground-level intricacies" -*Blueink Review*

"Sea of Red is exemplary in production quality and cover
design...and will appeal to many readers... This book is exemplary
in character appeal (or interest) and development. All main
characters (including antagonists) are unique and fully fleshed out
with compelling, layered motivations and traits...Sea of Red is
exemplary in its voice and writing style...The premise is something
out of today's headlines and with the addition of the glossary, and
maps will appeal to readers of military and war fiction."

# Sea of Red

James Bultema

## ALSO BY JAMES BULTEMA

Non-Fiction
*Guardians of Angels: A History of the Los Angeles Police Department
1869 – 2019*
*Unsolved Cold-Case Homicides of Law Enforcement Officers*
*The Protectors: A Photographic History of Police Departments in the
United States*
*Gangsters and Cops: Prohibition, Corruption, and LAPD's Scandalous
Coming of Age (2023)*

Documentary
*Behind the Badge: An Insiders History of the Los Angeles Police
Department*

# Contents



Chapter 1

*ROYAL MALAYSIAN NAVY GUIDED MISSILE FRIGATE KD JEBAT, ARLEIGH BURKE GUIDED-MISSILE DESTROYER USS CURTIS WILBUR*
South China Sea



*UNITED STATES NAVAL ACADEMY*
Annapolis, Maryland



*THE WHITE HOUSE*
Washington DC



*NAVAL BASE SAN DIEGO*
San Diego, California



*BEIDAIHE BEACH RESORT*
Beidaihe, China



*ANQUING TIANZHUSHAN AIRPORT*
Anquing Tianzhushan, China



*NORTHROP GRUMMAN E-2D ADVANCED HAWKEYE*
South China Sea



*USS RONALD REAGAN*
South China Sea



*MINISTRY OF NATIONAL DEFENSE*
Beijing, China

# Glossary of Acronyms

| | |
|---|---|
| A2/AD | Anti-access/area denial |
| ADIZ | Air Defense Identification Zone |
| Aegis | Advanced command and control system |
| AESA | Active Electronically Scanned Array (radar) |
| AMRAAM | Advanced Medium Range Air-to-Air Missile |
| ARG | Amphibious ready group |
| ASCM | Anti-ship cruise missile |
| ASUW | Anti-surface warfare |
| ASW | Anti-submarine warfare |
| AWACS | Airborne Warning and Control System |
| BARCAP | Barrier Combat Air Patrol |
| BMD | Ballistic Missile Defense |
| BMDO | Ballistic Missile Defense Operations |
| BMDS | Ballistic Missile Defense System |
| BVR | Beyond Visual Range |
| BVRAAM | Beyond visual range air-to-air missile |
| C2BMC | Command, Control, Battle Management, and Communications system |
| CAP | Combat Air Patrol |
| CCDI | Central Commission for Discipline Inspection |
| CEC | Cooperative Engagement Capability |
| CEP | Circular Error of Probability |
| CIC | Combat Information Center |
| CICO | Combat Information Center Officer |
| CJCS | Chairman of the Joint Chiefs of Staff |
| CMC | Central Military Commission |
| COMCARSTRKGRU | Commander, Carrier Strike Group |
| CSG | Carrier Strike Group |
| CWA | China World Airlines |
| DNI | Director of National Intelligence |
| EOTS | Electro-Optical Targeting System |
| FONOP | Freedom of navigation operation |
| HCDS | Harpoon Coastal Defense System |
| HUD | Head up display |
| JASSM | Joint Air-to-Surface Standoff Missile |
| JDAM | Joint Direct Attack Munition |

| JSDCMC | China's Joint Staff Department of the Central Military |
| LAPD | Los Angeles Police Department |
| LCAC | Landing Craft Air Cushion |
| Link 16 | Datalink system for whole-force comms |
| LRASM | Long-range anti-ship missile |
| L-T | The spoken form of lieutenant |
| MC-1 | Shipboard comm system |
| M-SHORAD | Maneuver-Short Range Air Defense |
| MSS | Ministry of State Security (China) |
| NATO | North Atlantic Treaty Organization |
| NFO | Naval Flight Officer |
| NSA | National Security Administration |
| NSC | National Security Council |
| NSM | Navy Strike Missile |
| OOD | Officer of the Deck (Navy) |
| PAL | Permissive Action Links (codes to launch missiles) |
| PAVE PAWS | Precision Acquisition Vehicle Entry Phased Array Warning System |
| PLA | People's Liberation Army |
| PLAAF | People's Liberation Army Air Force |
| PLAN | People's Liberation Army Navy |
| PLARF | People's Liberation Army Rocket Force |
| PRC | People's Republic of China |
| PSC | Politburo Standing Committee |
| RED HORSE | Rapid Engineer Deployable Heavy Operational Repair Squadron Engineer |
| RO | Radar operator |
| ROC | Republic of China - Taiwan |
| ROE | Rules of engagement |
| ROTC | Reserve Officer Training Corps |
| RWR | Radar Warning Receiver |
| SAM | Surface to Air Missile |
| SAR | Search and Rescue Swimmer |
| SAR | Synthetic Aperture Radar |
| SCS | South China Sea |
| SEAD | Suppression of Enemy Air Defenses |

| SRAAM | Short-range air-to-air missile |
| SRBM | Short Range Ballistic Missile |
| SWO | Surface Warfare Officer (Navy) |
| TACTAS | Tactical Towed Array Sonar |
| THADD | Terminal High Altitude Area Defense |
| TSA | Taiwan Security Act |
| UAV | Unmanned Aerial Vehicle |
| USINDOPACOM | United States Indo-Pacific Command |
| USPACFLT | United States Pacific Fleet |
| VLS | Vertical Launching System |
| WVR | Within Visual Range |

## Principal Characters

### Royal Malaysian Navy

| | |
|---|---|
| Captain Ahmad | Captain of the Royal Malaysian Navy Missile Frigate KD *Jebat* |

### United States Government

| | |
|---|---|
| Mark Taylor | President of the United States |
| Brad Kelly | Secretary of State |
| Elena Ramirez | Director of National Intelligence |
| General Robert Matthews | Chairman of the Joint Chiefs of Staff |
| George Mitchell | Secretary of Defense, |
| James Richardson | Vice President of the United States |
| Logan Wright | Chief of Staff |
| Robbie Spencer | Assistant to the President for National Security Affairs |

### United States Military

| | |
|---|---|
| Billy Ottenberg | Radio operator - E-2D Hawkeye |
| Brett Jansen | Ensign, a recent graduate from Naval Academy and assigned to USS *Mustin* |
| Carlos Martinez | Lieutenant Junior Grade, Pilot P-8A Poseidon maritime patrol aircraft |
| Elam Feldner | Commanding officer of the submarine USS *Missouri* |
| Harley "Snake Eyes" Jennings | Gunny Sergeant, Marine NCO with Naval Strike Missile Defense System on Woody Island |
| Henry "Hank" Winston | Colonial, USMC, Commanding officer of Woody Island |
| Horace Washington Smith | Chief Master Sergeant, Red Horses, the Rapid Engineer Deployable Heavy Operational Repair Engineers |
| Jason Roberts | Captain, Commanding officer of the USS *Reagan* |
| Jerome Albright | Petty Officer 3rd class, Sonar operator aboard the USS *Missouri* |
| Jessie Hampton | Lieutenant, F-18 pilot from the USS *Ford* |

Liam Javernick                    PO3, ATO/SAR on MH-60R Seahawk
                                  helicopter
Lucy Wu                           Lieutenant, Pilot of Sikorsky MH-60R
                                  Seahawk helicopter, USS *Reagan*
Nathan Hubbard                    Captain, Company commander in the
                                  82nd Brigade, 2nd Battalion, 504th
                                  Parachute Infantry Regiment, Fort Bragg
Roy "Rogers" Calhoun              LTJG, Copilot on E-2D Hawkeye
Sarah "Danger" Freeman            Lieutenant, pilot of US Navy E-2D
                                  Hawkeye
Theodore Cummings II              Captain, Commanding officer of the USS
                                  *Michigan*
Thomas "Solo" Kronbach            Major, USAF B-1B pilot
Tod Bailey                        Captain, Commanding officer of the USS
                                  *Mustin*

## People's Republic of China

Zhang Wei                         President of the People's Republic of
                                  China
Li Chang                          Captain, Commanding officer of a PLAN
                                  submarine
Jian Ts'ui                        Colonial, Commander of Woody Island
Dr. Dong Liang                    Assigned to Central Military
                                  Commission. Missile code expert
Li Jung                           General, third in command behind the
                                  president and General Wang
Sun Tong                          General, former H-6 pilot
Wang Yong                         General, second in command of the PLA
                                  behind the president
Li Zhang                          State Council of the People's Republic of
                                  China
Chang Huang                       Major, J-20 pilot, married to the
                                  president's daughter
Jia Xiao                          Read Admiral, commanding officer of
                                  the PLN amphibious assault ship the
                                  Hainan
Wan Jun                           Former president of China
Ye Jiang                          Premier of China

## Republic of China (Taiwan)

| | |
|---|---|
| Chen Guang | President of the Republic of China – Taiwan |
| Albert Chang | Supervisor of Taiwan's most valuable radar site |
| Jimmy Chen | Pilot of the F-16V fighter |
| Randy Sha | Master Sergeant assigned to Presidential Security and Protective Service |
| Sang Sen-fan | Military police officer |

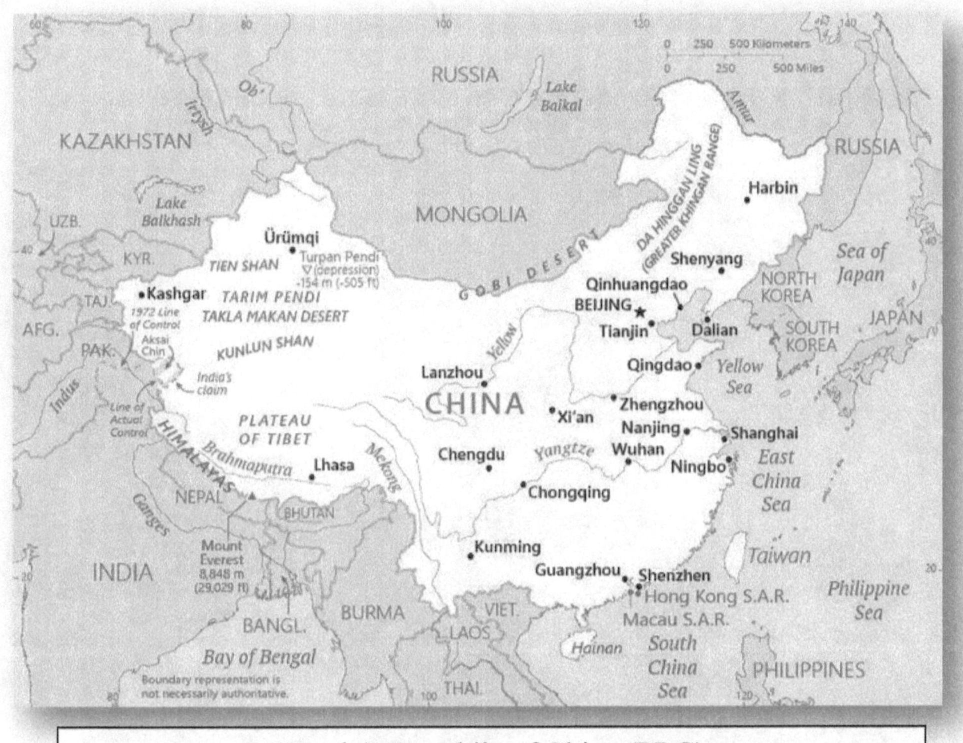


People's Republic of China (PRC)

Courtesy of Central Intelligence Agency - Maps

Woody Island, South China Sea

Courtesy of Mapcarta

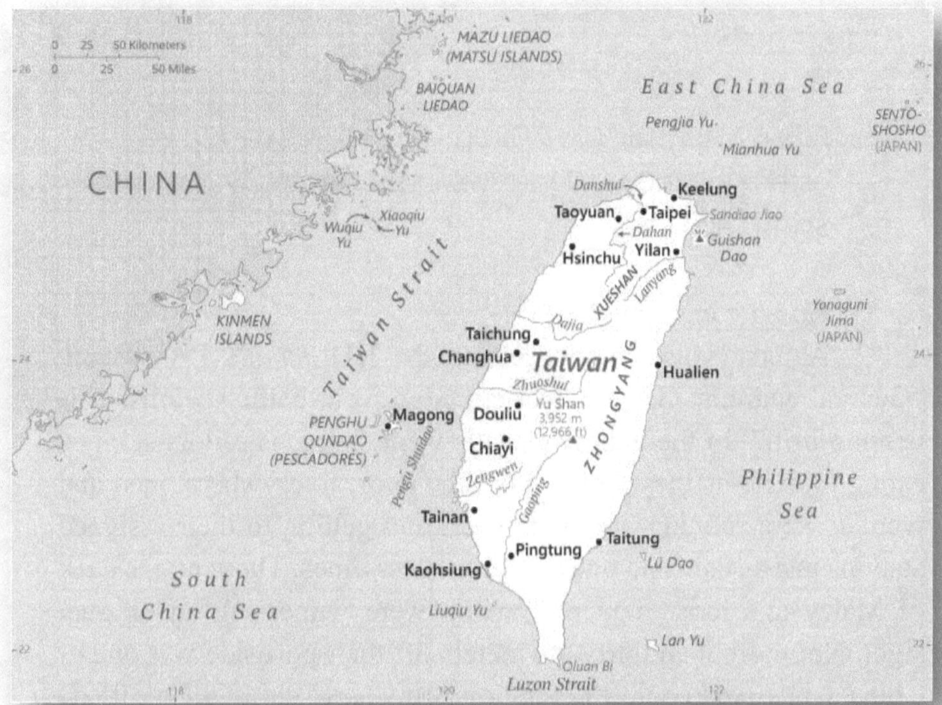


## Republic of China (ROC) Taiwan

Courtesy of Central Intelligence Agency – Maps

# Chapter 1



*Gong, gong, gong.*

A terse voice announced on the KD *Jebat*'s PA system, "General quarters. General quarters. Man, your battle stations. This is not a drill." In the galley, utensils went flying as sailors stopped eating midbite as they sprinted out the door. Everywhere, men and women were running, grabbing gear, and getting to their assigned stations just as they had practiced countless times. Those on the deck of Malaysia's most modern warship were witnessing an unusual sight. Not more than thirty-six meters off their port side was one of China's massive People's Liberation Army Navy ships, a Type 052D guided missile destroyer identified by NATO as a Luyang III ship of war. It was immense and dwarfed the much smaller frigate. The sight of the Chinese destroyer wasn't rare, but the vessel's disregard of their warnings to give way to the *Jebat* was bold.

The crew of the United States Navy's USS *Curtis Wilbur* observed the Chinese destroyer's tactics. The *Curtis Wilbur* and the *Jebat* had been participating in joint military exercises and Freedom of Navigation Operations in the South China Sea for the past week.

Using the partner-nation, classified CENTRIXS comms, Captain Ted Fletcher contacted the KD *Jebat*. "Storm Hawk, Steel Hammer. Captain Ahmad, keep your ship steady and on course. Don't give the Chinese a reason to ram you. USPACFLT doesn't want us to provoke them."

Sounding perturbed, Ahmad answered, "That's fine for you, Captain, but it was my country's drone the Chinese shot down last month. In my way of thinking, that's an act of war."

"I understand, but let's not turn this exercise into a shooting situation."

With the two warships traveling at 15 knots and nearly side-by-side, the Chinese destroyer inched closer to the much smaller frigate, so close that sailors on the *Jebat* could practically read the Chinese sailors' name tags.

Across the static-ridden international distress and emergency frequency that all vessels are supposed to monitor, the Guard frequency, a male voice warned in accented English, "Attention, all military vessels, this is Chinese territory. China has sovereignty over these islands. You are in violation of our region. The Chinese government demands that you leave the area immediately."

Ahmad quickly grabbed the radio mic. "This is Captain Ahmad of the Royal Malaysian Navy. We are not altering our course until you explain why you shot down our unarmed UAV without provocation."

In broken English, the Chinese captain replied, "The captain of this ship denies shooting down any drone and again demands all foreign vessels leave our territorial waters—now."

Not interfering with the exchange for fear of escalating the tense situation, Captain Fletcher listened to the discourse and kept USPACFLT updated. A message flashed on his comms screen: "From USPACFLT, do not engage the Chinese and use safe maneuvers to remove your ship from the situation."

Captain Fletcher keyed the CENTRIXS mic. "Storm Hawk, Steel Hammer. Orders from USPACFLT are to disengage. I am maneuvering away from this area, and you are to do the same. The UAV situation is above our pay grade and will be managed by senior command. Do you copy?"

Several long seconds passed with no reply. Captain Fletcher lifted the mic to make another transmission.

"Steel Hammer, Storm Hawk," Captain Ahmad finally replied, "I'm afraid I have to disagree, but we will follow orders and are maneuvering from the area."

# Chapter 2



*United States Naval Academy*
Annapolis, Maryland


Soon-to-be Ensign Brett Jansen could barely contain himself. Standing smartly in his dress whites outside of the Navy-Marine Corps Memorial Stadium with his classmates, he examined every detail of his best friend Robbie Cantler's uniform for anything out of place—a piece of lint, hair, anything. Cantler did the same for him, just as they had done countless times for other inspections. But this time was different. It was graduation day at the United States Naval Academy. Jansen felt his phone vibrate. He thought about looking, but not today. If he had, he would have seen his news feed headline a blurb about a Chinese vessel encroaching on a Malaysian frigate yesterday in the South China Sea.

Jansen exclaimed, "Dude, we've marched together for four years, but nothing will be as memorable as this one. I can't believe we've finally finished, and we're going out into the real Navy."

"Yeah, bro, we did it. I'm so damn proud of us. Think about it. We're officers in the United States Navy—amazing."

"I'd bite my tongue," replied Jansen. "We haven't been commissioned yet—and with you, anything's possible."

"Now hear this," boomed a voice over a loudspeaker. "All Midshipmen form up in your assigned lines."

The two friends hugged and patted each other on the back. Jansen said, "After this shindig, let's meet in the end zone for a photo op."

They found their positions in the two lines that the 1,013 other Midshipmen had started to form. They marched proudly into the stadium and onto the field a short time later. Standing as erect as humanly possible, they were both bursting with pride for their country, the Navy, and themselves. As the order came to take their seats in front of over twenty-five thousand people, the men and women, soon to be the Navy's newest officers, took it all in, each with visions for the future. They were instructed to sit at attention with their hands neatly placed in their lap but forget that. As Jansen looked around the expansive field, everyone smiled, laughed, and squirmed in their seats as if tomorrow would never get here. His thoughts were now about life after the academy, his first assignment—and if he was ready.

For Jansen, graduation was the fulfillment of a childhood dream. His grandfather fought in Vietnam, and his dad fought in the Gulf War as enlisted soldiers. He continued the family's military tradition but followed their advice to be an officer and had picked the Navy because of his love for the sea. Growing up in the beach city of Grand Haven, Michigan, situated on Lake Michigan, he could swim before walking and operating a boat before he had a driver's license. His entire youth was spent on or in the water.

Jansen was a certified scuba diver because of the encouragement from Gramps, who loved the old TV hit *Sea Hunt,* in which a former Naval diver went after bad guys and saved lives. Jansen loved diving in the clear lakes around western Michigan, especially near Traverse City.

As for his first boat, his dad, a do-it-yourselfer, had ordered some plans from *Popular Mechanics* to build a three-point hydroplane in their walk-out basement. Jansen would never forget their fun building it from scratch, laying on the fiberglass, smelling the unique odors, and adding all the small details to make his boat memorable. But in their excitement of construction, they failed to notice it was too large to fit out the basement door.

His dad, always calm under fire, shrugged his shoulders and tore a portion of the wall down. After some back-breaking work, they got the twelve-foot racing boat out of the basement to marvel at their craftsmanship under the bright summer sun.

The boat's maiden voyage on Spring Lake epitomized his relationship with his father. Powered by a souped-up Mercury motor with a speedy Quicksilver unit, the boat was super-fast and could jump wakes so high that his knees—hell, his whole body—would bounce high into the air. Always one to push the envelope, Jansen knew that to be fast, you had to find the edge between control and losing it. It was no easy task driving the hydroplane. He had to get on his knees to operate the boat because the hull was too shallow for a seat.

Jansen sped by with his dad and older sister, watching from a long dock jutting into the lake. To demonstrate the boat's maneuverability, he decided to speed toward the dock and abruptly turn away at the last moment. But he waited too long to make his turn, and as he tried to save it, he flipped the boat right next to the dock.

The next thing he knew, his dad was in the water, ensuring he was still in one piece. The two dragged the boat to shore. While standing on the beach with water dripping down his face, he could only sheepishly apologize.

His father was not impressed. "Let that be a lesson, son. Always stay within yourself and what you're capable of. It's great to test your boundaries but do so with the knowledge of what might happen if you miss your objective."

Lesson learned.

Besides boats, Jansen and his buddies enjoyed the beach at the famed Grand Haven oval, where every week, a new set of girls, mostly from nearby Grand Rapids, would come to town wanting to have some fun. Jansen and the boys were always there to make sure that happened.

It was a simple weekly operation. They drove around the sandy oval that had scores of RVs lined up with tents scattered in between. The trick to success was always having your head on a swivel, looking for any nice-looking girls. Once spotted, the boys would stop, make some small talk, and, when successful, load the car with the giggling girls. There were always some parties at the cottages on Five Mile Hill, which was a good stopping point to show the girls the view. At the week's end, the guys got the phone numbers of their "girlfriends." When the nasty Michigan winters arrived,

Jansen and his friends would drive to Grand Rapids to connect again. It was a flawless plan that worked perfectly.

During his junior year of high school, his thoughts turned to his future, and he set his sights on Annapolis. He gathered letters of recommendation from his friend's dad, the mayor, a Navy recruiter he had befriended, and his school principal. He created an impressive package and sent it to US Senator Joseph Riddle of Michigan. In the fall of his senior year, he received an invitation from the senator for an interview at the senator's Detroit field office.

The timing was perfect for Jansen's football-loving family. The meeting with the senator was on Monday, leaving Sunday open for Lions football. Everyone in his family was afflicted with the self-diagnosed disease of Lion's Fever. The symptoms were universal: never miss a game no matter the Lions' record, proudly tell anyone who cared how much you loved your team, and continually repeat with conviction that there's always next year.

Jansen and his father went to Ford Field that Sunday to watch a game against the dreaded Green Bay Packers. True to form, the Lions lost on the last play after leading the entire game. Perhaps he thought becoming a Midshipman might change the bad luck of the Lions.

The young Jansen met with Senator Riddle the following day and sat alone with the senator in his office for a half hour. After the meeting, Jansen's father asked about the interview, but he couldn't remember what he'd been asked or what he'd said. He had to admit he was a little intimated. All this was a lot to take in for a kid from a small town. All he knew was what the office staff had said on his way out—the senator had two of his allotted five nominations open for Annapolis.

A few weeks later, Jansen received an email from the senator's office. Instead of grouping Jansen with ten other candidates and letting Annapolis pick the most qualified person, Senator McConnell had used his option to designate one principal nominee and nine alternates. Jansen was the top nominee.

He was incredibly proud of his nomination, but he had to temper his pride because the nomination was only a part of the process. A few months later, when the ice on Lake Michigan began to break up, Jansen got his notification of appointment to the US Naval Academy.

At the end of his graduation ceremony, he yelled his "hoorays" as loud as he could and tossed his cap high into the blue sky. He wove through his hugging classmates to the end zone to meet Cantler. To his surprise, his father was also there to greet him. The young Jansen would never forget as his dad stood at attention and rendered a perfect salute to the first military officer in the history of the family.

# Chapter 3

*THE WHITE HOUSE*
Washington DC

In the Oval Office, President of the United States Mark Taylor loved nothing better than to take off his shoes, stretch his long legs, and settle his stockinged heels on top of the Resolute Desk, one of the most famous desks in the world. It was 6:10 p.m., still too early for him to call it a day, but he allowed himself this little sin when he knew it might be a long night and he was alone. Entering the room was his Secretary of Defense, George Mitchell; Chairman of the Joint Chiefs of Staff, General Robert Matthews; and Chief of Staff, Logan Wright, who always had an opinion. They gathered around the coffee table before a National Security Council meeting.

"Sir, I'll be frank," said SecDef Mitchell. "For the past two decades, while we chased terrorists around the world, the Chinese People's Liberation Army built a force of conventional missiles that rivals and potentially outperforms ours. Their shipyards have spawned the world's largest navy that now rules the waves in East Asia and can launch nukes from ballistic missile submarines. In the South China Sea, the PLA is fortifying almost every island. At times, I seriously wonder if they aren't about to invade our friends in Taiwan."

Putting his stocking feet up on the coffee table, the president nodded. "I tend to agree with your assessment, George." Taylor looked at his closest advisers. "I see an overt challenge to our mission in the South China Sea. But I'll not sway from our commitment to our allies. The United States will maintain a strong military presence in the Indo-Pacific to preserve peace and stability and to uphold freedom of the seas consistent with international law. As long as I sit in this chair, I will not allow Beijing to assert their maritime claims or to treat the South China Sea as their empire—not on my watch."

"Mr. President, if I may," said General Matthews, "I see China's ambitions in its near seas as the greatest single threat to the interest and security of the United States. China believes the East China Sea and most of the South China Sea are undisputable regions of their domain. The list of nations they intimidate gets longer each year. There is Indonesia"—he tapped his forefinger on the armrest of his chair—"Malaysia"—another harder tap— and tap, tap, tap, "the Philippines, Japan, India, Vietnam, and Taiwan." Each country had received the same emphasis, and it was crystal clear to the others gathered that the general was not happy. "By their actions, China reveals that they want complete sovereignty, and by that, I mean absolute control of the airspace and sea lanes from the western Pacific Ocean through the Indian Ocean. This means they will wish to complete the expulsion of the US military from the first island chain. As we know, almost all the waters are claimed by the PRC. These are the significant archipelagos from East Asia's continental mainland coast, the Kuril Islands, the Japanese archipelago, the Ryukyu Islands, Taiwan, the northern Philippines, and Borneo. Such a move would abrogate our treaties and obligations to our allies because we would no longer be able to defend them."

"And let's not forget," added Chief of Staff Wright, "when China sank that Vietnamese fishing vessel near the Paracel Islands, they argued the ship had violated its territorial claims, which was bullshit. Then they held live-fire military drills at the northern end of the Taiwan Strait as if it was their God-given right."

"All right, I hear your points," said the president. "Suggestions?"

"Sir," SecDef began, "the US must maintain its ability to operate in those waters to deter Chinese aggression and to maintain regional peace and stability. This administration should consider expanding and increasing the tempo of our military operations in the South China Sea. Freedom of Navigation Operations should include everything from escorting fishing vessels to simply sailing through the Taiwan Strait. We must make it clear that we will not back down from their intimidation."

"But we also can't underestimate the danger of FONOPs in the South China Sea," added the National Security Advisor, Robbie Spencer. "Recall back to 2001. A Chinese fighter jet crashed into one of our intel birds. Just a few years ago, a Chinese destroyer came within forty meters of the USS *Decatur*, a near collision. And last week, we had an encounter between Malaysia, China, and our own destroyer, *Curtis Wilbur*, over the downing of a Malaysian drone. We must harden our stand or lose respectability in the Indo-Pacific."

"Okay," said the president with conviction. "You all have some great points. There's so much on the line, we must get this right. I'm sure we'll talk about this more in a few minutes, but I want you three to take the lead on coordinating suggestions for a revised policy on China and the South China Sea. We'll meet again in a few days."

President Taylor took his feet off the coffee table and stood up. The power brokers of the US stood and left the office. Taylor slipped his feet into his shoes and followed them to the NSC meeting.

# Chapter 4

*NAVAL BASE SAN DIEGO*
San Diego, California

After enjoying six weeks of post-graduation leave, newly commissioned Brett Jansen was sweating bullets. Not that it was a hot day as he sat at his kitchen table at his on-base billeting in San Diego, but Navy bureaucracy had him confused and frustrated. He kept reviewing his orders on when to report to the guided-missile destroyer USS *Mustin.* His stomach was in knots while he studied his *Shipboard Etiquette* pamphlet, which Annapolis graduates use as a "brief." He had thumbed through the twenty-page reference guide regarding how officers should conduct themselves when reporting for duty. But he couldn't find any specific information about when to report. It was very frustrating. He felt his career would end before it began.

Somehow, he had to find when to report layered in the small print of his orders. If it was "immediately," he had twelve hours exclusive of travel time. If it was "without delay," he had forty-eight hours; if it was "proceed," he had four days.

Give me a break, he thought.

But it got worse as he reread the same paragraph. "Take the day on which the four-day allowance would have expired and add the number of whole days to the travel time. This will give the date on which the officer would report without any authorized delay. To this, add the authorized delay, which will give you the latest day to report."

Holy shit, are you kidding me? He muttered, "How about just telling me when to be there."

He continued reading only to find one more clear instruction. "If, when reporting to a certain port to join your ship, you find that the ship is not present, you should go aboard another ship."

Great, he thought, who knows where the shit I'll end up.

He had an idea. Like in the old TV game show *Who Wants to Be a Millionaire*, he was going to phone a friend.

"Hi, Dad. You won't believe this . . ."

When his day came to report, Jansen stood on the pier looking at his new home for the next two years, the USS *Mustin*, an Arleigh Burke-class guided-missile destroyer. He stood frozen in time as he took in the magnificent ship. He was so proud of himself. It was now time to report.

Never ill-prepared for anything, Jansen had done his homework and could answer any questions about his new digs. The ship was named after an Academy alum, Henry C. Mustin of the class of 1896, a man most considered the "Father of Naval Aviation." His eldest son, Lloyd, a 1932 graduate, helped develop the antiaircraft gunsight. Jansen was prepared.

He walked up to the Coxswain at the base of the gangway. In his excitement, Jansen saluted first, which surprised the young sailor.

"I'm Ensign Brett Jansen, reporting for duty." He handed his orders to the Coxswain.

"Welcome to the USS *Mustin*, sir." The sailor returned the salute, a bit uncomfortable as the one receiving the honor instead of giving it. "These sailors will help you with your gear." He motioned to a couple of young men who took Jansen's gear. Watching the Ensign and his helpers ascend the gangway, the Coxswain wondered how this officer who salutes first would do under the pressure of command.

When Jansen reached the top grating, he faced aft and, with his best military bearing, snapped a picture-perfect salute to the colors. Then, he just as smartly turned and saluted the Officer of the Deck.

"Sir, Ensign Brett Jansen reporting for duty."

Permission to board was granted, and Jansen stepped onto his first vessel as a commissioned officer. After a short visit with the Executive Officer, Jansen was shown his room and told to report to his division officer, Lieutenant Junior Grade Robert Broersma. Another Dutch name, Jansen thought while he collected himself in his room. He couldn't believe how modest his berth was as he shoved off for his division officer's office.

After knocking on the door, he heard "enter." Once in the office, he promptly removed his cover and stood at attention in front of a young and very fit LTJG Broersma. "Sir, Ensign Jan—"

"Relax, ensign, this isn't Annapolis, and I won't take your head off, okay?"

"Yes, sir."

"That's much better, but no need to yell. So, tell me about yourself and how you ended up standing here?"

Jansen gave him the rundown and said that he was Dutch from both sides of his family, which he was incredibly proud of.

"Well, we've something in common there," said Broersma. "I'm with you. I really appreciate my heritage, and I tell anyone who will listen. There are a few others aboard." Pausing a moment, the division officer said, "You know you'll be sitting in my chair soon enough, right?"

"I thought so, sir. At the Academy, they said most of us would be a division officer in charge of twelve to fifty personnel. My goal is to be a Surface Warfare Officer. I don't want to sit behind a desk. I like to be where the action is, so I've asked to work in Combat Systems."

"Then you found the right room on the right ship. Welcome aboard, Jansen. We'll head out in two days to join the Seventh Fleet at Yokosuka Naval Base in Japan." Broersma shook hands with his new ensign, and Jansen started his new journey.

# Chapter 5



*Beidaihe Beach Resort*
Beidaihe, China


To the casual passersby, they looked like seven older men taking a dip in the sea to beat the heat of a hot August day. It wasn't a wrong assumption to make in a famous resort town on China's Bohai Sea. Known for its long beaches and shallow water, the resort had all the personal amenities of any famous Western beach, plus fabulous bathing areas, hiking trails, boat cruises, a large amusement park, and Tiger Stone Park, which drew its name from the shapes of boulders. There was even an area for bird watchers at Lianfengshan Park, known for its large population of migratory birds.

But the seven men who played like schoolchildren in the sea weren't ordinary swimmers. If any tourist had bothered to look closer, they would have noticed a boat just offshore carrying several beefy men, fully clothed, who watched the swimmers like the local White-Bellied Sea Eagle-eyed its next meal. The seven men splashing in the water were China's most elite. They were responsible for every significant decision affecting China's 1.4 billion souls.

Most Chinese citizens thought the twenty-four-member Politburo made all the decisions that affected daily life. However, the actual decision-making power belonged to the smaller Politburo Standing Committee, which appeared as just an inner-cabinet advisory board. Seven of the most powerful men in the country were the PSC, and the head of it was the President of the People's Republic of China, Zhang Wei.

Zhang not only held the mostly ceremonial position of president, but more importantly, he had consolidated power over the last few years to ensure that he also carried the title of General Secretary and Chairman of the Central Committee of the Chinese Communist Party. Those two positions put him in charge of all matters dealing with his countrymen and short and long-term goals for the Chinese Communist Party. Along with those two positions came the title of Chairman of the Central Military Commission, or CMC, so he was also the military's commander-in-chief.

Like the rest of China's elite, the seven men swimming had come to the beaches of Beidaihe because the heat in the capital of Beijing had soared. Their swim appeared all fun and play, but underlying it all was serious business. The Chinese leaders were discussing plans and proposals that would decide China's future, which were to be formalized in the last three months of the year.

As he bobbed up and down in the swells of the Bohai Sea, Zhang signaled for the other six men to swim closer. When they surrounded him, he said, "At dinner tonight, I want to get a head start on the numerous issues we must all discuss as we plan for next year and beyond. While getting away from the sweltering city is nice, work will always trump play. I suggest you enjoy your afternoon and plan on a late evening."

Not waiting for a reply, one of the most powerful men in the world, a former competitive swimmer, whirled away from his subordinates. Using his favorite stroke, the freestyle, he glided through the water like a shark.

Once he returned to his vacation home, Zhang told his lead chef, Bingwen Lai, to ensure dumplings would be served at dinner. Dumplings were his favorite, and he marveled at how minced meat and chopped vegetables wrapped in a thin dough had a history of more than eighteen hundred years. Zhang loved history and thought the dumplings appropriate since he planned on making some history of his own.

Before his dinner guests arrived, Zhang surveyed the table. The centerpiece had been his idea too. It was a vintage bronze statue of a PLA private with his arm raised and holding the Chinese national flag. It was a victory pose, and the beauty of the sculpture sent chills down his spine.

The six men arrived to dine as commanded. While the gathered elite enjoyed the dumpling course, Zhang happily ate and surveyed the men of the PSC and several party elders who at one time had either sat in Zhang's chair or had been members of the PSC. The room had gone silent, a sign that everyone enjoyed the dumplings. When they began to wipe the last morsel of food from their faces, Zhang addressed them.

"I want to honor all those sitting at this table, especially those who came before me and cleared the path we now travel." He bowed toward the elders. "Thank you for your service to our country. With your help, we shall widen that path to an expressway."

Zhang's eyes welled, but there was only polite applause around the table. His watery eyes didn't prevent him from taking note of each person's level of enthusiasm. When the clapping stopped, he continued.

"We have much to discuss, many topics of real importance. But first, we must address what I wish to make our top priority—the reunification of Taiwan with our beloved country. Hong Kong, Macao, and Taiwan have been integral parts of China since ancient times. We must return to those ages."

Pausing to let his words resonate around the room, Zhang noticed some men squirming. They were the same ones who had merely gone through the motions of clapping. He made a mental note to have his security staff secretly see where their allegiances truly were.

"Forty years ago, we took a different policy approach by moving away from the liberation of Taiwan and focusing on a peaceful unification. Well, I ask you—how has that worked? When we were children, Chiang Kai-shek's Republic of China and its ruling Nationalist Kuomintang Party defeated our great Mao Zedong's Communist People's Army. We have been hiding away ever since."

Zhang slammed his fist on the table, causing several dinner plates to bounce. "Enough!"

He noticed how the elders were becoming uncomfortable with his bold comments. After all, it was their policy he was referring to. So be it, he thought. Their time has passed with no results. Mine will be much different.

Zhang righted a chopstick that had fallen off its ceramic rest. "As some of you, no doubt, have heard or suspected, I've been devising a plan with my top generals and most trusted staff that will bring Taiwan back under our control now, not another fifty years from now, some nebulous time in the future. I—"

"With respect, President Zhang," interrupted Premier Ye Jiang, "the PSC is seven men who make decisions based on a consensus. I, for one, have not heard anything about this plan. Before we go any further, may I suggest we make your proposal for Taiwan reunification as the lead agenda item at our formal talks later in the year? This will allow us all to be involved and to come up with specific points that can be argued and universally approved."

Wan Jun, one of the oldest men of the group and a former president of the PRC, added, "If you think we can take over Taiwan by force without the United States coming to their rescue, you're mistaken. That is why we must not get brash about reunification. We're not there yet."

Mumbling around the room grew louder. President Zhang held up his hand. Most in the room understood and immediately stopped talking—a few holdouts hushed after a few seconds. Everyone knew from his gesture that any more open opposition could land them in jail for corruption charges. It was Zhang's preferred method to eliminate those who disagreed with him. There were thousands who could attest to it.

"As chairman of the CMC, I'm privy to much more information than even some of you in this room. I feel confident we should proceed through the proper channels to develop my proposal further. You have my assurances that you all will be involved, some more than others, in bringing twenty-four million of our countrymen back to where they belong."

One person in the room, Wan Jun, had different ideas and thoughts, not if I can help it, Mr. President.

# Chapter 6



Captain Qiang of China World Airlines was not one to ask questions. Life seemed simpler that way. When he had reported to the airport in Beijing at 2100 hours, he had expected to fly a Boeing 747-8 to New York City with its 410 seats full of customers. But his supervisor told him there had been a change of plans, and he and his copilot would fly the plane to Anquing Tianzhushan Airport. Qiang knew the new destination was an airport shared with the People's Liberation Army Air Force, twelve hours flying time south from Beijing.

"One more thing," his supervisor said while tapping on a tablet. "There won't be any passengers. It's a routine flight to deliver the plane to the base."

"Yes, sir, I would be happy to complete this flight." Silently, he wondered why there were no passengers, but that was none of his business—doing as you were told made life easier.

"Thank you, captain. Also, our company is honored to supply the PLAAF with an aircraft they will convert, so our president has a plane like Air Force One for the American president."

Qiang couldn't argue with an explanation like that and suspected his supervisor knew it too. An hour later, he was airborne. The flight had smooth air as his copilot flew the plane into the approach pattern.

"Anquing Approach, China World two-four-six. Request permission to land."

"China World two-four-six cleared for runway two-four left. Maintain course and speed."

"Roger, runway two-four left." To his copilot, he said, "I've got the controls."

Upon landing, ground control directed the Boeing 747-8 to the hot brakes parking ramp. Qiang went well past the terminal to a concrete square where two trucks sat, one outfitted with stairs. A man exited the pickup and used flashlights with red plastic tops to marshal the plane into an exact spot. Qiang followed the signals, glad to have helped since there were no taxi lines to follow. When he stopped the plane, he was told by ground control to shut down. No sooner had he and his copilot finished their checklist than a PLAAF Colonel entered through the open cockpit door.

"On behalf of the People's Liberation Army Air Force, thank you for participating in this historic flight. Soon this aircraft will carry our esteemed president to wherever he is needed. My men will drive you to the main airport. We have reserved two first-class seats for your return flight to Beijing. Again, thank you."

"Colonel, it was our sincere pleasure to help you and our country in any way we can," said Qiang.

With that, the two pilots departed the aircraft. As they walked away from the airliner, the PLA Colonel turned toward his second in command and couldn't help saying, "Excellent work. They have no clue that our president will never use this bird."

# Chapter 7

*NORTHROP GRUMMAN E-2D ADVANCED HAWKEYE*
South China Sea

Lieutenant Sarah "Danger" Freeman was bringing her Northrop Grumman E-2D Advanced Hawkeye to a cruising altitude of twenty-seven thousand feet over the South China Sea. Left behind, for now, was her Carrier Strike Group consisting of the USS *Reagan* aircraft carrier, one cruiser, one submarine, a destroyer squadron of two anti-aircraft warships, and a carrier air wing of seventy aircraft. That's enough firepower to rival the air forces of entire nations.

As she slowly reduced thrust to the two Rolls Royce turboprop engines, her thoughts drifted to her recent successes in the Navy. She had been promoted to lieutenant with the minimum time in grade. More importantly, she was upgraded to aircraft commander of the Navy's most advanced battle management command and control aircraft before many of her peers. This was a significant milestone in her young career because she was chosen over several other competent pilots. Flying was different now that she was responsible not only for her aircraft but also for the other four souls on board who trusted her to make all the right decisions to get them back home safely. Freeman was comfortable with that responsibility because she trusted her judgment and training.

Freeman was used to competing—and winning. She was a scholarship swimmer in the butterfly at Colorado State University and liked nothing better than to leave her competition in her wake. She was elected captain of her high school and college teams and noticed early how her teammates listened to her when discussing swimming and competing. At a young age, she learned to lead.

When a friend told her about the Reserve Officer Training Corps military program in her first year at college, she discovered new opportunities she'd never considered. Picking up some pamphlets at the Naval recruitment center, not only did she learn about ROTC, but she browsed the brochure that encouraged a career in submarines, destroyers, big deck aircraft carriers, or aviation. To this day, she would admit that she didn't know why the photo of a Boeing F/A-18E Super Hornet, with its afterburners lit as it took off from the deck of a carrier, had thrilled her. She decided right then and that was what she wanted to do—to be a Navy pilot. And, as her father would tell you, watch out when Sarah got something set in her mind.

Glancing over at her copilot, Lieutenant Junior Grade Roy "Rogers" Calhoun greeted her with his smile.

"Hey, Danger, what's the smile all about?"

Glancing back at her gauges, Freeman's smile grew. "Just livin' the dream, Rogers."

"I hear ya."

To keep that invisible wall between a commander and a subordinate, Freeman asked, "Did you hear what the SecDef had to say yesterday about China's claims to the water we're flying over?"

"No, I was catching up on some sleep."

"He said the US is tired of Beijing's claims to the South China Sea. He used the word 'harassment' for China's treatment and threats to our regional allies. He was pretty PO'd. I'd bet you a day of liberty; that's why we pulled this assignment. Flying directly over the Spratly Islands is throwing a challenge to a country that thrives on them."

"Lieutenant Freeman, we're up and running," said the Combat Information Center Officer, who went by CICO. He sat behind her with two other air battle managers. "Just the usual contacts, nothing out of the ordinary. There's a large container ship twenty kilometers northeast of the CSG."

Sitting in the tunnel of the E-2 in the most forward seat of three officers was the RO or Radar Operator, who was responsible for maintaining all passive detection sections, radar, and data links. Furthest aft was the ACO or Air Control Officer, who controlled most of the air wing assets. To move up to the CICO position, a

Naval Flight Officer, or NFO, had to do their time in the other two seats and prove they were worthy of moving up.

The three NFOs were all squeezed together and looking at their screens showing the output from the aircraft's state-of-the-art AN/APY-10 advanced radar, which was smaller and lighter and used less power than its predecessors. Supplying high-resolution radar, it could spot and track thousands of contacts from hundreds of miles away. It could even detect small, highly maneuverable targets and distinguish them from dense littoral and overland surroundings. Not only could the AN/APY-10 detect both air and sea surface targets simultaneously, but it could also suppress clutter, jamming, and other electromagnetic interference to keep a tight focus on a target. Nothing hid from its prying eyes.

"Okay, people, let's be alert," warned Freeman after looking down at an archipelago, "those are the Spratly Islands we're flying over. Three of our friends, Taiwan, the Philippines, and Vietnam, call it home, but unfortunately, the big bully on the block, China, has put up the only mailbox. RO, I want constant updates."

"Yes, ma'am," came the instant reply from RO Billy Ottenberg, the youngest and most inexperienced five-person crew on board the E-2. Freeman observed that he seemed overly fidgety and nervous on his first flight with his new crew. She hoped he could be counted on if the shit hit the fan.

"L-T, as a reminder, we have no air assets in the vicinity. It's us and the big blue sky," came the heads-up from the CICO.

"Roger that," she replied.

They all understood they were an integral part of the United States policy of conducting freedom of navigation through the contested South China Sea. Beijing claimed that the expansive maritime area belonged to them and demanded that all others seek permission to access the region—from sea or air. The People's Liberation Army Navy, or PLAN, was unhappy with earlier American excursions into the area. So far, no one had been hurt, but today was a new day. Freeman wanted the crew to be prepared for anything that might confront them. Be Prepared was more than a Boy Scout motto to her.

"Bandit, northwest bullseye, thirty-four miles, taking off from the island," reported the RO in a calm voice which Freeman at once noted.

"Roger." Freeman switched from intercom to UHF radio to call their carrier, the USS *Ronald Reagan*. "Ranger, Freedom 21. Request immediate air support. Bandit airborne from the Spratly Islands."

"Freedom 21, Ranger. Okay, your request, scrambling now."

RO, somewhat more excited, called out, "Bandit, Chinese J-20, southwest, thirty-one miles, flying low, heading north, changing course to our heading."

Freeman knew that standard procedure on the *Reagan* would call for the ship to monitor the airspace for additional bandits. Plus, the on-call Lockheed Martin F-35 Lightning IIs scrambling to her E-2's position would see the situation in real-time on their HUD via her Hawkeye's radar data link—one less detail to be concerned with.

Freeman hoped the Lightnings were pushing the envelope because one thing was for sure, China's new fifth-generation fighter, the Chengdu J-20 flown by the PLAAF, could travel at speeds up to 1,300 mph. It would take just minutes for the J-20 to close the distance to her aircraft. Just then, the Chinese fighter did a flyby mere feet over the top of the Hawkeye. The exhaust blast from the J-20's dual engines shook the E-2 aircraft severely. Instantly, the controls in her hands were unresponsive.

The Hawkeye plunged into a violent nose-dive, dropping and spinning a thousand feet in seconds. Images from training simulator sessions clashed with her consciousness of what to do.

But Freeman trusted her instincts. "Rogers, I have the controls. Give me full power." She ordered.

After Rogers applied full power, the aileron began to respond to her input. With steady hands, she pulled back on the elevator and applied forward pressure to the right rudder pedal to get the E-2 to start a turn which would force the plane to come out of its spin.

Within seconds, Freeman felt the aircraft come back under her control. She was pumped—she was saving it.

"Danger, watch out," shouted Rogers.

Looking up from her controls, Freeman saw the J-20 heading straight at them.

There was only an instant to decide to dive, climb, or stay on course in this aerial game of chicken.

She stayed on course.

The J-20 went vertical just as the two aircraft were about to collide.

This time, Freeman was ready, and she fought through the turbulence.

Over the intercom came a frightened scream from her RO. "That pilot's crazy. We're going to die!"

"Calm down, RO," Sarah fired back. "They don't want to die any more than we do. Now, do your job. The pilot is just trying to intimidate us into reversing course and leaving the area—which I can guarantee to that asshole is something that won't happen. I don't give a shit what he's flying."

*LOCKHEED MARTIN F-35C LIGHTNING II FLIGHT*
South China Sea

Airborne and with his throttle pushed to the stops at Mach 1.8, Lieutenant Commander Dick "Mad Dog" Johnson, mission call sign Boxer 11, led a flight of four F-35s. Their Lightnings' computer-controlled, powerful Active Electronically Scanned Array, or AESA, radars had an immediate lock on the J-20 the moment they left *Reagan*'s flight deck. All four pilots had been briefed that their scramble wasn't a shooting mission, but they also knew if the mission changed, their stealth would allow them to shoot first. And as every fighter pilot knew, those who shot first had all the advantages.

As the F-35s approached the Hawkeye, they saw the J-20 roll to the left dangerously close to the Hawkeye on their HUD.

What they couldn't see was Freeman staring face-to-face with the pilot who had almost killed her and everyone on board the E-2 and smartly giving the PLAAF pilot the one-finger salute as crisply as if she was saluting a four-star general.

Closing in on the E-2, Mad Dog saw the Chinese fighter go to afterburners and thunder away. In the old days, he might have given chase, but in today's Navy, the keyword was situational awareness, not engagement. Besides, why get in a dogfight when you could launch a missile that rarely missed?

As the J-20 ran for home, Mad Dog knew the pilot had so many alarms going off that his ears would be ringing for days. If this encounter had been a real fight, an AIM-120 missile would've taken China's most advanced fighter out of the PLAAF's inventory.

"Freedom 21, Boxer 11. Apologize for taking so long. From what I saw, fantastic job. You kept your cool and stuck with your mission. Congratulate your crew for me. We'll hang in the area until you're relieved. See you in debrief."

"Boxer 11, Freedom 21. Thanks for having our six. See you back at the boat."

# Chapter 8

*USS RONALD REAGAN*
South China Sea

Captain Jason Roberts, commanding officer of the USS *Ronald Reagan*, sat next to his executive officer, or XO, while staring at the split-screen TV monitor that showed the commander of the US Seventh Fleet, Vice Admiral Ronald "Ronnie" Stanberry, and a conference room filling with people. A command logo popped onto the screen and muted the video conference. At the same time, they waited for Admiral Christopher "Chris" Jenkins, the commander of the United States Indo-Pacific Command, to arrive, and COMCARSTRKGRU, Rear Admiral (lower half) Robert Wisniewski in charge of Carrier Group seven and eleven, designated Task Force-70. While his XO fidgeted in his chair, Roberts knew this video conference was big. Admiral Jenkins was at the top of the world's most extensive geographic combatant command, USINDOPACOM. His boss was the president of the United States through the SecDef. The expanse of his area of command was mind-boggling: 380,000 military personnel, thirty-six nations, fourteen time zones, and more than 50 percent of the world's population.

Yes, today would be a crucial meeting.

Roberts was used to big days. Growing up in Minnesota on a dairy farm, every day was a big day to complete his chores before and after school. He had hated the smell of manure, which seemed to get into every crevice of his body. He told his dad that while he respected what he did, it was not for him. No, he wanted to see the world, and the Navy sounded perfect. A three-sport athlete in high school, Roberts was popular and outgoing. He had no trouble getting an appointment to Annapolis.

When he was home, the widowed father of two had his kids trained to care for their dad—command and leadership. He had always been a strong leader, a top-notch pilot flying F-14s who worked his way up the ranks by maintaining a spotless record. As a young pilot, he experienced his first taste of war in 1991 during Operation Desert Storm as part of Task Force 155. From the beginning, Roberts had ambitions to command a carrier and accepted the challenges he now faced in command of *Reagan*.

Abruptly the TV screen went from the USINDOPACOM logo to a room filled with many people with lots of stars on their shoulders.

"Sorry, Ronnie," said ADM Jenkins, "I just got off the phone with SecDef. Of course, he and the president are anxious to hear from you about what happened out there."

"Yes, sir," answered the VADM Stanberry. "As you know, we've had several incidents with the PLAN, mostly with ship-to-ship confrontations. But these last two were a serious escalation. First, the shooting down of Malaysia's airborne drone and now a near collision with our E-2 have us all asking why there's an obvious escalation by the Chinese."

"Ronnie, we're asking the same questions here and in the White House. Captain Roberts, I've read your after-action report, but I want your take on what happened."

"Yes, sir," replied Roberts. "We were performing a freedom of navigation exercise when the J-20 jumped our aircraft. The first flyby caused the pilot to temporarily lose control of her aircraft. She was able to keep it in the air using her skill and with some luck. Statements by the aircrew substantiate this, as well as the cockpit data. The situation was about as close as you can get to a shooting situation. If the E-2 had gone down, so would have the J-20, and I'm sure the F-35s would've been dodging surface-to-air missiles too. Sir, this was a close one."

"Okay, thank you," said ADM Stanberry. "President Taylor has made it very clear to SecDef and me that in the wake of China's aggressive behavior, our need to reinforce our commitment to defend the right of navigating the seas for all nations is paramount. China's claim that international waters begin over one thousand miles beyond its land stands in direct contrast to the twelve nautical miles adhered to by everyone else in the world."

Looking down for a moment to collect his thoughts, the admiral looked into the camera and said, "Therefore, formal orders will be coming down shortly that will CHOP the Carrier Strike Group supporting Fifth Fleet to you, Ronnie. Create a dual-carrier task force for operations in the South China Sea. You will conduct round-the-clock flights testing the striking ability of our carrier-based aircraft. It's time we put our foot down, and that foot will have two CSGs attached to it. I suggest you get ready. That is all."

The USINDOPACOM feed went black.

"Okay, Jason," said VADM Stanberry, "we have our orders. Let's get ready." Then Seventh Fleet's feed went black.

Robert's XO had a wide-eyed expression. "Wow, another CSG with ours. A task force."

Roberts had known it would be a big day. He stood up and said, "Let's do this."

# Chapter 9



President Zhang Wei looked around the room inside the sprawling Ministry of National Defense building where the Central Military Commission was located and considered the faithful and devoted group he had so carefully assembled. Included were the fifteen commanding generals from all departments. He knew he could trust these men with his strategy to make China the singular power in the Indo-Pacific, supplanting the United States' influence and forcing their former allies to become subservient nations to the cause of China—his China. Heading the list would be reunification with Taiwan. Those who didn't share his vision were not in the room but in a stank one-room "tiger cage" prison.

Sitting next to him, General Wang Yong reviewed the notes for this crucial meeting. Zhang had noticed the devoted leadership ability of General Wang in the ongoing civil war in Syria. The president thought so highly of him that he specially groomed him for command in the Central Military Commission. He was now his second in command of the PLA.

The president looked over at his other handpicked men—all members of his inner circle. One, Liang Chao held the vital position of Chairman of the Standing Committee of the National People's Congress and had a background in technology that had catapulted him into the inner circles of power. Zhang liked his constant innovation and leadership in the field of military arms. Plus, it didn't hurt that Liang knew all the right people.

Zhang surrounded himself with people he could trust. Those he doubted were no longer a part of his inner circle, nor would they ever be since he used China's bureaucracy to eliminate them. The name he adopted for his enforcement agency was the Central Commission for Discipline Inspection. The CCDI was, on paper, tasked with enforcing internal rules and regulations and, more importantly, sniffing out corruption at all levels of government—his favorite task.

It was simple. If he found someone he could no longer trust or someone he saw as a threat, he sent agents from the CCDI to knock on their door. Soon after, stories would appear in the press about so-and-so being found guilty of corruption and sentenced to prison. He chose Ho Cheng to head the agency because of his sworn allegiance to Zhang. Between them, their anti-corruption campaign snared 1.3 million officials from various levels of government, including top generals, party bosses, presidential aids, down to a snooping janitor.

And last, there was Chao Guanting, Zhang's vice president. Growing up poor in central China, Chao was adopted by a wealthy relative who ensured he received a superior education. From there, Chao made inroads through the party and was noticed by Zhang, who had directed his career since 2012. Zhang only had to ask, and Chao would deliver.

The president felt very secure in his choices.

"Okay, I believe you all have had time to look at the agenda and supporting material," said Zhang. "I've called this special security meeting to go over our global strategy in the Indo-Pacific region, a strategy that I like to refer to as our 'China Vision'—meaning a modern China of unprecedented power and influence. Our two primary objectives are the reunification of Taiwan and the recognition of various contested islands as ours. These objectives will put us up against the United States and its allies. A victory would enormously expand our power and position in Asia and add the entire South China Sea into our maritime territory. Our homeland would continue as the most dominant power in Asia."

As the president scanned the room, he saw he had everyone's attention, so he continued. "All our efforts must focus on achieving these national goals. We must safeguard our sovereignty and security and firmly oppose all attempts to divide us. I believe, along with our generals, that while the US has been busy chasing terrorists from country to country in the Middle East for two decades, our long-range plan, developed years ago but given renewed attention by me in 2012, has developed the Navy into the largest one in the world. Our Air Force has caught up with those in the West and, in many areas, has surpassed them. We have the world's most technologically advanced fighting force." Glancing over at General Wang, he nodded for him to continue the orchestrated meeting.

"Thank you, Mr. President," said Wang. "My staff, under my direction, was tasked to develop a plan to eliminate the threats that the US aircraft carriers present to our objectives in the Indo-Pacific. If one examines the mistakes made by the Japanese in their attack on Pearl Harbor during World War II, their failure to account for the aircraft carriers and sink them eventually led to their defeat. Lesson learned."

After taking a moment to let his remarks sink in, General Wang continued. "In our version of Pearl Harbor, we'll go after the carriers first and then the escort ships. The Americans have eleven carriers. Two are in California, and two are in drydock in Virginia. We're currently refining our plan to neutralize all four. The other carriers of concern are the *Reagan* and the *Nimitz*, currently deployed off our shores. Destroy them, and we'll have the freedom to do as we please in the China Sea. I feel confident we can sink all of them with our newly upgraded hypersonic glide missiles. We've flight-tested them nine times—all successfully. In the last test, our Navy purposely demolished one of our decommissioned destroyers using our DF-17.

"Understanding the key roles of Kadena and Anderson Air Force Bases on Okinawa and Guam, our Rocket Force has strategies to suppress air operations by cratering runways. Our missile superiority will allow us to keep them inoperable for the needed time. Using DF-21Cs carrying submunitions, we will attack large areas so that every parked aircraft would have a high probability of being taken out of the battle."

"General Wang," interjected Zhang, "please explain how this all ties into our invasion of Taiwan."

"Yes, Mr. President. The key to success in our campaign is air superiority. While we engage the enemy and destroy their carriers, support ships, and airfields, we'll begin sustained air attacks on Taiwan using our upgraded aircraft with air-to-ground sensors and precision munitions. At the same time, we'll strike select Taiwanese targets with our ballistic missiles. We'll overwhelm their inferior defenses by using most of our 152 air bases, nearly 400,000 service personnel, and our 3,100-plus aircraft, of which well over 2,000 are combat planes. We'll use all the air bases for forward deployment, positioning forty fighters and six bomber regiments, all of which can operate with unrefueled operations. With the US carriers and their proximity bases out of service from our bombings, we can obtain our operational objectives before the US can rally and bring its entire forces to bear.

"Geography will also play a critical role, a distinct advantage to our forces. The US has only one base within eight hundred kilometers, while our Air Force has forty-one within the same range. This basing mismatch will allow our most modern fighter force to reach the battle area, putting the US fighter aircraft at a significant numerical disadvantage."

"Excuse me, General Wang," said the president, "thank you for that detailed report, but let's leave the specifics for later." Addressing his trusted allies, Zhang said, "Please, any questions?"

Liang Chao quickly spoke, "Being an expert in the field of technology, I can say for certain that we lead the world in military advancements. I strongly agree with our president about our success in gaining control of our region. Now is the time."

"Thank you, Liang. Other comments?" asked Zhang.

"As your Vice President," said Chao, "I, too, strongly agree with the strategy to regain power over Taiwan. Control of the Indo-Pacific is paramount to our China Dream. Our unified national ideology will strengthen the ties between our citizens and the Communist Party. As our great leader Mao Zedong said, 'Party, government, military, civilian, and academic; east, west, south, north, and center, the party leads everything.' And we'll lead our country to victory."

# Chapter 10


*USS Mustin*
South China Sea


As Ensign Brett Jansen hurried to catch up to his training officer for the day, Lieutenant Tom Whitlock, he felt somewhat overwhelmed with his duties as a Surface Warfare Officer or SWO. He could hear his Academy instructor now, "Your role will be manager, and that role varies immensely. You will lead engineers, technicians, and quartermasters. When you are out to sea, you'll navigate from the Bridge, serve as a tactician in the Combat Information Center, better known as the CIC, and even oversee the engineering plant. Your duties are interchangeable, and you better know each one."

Jansen and his training officer were headed to the Bridge to relieve the Officer of the Deck—or at least Whitlock was. Jansen understood his role today was to shut up and be an attentive fly on the wall. Minutes ago, they were in the heart of the ship, the CIC. Whitlock had noted if any specific actions were to occur on his watch, checked in with navigation, reviewed recent orders, and received an update on all nearby ship traffic.

After the two walked briskly onto the Bridge, Whitlock said to the OOD, "Lieutenant Barkley, I'm ready to relieve you, sir."

Barkley answered quickly and loudly, "I'm ready to be relieved. There are no current special orders. There's a large oil tanker 3.5 nautical miles NE of our current location, traveling east."

Satisfied he had received all the necessary information, Whitlock replied, "I relieve you, sir."

"I stand relieved. Attention on the Bridge. Lieutenant Whitlock has the deck." Jansen couldn't help but smile when he saw the two lieutenants give each other a sharp salute before Barkley departed the Bridge.

"This is Lieutenant Whitlock. I've got the Bridge. Lieutenant Broersma has the Conn."

"This is Broersma. I have the Conn."

Jansen was glad to see the Dutchman again, this time in new surroundings.

"Conn, maintain speed and course," Whitlock ordered.

"Aye, aye, sir. Maintain speed and course."

"Attention on the Bridge," announced Whitlock. "Ensign Jansen is here as an observer only. Any questions?"

"No, sir," echoed the crew on the Bridge. Whitlock nodded for Jansen to approach his seat overlooking his home for the next four hours. "Ensign Jansen, did you attend the Mariner Skills Course?"

"Yes, sir. Immediately after leave."

"What was your takeaway from that course?"

Jansen thought for a moment. "May I be frank, sir?"

"Fire away, Jansen."

"We went over, in detail, the two incidents involving collisions of our ships that killed seventeen sailors a few years ago. Based on those studies, I've concluded that we're not doing enough to ensure that SWOs are adequately trained. I think those incidents happened because people lacked knowledge about navigation and shipborne systems."

Whitlock looked straight at Jansen. "And that is precisely why you are standing watch with me today. The CO and many others, including myself, believe we must improve shipboard training and qualifications for Bridge watchstanders by dividing SWOs into specific specialties and training them accordingly. Being a jack-of-all-trades is good for understanding the function of a destroyer. Still, I believe there's a need for specialization. Think about it, Jansen. Right this minute, I'm responsible for the lives of every sailor on this ship. There's no wiggle room. We must get this right."

"Yes, sir, I'll do my best."

"Okay, I want you to walk the Bridge and pay attention to everything. Peak over shoulders, ask questions, learn—got it?"

"Yes, sir, shoving off."

# Chapter 11



*PLAAF Chengdu J-20 flight*
Quzhou, China

Some would argue that the only reason *Kong Jun Shao Xiao* (Air Force Major) Chang Huang, of the Eastern Theater Command's 85th Air Brigade, was piloting the PLAAF's Chengdu J-20 stealth fighter was because he had married the daughter of the president of China. Chang would disagree. He would like to think it was because of his prowess as a fighter pilot. But then the connection sure didn't hurt, he thought with a smile. Marrying the love of his life arguably opened many doors for him.

From the time he was born, Chang was destined for glory. He came from a wealthy family in Beijing. His father was in the upper echelons of power in the Chinese Communist Party and knew all the right people, so President Zhang looked after him as a devoted supporter of his policies. It was only fitting that Chang met his future wife at an elaborate state dinner. She would never admit it, but Chang knew his dress uniform, heavily adorned with medals, caught her gaze that night. She couldn't keep her eyes off him. Their first dance together sealed the deal. He could tell by the look in her eyes as they moved as one across the dance floor. As it turned out, she was as great a wife and he an exceptional pilot—a perfect bonding.

Today, Chang and his wingman, callsign Jaeger 2, were flying their J-20 fighters from Quzhou on the eastern coast of China toward Taiwan to remind the breakaway province that the PLAAF ruled the skies. Quzhou was only 500 kilometers, or 310 miles, from the runaway state. Both pilots did the math. It would take only eight minutes before Taiwanese warplanes would enter their air-to-air missiles' kill range. Hell, in fifteen minutes, they would be flying unseen in their stealth fighter over the capital, Taipei.

In the bellies of their fifth-generation fighters were PL-15 beyond visual range air-to-air missiles, called BVRAAMs, and PL-

10 short-range air-to-air missiles, or SRAAMs for short. The PL-15 was equipped with an AESA-seeker, satellite-enabled inertial guidance system, and a dual pulse motor capable of 200 kilometers or 124-mile combat range.

Chang and his wingman were using their AESA fire control radar with a chin-mounted electro-optic sensor linked with six electro-optic apertures around the aircraft, a design to provide a 360-degree situational awareness system to warn pilots of incoming aircraft and missile threats and for day and night-vision fire control capability.

"Jaeger 2, Jaeger 1. Ready to make history?" said Chang.

"Jaeger 1, Jaeger 2. On your command."

"Jaeger 2, Jaeger 1. On my mark, go to 300 for a flyover of Penghu Island. 3—2—1—mark."

At the command, instead of operating in stealth mode, the two J-20s buzzed Taiwan's Penghu Island, screaming overland at one thousand feet for all to see.

A sonic boom shook the few buildings of the defense forces stationed there. By chance, the commanding officer was walking to his jeep as the two jets skyrocketed over his base. He was Army, but he knew that the Taiwanese Air Force didn't have any jets that looked like those. He immediately turned and sprinted back to his office to notify his superior on the main island.

"Jaeger 2, Jaeger 1. That should get their attention," said Chang. "As planned, maintain this altitude and take a heading of zero-five-one degrees for our flyover of Tainan and then of Kaohsiung City. Slow to 450 to give them a chance to see us."

"Copy that, Jaeger 1."

A few minutes later, the two J-20s completed their flyover of the main island, directly violating Taiwanese airspace and causing an immediate international uproar that made headlines worldwide. Mission accomplished.

# Chapter 12



*THE WHITE HOUSE*
Washington DC


At 5,525 square feet, the Situation Room was not your typical conference room. Containing secure advanced communication systems, the president and others in the room could communicate with anyone, anywhere in the world, and with a video feed if needed. President John F. Kennedy developed the capability in 1961 after the botched Bay of Pigs invasion of Cuba when the US had no real-time communication with frontline troops. The Situation Room was used today to decipher China's actions and intentions in the South China Sea. President Taylor had called in the NSC to ensure he had the best minds in the nation working to solve the same dilemma: how should the US handle the PRC and its brazenly overt campaign toward Taiwan without escalating to all-out war?

Like several presidents before him, Taylor had a military background. A graduate of the Naval Academy, class of '74, he had missed the war in Vietnam. Still, he found a home with the Office of Naval Intelligence. The Cold War was raging, and Taylor became an expert on Russian military threats posed against the United States. One takeaway from his experiences was the need for solid, feet-on-the-ground intelligence. After serving for six years, he returned home to Pennsylvania and decided he wanted to be involved with the state's decision-making process. He successfully ran for the state Senate and, from there, for the US Congress and, eventually, the White House—never losing an election. People loved him for his honesty, a man who adhered to the dictates of his conscience and who was a relentless investigator of the facts. It was said that after people who disliked him spent some one-on-one time with him, they came away respecting the man and, many times, becoming an ally. Married to the love of his life, Shannon, who had his back throughout his political career, was the best-sounding board a man or president could ask for. They had one child, Jennie, an outspoken, free spirit who never held back and let him know exactly how he was doing, whether asked or not. But when things were tough, his daughter was always there for the both of them.

"Okay, folks," said the president to a packed room, which included all the aides seated around the room's perimeter, "let's get started. I called this meeting so we can begin to put a collective hat on just what the PRC has in mind with their ramped-up muscle-flexing moves in the Indo-Pacific. I feel uneasy concerning their movement like they're getting ready to move on Taiwan and, for that matter, the US." Looking down the long table at SecDef Mitchell, he said, "George, please bring us up to date on the recent provocations by the PLA."

"Yes, Mr. President. One month ago, a PLA naval destroyer used a weapons-grade laser to shoot down an unarmed Malaysian drone operating in international waters. As a Malaysian destroyer entered the same area, it was nearly rammed by the same destroyer, as witnessed by the crew of the USS *Curtis Wilbur*. USPACFLT ordered both allied ships to leave the area to avoid escalating the encounter. A few days after that event, a PLAAF J-20, China's most advanced fighter, flew so close to one of our E-2s that the pilot lost control of the aircraft, barely saving it at the last minute. Four of our F-35s chased it away."

Pausing for a moment to let the information be absorbed, SecDef continued. "A few days later, nineteen PLAAF jets approached Taiwan and crossed the sensitive midline of the Taiwan Strait. The Republic of China Air Force scrambled jets and activated their air defense missile batteries. That was enough for the Chinese, and they returned to the mainland. And yesterday, two PLAAF J-20s violated Taiwan's airspace with a low-altitude flyover of a small island that continued over the main island, where they flew over two cities before returning to China. They could have flown over Taiwan with their stealth capability, and no one would have noticed. But they clearly wanted to be seen and to send a message to Taiwan."

"If I may," interjected the Secretary of State, Brad Kelly, "not since the Third Taiwan Strait Crisis of 1995–1996, when the PRC fired missiles in the waters surrounding Taiwan, have we had such a provocative military move by China. In 1995, it was to send a message about the ROC's movement away from the One-China policy, and then, in 1996, it was to influence the ROC elections. It's obvious the PRC is striking back now as they did in the '90s because of our Deputy Secretary of Defense's visit to Taiwan, the most senior official to visit the island in four decades."

"The dialogue between the two countries is escalating by the day," added the SecDef. "Taiwan's Defence Ministry complained that the PRC was carrying out provocative acts destabilizing the region and that China should stop and, in their words, 'pull back from the edge.' The PRC's widely read state-backed paper, the *Global Times*, said that the drills were a rehearsal to take over Taiwan. That could be more than just self-aggrandizing."

There was a brief pause, then the president said, "What we have here is a conflict over the balance of power between the US and the PRC. China has been preparing to replace us as the dominant power in the region for longer than we've been preparing to maintain it. Their anti-access, area denial strategy, the A2/AD, relies on a modern blue-water naval fleet, an armada of attack submarines, and an enormous inventory of anti-ship ballistic missiles. As the PRC has warned countless times, any intervention by the US will be met by the entirety of its forces. With the escalation of events in the region and the recently introduced Taiwan Security Act, it's time this administration takes a position and makes our solidarity with Taiwan known not only to China but the entire world."

"Mr. President," said Robbie Spencer, the Assistant to the President for National Security Affairs, "we at the NSC recognize that just a few years ago, we had complete control of the Indo-Pacific region and had a strategic and technological advantage over the PRC. This has all changed. With few outside distractions, China has spent billions on their A2/AD systems of attack aircraft, warships, and state-of-the-art ballistic and cruise missiles designed to strike key targets, such as our two carriers in the region. Their boast that they could easily sink our two carriers and kill ten thousand sailors to teach us a lesson—I hate to say—has merit."

General Mathews couldn't restrain himself. As the CJCS's face reddened, he said, "Mr. Spencer, that comment is unproven and, I believe, inaccurate. Most of us making a living in the military know our assets and their capabilities because if we didn't, the enemy would pounce on us. I could discuss with you for hours why China or anyone else could not sink one of our carriers. But I'll be brief.

"With their unlimited range and the fact that they are always moving, our carriers are tough to locate. As you know, carriers never deploy alone, and they have layers of protection within a Carrier Strike Group. Because of their vast size, they would be difficult to sink. Carrier aircraft can destroy enemy combat systems and—"

"Okay, General Mathews," said the president, "thank you. We must move on, but your points are well taken. Elena, your opinion, please." President Taylor thought the world of his Director of National Intelligence. She had been with him since those early days in Pennsylvania politics. He trusted her judgment like no others.

"Thank you, sir," said Elena Ramirez, the DNI. "I believe we need to tread lightly. If war were to break out between the US and China, a battle between the two most powerful militaries on Earth, the outcome would be shocking and horrendous. Make no mistake, the US could lose. As we've discussed, China's rapid military buildup across the board—from cyber to space to air, sea, and land— makes the outcome very uncertain. With that said, we must also examine the credibility issue with our allies in the area. The world knows that the Taiwan Security Act was introduced in Congress. If the bill is defeated, the outcome will devastate American integrity and our influence in the region and the world. Quite simply, we would lose creditability. Despite the possible negative outcome of a war, I believe we should support the TSA legislation. It will make a statement to all the nations in the region that the US will support Taiwan and, by association, them. By passing the bill, the world will not doubt our intentions and our defense commitment to Taiwan. We cannot turn our heads from the country's shining example of democracy."

"Thank you, Elena, well stated." Scanning the room, the president noticed a lot of approving nods. "Okay, in the interim, I will approve General Mathew's earlier written recommendation of sending the CSGs *Reagan* and *Nimitz* on freedom of navigation operations through the Taiwan Strait and the Spratly Islands and then circling back through to return to their base in Japan. Mr. Vice President, I want you to take the lead and talk with our friends on the hill about our support of the TSA. I also want you to draft a statement for my announcement about this country's support of Taiwan and the bill. Are there any objections?" No one stirred. "Okay, good. We're all on the same page—one more thing. I want the NSA and the DNI to make a concentrated effort to gather as much intelligence as possible on the PLA, their capabilities, and their numbers. I know you do this daily, but I want a renewed effort. Have a report to me within one month. Thank you, everyone, for your thoughtful input. Now, let's get to work."

# Chapter 13



*Task Force-70*
East China Sea

As the rising sun slowly washed over the Bridge of the USS *Ronald Reagan* with a brilliant yellow light, Captain Jason Roberts took a moment to take it all in. He gazed upon the calmness of the East China Sea. It was as flat and calm as the lakes in Minnesota where he had grown up. Looking up, he appreciated the cloudless deep-blue sky. The magnificence of the moment would make the perfect Navy recruiting poster—but only with the addition of what surrounded him. The Aegis guided missile cruiser USS *Cowpens* and two missile destroyers traveled directly off the bow. Not appearing in his recruiting poster were two attack submarines looking for any hostile ships and, especially, any unfriendly submarines that would want to harm the newly formed Task Force-70.

But there was more. TF-70 assortment of warships accompanied the USS *Nimitz*. Escorting the *Nimitz* was Destroyer Squadron 23, with two cruisers, three Aegis-guided missile destroyers, and one submarine.

These two combined CSGs were not just a photo op for the Navy but Task Force-70, formed so the PLA could examine and grasp exactly what they were facing. Staring down from their satellites, they were witnessing the overwhelming power of the United States Navy, warships carrying more than twelve thousand military professionals and one hundred and twenty state-of-the-art combat aircraft. It was a message sent in the open, warning China to think twice before deciding to confront the US.

In the Indo-Pacific, the PRC claimed nearly 1.3 million square miles of the South China Sea, disregarding other nations' claims of ownership and the International Court of Justice, which had ruled against China's claims. The United States was making it clear, with their FONOP aimed directly at the PRC, that the US stood with their Southeast Asia allies and partners in protecting their sovereign rights to travel in international waters.

"Sir," the XO brought Roberts out of his thoughts, "Admiral Wisniewski is requesting you in his stateroom."

"Thank you, XO. You have the Bridge."

"Aye, aye, sir. XO has the Bridge."

As he briskly walked to meet RDML Wisniewski, the commander of the beefed-up Task Force 70, a man who also wore the hat of the commander of CSG 5 and was also called COMCARSTRKGRUFIVE, Roberts wondered what his boss wanted. Arriving at the CTF's stateroom, Roberts knocked once and walked in the door after he heard a loud command to enter.

"You called for me, Admiral?"

"Yes, Jason. I want to go over our orders one more time. I've already discussed this with Captain Samson from the Nimitz. As you know, this mission is code-named Operation Open Seas and has been blessed by the president. We have been ordered to stand our ground when confronted by any PLA aggressive and threatening actions. If we're challenged in any way, we'll return in kind. As you're aware, since we've moved from our home base, the PLAAF's combat aircraft, on numerous occasions, have crossed the median line in the Taiwan Strait."

"Yes, sir," said Roberts. "Our C4ISR assets noted the latest run included two Xian H-6 bombers, four Chengdu J-10 fighters, four Shenyang J-11 fighters, eight Shenyang J-16 fighters, and they even threw in a Shaanxi Y-8 anti-submarine warfare plane."

"Correct," replied Admiral Wisniewski. "The sheer number of combat aircraft crossing the line has many in Washington believing the action should be viewed as a threat of force and in violation of the UN charter against such acts. These incursions are no longer just a single sortie. Still, the sheer number of aircraft suggests that China wants to punish Taipei for hosting the recent visit by our Assistant to the Secretary of Defense and several members of Congress who tagged along. As I've been informed, we'll treat this latest incident as an act of intimidation to change the status quo in cross-strait relations. When challenged about the last incursion, Beijing said its military operations are consistent with international law and that no violation occurred because Taiwan is part of mainland China."

"Excuse me, sir, but what bullshit," retorted Roberts. "Earlier, I was handed an intelligence report that stated Taiwan will not provoke China but will respond in self-defense. They scrambled a squadron of F-16s and used their land-based missile defenses to thwart any possibility of the Chinese jets buzzing the island—or, worse, of attacking."

"As they should," said the admiral. "Washington likes to keep China guessing about our resolve with Taiwan. Although there's no mutual defense treaty, everyone understands the 1979 Taiwan Relations Act and the newly introduced Taiwan Security Act before Congress. While the current act is not a guarantee of our protection in the event of an invasion, it does say that a threat to the peace and security of the Western Pacific area would be of grave concern to the US. I want you to brief the ship's crew, especially the aircraft crews, that the PLA will not push us aside. We'll stand our ground. We don't want a shooting war, but we don't want to be bullied by them, either. When TF-70 passes through the Taiwan Strait, I'm convinced China will be there and be ready."

"I understand, Admiral. I'll get to this immediately."

## Chapter 14



Captain Liu Ying, commander of the 1st Platoon of the 10th Tank Company of the Republic of China Army, carefully maneuvered his CM-11 main battle tank through the loose sand on Kinmen Island. It was a source of pride that his grandfather, Lieutenant Hu Ying, fought on the same beaches in 1950 in the successful war against mainland China. Lieutenant Hu was a national hero for his brave service to his country and for giving his life fighting the communists.

With his crew, Captain Liu was participating in a five-day live-fire drill. In most war game scenarios, they had some evidence pointing to an impending invasion of Kinmen Island by the PLA, unlike the surprise one in 1950. Liu planned on being ready.

Like his grandfather, Liu dealt with hand-me-down tanks. The CM-11 Brave Tiger was the country's most modern tank at twenty years old, an upgrade to the old American M60 main battle tank. It remained a slow mover, and its kinetic protection was poor. It would be game over if struck with China's armor-piercing fin-stabilized discarding-sabot or APFSDS round. Still, the old boy had a 105mm gun. And with the CM-11's thermal sighting and DM63 APFSDS rounds, it could dish out some serious damage, just at a much slower pace.

Because most nations were wary of China's wrath for selling modern equipment to Taiwan, the tankers did their best with what they had and developed tactics around sticking their nose out, getting off a shot, and then trying to hide. The key was to shoot first, take cover, and not get hit in return.

On the positive side, under President Taylor, the United States had agreed to sell to Taiwan 106 state-of-the-art M1A2T Abrams tanks to modernize its fleet of a thousand battle tanks. Liu thought highly of the US president for supporting Taiwan, someone willing to accept whatever the PRC decided to dish out. And Liu was exceptionally proud that he was chosen as one of one hundred ROC Army personnel to travel to the US to be trained to instruct people about the M1A2T tank upon their return to Taiwan.

# Chapter 15



*CHINA GRILL*
Beijing, China


In China, one couldn't be too careful who their friends were because the difference between the high and low life was prison. Premier Ye Jiang, second in power to only President Zhang, looked at General Li Jung, wearing his dress uniform that contained more medals than emails in his inbox. That was the man's style, pomp, and circumstance. But General Li was also a man who could be depended on to get the job done. And most significantly, he was the third in command of the PLA Rocket Force. The homeland had many secrets—today would add to that number.

"What time did you tell him?" asked Li Zhang from the State Council.

"Our devoted leader will be here when he chooses," said Premier Ye. The small group was out in the open, but the subject wouldn't be. They were sitting atop the Park Hyatt in the China Grill, which had some of China's most delicious meat dishes—if you could afford it. The 360-degree view allowed them a peek, albeit through smog, of their great city.

"I told our security detail," explained Ye, "I would allow one agent inside the restaurant to keep an eye on us, but they wouldn't be privy to any of our conversation. For all they know, we're just taking former president Wan Jun to a nice dinner—speaking of which, here he comes."

The three men quickly stood up to greet the former president of China, Wan Jun, now just an old man in retirement, or so it appeared. Unlike the Japanese, the Chinese didn't bow as a greeting; it was an honor reserved only for their respected elders. All three men bowed to Wan Jun.

After sitting down, the power brokers of China took a minute to catch up, just as any group of close friends would do. The restaurant staff had been instructed not to approach the table until Ye gave them a wave.

Focused on the four powerful men, Major Guiying of the Central Security Bureau sat at the bar where he could take it all in. He adjusted his Norinco NP22 9mm pistol to keep it from jabbing him in his rib cage. Just out of sight, he had three additional men, each carrying a compact Chang Feng 05 submachine gun—just in case. The major also had two men in an unmarked vehicle covering the front of the building, and his last man was in an alley watching the back door. Guiying was not about to have any trouble on his watch—he didn't care much for jail cells. As Wan Jun entered, Major Guiying was surprised since he thought the man had died from old age.

The group ordered drinks. Three of the men drank *baijiu* while the former president ordered *tieguanyin*. Now it was time to get down to business.

"While I respect President Zhang," said Ye, "although he's done much for our country, I can't stand by and allow him to jeopardize all that progress with his plan to battle with the US over Taiwan." The other men nodded in agreement.

"My sources in the missile force," said General Li, "told me that the DF-26 and DF-21D ranges of 2,400 km/h are an exaggeration and that the precision guidance systems have problems. In several exercises, our forces had difficulty hitting a moving target, let alone a US carrier that can travel at over 30 knots. Additionally, my intelligence reports that the Americans have advanced new technologies to improve its layered ship defense systems, especially against ballistic and cruise missiles."

"I would add," said Ye, "that a war with a peer adversary like the United States will be highly contested, and you could see thousands or even hundreds of thousands of deaths, not to mention large-scale destruction akin to World War II or Ukraine. Do we want to take this risk to control the Indo-Pacific? I, for one, don't think so."

"Add to this," said the general, "the price in global economic terms. Our economy would be shattered for years if not decades. I strongly believe it's not worth the risk. The reunification of Taiwan is just one step away from occurring. Once we have pro-reunification people in power—it will happen. It just takes time. We've been around for three thousand years, and a few more years is nothing."

As the conspirators continued their collusion, they were under surveillance by a nicely dressed young couple from the Ministry of State Security. The MSS was the highly feared secret police of the PRC. The four senior PRC power brokers were receiving lots of attention from the current Chinese president, who didn't trust any of them.

The make-believe young lovers out for a nice dinner were two of MSS's finest agents. Both were chosen for this assignment for their undistinguished looks. They appeared like the couple next door you could never remember anything about. Both were unarmed to avoid raising suspicion from the likes of Major Guiying of the CSB, who didn't miss a thing as he continually scanned the room. As the four men conversed, the couple never looked over in their direction but instead murmured while sipping glasses of wine.

Hidden in the metal frame of the female's purse was a miniature mic programmed with a precise directional spread that was designed to pick up the conversation of subjects up to nine meters away. In an ideal world, the mic picked up discussions where it was pointed and filtered out surrounding ambient noises. The two agents wanted nothing to go amiss since they knew they were on a career-enhancing assignment directed from the top echelons of the PRC. The agents ordered their main course because the conversation had no signs of letting up at the table of the retired president.

"During my term," said Wan Jun, "we had a balanced dialogue with the United States, and each of us profited. There was little saber-rattling as there is today. For the long-term security of our country, we must find a way to stop President Zhang and the PLA from destroying everything we all worked so hard to achieve."

"The war with the United States begins and probably ends with the rocket force," said General Li. "The six missile brigades are independently deployed throughout the country. With two thousand missiles and hundreds, if not thousands, of advanced cruise missiles in their arsenal, stopping them will be most challenging. The order to launch comes from the president. In my opinion, and we've discussed this, the key to preventing any launch of our missiles is through the infiltration of our communications system. We can approach this in two ways.

"The PLARF has a separate command and control structure. The nuclear command, control, and communications system are kept separate from the conventional side. This is to ensure tight control of not only nuclear missiles but conventional, carrier-busting missiles as well. Like all communications, it's vulnerable to cyber and other attacks against the network. I've got a top-level source that might provide the penetration we need to stop all missile launches. Doing so ensures President Zhang has no recourse but to sue for peace.

"The second part of my plan is to have our other source in our Information Operations and Warfare branch move forward with his hacking to get into the command and control structure. Between the two, I feel quite confident in success. Are we all agreeing to put this on the fast track?" As the general surveyed the other three men around him, he saw all nod in agreement.

Ye waved over to the waiter. "I suggest we order, maintain our party decorum, and speak a little louder about everything except what we're here for."

# Chapter 16



*USS MUSTIN*
East China Sea

It was a thrilling time for the crew of the USS *Mustin* as an integral part of Task Force-70 heading for the Taiwan Strait. Compared to the open sea, they would be in tight quarters in the ninety-mile-wide strait with Taiwan on one side and the behemoth China on the other. For most in the carrier groups, it was a new experience, but for the crew of the *Mustin*, it was almost old hat because they had sailed through the strait earlier in the year.

During the officer's briefing, it was pointed out that Operation Open Seas would openly challenge the PRC with a FONOP exercise through the Taiwan Strait—China's front doorstep. It will demonstrate how the US vehemently rejects China's claims that nearly the entire western Pacific Ocean was its territorial waters. Their claim was the equivalent of saying Hawaii was in China's domain. Like during the Battle of the Bulge in World War II, when the Americans were told to surrender or else and gave the Germans "NUTS!" as a reply, the United States Navy was also implying NUTS but with a two-carrier task force as their exclamation point.

As Ensign Jansen looked around the dim light of the Combat Information Center, he was in information and visual overload. There were so many computer screens that it made his Academy cyber warfare training room seem pale in comparison. Despite his post-graduation training with the Aegis Cruiser Air Defense Simulation program that models the operations of a CIC, the reality of being immersed in the technology made his palms sticky. Everyone had headphones on and seemed to be talking with someone about something. Yet, it was eerily quiet. There were numerous sailors and officers, all tightly packed into the CIC. For Jansen, it was all very invigorating.

"Okay, Jansen, let's review the overall picture again," explained Lieutenant Whitlock. "Then we'll go over the precise details of each component. The Aegis Combat System is the world's most advanced integrated radar and combat system. Our job as an Aegis destroyer is to protect the fleet and, most importantly, our carriers against air and missile threats."

"Yes, sir, our instructors went into some detail, but the classes were nothing like this where it's right in front of you."

"Well, that's why the CO and I want to take the time to introduce you to Aegis because this is where we're going to have you specialize."

"Excellent, this is exactly where I hoped to be," said Jansen.

"Now for the meat and potatoes. The Aegis Combat System has a combined architecture with four subsystems; the newly installed AN/SPY-6 multifunction radar can handle thirty times the target as the old one. It has a track capacity of more than one hundred targets, a command and decision system called CDS, an Aegis display system called ADS, and the weapon control system called WCS. When a threat is detected, the CDS receives data from the ship's external sensors via our satellites and delivers a command, control, and threat assessment. Based on the CDS output, the WCS immediately calculates engagement instructions, selects weapons, and interfaces with the weapons' fire control systems. With me?"

"Yes, sir. What about our ability to defend against ballistic missiles? I've read so much about the supposed capabilities of the Chinese missile program. If you were to believe every report you read, you would wonder why we shouldn't turn tail and run."

"I was just getting to that, but a solid question," declared Lieutenant Whitlock. "Ours is the sea version of the Ballistic Missile Defense System. Our Aegis Combat System provides air and fleet defense against enemy aircraft and cruise missiles using variations of our Standard Missiles, the SM-2 and SM-6. In addition, we have the Evolved SeaSparrow Missile, the MK 15 Phalanx Close-in Weapon System, the TLAM cruise missile, and the Tomahawk Land Attack Missile.

"For this watch, I'm the CIC Watch Officer, and I want you to be my shadow and take in everything. In normal circumstances, which the next few days will not be, the CICWO is responsible for the functioning of the room and for training and welding the CIC team into an efficient unit. My battle station is any place I'm needed when we're at general quarters. And in GQ, I'll ensure everyone is doing their job. I'll keep radar operators and lookouts informed of expected contact sectors and ensure the navigator and fire control receive all necessary assistance.

"Let's go over to the surface plot officer and check on how the formation of the task force is going and ensure that we're holding our position as ordered by the boss." With that, the two officers moved out, with Jansen looking on with wonderment and pride in his new assignment.

# Chapter 17



*MINISTRY OF STATE SECURITY*
Beijing, China

The Ministry of State Security was contained in a nondescript multi-story building located on the edge of Tiananmen Square. The MSS was responsible for counterintelligence and political security. It's one of the tools President Zhang uses to ensure no one usurped his authority and to gather intelligence on any potential threat to his position as the most powerful person in China, if not the world.

The Comprehensive Intelligence Analysis Division was inside one of the building's rooms, identified by a stark sign on the wall. Sitting on a table surrounded by four MSS agents was a designated computer with a high-quality speaker pointed at the three men and one woman.

As the audio indicator moved across the screen, the agents were treated to enhanced audio with most of the ambient noise removed. Consequently, there were no clanking plates and utensils but an acceptable audio record of four of China's elite talking. They all listened intently, waiting for each power broker to incriminate himself.

"What time did you tell him?"

"Our devoted leader will be here when he chooses."

"I told our security detail I would allow one agent inside the restaurant to keep an eye on us, but they wouldn't be privy to any of our conversation. For all they know, we're just taking former president Wan Jun to a nice dinner . . . speaking of which, here he comes."

"Please be seated, my friends. You're too kind—"

The MSS office chief stopped the playback. "As you know, everything was working as it should, perhaps even better than expected given the distance and environment. We recorded the conversation, even Premier Ye Jiang admitting that the dinner was just a front for a more serious conversation. And then this." The chief started the playback again:

"While I respect President Zhang, and although he's done much for our count—" Suddenly, a loud, distinct beep sounded throughout the room.

"And then just this annoying beep," the chief said. "No voices, no ambient sound, no nothing until they were having a drink and talking about the weather. I ask you, what the hell happened?"

"Sir," one of the field agents replied, "I know it was not us. We had everything set up to perfection and had no idea this was occurring."

"Yes, sir," said the female agent, "I had eyes on the group and, using my peripheral vision, didn't see anything unusual."

"If I may," said the second in command, "Premier Ye Jiang and especially General Li Jung have uncontrolled access to countersurveillance tools, including an audio jamming device used against clandestine recordings such as we were attempting. A small device that, with a switch of a button, emits a constant, undetected sound that disrupts any recording. I'm sorry, sir, but we cannot defeat it."

"I can't believe these men outdid us," the office chief said. "This recording was the evidence we needed to prove their conspiracy against the president. I'll report this personally to President Zhang and hope we all don't end up in prison. Failure isn't an operative word for our leader. In the meantime, I want to use all our available resources to get something on these men so we have evidence to charge them with corruption." The chief stormed out, unsettling the air in the room.

# Chapter 18



USS *Ronald Reagan*
East China Sea

"Attention on deck, this is the captain speaking. As we approach the Taiwan Strait, we will go to GQ, as will the entire task force. While missions through the strait have occurred before, this one is different because we'll meet force with force. With Operation Open Seas, we're carrying out Freedom of Navigation Operations in support of our president, who recently stated that the US would no longer accept Chinese declarations of claims to most of the western Pacific. The overt aggressive behavior of China will no longer be tolerated.

"I'm asking each of you, no matter your rank or position, to give me and your crewmates everything you have to fulfill this mission. We all pray this does not become a shooting confrontation, but by God, if it does, the United States Navy will prevail."

With that, the klaxon sounded. "General Quarters. General Quarters. All hands to your assigned stations. Go up and forward on the starboard side. Down and aft on the port side. Report readiness to CIC in five minutes. Set condition Zebra throughout the ship. Air boss, launch aircraft."

Lieutenant Sarah "Danger" Freeman was already on the launch ramp behind the controls of her E-2. She and her crew of four would first quarterback the airspace around the two fleets. A second E-2 from the *Nimitz* would join her. Their mission was to give battlespace awareness, especially in theater air and missile defense.

"Grab anything but my ass, and here we go," shouted Freeman over the noise from the turboprops. Throwing a salute back at the yellow shirt who would command their helper to push the button and release the pressure on the catapult, she applied full throttle to the plane's Rolls Royce engines. The Hawkeye was hurled off the deck along with a huge grin on the pilot's face.

With the ability to launch aircraft every twenty-five seconds, Lieutenant Commander Dick "Mad Dog" Johnson was quickly up next on the catapult so he could establish the Combat Air Patrol, called the CAP. Mad Dog had launched hundreds of times, but he could feel the butterflies flying around his stomach as he taxied into position for this flight.

He was always amazed at the crew's performance as they worked as one to get the aircraft into the air. It was the finest choreographed performance he'd ever seen. Mad Dog looked over and made eye contact with the flight deck controller wearing a bright yellow shirt while the deck team directed him to the catapult. As he nestled deeper into his seat, the last yellow shirt directed Johnson to look over to the ordnance handler in their bright red shirt. Mad Dog quickly held up his hands to show he was not touching the controls, and the red shirts armed his ordnance. Completed, he was directed back to the yellow shirt, who aligned Johnson to the final point. With his head on a swivel, the yellow shirt looked forward and aft as he motioned the aircraft into tension while Mad Dog rammed the stick to all four corners, then pushed the throttle to full power. Next, he cycled the rudders, showing the deck his controls were free and clear. As the yellow shirt sharply pointed at the shooter, the catapult was cranked up to pressure. As he did for every launch, Mad Dog smartly saluted the officer before the helper hit the release button. Just as the sound became almost deafening, the catapult fired the F-35 down the deck, reaching 150 knots in two-and-a-half seconds. As the flight deck and color shirts streaked by at an ever-increasing speed, the visual rush was exhilarating. Then Mad Dog was consumed by quiet as he hung over the ocean at eighty feet. A quick scan of his instruments indicated everything was as it should be, and Mad Dog roared off.

Satisfied, he mentally restarted his heart and went to altitude to await his wingman. Simultaneously, the *Nimitz* was launching aircraft. Two squadrons of mostly F-18s, half from the *Reagan*, took to the skies for the country's defense—twenty-four advanced fighters totally ready for any Chinese intrusion.

Ensign Brett Jansen had reacted to GQ as the carrier aircraft were forming up and was in the CIC watching over the different weapon stations. Lieutenant Whitlock was the CICWO. With a three-mile battlespace established, the entire crew in the CIC was diligently searching, detecting, tracking, and readying to engage and destroy any threats to the carriers and the task force. Working against the fleet was the compressed area of the battle space that hindered their maneuverability and allowed the Chinese to know their precise location—not a good thing.

# Chapter 19



On the forward edge of the battlespace, three nautical miles from the task force, Commander Elam Feldner was skillfully guiding the USS *Missouri*, a Virginia class fast attack submarine, in a sea filled with other submarines and was at a depth of two hundred feet. US intelligence had indicated that half of the five hundred subs in the world were in the East and South China Seas. Being from Brooklyn, Feldner was used to traffic, but not traffic carrying torpedoes and missiles that could obliterate him and his crew of 135 in the blink of an eye. Stealth was critical to survival.

The difference between Chinese and American submarines was extreme, like the difference between hot sauce and ketchup. The US fleet of sixty-eight submarines, all nuclear-powered, were built for vast distances and could remain underwater indefinitely. While China had thirteen nuclear-powered submarines, they also had seventy more affordable diesel versions, including those driven by air-independent propulsion. China's modern non-nuclear submarines could be considerably stealthier than their nuclear counterparts, emitting detectable sounds via the vessel's nuclear-powered pumping coolant. The diesel subs threatened a less-maneuverable nuclear sub at home in littoral waters.

Feldner and his crew patrolled the outer layer of carrier defense, providing long-range anti-submarine screening. Their tactic for this mission was simple: sit on the bottom—still, quiet, and ready to strike like an eel. The commander knew from previous assignments in the area that he could be sure of more than one Chinese sub shadowing their every move or, at worst, lying in wait for a US carrier. Feldner knew two other Virginia class submarines were protecting the task force, but none were in his assigned zone. If Sonar picked up anything, it would not be a friendly.

As they traversed the Taiwan Strait at General Quarters, the captain had his best personnel in the control room running the latest anti-submarine warfare, the multi-layered AN/BLQ-10 Submarine Electronic Warfare Support System, to warn them of potential hostile threats, including the number and location of them. In addition, his crew used the AN/BYG-1 Combat Control System, the Navy's undersea weapons and tactical defense system, for tracking and analyzing other submarines.

In the never-ending game of hide-and-seek between adversary and hunter, sonar reigned supreme—for both sides. Sonar Technician (Submarine) Third Class Jerome Albright, wearing his Bose headphones, was working his AN/BQQ-10 passive sonar and attempting to distinguish the ambient ocean noise from the distinct sound that would give away a PLAN submarine. Included were biological sounds ranging from snapping shrimp to whale songs, plus noise emitted from nearby boats. He was listening on the lower-frequency bands, less than 200 Hz, because that was part of the radio spectrum for the sounds emitted by most engines, machinery, gears, and auxiliary systems—meaning other submarines.

Operating in the Taiwan Strait, where the depth was usually less than five hundred feet, made Jerome's job as the go-to sonar operator considerably more difficult. Shallow water amplified ambient noise in the low frequencies to around 70 dB but could get as high as 90 dB in shipping lanes. Jerome always compared the amplification difference to a vacuum cleaner and a power lawn mower. These are amusing examples, he thought, considering he tried hard not to use either in rural Georgia.

Besides discovering other submarines, as an avid basketball player, Jerome had enjoyed the groan from a buddy when he drove by them and planted a well-placed elbow in their rib cage to open the lane for his trademark dunk. Such sounds had been frequent for two years before he joined the Navy at eighteen.

But the sounds he made his living from now came from such things as a modern Chinese Jin-class ballistic missile submarine with a sound level of approximately 110 dB. At one meter, it was comparable to standing on a runway with a jet airplane taking off right over your head. Unfortunately, that loud son of a bitch class of sub wasn't significantly noisier than the surrounding ocean, which mainly carried amplified sounds of small and large boats and ships and hidden in the din, submarines not prefaced with USS. Additionally, PLAN diesel submarines ran on extremely quiet batteries and were most difficult to detect. As the task force entered the shallow waters of the Taiwan Strait, there would be little room for error in protecting two of America's supercarriers.


Twelve miles from mainland China

Mad Dog flew his flight of four F-35s with twenty-four mostly F/A-18Fs from VFA-27, the Royal Maces, along the coast of mainland China in international waters. He lived for missions like this, flying CAP 144 miles from his home aboard the *Reagan*, and he was all strapped for combat—should it happen. It was a military axiom that the country with the most advanced weaponry held the upper edge—advantage USA. Designed for air-to-air combat, a US F-35 could dominate the aerial battlefield and change the course of a fight in a heartbeat.

On the command net radio, CNR Mad Dog checked in with Lieutenant Freeman, piloting her AWACS aircraft. "Freedom 21, Boxer 11. What do you have for me?"

"Boxer 11, Freedom 21. Nothing on the screen that would interest you, but we have eyes on China's airspace with nothing moving."

Of the twenty-four F/A-18s and four F-35s flying CAP, fourteen were armed with the new Joint Advanced Tactical Missile, designated as the AIM-260, replacing the aging AIM-120D, Advanced Medium-Range Air-to-Air Missile, AMRAAM. With many of China's fighters now armed with the PL-12 advanced medium-range air-to-air missile and the PL-15 BVRAAM with ranges up to 180 nautical miles, the US found itself outmuscled in the sky. Alarm bells had sounded in Washington DC and soon became a shriek after an Indian Air Force's Sukhoi Su-30MKI Flanker-H fled from several Pakistan F-16s and successfully evaded several AIM-120s. The pilot had used a combination of jammers, flares, and superior maneuverability to outdo the pursuing missiles in seconds. Consequently, the four missiles crashed harmlessly back to earth without success, and the US defense industry took note.

The advanced AIM-260 had a range of over 180 miles, partly by using ramjet technology, an air-breathing jet engine with no moving parts, and relying on forward motion to draw air through a unique intake design that compresses the air for combustion. When the fuel sprayed into the engine ignited, it became self-sustaining. While the AIM-120 had speeds of Mach 4, the AIM-260 could do up to Mach 5. With near hypersonic speeds, the response time for enemy fighters to evade shrank. Using radar and infrared seekers, the new missile also had a much higher survival rate against enemy jamming.

"Boxer 11, Freedom 21. Bandits, twenty times J-11 fighters, west three-five miles, bearing zero-two-one, heading northeast flight level one-niner-zero at five hundred."

Mad Dog keyed the CNR. "VFA 11 and 12, Boxer 11. Close distance on bandits. VFA 11, run parallel on the same heading, flight level three-one-zero. VFA 12, same at flight level one-niner-zero. Negative bandits toward task force. Maintain distance from coastline."

Efficiently, both squadrons simultaneously went full throttle to their assigned sectors. A new US policy was about to give the Chinese notice: none of their fighters would be allowed a close-in flyby of any American ship of war—not now, not ever again.



Using the Cooperative Engagement Capability, Ensign Jansen saw on the CEC all the information being shared by Freedom 21. CICs on every ship were analyzing the path of the Chinese J-11 fighters as they streaked northeast, just on the edge of their coastline. All Aegis radars in the task force were integrated into a single network. It was a team effort with no aircraft or ship oblivious to the entire tactical picture.

The CO's voice came over the MC-1, temporally breaking their collective concentration on the path of the J-11 fighters. "All hands, be especially vigilant. We're the closest vessel to mainland China's outermost ship. Should bandits turn this way, we will engage first. Stay alert."

"Okay," Jansen spoke to his crew, "let's run another weapons check to ensure we're battle ready and there are no surprises. We're so close to China, so you know they have scores of truck-mounted, anti-ship cruise missiles following every move we make. I want all warfare mission areas double-checked. Antiair Warfare, Anti-surface Warfare, Anti-submarine, and Strike Warfare report when checks are complete. We don't get a second chance at this, so full concentration."



Using his radio presets, Mad Dog switched to the radio used for intra-flight comms. "I'm receiving a message from our dear friends, which I'm putting through."

A voice in broken English said, "This is the People's Liberation Army Air Force on Guard. You're intruding on the Chinese air domain. Change your course immediately, or you'll be intercepted. I say again, change your course now, or our superior fighters will intercept you. You're violating Chinese sovereignty."

When the purported official repeated the message in Mandarin, Boxer 11 went back on the radio. "Maces 11 and 12, Boxer 11. Prepare for hostile actions. Do not fire unless as a last resort and given permission. No aircraft will be allowed to penetrate our CAP. Any changes to the Rules of Engagement will come from COMCARSTRKGRU."

"Boxer 11, Freedom 21. Bandits, twenty times J-11 fighters, course change. Three-zero miles out, bearing zero-eight-zero, heading east flight level one-niner-zero at seven hundred. Will intercept your current position."

"Boxer 11 to all flights. Go active on your AESA radar. Communicate with your wingman specific threats and act on them. Stay twelve miles from the coastline. Boxer 11 flight, go active with your NIFC-CA." Speaking to the two Boeing EA-18G Growlers, he added. "Spooky 11 and 12, Boxer 11. Initiate jamming now."

With a complete picture of the entire battlespace being relayed to the task force commander, tactical decisions would be made in real time using all available CAP data.

*USS Mustin*
South China Sea

As they watched the air skirmish from fifty nautical miles away, Jansen observed the twenty bandits turn toward the fleet. "Okay, we've been ordered by the CO to go weapons tight on our SM-2. Execute." With a push of a few buttons, twenty-four RIM-66 SM-2 Block IV medium-range surface-to-air missiles were one step from being fired. All Aegis ships used missiles with a range of ninety nautical miles and an altitude of sixty-five thousand feet; the SM-2 was an integral part of the layered defense of all naval assets. A solid propellant-fueled, tail-controlled missile could counter high-altitude anti-ship cruise missiles and other ASCMs that used midcourse guidance from radar illumination of the target for homing during the terminal phase—the right tool for the right job.

# Chapter 20

*COMBAT AIR PATROL*
South China Sea


Using AESA radar, the fighters used BVR tactics, or beyond visual range, that employed total information awareness from Link 16 advanced data link capabilities.

"All flights, Boxer 11. We're being spiked with their radar, but no missile threat. Do not violate Chinese airspace. Stay twelve miles from their coastline. If they switch to their missile radar, do the same."

The PLAAF aircraft were loaded with long-range missiles. They used semiactive radar homing that required the fighter to maintain a lock on the enemy until the missile's radar could take over. In this confrontation, it was a push since the J-11s were armed with R-77 missiles, close matches for the US AIM-260s. The Hornets were also armed with AIM-9X Sidewinder heat-seeking missiles.

With a closing rate of over 1,000 knots, forty-four fighters were on each other in minutes and operating using Within Visual Range, WVR tactics. The radio crackled in Mad Dog's earpiece as pilots called out targets, direction, and strategy, and some broke off their formation to give chase. Using the same tactics as the Americans, the Chinese attempted to single out aircraft and pursue them. Radar jamming only complicated the aerial arena.

WVR tactics were developed during the first biplane dogfights of World War I. The tactics involved the basic concept of angles, attempting to out-turn your enemy, and the idea of energy equations, or using one's superior speed or altitude to make attacks while maintaining enough energy to prevent the enemy from giving chase. Today, WVR was déjà vu but at just under Mach speeds.


*PLAAF CHENGDU J-20*

Major Chang Huang had had enough of this flying-in-circles bullshit. Throwing his J-20 toward the sea, Chang ordered his wingman to entertain the Americans. At the same time, he would demonstrate his stealth that would allow him to penetrate the American layered defense in a show of superiority by him and China's fifth-generation fighter.

As he leveled off and skimmed fifteen meters above the sea, Chang thought about how his wife would be upset about the risk but proud of his actions—she was that way. Her father, President Zhang Wei, had singled out his son-in-law for this vital mission to demonstrate the capabilities of China's most advanced fighter and the nation's resolve to challenge any passage through their territorial waters. He would give a show of force that would draw the world's attention.

From his Type 1475 AESA radar, Chang had a HUD carrier on his holographic head-up display, pushing the throttle to the stops. He couldn't believe the rush he felt, traveling at Mach 1.7 and at what seemed like inches over the water. So far, so good, he thought, and the missile approach warning was silent—stealth, baby.

*NORTHROP GRUMMAN E-2D ADVANCED HAWKEYE*
South China Sea

The CICO caught something on his radar. It appeared to be a bandit moving away from the aerial dogfight and heading toward the Task Force. He adjusted his radar to extremely low frequency in case the contact was a stealth fighter. The CICO was still getting up to speed with the aircraft having just been outfitted with this new technology.

Yep, there it was again. "Lieutenant, bandit breaking away, one time J-20, east one-five miles, bearing zero-eight-zero at nine hundred. Ma'am, he's heading directly toward the Task Force carriers."

"Boxer 11, Freedom 21. Bandit breaking away, one times J-20, east one-five miles, bearing zero-eight-zero at five hundred, heading towards the *Reagan*." Freeman switched to her intercom. "Nice job, CICO."

As Mad Dog made a hard 9G bank, the pressure suit's squeeze and the g-forces' effects on his body only allowed him to grunt over the radio. Leveling off and racing toward the J-20 at full throttle, he could finally talk. "Freedom 21, Boxer 11. Roger, I'm on it. Break. Boxer 12, Boxer 11. Take mission command. I'll handle the stray."

"Boxer 11, Freedom 21. Bandit speed now one-three-zero-zero."

"Freedom 21, Boxer 11. Roger. I don't have him on radar. Direct me to the bandit."

"Roger, you should have it on HUD . . . now."

"Pepper 06, Boxer 11 Confirm, weapons are still tight."

"Boxer 11, COMCARSTRKGRU. Activate targeting radar, but do not fire. I say again, do not fire. Only fire if fired upon."

"Boxer 11, Pepper 06. Copy activate targeting radar and do not fire unless fired upon. Confirming bandits are passive now."


South China Sea

*Beep-beep-beep.*

Shit, thought Chang, looks like I've got company.

His radar HUD told him an American fighter had locked its missile guidance system on his J-20.

"Chinese aircraft, this is American fighter Boxer 11 on Guard. You are ordered to change course immediately, or I will terminate your flight. I have missile lock. Do you copy?"

"Boxer 11, this is Chinese fighter Jaeger 01. You're violating Chinese airspace, and I demand that you and your carrier group turn away. Failure to do so will initiate my order to our missile command and a subsequent launch of our carrier missiles. I'm on a reconnaissance flight and have no intention of firing on you or your carrier force. If you fire on me, the command goes out instantly."

"Jaeger 01, the United States Navy is operating in international waters and takes your presence as a threat to our security. Turn away now—this is your last opportunity, or I will fire." Mad Dog knew that the J-20 was still using only passive radar, and he was guessing the pilot just wanted to buzz the *Reagan*. Still, he was eager for just one error on the part of the PLAAF pilot so he could send an AIM-260 right up his ass.

Although Mad Dog was closing the gap, he wasn't fast enough to catch the J-20 and escort him from the area. With nothing but silence on Guard, Mad Dog knew Jaeger 01 was calling his bluff.



"Roger, sir," Jansen calmly said. "Standing by, missiles tight." Jansen calmly said. "Sir, we still don't have a firing solution on the J-20."

"Roger that," said the CO. "Use caution. We have one of our own thirty miles out giving chase."

Jansen glanced down at the weapons console and saw that PO3 Foster had the wrong radar up. "PO3, why aren't you on CEC? Switch immediately so we can receive the bearing from the Hawkeye."

"Yes, sir. I have a firing solution for the bandit. Permission to fire?"

"No, he's on passive only. We have no orders to fire," exclaimed Jansen.

Excited, Foster replied loudly, "Sir, he's almost on us. We must fire now, or we're going to be hit." The young weapons sailor started the launch sequence.

Jansen quickly reached over the back of the sailor's chair, knocked Foster's hand away from the console, and then spun the PO3's chair around. Jansen yelled for security. Positioning his body between the Foster and the console, Jansen repeated his security request on his comms. Within a minute, two burly armed Marines arrived and escorted the sobbing Foster from his weapons station. As he was escorted from the CIC, Foster kept yelling they were all going to die. Just at that moment, a roar came from overhead. Jansen knew the J-20 had arrived.

He quietly took the seat of the now departed PO3 weapons launch operator and ensured all was safe. On his comms, he heard the CO say, "Bandit on us, still on passive radar. Do not fire. I say again, do not fire."

Sitting in the adjacent chair, the operator said, "Sir, that was close. One more step, and he would have launched."

"Yes, but he didn't," said Jansen. "Carry on with your duties. We still have a Chinese jet buzzing around us, and we could be ordered to go active any second."

"Yes, sir, I'm on it."



The president of China looked at the vast six-meter screen as radar tracked the aerial skirmish and the progress of his son-in-law as he skillfully flew his J-20 right at the heart of the American carrier fleet and the *Reagan*. Despite the success, there was apprehension in the air because the top leaders of China knew that an F-35 was pursuing Chang and had activated its missile radar.

The consensus among those in the Central Military Commission who were in the room with the president was that the Americans wouldn't shoot down an aircraft that was not targeting their fleet but was only doing a flyby, something that had been down countless times before. Flybys were just a continuation of China's strategy of intimidation. If the US were dumb enough to shoot down the fighter, China would have the excuse to escalate the tit-for-tat to an all-out shooting war that Zhang knew the Chinese would win. If the flyby plan were successful, as most thought it would be, Zhang would order the next surprise.

"General Wang, prepare our ballistic missiles for launch," stated Zhang calmly.



South China Sea

With the USS *Ronald Reagan* in sight, Major Chang pulled back on the stick. He did a vertical climb, draining off speed as he slowly rolled over for a parallel run by the carrier at near stall speed. As he flew by, he could see the officers on the Bridge staring at him in disbelief. His mission nearly accomplished, Chang went to full throttle and pulled a tight bank toward home. As he was mentally congratulating himself, there was a tremendous explosion at the rear of his jet. In a millisecond, Chang saw all his instruments respond erratically. He lost control of his aircraft and pulled the ejection lever as his J-20 started to tumble toward the sea. After that, everything went black.

*LOCKHEED MARTIN F-35C LIGHTNING II*

South China Sea

Mad Dog Johnson could only smile as his finger relaxed on the trigger of his SM-6 as the J-20 splashed into the sea. If there were a prettier site than this, he'd love to see it.

"Boxer 11. Splash one bandit."

*AUGUST 1ST BUILDING*

Beijing, China

"What just happened?" screamed President Zhang.

"Mr. President, it appears Major Chang was shot down," exclaimed General Wang. "Our radar did not detect a missile launch but detected an explosion at the aircraft's back. Perhaps the Americans used their new laser technology to take down our fighter."

"Is Chang okay?"

"I'm not sure, sir. The Americans are jamming the area. It was a large explosion, sir."

"They may have killed my son-in-law, but our mission remains unchanged. General, give the order to fire ballistic missiles."

*PEOPLE'S LIBERATION ARMY ROCKET FORCE*
Qinghe, Haidian District of Beijing, China

The order to fire missiles went through General Zhou Kwon, who was in command of the PLARF and took his orders only from the president. He commanded 125,000 personnel divided among six ballistic missile brigades across China. The PRC had the world's most prominent land-based missile arsenal, with well over two thousand ballistic missiles and hundreds of cruise missiles. General Zhou was preparing to launch two of his most powerful ballistic missiles. The first would be a Dongfeng DF-26B, able to strike targets between 1,864 and 3,417 miles away. The second, the Dongfeng DF-21D medium-range missile with a range of 621 to 1,864 miles, was called a "carrier killer" for all the right reasons. And both missiles had enough maneuverability to hit large, moving warships.

"General Zhou, we're prepared to launch and are awaiting your order," stated his second in command.

"Give me the parameters again."

"Yes, sir. We're firing the DF-26B from Qinghai Province and the DF-21D from Zhejiang Province. Both are programmed for our target in the South China Sea."

"Permission granted. Launch the missiles."

# Chapter 21

*USS Ronald Reagan*
South China Sea

No one on the deck of the *Reagan* could believe their eyes when the Chinese J-20 did a vertical climb followed by a slow pass alongside their ship. Later, sailors would exchange stories about how they could see right into the cockpit as the pilot calmly buzzed their ship—waving. But that was nothing compared to the fighter blowing up nearly right over the deck. No one knew for sure what had happened. Some speculated that Mad Dog put an SM-6 up the J-20's tailpipe. Others thought it was a combat laser from one of the nearby Aegis destroyers that brought the jet down. Speculation only added to the mystery. But what was certain was that *Reagan*'s alert lookouts had spotted a pilot ejecting, a chute deploying, and what appeared to be an unconscious or dead person drifting down into the sea.

"Pedro 21, Starlight," called the *Reagan*'s Air Boss to an airborne Sikorsky MH-60R Sea Hawk helicopter. "We have a Chinese fighter down with the pilot in the water two miles northwest of our location. Commence rescue operations."

"Starlight, Pedro 21. Roger that, four miles out."

Lieutenant Lucy Wu went into action piloting the Sea Hawk as she twisted the collective to maximum throttle. A native of Taiwan and a graduate of Annapolis, Wu was close to her homeland while on her way to rescue a Chinese pilot—that was hard to compute for the twenty-eight-year-old.

Wu told her copilot, "Lieutenant, mark the carrier position and give me a heading to the downed pilot's location. SAR, suit up. You have just a few minutes."

Both answered simultaneously, "Roger, L-T."

For Naval Aircrewman (Helicopter) Third Class Liam Javernick, this search and rescue mission culminated from some of the Navy's most rigorous training. A star swimmer back home in Iowa, Javernick had wanted to become a rescue swimmer since he saw a movie called *The Guardian*, starring Kevin Costner. Soon after enlisting in the Navy, Javernick went through a four-week Aircrew school, followed by a five-week Aviation Rescue Swimmer school. After graduation, he attended the "A" school for the type of helicopter he would become qualified in. When completed there, Javernick was off to the Fleet Replacement Squadron for eight months of training on in-flight procedures, such as hoist operations and in-flight troubleshooting. Finally, he went to the dreaded school: Survival, Evasion, Resistance, and Escape. It was a brutal two-week school that many failed. But for the Iowan, it was like husking corn—you don't like it, but you get the job done. Now here he was, suiting up to do an actual search and rescue while the Sikorsky SH-60 shot across the South China Sea to pick up a Chinese pilot. He was pumped and ready.

"Lieutenant, I have a body off the bow at one o'clock," said the copilot. He pointed across the cockpit at a body bobbing in the calm sea.

"Roger, I see him. SAR, are you ready?"

"I sure am, L-T."

"Okay, coming in for your drop. Stand by."

As Wu trimmed speed, she lowered the collective to hover the helo fifty feet above the sea. Controlling the cyclic perfectly, she gave slight pressure to the left rotor pedal and aligned the aircraft for Javernick to exit. In position, Javernick threw open the side door and looked down at the churning water caused by the powerful rotors. Sitting on the edge of the Sikorsky, he felt adrenaline stimulating all his muscles. He was ready.

Sliding out the helicopter's side door, he jumped into the sea. The cold water shock only added to his determination to make it a successful rescue, no matter the pilot's condition or country. As he scanned the area, he saw a body floating near him. Swimming the last few feet to the pilot, he noticed their head was upright due to the support of an inflated vest. Flipping open the visor, he saw that a man's eyes were shut.

Javernick yelled, "Can you hear me? Talk to me."

Nothing.

Javernick signaled to the helicopter for the rescue sled. As the metal rack reached him, he carefully wrestled the body into it and raised his hand in the signal to take it up. As he watched the sled rise, Javernick silently prayed the man was still alive—everyone deserved to live.

With the Chinese pilot safely in the Sikorsky, the crew lowered the cable for Javernick, who promptly clipped it to his rescue vest and was efficiently pulled up. Once aboard, he checked the man's vitals. With his cold, wet hand slipping along the pilot's neck, Javernick finally hit the carotid artery and was rewarded with a weak pulse. Thank you, Lord, he whispered to himself.

Excited, he shouted above the roar of the blades pounding the air, "L-T, I have a pulse!"

Wu reacted quickly, slamming the collective to full military power as she thundered toward the *Reagan*. "Starlight, Pedro 21. Popcorn plus one. The pilot is alive but unconscious. Have medical personnel standing by."

After expertly lowering the Sea Hawk to the deck of the *Reagan*, sailors ran to the helo and chocked the wheels. Just as quickly, five medical corps crew members rushed up and gently lowered the rescue sled to a gurney. As they did so, they heard an audible groan from the PLAAF pilot. And then they heard over the loudspeakers, "We have enemy missiles inbound! Institute incoming missile protocol."

Missile Defense Agency, MDA
Guam

"Sir, two confirmed launches of missiles, both from China," said the Army technician as calmly as he could.

"Give me the specifics," instructed the watch officer on duty as he hit the emergency warning switch on his console to alert all commands about incoming missiles.

"Sir, a DF-26B as Target One, from China's northwestern Qinghai Province, and a DF-21D as Target Two, from Zhejiang Province on China's eastern coast."

The radar specialist was confident with his information because he was tied into the Early Warning Radar and the C2BMC radar, which integrated individual ballistic missile defense systems using land, sea, and space components. Together, they created a global, networked, and layered missile defense apparatus capable of identifying, tracking, and intercepting ballistic missile threats in all phases of flight. Forward-based AN/TPY-2 theater missile defense systems operated under one battle picture.

With the launch of two ballistic missiles toward a task force of two Carrier Strike Groups, the United States faced an unprecedented attack.

"COMCARSTRKGRU, MDA Guam. Fireball, fireball. Incoming missiles your location. Two targets. Stage zero separation."

"MDA, COMCARSTRKGRU. We're on it, and the entire fleet is taking appropriate action."

A few moments later, the specialist reported, "We have stage one separation on Target One, negative on Target Two. Sending tracking data." He added not long after, "Target Two stage one separation. Target One stage two separation."





"USS *John Finn*, COMCARSTRKGRU. Go active with SM-3 Block IIAs. Permission granted to fire when appropriate," said Admiral Wisniewski.

"*John Finn*, SM-3s going active on Target One and Target Two using system data track from C2BMC." The Arleigh Burke class destroyer was locked on both targets.

In the CIC of the *John Finn*, the weapons control center crew awaited the final order. "CO," said CICWO, "we have a final firing solution. Standing by."

"You have permission—fire."

"Two eagles away!"

Two SM-3 missiles ignited in a large plume of flames and smoke from the vertical launch tubes and began their journey.

The SM-3 interceptor was a defensive weapon designed to take out short and intermediate-range ballistic missiles in their third and final stages of separation. After launch, the SM-3 kill vehicles used onboard navigational thrusters to maneuver toward the incoming target. It used sheer force instead of an explosive warhead to destroy its target. It was like sending a ten-ton truck traveling at 600 mph at an incoming ballistic missile.

*John Finn* reported the SM-3s' activities on the net. "Eagles receiving and processing track data . . . maneuvering toward the target . . . performing discrimination and target selection . . . performing aimpoint selection. Mark–successful intercept on both targets."

The roars of the two successful intercepts went up across half the world as scores of ships, MDAs, seventy C2BMC workstations, and the White House celebrated. Flying over the South China Sea in an E-2 came another celebratory shout from a brash Lieutenant Sarah "Danger" Freeman, who screamed with joy and said it all, "We got them, assholes! Go, Navy!"

All nineteen Chinese fighters engaging the CAP turned back to the mainland. In the skirmish, there were no causalities on either side except for the Chinese president's son-in-law.

"General Wang," said the president, "you're my second in command of all forces in the PLA. If you want to keep that position, you had better explain the two major setbacks we've encountered in just a few hours."

The general quickly replied, "As for Major Huang, our satellites and his radar showed no signs that the US shot him down. While possible, I believe a catastrophic engine failure caused the plane to crash. His aircraft had the WS-15 engine, which we've had serious problems with, and they are being replaced. We're still analyzing the data as we talk."

"I don't believe that for one minute, general," exclaimed the president. "That was a huge explosion. It had to be caused by the Americans striking our brave pilot with an air-to-air missile. To blame our most advanced fighter for engine problems is ludicrous. And what about our two missiles that were shot down? Did those engines also blow up?"

"As we had planned," the general explained, "this was to be a day that we flexed our muscles to show the Americans the might of our military—the combat sortie to challenge their CAP, Major Chang's flyby of the *Reagan*, and missiles programmed to hit near the carrier fleet. In all our previous missile firings, we have heard their objections, but no one acts. Obviously, the US has decided to challenge us at another level in the Indo-Pacific—our home waters. This blatant shooting down of our two missiles gives us the excuse to move forward. Operation Safe Net is on schedule, and it won't be long under your leadership that the American influence in the area will be eliminated, and Taiwan will be reunited with our homeland— I can guarantee this, Mr. President."

# Chapter 22



*USS Missouri*
South China Sea


Things were no longer status quo, thought Commander Elam Feldner aboard his Virginia class attack submarine. Events were transpiring quickly, fast turning into an all-out war. A Chinese fighter was shot down, missiles fired in the direction of the US task force, and aerial engagements—all an abrupt change from the days of playing the high-risk tag game of I buzz you; you buzz me. The stakes were being raised, and the man from Brooklyn didn't want his submarine to be part of the next ante with a winner-take-all pot—unless he could rig the game to his favor. His mission was to locate all PLAN submarines in his sector and to keep them from being within firing range of the carriers.

"Captain, Sonar. I've got a faint contact, bearing one-eight-seven, unknown range." Sonar Technician (Submarine) Third Class Jerome Albright had been analyzing the contact for an hour but couldn't confirm it until now.

"Sonar, Captain. Roger. Let's try to get direction and speed. Designate contact as Sierra One. Stay with him, Jerome. Break. OOD, left rudder to three-zero-zero, speed 5 knots."

"Captain, OOD. Left rudder to three-zero-zero, speed 5 knots." As the OOD repeated the command, a junior sailor who was the sub's pilot used his four-button, two-axis joystick to change the course.

In underwater seek and destroy, the game was ruled primarily by math. Passive sonar could only tell you the direction of the contact. By maneuvering and being patient, the crew in the plotting room would determine how fast the contact's direction changed by comparing the data to their direction and speed. With additional course changes and measurements between the good guys and the contact, one could estimate the distance to the submarine. After an hour or two of plotting course changes, the crew could also conclude how fast the contact was going and its course. Eventually, they could calculate a firing solution, should it be needed. But it had to be done silently, not to reveal your position, or the roles would change instantly, and the hunted became the hunter.

"Conn, Sonar," said Albright, "after running data through the computer files, I designate Sierra One as a Chinese Yuan class, Type 039A/41 diesel-electric submarine."

This information is essential. Feldner now knew several vital factors about his adversary, such as that the Type 039 was covered with rubber anti-sonar protection, used advanced noise reduction techniques, and was as quiet as anything prowling the seas. The captain knew it carried Yu-6 torpedoes and the supersonic YJ-18 series anti-ship and land-attack cruise missiles with inertial plus terminal active radar guidance and a range of seventy-five miles. The Yuan-class submarine also had enhanced sonar, either provided by the Russians or copied and produced by Chinese companies. Feldner was surprised they could get a return on their passive sonar, advantage *Missouri.* The submarine was ninety miles from the fleet. That was close enough.

An hour passed.

"Conn, Sonar. I've lost contact with Sierra One. Working to reacquire."

Feldner had a decision to make. With the task force quickly cruising within the range of Sierra One, it was crunch time. He knew he was probably close, but that could be changing by the minute. He could use his active sonar and likely find the exact location of the 039A. Still, he would also reveal his precise position. Both submarines would then have firing solutions, and the chances were neither would survive a torpedo attack on the other. But the Chinese sub might also hightail it out of the area and speed away from the oncoming fleet. He could hope to reacquire the 039A, get a fix, and be prepared to take him out should Sierra One's commander become aggressive by preparing to take a shot at one of the carriers. A second choice would be to call for reinforcements to force Sierra One out of the area or to sink it.

Acting on his instincts and experience chasing submarines for ten years, Feldner ran through the scenarios again, taking less than a minute to compute the potential life-and-death decision.

"Sonar, Conn. Any hint of a reacquire?" asked Feldner.

"Conn, Sonar. Sorry captain, nothing."

"Comm, Conn. Send the following message to COMCARSTRKGRUFIVE. Lost contact with Chinese Yuan class, Type zero-three-nine-alpha sub, coordinates 26°30' north, 121°23' east. Last bearing zero-eight-five at 5 knots. Request ASW support."

Since the first submarine entered service, communications with the outside world were restricted by the depth at which the vessel could exchange information and by the speed at which they could do so through the medium of water. The submarine would have to travel near the surface to transmit, allowing the communication antenna to break the surface. While it worked, it could jeopardize a sub's location and expose it to Anti-submarine Warfare efforts.

*Missouri* didn't have this problem. It was freshly fitted with a top-secret communication device called Quantum Key Distribution. The submarine didn't have to sacrifice speed or rise near the surface. With QKD, the craft used laser optical communication to a satellite or an airborne platform, such as the Boeing P-8A Poseidon. It was a game changer, especially now.

# Chapter 23



*KADENA AIR BASE*
Okinawa, Japan


Sitting around the ready room at Kadena Air Base, on a large island in the middle of the Pacific Ocean, Lieutenant Junior Grade Carlos Martinez was daydreaming about how he came to be on this nondescript island. It began simply enough when he became friends with his neighbor Jose Gonzales in East Los Angeles, a man who flew McDonnell Douglas F-4 Phantom IIs in Vietnam back in the day. Carlos could only dream of flying after hearing about his exploits during the war. When Jose bought a Cessna 172, the first person he took on a ride was Carlos, whom he eventually taught how to fly. Although Carlos couldn't afford to get an FAA license, he knew he was a good pilot. Fortunately, Jose was a good friend who could have been his granddaddy and a mentor who encouraged Carlos to go to college and let Uncle Sam pay for flying. So, it was off to the University of California Los Angeles and its outstanding ROTC program, from which Carlos graduated, the first from his family to do so. He got commissioned into the Navy and earned his golden wings. Years later, here he was, deployed from his unit's home base at NAS Jacksonville as a pilot of a P-8A Poseidon maritime patrol aircraft, a bird described as one of the best all-purpose planes in the Navy.

Carlos would have enjoyed bragging to Jose about the latest addition to the P-8, but it was classified. But what he had been able to tell Jose about the aircraft's capabilities had impressed the ol' fighter jock. The multi-mission Boeing jet, modified from the civilian 737-800 aircraft, performed anti-submarine warfare, ASW, anti-surface warfare, ASUW, and shipping interdiction missions. The plane was armed with torpedoes and Harpoon anti-ship missiles and carried sonobuoys. Upgraded additions included the Lockheed Martin AGM-158C Long Range Anti-Ship Missile. On the drawing board was the integration of 500 and a 2,000-pound Joint Direct Attack Munitions, simply called JDAMs, and slight modifications for MK 62/63/65 Quickstrike mines, the Small Diameter Bomb, the Miniature Air Launched Decoy or MALD, the Bomb Rack Unit BRU-55, and a Universal Armament Interface, or UAI—an alphabetic list of killer upgrades.

*Gong, gong, gong.*

"VP-45, patrol crew Alpha. Emergency mission. I say again, emergency mission."

After the second *gong*, nine crew members had already started to sprint to their P-8, with LTJG Carlos Martinez leading the way.

Sliding into the left seat as the mission commander, he grabbed his headset and contacted operations to learn about their mission.

They replied, "Switchblade, VP-45. Just received from *Missouri* the following: lost contact with a Chinese Yuan class, Type zero-three-niner-alpha sub, 26°30' north, 121°23' east. Last bearing zero-eight-five at 5 knots. Request ASW support. Stop. Proceed at the best speed to the target area and assist; contact airborne Hawkeye, call sign Freedom 21. Per COMCARSTRKGRUFIVE, you have permission to engage if the torpedo or missile tubes are flooded. Task force is sailing within strike range of the Chinese sub. Chinese ballistic missiles were just shot down that targeted the task force. And PLAAF has skirmished with US fighters."

"VP-45, Switchblade. Roger. En route."


South China Sea

PLAAF Major Chang Huang slowly tried to open his eyes and wondered where the hell he was. Dammit, why is it so hard to open my eyes? As Chang tried to force them open, squinting, he could only distinguish bright lights and thought he must be in the process of rebirth, just as he was taught in his religion. He wondered what was in store for him now.

"Major Chang, can you hear me?"

Crazy, he thought, someone's calling my name. I guess I'm still alive.

"Major Chang, I'm the Naval Surgeon aboard the USS *Ronald Reagan*. You've been injured, but we're taking care of you. Do you understand?"

Wait a minute . . . USS *Ronald Reagan* . . . okay, I remember. I was on a mission to that ship.

"Major Chang, you're alive and should have a complete recovery. Try and open your eyes, and we can talk."

So, I'm not in the process of rebirth. I'm still in this world— I'm still alive! That means I can open my eyes.

Slowly, the major forced his eyes open and saw a Black person staring at him from just inches away.

"Hello," was all Chang could mutter, but in near-perfect English.

"Hello to you, major," said the Black man.

Chang finally got his eyes fully open, and he scanned the room. He was in some hospital with two other uniformed people smiling at him, and a third person had a stern look and daggers for eyes that probably never smiled in his life.

"We're going to prop you up a little," said the Black man who had said he was the surgeon, "so we can explain what is happening. We gave you a sedative because you got a little frisky while on the edge of consciousness." Chang felt his back rising, and he was no longer prone in the bed.

"Welcome to the USS *Ronald Reagan*. As I said, I'm the ship's surgeon, Commander Jackson. That was some entrance you made!"

"What do you mean?"

"It appears you don't recall, but that's normal trauma after ejecting from an aircraft and splashing into the sea."

"What do you mean ejecting?"

"There was an explosion as you were flying away from our ship, and a moment later, you ejected—just in time, I might add."

Just then, Chang remembered. He had made a flyby of the carrier and was heading home when his jet blew up. Oh shit, he thought, I bet my wife and father-in-law think I'm dead. "Sir, we must get word to my people that I'm alive, or I fear there may be retribution. Please get word to the Chinese authorities that I'm alive."

"Commander, I got this," said the man with no smile and in a uniform different from what the others wore. He lightly pushed the doctor to the side. This was the man with no smile. "I'll be happy to make notifications shortly. Let me ask, what was your purpose for flying at the USS *Ronald Reagan*?"

"Please, contact my people first so we don't have another incident. Believe me, the next one will be much more serious. We can talk after."

The man with no smile looked at him and seemed to decide what to do next. Suddenly, a woman entered the room and gently pulled the man away from the bed. A few seconds later, he was back.

"Major, any specific message to your people?"

"Besides the obvious, tell them I was not shot down but had a catastrophic engine failure. That would be a good start."

"We'll do that immediately." Mister No Smile then quickly turned and left the room with the woman.



"HSM-77, crew delta," blared a voice over the MC-1. "Report to your aircraft for emergency deployment."

Lieutenant Lucy Wu, who was trying to get some shut-eye in a ready-room chair, instantly snapped awake, grabbed her gear, and was off. Sprinting to her Sikorsky MH-60R Sea Hawk helicopter, she saw her other two crewmates just climbing on board: the copilot, the Airborne Tactical Officer, or ATO, and the sensor operator and the SAR specialist, Naval Aircrewman (Helicopter) Third Class

Liam Javernick. At the helo, Wu jumped into the right seat as the pilot, which differed from a fixed-wing pilot's position, mainly because helicopter pilots held a cyclic stick in their right hand.

"Ramrod, Starlight. The message from *Missouri* follows. Lost contact with a Chinese Yuan class Type zero-three-niner-alpha sub at 26°30' north, 121°23' east. Last bearing zero-eight-five at 5 knots. Request ASW support. Stop. A P-8 will assist and be on station by the time you arrive. Communicate with Freedom 21, our Hawkeye playing quarterback in the area."

"Roger Starlight comm." As she ended her communication, she noticed that Lieutenant Junior Grade Jennings had powered up the electrical system, which hadn't reached fifteen volts. He was about to start the engine. Doing so would cause a hot start—not good.

"Slow down, Jennings. The voltage is too low. Wait until it's in the green."

"Sorry, L-T, my bad. I just want to get going as fast as possible."

"We all do, but even on our slowest day, we're airborne within four minutes. Let's slow it down and ensure we don't compromise the engine—or the crew."

"Chock and chain handlers clear," reported the copilot.

"Tower, Ramrod. Ready for takeoff," said Wu.

"Ramrod, Tower. You have priority. Check with your LSE, and you're green to go."

"Ramrod," acknowledged Wu on the radio. On the intercom, she said, "I have the controls." The landing signal officer gave the crew hand signals to marshal a safe ascent, and they were on their way.

# Chapter 24



"Alfa Conn, Freedom 21. We're on station and request your Bullseye. We have a P-8 and a Sea Hawk arriving in minutes to assist," said the E-2's RO. "Have you had any further contact with Sierra One?"

"Freedom 21, Alfa Conn. Negative on contact. Sending location. Heading one-eight-five, five hundred feet at three knots."

"Alfa Conn, Freedom 21. Roger, relaying to support ACs."

"RO," said Lieutenant Freeman, "make sure all assets are on the same frequency so we all receive the same information."

The RO made the necessary comms, and a once-silent frequency carried the beautiful audio of US Navy efficiency.

"Ramrod, Switchblade. We will lay a field of active sonobuoys in the direction Sierra One was last traveling. Suggest dipping sonar in the opposite direction."

"Switchblade, Ramrod. roger, dipping sonar." Lieutenant Wu dropped the nose of the helicopter, applied throttle, and was off to a spot in the wide-open sea to look for a very silent Chinese submarine. Using a durable and reliable reeling system, Javernick lowered the six hundred-pound AN/AQS-22 Airborne Low-Frequency Sonar into the water by sampling the twenty-five hundred feet of cable available. Hovering fifty feet above the rotor wash-induced frothy sea, the helo crew listened carefully on active sonar for any sound of the Chinese submarine. Nothing. Just like fishing, Wu thought, you reel in your line and look for the next likely spot to catch a sub, then repeat.

On board the P-8A Poseidon aircraft, mission commander and pilot LTJG Martinez led the crew of nine, the same group of people he had been flying with since he got to Kadena Air Base. This was important. In the high-stakes mission of ASW, knowing how the person next to you will react to threats and detections was imperative to one's survival and discovery of the enemy. Decisions from a tight crew were quicker and more efficient.

Behind the Poseidon's dual-pilot cockpit was a row of side-by-side seats for the two sensor operators, or ASOs, plus relief pilot and in-flight technician. Weapon Systems Officers handle weapons above the surface and a submarine hunter for anything below the surface. The ASOs used an integrated suite of instruments that included radar and electro-optical and electronic signal detection sensors to provide search, detection, location, tracking, and targeting capabilities against surface targets. Sensor systems also provided tactical situational awareness information for dissemination to fleet forces and intelligence, surveillance, and reconnaissance information for exploitation by the joint intelligence community. Sending live updates with encrypted radios and communication systems was crucial because the information might be too dated to be helpful by the time the crew got back to base.

"Okay, ASOs," said Martinez. "Do you have a grid for me to lay our field of sonobuoys? They've got a big head start on us."

"Sure do. Computer analysis completed. I just sent the coordinates."

"Roger. Got it." With the grid information, Martinez executed the suggested flight pattern, making a tight bank angling down to two hundred feet above the seemingly never-ending South China Sea. Flying so low for an aircraft frame that was engineered for cursing at thirty thousand feet was challenging. With the thicker, more turbulent air of lower altitudes, the reinforced structure of the P-8A could cope, but the pilot's skill was key. There was little room for error at 260 knots and just feet from the surface.

"WSO, launch sonobuoys at five-second intervals," said Martinez.

"Roger. Launching now in five-second intervals."

At that moment, in the rear of the aircraft, the L3 Harris Sonobuoy Rotary Launch System, with the ability to launch a buoy every three seconds, was activated. Each buoy had a small parachute that allowed the AN/SSQ-62E Directional Command Activated Sonobuoy to enter the water gently. With the water depth in the grid area at only four hundred feet, the buoys were preprogrammed for three hundred feet. The new and improved thermal batteries in the buoys had a life of eight hours. Modifications to depth by UHF and VHF radio signal commands could be made from the Poseidon.

The crew decided to set the buoys in active mode, understanding that it would give away the location of the sonobuoys but also provide the best chance to locate Sierra One.

The monitoring system provided search, detection, location, tracking, and, once located, targeting data for Sierra One. Both sensor operators were listening to the feeds from the sonobuoys. They observed as their computers translated noise in the water into colorful graphs and suggested new locations to drop additional sonobuoys.

"JG," said the ASO, "monitoring, but no positive returns."

"Roger that," said Martinez. "Give me the coordinates for the next drop." Shit, he thought, every second we don't locate the bandit increases the search radius, and the advantage goes to the submarine captain.

"Ramrod, Switchblade. Any luck?" asked Martinez.

"Switchblade, Ramrod," answered Wu. "Not a beep."

In the helo's cockpit, the copilot leaned forward.

"Just a minute," said the copilot on the intercom. "I have a faint return on active sonar, bearing one-one-seven, unknown range."

Wu toggled the radio mic. "Switchblade, Ramrod. Hold everything. Contact one-one-seven, unknown range. We're repositioning."

"Ramrod, Switchblade. Heading your way."

Martinez turned the yoke, applying throttle to close the distance to the Sea Hawk, who had caught Sierra One heading back from where it had come. The sub's captain had to know the United States Navy was on to him—not a pleasant feeling, Martinez imagined.

"JG," the young radar operator sitting at the Inverse Synthetic Aperture Radar station shouted on the net, "pop-up contact bearing zero-four-five, range 10 miles. Signature of periscope. Designating contact as Sierra One."

Martinez knew the ISAR had a perfect detection system for this event. "Ramrod, Switchblade. We're coming in fast. Go to five hundred feet west of the bearing and standby."

"Switchblade, Ramrod. roger."

As the P-8A Poseidon entered the search area, the crew was rewarded.

"Madman! Madman!" the same radar operator yelled.

The callout meant only one thing—they had just flown over Sierra One. Thanks to the sensor's magnetometers that detected ferromagnetic materials, a submarine's presence in the Earth's magnetic field would distort that field around it and give its position away to an airborne sensor.

Now the playing field changed. No longer was the Chinese submarine on the hunt for prey. It was the hunted. The crew of the P-8 worked on a firing solution and quickly let the mission commander know when it was complete.

"To all commands on the net, Switchblade. We have a firing solution for Sierra One. Will fire on Sierra One if they flood torpedo or missile tubes."

"Switchblade, COMCARSTRKGRUFIVE. Copy. All assets standby at a tactically safe distance."

Aboard *Missouri*, the crew had received the Chinese sub's exact location and was monitoring it.

"Conn, Sonar," said Albright. "Sierra One is surfacing bearing two-six-zero, heading toward the mainland."

Circling above the water, the P-8's pilot and copilot noticed a distinct white pattern in the sea.

"To all commands on the net, Switchblade. We have a visual on Sierra One," reported Martinez. "Sierra One is surfacing."

"Switchblade, COMCARSTRKGRUFIVE. You have permission to let the Chinese captain know we're heading his way."

"COMCARSTRKGRUFIVE, Switchblade. roger that, with pleasure." Martinez warned his crew on intercom, "Hang on, boys and girls, here we go!"

From five thousand feet, the JG pushed the yoke down hard and watched his speed increase as the altimeter spun backward faster than a berserk clock. Martinez took aim and piloted the large aircraft straight toward Sierra One. Just as several of Sierra One's crew came topside, the P-8A Poseidon roared overhead, mere feet above their submarine and low enough to send shivers down the Chinese crewmembers' spines. They knew they had been compromised and needed to exit the area quickly.

And they did, heading for the safety of their shores and thankful for not being sent to the bottom of the South China Sea. To the person, it was humiliating as the large aircraft flew over again and waved its wings as if saying, see you next time.

As the US task force sailed out of the Taiwan Strait into the vast South China Sea, COMCARSTRKGRUFIVE ordered a stand down from general quarters. With no loss of life, the command staff of the task force and USINDOPACOM felt the Navy had conveyed the message that the United States would be more aggressive when sailing in the Indo-Pacific region to repudiate the PRC's claim to the area. It was now up to the Chinese to relent, or the Cold War could thaw and quickly become an all-out shooting confrontation.

# Chapter 25



*HANGER E-3, ANQUING TIANZHUSHAN AIRPORT*
Anquing, China

General Sun Tong was the ideal person for the PLA's top-secret project. As an aerospace engineer, he understood China's state-of-the-art YJ-12 advanced anti-ship missile and was a former pilot of the famed H-6 strategic bomber.

But above all else, what Sun valued most was his proven lineage to one of China's greatest generals, Qi Jiguang, who achieved fame with the defeat of the Mongol army after they breached the Great China Wall in 1549. After this success, Qi oversaw the defense of the Zhejiang coastal area against pirate raiders. The celebrated general contested Japanese pirate attacks by training volunteer soldiers in his innovative tactical formation called the Mandarin Duck Formation. Assigned to groups of twelve to protect their leader at all costs, if the soldiers' leader was killed, Qi ordered that all survivors be slain. The logic was simple to Qi, and it instilled in the twelve-man protection squad the mentality to fight with every ounce of their being to ensure the survival of all. The concept worked, and Qi was promoted to China's highest military rank, Commissioner in Chief, which influenced the Chinese military's overall success and defensive tactics.

Sun thought he had good blood flowing through his veins. And he was about to become a legend in his own right as the person in charge of one of the most daring schemes in military history—the destruction of four American carriers in one strike. President Zhang believed in him—had handpicked him—and Sun would not disappoint.

The highly secret plan was ingenious in concept but problematic in execution. Ingenious that two civilian jetliners would appear to air traffic controllers as just two passenger aircraft from China World Airlines. But like a wolf in sheep's clothing, these apparent civilian jets would be converted to long-range strategic bombers. The plan was also problematic because the aircraft would have to fly through American airspace and get close to their targets: two carriers at Norfolk, Virginia, and two others in dry dock at San Diego, California. With four carriers destroyed, America would be left with just seven—and there were plans to make that number even smaller. Unlike the Pearl Harbor attack in 1941, when the Japanese mistakenly left the US carriers unaccounted for and soon after paid a dear price for that oversight, China wouldn't make the same error. Taking out the American carriers would most certainly ensure victory.

Overseeing the aircraft conversion project, Sun was impressed with his design. The Boeing 747-8 aircraft could carry four YJ-12 anti-ship missiles in their bellies.

The YJ-12 was the perfect weapon for the attack. With a range of 248 miles, if flying at a very high altitude, it could achieve Mach 3 speeds of over 2,300 mph depending on the launch altitude and flight path. Armed with a five hundred-kilogram or 1,102-pound warhead, supersonic speed raised its destructive power even higher. Such power would guarantee the aircraft carriers' destruction or, at the very least, would disable them for an extended period. The YJ-12 also had a superior inertial navigation system to direct it to the target. The difficulty was getting the weapons within range of the carriers to release the ordnance before being shot down by the Americans.

But the Chinese had two things working for them: first, the element of surprise, and second, the US did not shoot down civilian airliners. In fact, throughout the history of aviation, the United States has never shot down a civilian aircraft within its borders.

Today was Sun's fourth live trial of the aircraft named 勇, *The Brave One*, while the second, named 无畏, *No Fear*, would duplicate any changes needed. Sun fancied naming his plane, making them personal so the crews would feel closer to his dream. He emphasized that they should protect their aircraft as Qi Jiguang's warriors did for their leaders in the sixteenth century. The previous problems dealing with the proper extension of the weapons rack from the bomb bay doors were re-engineered by Sun, who was anxious to see the results. The target for today's test was in the China Sea, east of Shanghai. The plan was to launch a YJ-12 from 250 kilometers to target a retired destroyer sitting dead in the sea. Sun was also aware of the time factor. With tensions between his country and the US seemingly escalating daily, President Zhang wanted results and was waiting for the green light on this critical mission to his overall plan.

Once airborne and flying 11.5 kilometers, or thirty-eight thousand feet, Sun was at the controls of the China World Airlines Boeing 747-8. In a confident voice, he said, "Nearing launch point. Weapons Officer, lower the missile rack."

Now the real test begins, Sun thought, to ensure my alterations on the pylons worked. Once past this hurdle, Tong knew the YJ-12 would work to perfection.

The WO's radio call broke Sun's thoughts. "Opening doors . . . lowering ordnance. General, position of the weapon is confirmed. It's locked and ready to launch."

"Launch when ready."

The WO studied his computer screen and verified the telemetry; then, he pushed one button on his console. "Missile away!"

As the YJ-12 released from the pylon, the solid-fuel rocket booster ignited and sent the missile streaking away from the Boeing 747-8.

With a liquid fuel ramjet, the YJ-12 quickly reached Mach 3. Directing the missile to the target gently floating in the China Sea was the inertial navigation system with Beidou satellite positioning for any midcourse corrections. The terminal guidance used an infrared imaging sensor for precise targeting. With all the technology by China's best, Sun felt confident.

"General, we have a direct hit," said the adrenaline-infused WO.

Moments later, the crew could see smoke on the horizon as proof they were ready for one of the most clandestine missions in the history of warfare.

# Chapter 26



*USS RONALD REAGAN*
Philippine Sea

PLAAF Major Chang Huang was not a happy man. He strained his shoulder during his ejection from his Chinese fighter, and his left arm was now in a sling. Chang's sedative for pain was wearing off. Adding to his discomfort was some bullshit interrogation, or whatever it was, from the man with no smile and his female companion. They identified themselves as Naval intelligence officers. No Smile said he was Lieutenant Braxton, and the woman was Lieutenant Commander Anderson. Whatever.

"Again, I ask you," said Braxton, "what was your intention for flying by this ship in an unsafe and threatening manner?"

With near-perfect English, Chang answered in the most sarcastic voice he could muster, "As I've said, Mr. Personality, it was just another flyby to demonstrate the inferior defenses of your US Navy—which I proved until my fucking engine took a shit."

"Look," said Anderson in her best interpretation of a warm, loving person, "you understand how your actions could have turned your sortie into a war, don't you?"

"No, I don't. This was no big deal; you know it, I know it, the entire world knows it. So, let's stop playing games. Again, I demand that you get me on a fast plane back to China—got it?"

Moving in closer, Braxton couldn't refrain himself, "If it were up to me, asshole, I'd drop you in the middle of the China Sea and move on without giving you a second thought."

"Lieutenant," said Anderson in her sternest voice, "enough of that. Major Chang is our guest, and we'll treat him as such."

Staring right into his enemy's eyes, Braxton answered caustically, "Yes, Ma'am."

"Do you know why your country launched two missiles at our fleet?" asked Anderson. "Was it part of a strategic plan with the other aircraft flying toward our ships?"

"That would be need-to-know information, and I was not in the loop," said Chang. "But I should ask you, what gives you the right to encroach on our territorial waters?"

"Okay, we're not going there," said Anderson. "We've notified Chinese officials that you're alive aboard the USS *Ronald Reagan*. When we reach port in Japan, we'll turn you over to the Chinese Embassy. Good day, Major."

The two intelligence officers left, leaving Chang confident that his enemy had no backbone.

# Chapter 27

*THE WHITE HOUSE*
Washington DC

They were all there. The President's National Security Council sat around the Cabinet Room's long conference table surrounding their boss, President Mark Taylor. Everyone had sat in the same chairs countless times. If they chose, those facing the windows could admire the White House Rose Garden—but today wasn't that type of day. China was flexing its new military might for the world to see while demonstrating that the days of status quo, with the US running the show in the Indo-Pacific, were over—or soon would be. Adding grease to the growing fire was the passage of the Taiwan Security Act by the United States House of Representatives by a vote of 354 to 79. The TSA was now being debated in the Senate with passage all but assured.

While everyone got settled, President Taylor sat at the center of the table, silently complimenting himself on the new diet his daughter Jennie, a sworn vegetarian, had put him on after she noticed a slight bulge beginning to show on her pop's midsection. Along with his new workout regime, he felt fit for a guy closer to seventy than sixty-nine. With all the stresses of the presidency, he was convinced that being fit gave him an edge. And he thought today that would be something he needed.

"Good morning," said the president. "Well, it appears Beijing is getting the message. With the recent confrontation in the Taiwan Strait, the price of poker just went up. By launching two ballistic missiles in the direction of our carriers, sending several squadrons of fighters to test our defenses, and dispatching a sub to get close to our task force, China has seriously escalated tensions in the area. We need to develop our response to future relations with China." The president then glanced across the table to his Secretary of State, Brad Kelly. "Please lay the groundwork, Brad."

"Thank you, Mr. President. For years we've maintained a strategic ambiguity with Taiwan. Beginning in 1978, the US established full diplomatic relations with China under the Carter administration. After that, the US recognized only the PRC, meaning we affirmed by diplomatic omission their position on Taiwan that there is only one Chinese government—their One-China policy. Until your administration, Mr. President, the US policy has never changed. We've had formal diplomatic relations with the PRC but none with Taiwan. With the passage of the TSA all but assured, we have resolved this ambiguity with our friends from Taiwan and have sent a clear message to the PRC and, for that matter, the world. From this point on, a One-China policy ceases to exist, and the US recognizes the independence of Taiwan.

"With legislation moving to the Senate, we've committed to defending Taiwan at the expense of our decades-old mixed relations with China, a policy I support. I believe the PRC will, as a result, only increase its military adventurism. I'm not sure whether the PRC wants to escalate this into a real war. Still, the possibility looms larger than any other time in recent history."

"If I may, Mr. President," chimed in Robbie Spencer, the National Security Advisor, who had an office just down the hall from his boss. "We must ask ourselves how much we want to put on the table for an island of twenty-three million people, who on their own would have no chance against the PLA. I believe China would be all in with their desire to bring Taiwan back to the fold. And make no mistake; the Chinese are preparing right now, as we speak, to take us out should we get in the way. Just last week, President Zhang visited a PLA Marine base and exhorted his troops to prepare for war, maintain a state of high alert, and never forget their loyalties to their country. That comment was made as much for the US as for the Marines standing at rigid attention, throwing their fists in the air for their sworn leader and mission."

"And what should concern all of us," said Vice President James Richardson, a brilliant and informed gentleman from Harvard, "are the projections of almost every single war game we've run with just the scenario we're talking about—the high probabilities that we lose in a war with China. That equates to thousands of American lives." He tapped the table with his palm in obvious frustration.

"Excuse me, sir," interrupted General Robert Matthews, whose uniform almost sparkled because of all the badges and ribbons that covered it. "I know of those war games. And by the way, I hate the term 'game' because simulation is no game but a serious tool. But just like statistics, you can make the numbers represent whatever position you happen to be pushing. From the get-go, if you enter an equation with high percentages for a carrier kill by the Chinese DF-21D, you have a misleading outcome with the US losing. It's all data in and data out, but is the data reliable? I'm not convinced those results would happen."

Taking charge of the direction he thought the session should go, the president raised his hand slightly, "Gentlemen, all good points to bring up, but I want to hear about how we can best be prepared for war with China should it come to that. What do we need to do now that's different from what we've been doing? Do we have enough assets in the area? Are we prepared?" Taylor looked at his Secretary of Defense.

The country's brightest minds turned their heads in unison to hear from George Mitchell. "Mr. President, from the beginning, we must continue to counter public perception and opinion. President Zhang has been on a quest, through the control of his media, to show that it would be futile for the US to support Taiwan under any circumstances. We've all witnessed the enormous growth of the PLA. They have the assets to weaken any reinforcements that cross the Pacific to strengthen Guam, Japan, South Korea, and other Indo-Pacific nations. Zhang has promulgated that US forces would be so weakened and late to the battle that they shouldn't even try to do so. He has also iterated the cost to repel the PLA, who have just a short jaunt across the Taiwan Strait, compared to our reinforcements, who would have to travel over seven thousand miles to get there.

"We can continue contradicting his propaganda," SecDef went on, "but we must also consider the impact on our military. I believe we can all agree that we're already short on forces in the Indo-Pacific. If we lost a substantial portion of our Pacific Fleet and associated joint forces in a battle over Taiwan, our capacity to remain a force in the area would be enfeebled even if we prevailed. We have to ask ourselves: is it worth it?"

"I would argue it is," asserted Secretary of State Kelly. "To me, Taiwan represents a shining example of a free democracy right off the shores of a communist country that boasts legitimacy through seventy years of suppression. With the election of Taiwan's Democratic Progressive Party, tensions have risen dramatically. China sees that party's independence movement as a setback to its objective of reunification. Their answer was an increase in military exercises right off the coast of Taiwan. PLAAF fighters have made it routine to cross the actual line of control in the middle of the Strait to intimidate Taipei and test the island's defenses. It's a rehearsal for a takeover of the island.

"Beijing is now focusing on the US with a broadside of propaganda and belligerent military action. I believe we are obligated to the American people to ask ourselves if Taiwan's de facto independence is worth an armed conflict in which we have such an uncertain outcome. We might win the battle but lose the war, meaning our formidable presence around the world."

"I had a coach in high school football that had the philosophy of 'no risk it, no biscuit,'" said the president. "Sure, there's a risk of a negative outcome in Taiwan, but I feel strongly that the biscuit of freedom for the people of Taiwan justifies our actions. I appreciate the opinions expressed here today, but I want us to develop a unified plan to be prepared, as best we possibly can, for a conflict, war, or whatever, with China. We'll reconvene next week, and I want everyone in this room to formulate a solid plan for success and how we can accomplish it immediately. We've been sitting on our hands too long in the Indo-Pacific region. I want a unified strategy to be prepared for any actions brought on by China." The president quickly got up and left the room.

# Chapter 28



*GENERAL LI JUNG'S RESIDENCE*
Beijing, China

Sitting in his plush home office, General Li Jung of the PLA Rocket Force felt a bead of sweat slowly roll down his forehead. Word had filtered down to him that the meeting at the China Grill with Premier Ye Jiang, State Councilman Li Zhang, former president Wan Jun, and himself had been under surveillance by the feared Ministry of State Security. That meant only one thing: President Zhang suspected the meeting wasn't just a nice dinner among elite-level communist party loyalists. It was common knowledge that Ye wasn't a huge supporter of his immediate boss, President Zhang. Li also knew that his noise-canceling device must have saved their bacon that night, or they would all be hidden away in some dank cell or dead.

"I'm telling all of you there's nothing to worry about," encouraged General Li to his other three conspirators on his computer's screen. "Sure, the MSS was there, but they are always following some lead on people supposedly plotting to overthrow the president. It was just our turn in the bucket. They got nothing on us—and they won't. Nevertheless, I suggest no more late dinner outings. Instead, we'll use this video conferencing software on our computers.

"What we're using tonight is a software called Encryptoe—everything we say and do is encrypted. We have secure communications, and I have the parameters set to delete everything via burn-on-read timers. Each of you has had your home inspected to ensure no covert listening devices or video cameras. Now, turn on the audio jamming device for one additional security step. Then we're good to go."

"Thank you for looking out for our security," said former president Wan. "I wanted to report that I received information from two different sources, individuals that used to work for me, regarding something to do with a civilian aircraft that will somehow be used against the United States. Both sources said it's almost impossible to find anything about the top-secret project. I'll report back if I hear more, but we all should know this and keep our ears to the ground."

"Gentlemen," said Jiang, "we all have been reading about the United States Taiwan Security Act, so we need to move faster than we currently are. This bill, when passed, will push President Zhang further toward the brink of war. The key to our success is to stop missiles from ever launching or, at the very least, to keep them to a minimum. Without missiles, I give the edge to the US, which would force the president to cease hostilities. And then we hope the Americans agree to do the same. General, do you have anything to report on your sources along this path?"

"Premier, I can only comment that we're closer today than when we last met. I hope to have positive results to report very soon."

"Please keep us advised since this aspect of our plan is so important."

General Li squirmed in his chair as he thought just how challenging his assignment was.

# Chapter 29

Si De Park
Beijing, China

Dr. Dong Liang made it a point to avoid trouble even though he had serious issues with the Chinese Communist Party. As a senior at the storied Peking University in 1989, he saw many of his friends protest in a movement that focused on the Chinese f-word—freedom—a term not even remotely accepted in Beijing. His radical friends wanted freedom of the press, freedom of association, and free speech. They wanted an end to corruption in the Communist Party. The students took their demands to Tiananmen Square, where they faced off against the Chinese political establishment. Taking over the square, the student dissidents protested for two months. Dong could still hear their voices echoing, how they believed in their hearts they were making a difference. The exhilaration in their eyes still haunted him because they thought that the Party was listening, that change was coming.

Then it happened. On June 3, 1989, officials declared martial law and sent in the Army—large numbers of heavily armed combat soldiers. They came in droves with the support of tanks and heavy armor. It would be a lone student confronting a tank in Tiananmen Square and refusing to give up his ground that became the dissidents' rallying cry to the world.

But it was short-lived. With little warning, the PLA opened fire on the unarmed student dissidents with a barrage of bullets that literally cut protesters in half. There were body parts strewn around the square like discarded trash. Young students, some just wounded, were driven over by massive, armored personnel carriers. Thousands were killed and injured. Some of Dong's best friends were those that gave up their lives for something bigger than them all.

Dong didn't participate in the protest, which haunted him decades later. He was a thinker and a planner who wanted to make a difference like his friends, but his methods were subtle. Not drawing attention to himself would make him more effective when the time came. But as Dong grew older and his hair turned gray, he worried his day of dissent from behind the scenes would never come. He felt remorseful that he had let his long-dead friends down.

Dr. Dong Liang was a bespectacled, balding, five-foot-three, overweight fifty-five-year-old whom people paid little attention to other than when he was in the cafeteria. Dong loved to devour Lion's Head pork meatballs in the cafeteria's delicious brown savory sauce. One could get injured by Dong's flying elbows as he chowed down, caring nothing about what people thought but instead enjoying every morsel of his favorite food. But smoldering underneath the stains on his wrinkled white shirt, Dong was a brilliant and determined man. He strived to be the best throughout his career in computer information technology, his major at Peking University. And he was good, graduating at the top of his class and then receiving his Ph.D. The PLA sought out men and women to rapidly expand the military's use of technology and recruited Dong. During his interview with the PLA, both sides concluded that he was better suited as a civilian employee than an Army officer. So began the career of Dr. Dong Liang.

Through the years, Dong was a model worker. Never marrying, his life partner was his work. For the past eighteen years, Dong worked his way up the ladder in the Central Military Commission, the nation's leading military organ that commanded all armed forces and had President Zhang as commander in chief. The CMC had a direct command and control structure over the PLA Rocket Force, a separate entity from the PLA. The purpose of the split command structure was to ensure strict control of the stockpile of nuclear warheads and 1,250 land-based conventional ballistic and cruise missiles. The chain of command began with the CMC, went to the headquarters of the PLARF, from there to each artillery base, and finally down to the individual Brigades. The Brigades transmitted firing orders to the launch companies under their command. The entire C2 system used fiber-optic and satellite-based communication networks.

The network for missile launches was separated from all other computer networks. For an additional layer of security, the CMC headquarters was equipped with four separate and distinct computer networks. One was a dedicated command network; the others were an all-inclusive military information network, an internal office network, and one connected to the internet.

In 2016, through President Zhang's reorganization of the CMC's command structure, Dong was assigned to the prestigious Joint Staff Department, which carried out combat planning, command, support, and communications. Dong was the go-to expert on anything to do with programming. For this reason, his former boss, General Li Jung, contacted him. Dong would never forget the surprise call.

A long whistle cut the air and disrupted Dong's reminiscence. A referee held up a yellow card, and his former boss's granddaughter's soccer game resumed with the enthusiasm that only the young had. He and General Li had stood off to one side away from the screaming parents but not far enough away to miss the action on the field.

"I know," said General Li, pausing to stare into Dong's eyes and look for any hint of skepticism, "that you, like me, want what is best for our country. I also know from our years together what it means to you to see your beloved nation going down the wrong road. And I know you would want to correct it, not unlike your dear friends who were killed in Tiananmen Square so many years ago. Am I correct, Dong?"

Without hesitation, Dong answered, "Yes, of course, general. I've waited to be asked this exact question for decades. How can I be of service to you, sir?"

The eyes reveal everything about a person in a situation like this, and the experienced general saw nothing but assurance from his previous devoted subordinate. "What I'm about to tell you could get us both shot if it were discovered by the authorities." He paused and noted that the revelation did not affect Dong, who looked on attentively.

Li continued carefully while sneaking a glance at the game to look interested. "President Zhang is preparing to annex Taiwan and to destroy the United States when they come to their aid. He and his devoted generals have plans to sink all the US carriers that dare float in our waters by using our stockpile of ballistic missiles." He let the words sink in before continuing.

"There are several of us in positions of authority that believe this is wrong. We are convinced we should move slowly and cautiously to annex Taiwan. And that under no circumstances do we want to go to war with the Americans. Win, lose, or draw, a war like that could set China back decades, both militarily and economically. That is why you and I are meeting today and, in essence, putting our lives on the line."

"General, I say again, I share your convictions and ask what I can do to help."

"Thank you, Dong. I thought this was what you would say. We want you to develop a plan that will never allow those missiles to get off the ground. We don't know how it can be done, but we all agree if anyone can do it, you can. By sparing the US fleet from destruction, China would be overwhelmed by the sure weight of the US military, causing Zhang to sue for peace. This is a dangerous undertaking but one that must be taken to save our country."

When the general looked back at Dong, what he saw was a man already deep in thought. Li saw everything he needed to know. If there were a way to stop the launch of the missiles, this man would get it done.

A loud cheer went up when the general's granddaughter's team scored a goal. Both men clapped loudly.

# Chapter 30


*USS Ronald Reagan*
Yokosuka, Japan


Major Chang Huang was pissed. After his so-called rescue after his J-20 crashed, he was treated as a prisoner of war aboard the US carrier and was unable to gleam one piece of intelligence. Every time he tried to sneak from his room, some pimple-faced Marine told him to return to his room or he would put him in the brig. Hell, they brought him his food, some American magazines, a change of clothes—they gave him everything but a chance to look around the ship. He also had no way to contact his wife. But fortunately, they were now in Japan, and he was told he would be turned over to Chinese officials soon.

Wearing his PLAAF flight suit, which someone had patched up, he was ready to go. There was a knock on his door.

"Yes?"

"Major, this is Lieutenant Commander Anderson and Lieutenant Braxton. May we enter?"

"It's your ship."

Both officers entered the room and saw Chang in his uniform for the first time. They acted instinctively and saluted. Surprised, Chang returned the salute.

"Sir," said Anderson, "we're here to escort you from the ship and turn you over to Chinese officials. Do you have everything?"

"Everything but my J-20," Chang answered sarcastically.

"Yeah, that's too bad," replied Braxton in the same mocking tone.

"Follow me, please," said Anderson, and they were off.

They must have taken the most banal route because Chang didn't see anything noteworthy to report. Stopping at the top of the ramp off the ship, both US officers turned and saluted the national ensign and proceeded downward.

Chang noted several stiffs dressed in suits with two burly men behind them at the base of the ramp. As he and his two buddies reached the bottom, his escorts moved to the side to let him by. When he walked past Braxton, he heard him whisper, "Can't wait until we meet again, asshole."

Just as Chang was going to get in Braxton's face, he heard a scream from the most important voice in his life. His wife broke through the suits and sprinted toward him. Chang ran to her, and when they met, the major picked up his 110-pound darling and swung her in a big circle, kissing her the entire time.

Screw formality, he thought. He was going home.

# Chapter 31


Taipei, Taiwan


President Chen Guang was doing what he did twice a year, leading his country on the hallowed ground of the National Revolutionary Martyrs' Shrine. It was dedicated to those who fought and died for the Republic of China in the Sino-Japanese War, the Chinese Civil War, and the First and Second Taiwan Strait crises. Nearly four hundred thousand brave soldiers died fighting for their homeland.

As he listened to his country's national anthem, he knew the tears would flow again—they always did. It was just the lyrics, so powerful, so meaningful.

"Our aim shall be:
To found a free land
World peace, be our stand . . .
One heart, one soul,
One mind, one goal . . ."

Pulling his handkerchief from his pocket to wipe away his tears of pride, the president of twenty-three million Taiwanese found himself thinking back to what a tumultuous history his people had endured. After being settled by Austronesian-speaking Taiwanese Indigenous peoples six thousand years ago, the island was sought by many: the Dutch, the Qing dynasty, the Empire of Japan, and finally, the Chinese Communists. In 1949 the Republic of China's nationalists fled to the small island from the mainland. Then, in the 1980s and early 1990s, Taiwan transitioned from a one-party dictatorship to a multi-party democracy.

Kicked around like a mongrel dog stealing food, the PRC replaced the ROC in the United Nations, which refused diplomatic relations with countries that dared recognize Taiwan. Only 14 of 193 UN member states had diplomatic ties with Taiwan. The United States of America was not one of those fourteen until 2019 when both sides signed a consular agreement formalizing their partnership. With President Taylor in office and the Taiwan Security Act soon to pass, Taiwan and the US would be vital allies with the US's sworn commitment to the island's defense.

Chen fully understood how meaningful the relationship was and for Taiwan to have a strong ally like the United States. For over half a century, the PRC had an official policy to force unification if peaceful means weren't successful. The Communists had never wavered from their One-China policy, the insistence that Taiwan and mainland China were both parts of China and that the PRC was the only legitimate government of China. With recent events, Chen understood that hostilities with China were now more possible than ever. He also understood his fierce support of Taiwan's independence and outright rejection of the One-China policy. The only thing keeping them from war, he thought, was his support, for now, of the status quo, which was also the wish of the people. So far, so good.

# Chapter 32

*OFFICE OF THE PRESIDENT*
Beijing, China

Sitting in his office, alone for once, President Zhang Wei was going over his plans for reunifying Taiwan. He knew all too well that it began and ended with the defeat of the Americans. The destruction of the US carrier fleet would be the coup de grâce. He read over the report for a second time, wanting to make sure he missed no facts.

## <u>TOP SECRET</u>

Operation Safe Net

To: President Zhang Wei
From: General Wang Yong, Joint Staff Department Central Military Commission.
Subject: The below intelligence was obtained by MSS from United States Homeland Security. Below is the interpretation of this report as it applies to the "mission."

**Threat Assessment for US Aviation / Response to Violations of Restricted Air Space**

The Federal Aviation Administration, FAA, reported 3,432 violations of restricted airspace in a recent two-year survey. This raised concern that terrorists may deliberately enter restricted airspace to test the government's response, plan an attack, or carry out an attack.

The North American Aerospace Defense Command, NORAD, expanded its mission to include monitoring domestic air traffic and conducting air patrols when necessary.

In an audit, NORAD identified gaps in the simultaneous, time-critical, multi-agency response to airspace violations. They concluded that gaps happened because no agency took charge. Throughout all the involved agencies, the lack of shared protocols and procedures or even agreeing to what type of violation warranted an armed response confused the decision-makers. The US believes that terrorists (their primary emphasis) are interested in attacking targets with commercial or general aviation aircraft. NORAD reported that intelligence agencies couldn't agree on how significant the threat was from terrorists using available aviation aircraft in an attack. They cited that as many as seven key government agencies could simultaneously be involved in response to an attack. They are currently restructuring interagency cooperation and communication to define duties and responsibilities.

NORAD has the lead over all agencies to prevent air attacks against North America and to safeguard sovereign airspaces of the US by responding to unknown, unwanted, and unauthorized air activity. NORAD is tied into a worldwide system of sensors designed to provide leadership with an accurate picture of any aerospace or maritime threat. To accomplish their mission, they use a network of satellites, ground-based radar, airborne radar, and fighters to detect, intercept, and, if necessary, engage any threat. NORAD has an inventory of the F-15 Eagle, F-16 Fighting Falcon, and F-22 Raptor available to challenge any air-based threat.

The US is primarily concerned with the airspace surrounding Washington, DC, emphasizing the White House, the Capital, and areas where the president is traveling. Much less attention is allotted to the rest of the United States. Officials admit, "It's important to recognize that it may not be possible to prevent all restricted airspace violations or to deter all attacks."

A word of caution here. Any leak of our plans would be catastrophic to our success. The US uses its advanced intelligence network to supply NORAD with any information indicating an aircraft may present a potential threat. If they obtained this intelligence, our two planes would fly into a trap and be shot down.

The audit pointed out numerous times that without dedicated central leadership, as a problem evolved, precious time was lost in deciding who was responsible for responding to the violation of restricted air space. While this occurred, the violating aircraft continued to operate in restricted airspace. They could accomplish whatever they chose with the time they were provided. Additionally, the seven agencies that could be involved do not routinely share data.

There was also confusion over what constituted a restricted airspace violation because no standard definition has been defined. While NORAD uses the term "incursion," the FAA calls it "pilot deviation." Consequently, one report might elicit a response while the other may not. While they attempt to define the problem, the possible hostile aircraft could continue its mission. All agencies involved are working to solve these discrepancies, but this will take time. The advantage appears to be with us now and in the near future.

The salient point is that NO CIVILIAN AIRCRAFT HAS EVER BEEN SHOT DOWN in the United States. There aren't too many bureaucrats who would authorize the shooting down of a civilian airliner with four hundred people on board. Getting someone in the chain of command to authorize a direct attack on a passenger airliner would take time, allowing our pilots to continue their mission. Here are some examples of the response by NORAD and others to violations of restricted airspace.

### US Restricted Airspace Violations: Example: #1

In this first example, an emotionally troubled Canadian pilot decided to commit suicide by flying his Cessna 172 from Canada across the border into US airspace. Crossing into the state of Michigan that borders Canada, NORAD sent two F-16s to intercept. When they failed to communicate with the pilot, they escalated the intrusion by firing flares in front of the aircraft. When that failed, they used their landing lights to illuminate the cockpit, at which time the pilot made obscene gestures. When the perpetrator was within ten miles of a large population center, Homeland Security advised the governor to evacuate the state capitol building. Subsequent testimony about the incident indicated if the pilot had turned toward Chicago, he would have been shot down. Instead, the pilot, low on fuel, landed on a remote country road and was taken into custody by local police.

## US Restricted Airspace Violations: Example #2

In 2004, a twin-engine Beechcraft King Air carrying the governor of Kentucky was flying to Washington DC to attend the funeral of President Ronald Reagan. Unknown to officials, the transponder, a device that transmits an identifying signal to ground controllers, was not working. A Black Hawk helicopter was sent to intercept when the plane entered restricted airspace near the White House. With thick cloud cover, the helicopter could not locate the aircraft. When the plane got to within a few minutes of the capital, where thousands of dignitaries were gathering for the funeral, a general from NORAD was on the phone and was about to give the order to shoot down the transient plane. Just as the general was going to order the plane's destruction, it turned toward Ronald Reagan Washington National Airport and made a safe landing. Subsequent investigations revealed how little time they had to identify the governor's plane and make critical decisions. The consensus was the plane would have made it to the capital before being intercepted.

End of report.

President Zhang looked up from the document and could not help but smile. Even after 9-11, the ignorant Americans were still unprepared for anything like what China would release on them.

# Chapter 33

*HIGHWAY 134*
Changhua County, Taiwan

The Republic of China Air Force Major Sam Yi-Chun had flown in his Lockheed Martin F-16V Viper out of strange places, but nothing like this. Sam was one of his country's most celebrated fighter pilots. As he sat looking out of his bubble-like canopy with an unobstructed view forward and upward, it was hard to fathom that he was getting ready to take off from the middle lane of a civilian highway with a posted speed limit of 100 km/h. He would reach that speed in just a few meters.

The major was from the 5th Tactical Fighter Wing, participating in anti-PLA invasion drills. Today's operation was to land and rearm on the island's purpose-built highways because a simulated PLA strike had destroyed their home base. Taking part in the live ammunition drill were two Dassault Mirage 2000-5s, one Northrop Grumman E-2K airborne early warning aircraft, and six F-16V state-of-the-art fighters. All the aircraft would do carrier-like landings with specially deployed hooks to catch wires strung across the road to stop the aircraft swiftly on the limited space available. Once on the highway, the plane would all be refueled and loaded with ordnance. Sam was first in line as the squadron leader, awaiting orders to take off from the roadway.

One of the primary reasons for the exercise was to prepare for a war that targeted major home bases. Using several civilian highways was one way to disperse aircraft, refuel and rearm them, and keep them in battle. He had watched the efficiency of the ground crews and was confident they would do just as well with the aircraft yet to land.

Interrupting his thoughts, a transmission came over the radio. "Attention on the net, attention on the net. This is Command Alfa with an exercise knock-it-off. I say again, this is an exercise knock-it-off. Three zero-fighter bandits and two bomber bandits heading to ADIZ Charlie One. Scramble and intercept. Coordinates linked to HUDs. Additional assets en route."

"Command Alfa, Eagle 11. Roger, going airborne now." Roaring down the highway, breaking every motor vehicle speed law ever written, Sam reached 240 km/h and was quickly airborne.

He immediately went to his AN/APG-83 Scalable Agile Beam Radar AESA, newly added to the F-16V based on the F-22 and F-35 technology. Sam's screen was loaded with choices and could track twenty-plus target tracks. Switching to air-to-air missile mode and turning on his electronic protection radar, Sam was racing at Mach 2 toward the targets, hoping his wingman could catch up. As he traveled at 2,450 km/h, his Center Pedestal Display provided him with high-resolution target coordinates for the lead aircraft on his six-by-eight-inch color screen.

China was seriously upping the stakes. But as Taiwan's air defense forces had practiced hundreds of times, they were ready for the task. Piercing the atmosphere was their pulse acquisition radar for the island's improved Raytheon MIM-23 HAWK medium-range surface-to-air missiles. The low-to-medium-altitude radar system targeted the thirty-two aircraft crossing Air Defense Identification Zone Charlie One.

Also deployed with the HAWK SAMs were Taipei's indigenous-produced SAMs, Tien Kungs or Sky Bows, as the missiles were lovingly called. The Sky Bow was a medium-to-long-range system with a single-stage, solid propellant missile. It was deployed over the island as a mobile containerized system in a quad-box launcher. If those were not enough, Sky Bow SAMs were also in silo-launched sites.

Major Sam Yi-Chun slowed to 310 mph and called, "Eagle 11 to all Eagle aircraft. Strike formation."

Approaching the gathering, ROCAF fighters at supersonic speed were two J-16s, three J-11s, and two J-20s. Things were about to get dicey.

Using the Guard frequency, Sam radioed the PLAAF aircraft.

"This is Major Sam Yi-Chun of the Republic of China Air Force. You are approaching the median line, and I demand you turn your aircraft back toward the mainland. Failure to do so will be considered an invasion of Taiwan. Acknowledge."

After a few heart-pounding seconds of dead air, Sam's radio spit out the words from the Chinese commander. "We are in the airspace of the People's Republic of China and are on a military training exercise. Any interference will be considered an act of war and be treated appropriately."

Switching over to secure communications, Sam said, "All units, Eagle 11, break off current course and set up firing solutions. Do not fire unless fired on, or I give the order to fire."

Along with other ROCAF fighters from bases around Taiwan, the squadron sharply maneuvered into strategic positions. Using their AN/APG-83 SABR AESA fire control radar, they picked their targets for their AIM-120. At the same time, the ROCAF fighters were targeted by the Chinese fighters.

Sam thought there were too many fingers on triggers not to have someone fire for any reason—fright, orders, or just plain stupidity. Just as he was going to warn the PLAAF again, the entire formation of PLAAF fighters and bombers abruptly altered their course and turned toward the mainland.

"All fighters, Eagle 11. Break off contact and turn off your targeting radar. Return to base." The alarm warnings in his cockpit stopped while the air defense system operators secured their missile radars. Sam was unsure what China was up to, but he had an uneasy feeling about it.

# Chapter 34

*THE WHITE HOUSE*
Washington DC

"Good morning," said President Mark Taylor to his National Security Council in the Situation Room. "It's been a week, so I want to hear your strategy for how we best prepare for a conflict with China, should it come to that. Considering Beijing's recent bellicose move in the Indo-Pacific, the PRC appears to be moving toward a forcible reunification with Taiwan.

"As you all know, Taiwan has taken delivery of $3.85 billion worth of Harpoon missiles and eighty-six F-16 fighter jets. They have received Congressional approval for additional missiles, rocket artillery, and aerial reconnaissance sensors worth $2.8 billion and have purchased Stinger missiles and 106 M1A2 Abrams tanks from us.

"While critics will argue that our transfer of advanced weapons will only further enrage the PRC, I say it makes it abundantly clear to the world, especially China, that Taiwan has always been an American ally and that the passage of the TSA will stamp it as official. Taipei's pleas for help to defend itself have finally been answered. With these weapons, Taiwan can protect itself better and allow the US valuable time to respond in case of war. None of this will be lost on President Zhang.

"Beijing must understand that we are in this for the long haul and remain a force to be reckoned with. If this is a game of betting supremacy in the area, we must hold all the cards.

"Look, I get it. China will be China, and that will be a constant. But the United States must partner to a greater extent with our friends in Australia, Japan, and India—a quad of nations with the same vision. Determining the future of Asia is not the birthright of China or any nation. We must act in unison toward the bully on the block and keep our dialogue open. The quad should focus our dialogue on the freedom of navigation in air, sea, space, and cyberspace and work together to resolve territorial disputes and claims. We should be able to keep the PRC's aggressive behavior in check."

"Sir, along those lines," interjected SecDef George Mitchell, "we need to develop and invest in the means to move our forces quickly to the region to support our established military infrastructure. China understands that our forces are inadequate to cover our required global footprint. We must build our capacity by pushing more capability into this theater—and do it now.

"Currently, we have based 60 percent of our Naval forces in the region. I suggest moving more of our submarine force to Guam and deploying our long-range bombers to our forward-deployed bases.

"And I agree with you, Mr. President. We must reinforce our relations with like-minded allies and partners in the area. Deterring Chinese aggression will require us all to work together. I see this as one of the most important challenges today and for the foreseeable future. We must make the Indo-Pacific our priority theater and keep moving additional forces into the area. Our conventional deterrence has eroded over the last decade, and we need to change that. As one congressman recently said, 'It's time to put up or shut up.'

"While the Indian Ocean area in years past was questionable for our support, it's vital to counter China today. We need to enhance our relationship with India, both politically and militarily. Their recent battle with the PLA is a prelude to what is coming. Win India over, and we gain an ally with our defense of Taiwan. With limited bases and ports in the region, bolstering our strategic relationship with India will better allow us to project military power."

Glancing over to the Chairman of the Joint Chiefs of Staff, seemingly always at attention in his dress uniform, Mitchell went on. "Through the leadership and insight of General Matthews, the quad has been conducting naval and air drills in the Indian Ocean and western Pacific. This strengthens military cohesiveness among the four nations and sends a strong message to China about its persistent military ambitions. The working relationship between the quad's leading commanders and their staff adds tremendously to a cohesive defense partnership. In a conflict, these relations are the core behind success."

"I'd just like to add," said Secretary of State Brad Kelly, "that stronger economic ties are important too. We are strengthening our two-way trade and investments and encouraging US companies to invest in Indian firms, especially in technology. Already, Google, Adobe, and Microsoft have done just that. We can win wars with our militaries, but we can win over the people with stronger economic ties."

"I understand your point, Mr. Kelly," growled General Matthews, "but it will be our military with their butts on the line. The Joint Chiefs of Staff have recommended that Mr. Mitchell move more of our military assets to the Indo-Pacific region in preparation for any war and message China that we won't sit on the sidelines. At the same time, our flag officers will continue to engage with our partner national Chiefs of Defense and with every nation's flag officers within their spheres of influence. That will give some reassurance to our wavering allies and partners."

"Thank you, general," interrupted the general's boss, the SecDef, "Let me be very specific on what the Department of Defense has been doing with the president's approval.

"Even though we've restructured to eliminate nearly ten thousand billets from permanent stations in Germany, I don't believe we're basing enough personnel in the Indo-Pacific where we need feet on the ground. I recommend we increase that number, with the majority assigned to bases in Guam, Japan, and Okinawa. We haven't shifted fast enough from our twenty-year-long footprint. The new battlefield will not be on land but in the waters of the South and East China Seas and the Pacific and Indian Oceans. Joint operations with amphibious forces, Navy blue water and aviation forces, Air Force and Space Force forces, not to mention all services' cyber forces, will be crucial in a conflict with the PRC.

"Beijing, knowing this all too well, has strengthened their A2/AD to keep American ships and fighters at bay. With the addition of their precision missile systems, we must refine our footprint to face these increased threats. One way to accomplish this is by using our long-range bombers and submarines. Moving these assets closer to where they are needed can offset much of China's advantage.

"Additionally, as discussed, the USS *Gerald R. Ford* is cruising to be forward deployed from its home base in Singapore. The presence of an additional aircraft carrier and its attending battle group sends a strong message to all nations in the region that the security and freedom of the seas are of great importance to the United States."

"Mr. President, if I may?" asked Treasury Secretary Sullivan.

"Yes, June, please."

She stood up to emphasize what she was about to say. "Acting on the annual testimony of the commander of USINDOPACOM, Admiral Jenkins, Congress has funded twenty-two billion dollars over the next three years to defend American interests in the Indo-Pacific. While we talk of the importance of our mission in this newly identified priority theater, this funding allows us to put teeth behind the bark by funding our actions in the area."

The Secretary of Treasury, who loved her two pit bulls like her children, couldn't help but use them as an analogy whenever she was in the spotlight. "To ensure the US is like a junkyard pit bull guarding its turf, Congress allocated over half of the funds to increase the lethality of our military assets. This includes everything from defense radars to long-range missiles to more forward-stationed fighter squadrons and other forces. Sir, we have put up but won't shut up."

With a momentary lapse in the discussion, Robbie Spencer, the president's National Security Advisor, brought up what he thought was a relevant point to debate. "What keeps me up at night, folks, is China's superior numbers across the board. Their Navy is a battle force of 350 ships, including 130 major surface combat ships. By contrast, our Navy has less than 300 deployable ships. The

PLARF has more missiles than the US, many with a range of over 300 miles, compared to our in-theater missiles, with capacities of 185 miles.

"While our Patriot missiles and submarines in the area would wreak havoc with the PLA's incoming ballistic and cruise missiles, the problem exists when our magazines run empty. Then what? We've all seen the reports that say we don't have the numeric superiority to match China's. So, when our defensive measures begin to subside, the missiles from the PLA will not. Whatever the target, chances are it will be destroyed—including our carriers.

"Also, what will stop the third or fourth waves of missiles, enemy aircraft, and amphibious attack craft? To counter the numeric disadvantages, we must immediately ramp up land-based missiles for use in the area. I understand we're making strides in that area, but we must drastically move those assets forward to the region—now. The more tubes to shoot from, the better our chances for success. If we sit back and play the status quo, the US risks losing a war with China. Not pleasant to contemplate, but a reality."

The NSA noticed he had the undivided attention of everyone in the room, so he continued. "Currently, the entire eastern theater of the PLA is concentrated in Taiwan and Japan. China is outspending all peers in upgrading its military to prevent a move toward independence by Taiwan to control the Indo-Pacific region. Suppose China moves on Taiwan, and we push back. In that case, the conflict will be rapid and intense, with an extreme probability of high casualties—on both sides. I'm talking about what was encountered during World War II, something very few people alive today have seen. I believe these shared nightmares are what's keeping China in check for now."

"I agree with Mr. Spencer's assessment," added SecDef Mitchell. "If the time should come to strike back at the PLA, we have bases in the Pacific. The Air Force has fighters, C4ISR aircraft, and many other assets at Japan's Yokota and Misawa air bases and South Korea's Osan and Kunsan air bases. A bomber task force is rotating through Anderson Air Force Base in Guam. But we don't have the numbers to compete, so we're all on a level playing field. I suggest the US deploys more aircraft to Diego Garcia in the Indian Ocean, especially bombers and refueling tankers. I realize that stacking the deck in the area can come back and bite us, but the risk is tolerable and should be done immediately.

"Beijing continues in their aggressive modernization plan that most of us thought would take until the middle of the century to achieve. But evidence now indicates the time is nearing that their sphere of influence goes well beyond their borders. Their unchallenged success has emboldened the PLA in a military flexing of their muscles that is attempting to push the United States from the world stage as the protector for most countries in the region. We must adjust our National Defense Strategy to focus on future R&D and procurement to have an advantage over the PLA and expand our regional allies. By acting at warp speed on the recommendations made today, we can keep China in check, and if a conflict does occur, we'll be more than ready."

The president stood up and pounded his fist into his other hand. Everyone in the room felt their jaws drop two inches. The president rarely did anything like that, so he had their attention and then some.

"I'm a man of peace," said the president. "But I'm sick and tired of China threatening the peaceful nations of Asia with never-ending military threats. George, I want you to push forward on the issues presented today, and if there are any hiccups, let me know immediately."

Looking at Vice President Richardson, Taylor said, "James, I want you to pressure Congress for additional support to ensure our plans move forward uninterrupted and without bureaucratic delays. I want an all-out push on this."

The President stared into the eyes of his Secretary of State. "Brad, I want you to get on a plane to the Indo-Pacific region and personally deliver a message to our allies and those countries on the fence. We have their six and will be by their side if needed." The president turned his head. "And General Matthews, please get the word out to our troops that we're doing everything possible to ensure they have the best tools to do their jobs." Taylor told everyone in the room, "Now is the time to act as if we're at war to prevent ever having to pull the trigger to start one. But make no mistake, if that time comes, I pity the offender."

# Chapter 35



*CHAOYANG DISTRICT*
Beijing, China

As just a major in the PLAAF, J-20 fighter pilot Chang Huang led an opulent life. Married to the beautiful daughter of the president of China, Chang never took anything for granted. Living in the penthouse of a space-age high-rise overlooking Chaoyang Park Plaza, the largest green space in the sprawling city of Beijing, the major was always on alert, thinking someone would wake him from his dream.

As the sun streamed through large windows onto their table set for an early morning breakfast of tea and dim sum, Chang couldn't fathom how his wife, Mrs. Li Wei never had a hair out of place and looked simply ravishing every moment of every day. Besides her beauty, what he loved the most was her intellect—she was one smart woman.

He treasured the fact that despite her family's wealth, she chose to work instead of kicking back to enjoy a life of luxury—that was not her essence. Instead, she was an extremely successful corporate lawyer recently recognized as one of China's top ten attorneys.

"My love," said Chang, looking as confident as possible for his expected reaction, "I just heard from my commanding officer that he wants me back to the base in two days." After sipping his green tea to embolden himself, he continued, "I tried to buy more time, but he would not have it. I guess I'm a hero now. Not only did I almost single-handedly down a US aircraft carrier, but many believe the Americans shot me down for simply flying by it."

"But darling, you promised me a longer stay until your shoulder is fully healed."

"I know, dear, but I'm a fighter pilot whose place is flying our country's most advanced jet—not to mention they want to parade me around like some celebrated actor. No, I must report for duty. Even your father would agree."

"You don't get it," she half blurted out. "I was the one left behind, wondering if you were alive or dead for days. The pain from not knowing is something I have never experienced before and never want to experience again. And now you want back into the fight."

The military-decorated husband took a moment to collect his thoughts. "When we were dating, you knew that flying is what I live for. Sitting in some plush corporate office is not in my genes, but flying at Mach 2 is. If you could have seen the look on those smug, over-confident Americans, you would have kicked me out of the house to finish the job. I love you more than you'll ever fully realize, but now it's time to mount up."

He reached over, squeezed his wife's hand, got up, and left the room. He knew war was coming, and he sure as hell wouldn't miss it.

# Chapter 36


*AUGUST 1ST BUILDING*
Beijing, China

Dr. Dong Liang knew something was up within the Central Military Commission. For the past two months, there have been numerous tests of China's Nuclear Command, Control, and Communications System, better known as NC3. The tests also included land and sea-based conventional weapons. Interestingly, most of the scenarios tested involved conventional weapons. Although similar, there were nuances between the two. As one of the chief civilian leaders in the CMC, Dong was aware of most aspects of the test. He noted that his superiors and there weren't many, were examining the NC3 system and its orientation, moving toward negative versus positive control of both conventional and nuclear missiles.

He reviewed the details in his head while pretending to read one of many endless reports. With positive weapons control, there was 24-hour, 365-day monitoring, verifying, patrolling, and testing. With such a system in place, they could tell if NC3 had been compromised. Positive control was not limited to weapons systems but also applied to people—to uncover people with devious intentions. Dong knew about it all too well because he had pushed for it. Positive control was the overall system where every keystroke on every computer for every soldier and official was monitored to determine whether people were doing the work they were tasked to do and, if not, to find out what their intentions were. Was the individual trying to buy a new frying pan or trying to fry the electronics? With political stakes so high, Chinese officials would take no chances. Any hint of disservice to their county would land the offender in prison or worse. Quite a deterrent for most, Dong thought.

But Dong had also heard that President Zhang had misgivings about positive control of nuclear missiles and, to a lesser extent, conventional weapons. From his definition, negative control involved how weapons were deployed, the military procedures associated with them, and their design and delivery systems. The president's negative control was primarily making sure that nuclear or conventional weapons were not used without his authorization. So, Zhang was highly protective of the missile systems. He wanted assurance that the missiles were secure against efforts by people to gain unauthorized access, detonate them, or to prevent them from being launched. Simply stated, he wanted complete control of every missile in China's arsenal.

Dong was familiar with the technical and procedural solutions protecting the missiles because he either developed or approved the codes used to prevent unauthorized operations, primarily by using PAL or Permissive Action Links. These switches protected the missiles against unauthorized use and were put in place when a weapon was assembled. PALs were tamperproof and bypassing them was impossible. Dong's most recent PALs used a system of multiple eight-digit or sixteen-digit codes with a limited try capability. Since they were electronic locks, any effort to keep trying codes would lock out the offender. The entire PAL system was impregnable without the codes, which meant securing the codes was as crucial as preventing unauthorized access to the missile. Only a few top-level Chinese officials knew the codes and how they were secured. Dong Liang was one of them.

# Chapter 37



During some downtime while in the middle of a multi-national training exercise with frigates from Malaysia and the Philippines, Ensign Brett Jansen took another sip of his coffee to hide his red cheeks as his Dutch buddy, Lieutenant Broersma, congratulated Jansen for saving the United States from war with China. Broersma said that because of Jansen's heroics, there was talk that Jansen would be recommended for the Navy Commendation Medal. It was the same story he had heard so many times from so many sailors who had complimented him after he grabbed the hand of an overstressed PO3 from the launch button of an EM-3 surface-to-air missile. If the SAM had fired, it would've taken out a J-20, China's most advanced fighter—and who knew what would have happened next.

"Thanks, Bob," said Jansen. "I appreciate that, but I did what any other officer would've done. I saw a problem and took action to stop it. End of story. I'll tell—"

The Klaxon cut him off. "This is your captain. The *Liaoning* Carrier Strike Group is maneuvering close to our position. I want the CIC and Air Defense stations fully staffed. Further orders to follow."

Jansen and the other officers near him moved out quickly. Similar orders had been given to the KD *Jebat* and BRP *Jose Rizal* captains, so all three ships were abuzz with activity. What was just a training exercise a few moments ago had quickly become a real-life test.

The Arleigh Burke class destroyer and the two advanced frigates were completing joint exercises just off the shores of Malaysia's Layang-Layang Island Resort. The island was part of the Spratly Islands. It was claimed by Malaysia as their territory, but China, Vietnam, and Taiwan also claimed rights to the island known as Swallow Reef. The conflicting ownership claims of the militarily significant 86 acres of sand often brought the antagonists close to a shooting conflict.

Several months earlier, the PLA shot down a military drone belonging to the Malaysian frigate KD *Jebat*. The resulting showdown brought the two warships to a near-collision until a US destroyer stepped in, and cooler heads prevailed. Captain Ahmad of the KD *Jebat* remained furious about retreating from the Chinese. He hoped for revenge at the first opportunity.

Cruising at an altitude of 2,800 meters, or 9,186 feet, China's GJ-2, more commonly referred to as the Wing Loong II and known to be a medium-altitude long-endurance unmanned aerial vehicle, was reconnoitering the airport on Layang-Layang. Chinese intelligence had information that the airport's runway was being extended to facilitate Malaysia's jet fighters, such as the F/A-18, and they needed proof. To obtain that evidence, the Chinese violated Malaysia's airspace, presenting a threat to Malaysia's sovereignty and was especially troubling to the captain of the KD *Jebat*.

Unknown to the three naval ships' crews, their situations were about to escalate quickly. The PLAN's Type 055 guided missile destroyer CNS *Nanchang*, one of the world's most formidable destroyers, was using its stealth technology and heading straight for its operating area. At 180 meters long and 22 meters wide, *Nanchang* had 112 vertical launch missile cells that could launch surface-to-air, anti-ship, land-attack, and anti-submarine missiles—it had unprecedented defensive and offensive capabilities. As the primary escort of the *Liaoning*'s CSG, it had broken away to warn the unsuspecting ship captains to leave the area.

In *Mustin*'s CIC, Jansen was supervising his sailors as they were using the new AN/SPY-6 multifunction radar to get a fix on the *Liaoning* Strike Group.

"21MC, 20MC. We have seven ships spread out, range 64 miles, bearing two-seven-one," reported Jansen.

"20MC, roger. Let me know if there are any course changes," said the ship's captain, Tod Bailey, an Annapolis graduate and a man popular with his crew for his pleasant demeanor and always getting the most from each sailor.

While Bailey was contemplating whether he had a Chinese carrier within a few miles of his location, the ground radar station on Layang-Layang told Captain Ahmad of the KD *Jebat* that their high-resolution radar was tracking a drone. Returns identified it as a Chinese Wing Loong military UAV. Ahmad ordered a course correction to cut the distance to the drone so his radar could get a targeting solution. Now, it was his turn to equal the balance sheet. He paid no attention to Captain Bailey over comms as he sped closer to the island—his island.

Overhead, four KAI FA-50 Golden Eagle fighters from the Philippine Air Force had just taken off from an airfield in the archipelagic province of Palawan to provide limited air coverage for the ships participating in the partner nation training mission. The South Korean-made light combat fighters had just completed Block 10 and Block 20 upgrades. The Block 10 upgrade allowed using the Lockheed Martin AN/AAQ-33 Sniper targeting pod, and the Block 20 upgrade allowed using the AIM-120C. Major Carolos Mercado, a twenty-six-year Philippine Air Force Academy graduate and a former star of the institution's soccer team, led the flight of four fighters. Over six feet tall, he filled the entire cockpit of his fighter. The extremely popular major was loved by anyone who met him and was considered the finest fighter pilot in the Philippine Air Force.

Aboard the *Mustin*, Jansen noted something when it popped up on the radar. He keyed his mic and said, "21MC, 20 MC. Two bandits airborne. Shenyang J-15s from the *Liaoning*, bearing to intercept our current course."

Immediately after, over the MC-1, came the sound for GQ. "This is your captain speaking. General quarters. General quarters. We have incoming bandits. CIC, I need a firing solution."

Jansen reported, "21MC, 20 MC. The *Liaoning* carrier group has changed course. New course for our intercept."

Captain Bailey said from the Mustin's Bridge, "XO, ensure all this is going out on CENTRIXS to the *Jebat* and the *Jose Rizal*. Ensure that they are at GQ."

"Yes, sir," replied the XO.

*PHILIPPINE KIA FA-50 GOLDEN EAGLE FLIGHT*
South China Sea

Flight lead Major Mercado said over internal comms, "Golden 12 and Golden 13, two Chinese J-15s heading our way. If they come within twelve nautical miles of our territorial waters, go active on your AIM-120s. Position yourself for an intercept. Only fire on my command. Execute."

*KD JEBAT*
South China Sea

Captain Ahmad was moving around his CIC, looking over the shoulders of his subordinate officers to get all the information first-hand with nothing filtered. He had already decided that if the opportunity presented itself, he would shoot down the PLA drone violating his country's airspace. Deep within his soul, he was tired of being obedient to the Americans who were too compliant with the Chinese. No, it was time to demonstrate to everyone that Captain Ahmad and Malaysia were not to be ignored.

Using the BAE Systems combat data system, a lieutenant reported, "Captain, we have the Wing Loong UAV on radar, bearing one-two-one at 6,400 meters. Speed 115 knots, altitude 2,500 meters. Sir, we have a firing solution."

*USS MUSTIN*
South China Sea

"Sir," said the XO, "reports of visual contact, possibly the PLAN guided missile destroyer *Nanchang*, bearing zero-four-niner at twenty miles. Speed 15 knots."

"XO, have one of the FA-50s get a positive ID and report back."

"Aye, aye, sir."



"Golden 13, Golden 11. Buster to last sighting of possible Chinese destroyer and advise."

"Golden 11, Golden 13, copy." The pilot firewalled his throttles, and the General Electric turbofan engine used most of its twenty-two thousand pounds of thrust to propel the aircraft near 1,000 km/h. At 150 meters altitude, the sea was a blur, and Golden 13 was on his target quickly with his radar classifying the ship as the enemy. When he got a visual, it was the PLAN Type 055 guided missile destroyer *Nanchang*.

Slowing to 150 km/h for a better look, every alarm in his cockpit was telling him that the Nanchang had a missile lock on his fighter and a bandit in the area lighting him up. It was time to turn and burn.



China's GJ-2 UAV was highly effective as an aerial reconnaissance vehicle and a dangerous foe. Under each wing were six hardpoints capable of carrying bombs, rockets, and missiles. Protruding from the top surface of the aircraft was a satellite communications antenna that allowed the operator sitting hundreds of miles away to monitor everything around the aircraft. Not lost on the UAV's pilot was that the KD *Jebat* was tracking his every move.

Such aggression was somewhat unusual because the PLA had used UAVs to spy on the Layang-Layang reef island numerous times in the past and had only received token complaints and no resistance.

Going up the chain of command, the UAV pilot received permission to defend the aircraft using two FT-7 precision-guided munitions steered by the Beidou satellite guidance system. He could target the PGMs at the Malaysian frigate, but only if fired upon. With his orders, the UAV pilot continued his surveillance in and around the dual-purpose airport on the island.




Using their upgraded computer-based command and control system that integrated all weapons and sensors and allowed for rapid and effective weapons employment, the crew concentrated on the Chinese UAV.

"Captain, engagement coordinates received from CDS. The weapon control system has a lock on target. Vertical launch tube six ready with programmed Sea Wolf."

Captain Ahmad didn't hesitate. "Fire!"

With a push of a button, the GWS-26 Sea Wolf's solid-fuel propellant ignited, and the missile shot from its tube, hell-bent for one Chinese Wing Loong II drone. Programmed on auto mode, the Sea Wolf used radar tracking and the ship's surveillance radar that constantly measured the angle differences between the UAV and the missile. Guidance commands were issued to the missile through an Automatic Command to the Line-of-Sight device by transmitting on a microwave link to control the rear fins of the missile. As the Sea Wolf locked on its target, it fired a round tracked by radio beacons from the missile's tail.

When the Sea Wolf was about to impact its target, the Wing Loong II fired two FT-7 PGMs back at the attacking destroyer. One heartbeat later, the UAV burst into a massive fire, shocking tourists on the Layang-Layang resort beach. Fortunately for them, the debris fell harmlessly into the sea. Malaysia's pride and joy, the KD *Jebat*, now had two missiles headed its way.

It was surreal in the *Jebat*'s CIC—one second, there were cheers for the drone kill, then the next second, a quick blow to the gut as the room seemed to have the oxygen sucked from it as the crew saw two missiles tracked their every move. Even though the UAV had been blown to smithereens, the operator was still functioning in air-conditioned comfort and feeding the munitions tracking data. The frigate had only minutes to respond.

But this wasn't Captain Ahmad's first rodeo. Before firing the Sea Wolf, he'd activated his remaining missiles with fully automated Type 996 3D surveillance tracking radar. The two Chinese missiles had been automatically processing data faster than anyone thought possible.

"Two missiles inbound, two minutes until impact," *Jebat's* weapons officer exclaimed with an edge to his voice.

As two Sea Wolf missiles fired from their launchers, Captain Ahmad ordered, "Hard right rudder. Come to two-two-six, ahead flank."

"Both missiles on track," came a reply from the weapons officer. Efficiently, the outgoing missiles locked onto the two targets.

"Hard left rudder. Come to zero-four-five," said the captain as he attempted to trick the incoming missiles.

"We have a hit on missile one," said the weapons officer. "Missile two has missed its target. Enemy missile inbound, impact in one minute."

Another Sea Wolf auto-fired and headed toward the remaining incoming missile. Captain Ahmad knew he had only seconds to save his ship and crew.

"Bring the 30mm to bear on the incoming," ordered the captain.

Within the CIC, a nineteen-year-old sailor, who had finally grown enough whiskers to start shaving the previous week, did as he was trained. He used his electro-optical director from his console and frantically searched for the incoming missile. With a range of 5,100 meters, or 3.1 miles, his gun was set in the AUTSIG mode, allowing the computer to acquire the missile bearing down on the ship.

The 30mm DS30M Mark 2, which sat on a gyro-stabilized, electrically operated, self-contained, single-cannon mount, began putting metal in the air at a rate of 650 rounds per minute. Using a chain drive that moved the bolt assembly that loaded, fired, extracted, and ejected the cartridges—including any duds—the gun fired into the sky. At the same time, the youngster in the CIC prayed something would hit home because he sure as hell couldn't see anything.

A moment later, there was a massive explosion. Debris from the missile smashed onto the destroyer. One piece of shrapnel penetrated a sailor's helmet, who fell to the deck with part of his head missing. Three other sailors lay wounded nearby, their blood making the deck slippery for medics.



The CIC informed him of his situation as Captain Bailey absorbed what had just transpired between the Malaysian Frigate KD *Jebat* and one destroyed Chinese UAV.

"21MC, 20MC," said Jansen. "Bandits one and two, both J-15s from the *Liaoning*, still on a bearing to intercept our current course. Eleven miles out, speed 270—correction, bandit one just changed course, bearing zero-five-eight, heading toward the *Jebat*. His targeting radar is active. The frigate is painted."

"WCS, light him up and be prepared to fire," ordered the captain.

"Roger," came the reply from the WCS.

"21MC, 20MC. Positive ID on PLAN ship *Nanchang*, speed 30 knots, bearing zero-five-five, eleven miles out," said Jansen. "Destroyer is headed for our location, as is the *Liaoning* at forty-three miles out."

"Golden 12, assist Golden 13," said Major Mercado. "Bandit one has a missile lock. Return the favor but don't fire unless ordered to do so or unless the bandit fires. I've got Bandit two, who has targeted the *Jebat*."

Going to full military power, Mercado swiftly closed on the Bandit. Major Mercado received targeting information, autonomous tracking, GPS coordinates, and precise weapons guidance for an extended standoff range using his new Sniper targeting pod.

As soon as he lit up the Bandit, alarms sounded in his cockpit. Shit, he was targeted too. The question seemed to be who would blink first.

*KD JEBAT*
Near Pulau Layang-Layang, South China Sea

"Sir, Bandit one has a missile lock," came a tense voice from the CIC. "Weapons officer reports he has a lock on the Bandit. Standing by."

"Roger, wait for my command," said Captain Ahmad. "I want four GWS-26s fired five seconds apart."

"Roger four 26s," replied the CIC. "Bandit's 9 miles out, converging on our location at 868 knots."

Knowing the effective range of the Sea Wolf missile was 5.4 miles, the captain waited anxiously to pounce on the J-15.

*PHILIPPINE KIA FA-50 GOLDEN EAGLE FLIGHT LEAD*
South China Sea

"Stormhawk, Golden 11," said Major Mercado to the KD *Jebat*. "I have missile lock on the Bandit. Awaiting orders."

He had barely finished the transmission when Bandit one fired a PL-12 radar-guided BVRAAM at the FA-50.

Mercado received a missile approach warning from his MAWS radar. He was the best fighter pilot the Philippines had, so without hesitating, he used his Sniper pod for an exact lock on the J-15 and fired one AIM-120C.

"Fox Three," shouted the major into his mic as he released chaff to misguide the Chinese missile. He went to afterburner, flying toward the incoming missile to reduce the closure rate and minimize the Doppler effect.

The Chinese PL-12 missile used active radar homing; the latest technology provided by the Russians from their R-77 missile. It flew by the chaff, as it was programmed to do, and smashed into the FA-50. The jet dissolved into a giant fireball. Major Mercado, Philippine Air Force fighter pilot, didn't even have time to register what killed him.

Having already fired his AIM-120E at the J-15, the Chinese pilot was forced to take evasive maneuvers. He also released chaff as he dove for the deck, hoping the China Sea would be his ally and confuse the Americans' most popular missile. There was a reason the AIM-120E was so popular—it worked. Credited with over sixteen air-to-air kills, the J-15 pilot had made his seventeenth and final kill just before the AMRAAM tore him and his fighter into little pieces of metal and flesh.



"21MC, 20MC. Radar has confirmed two planes down," said Jansen matter-of-factly. "One a Philippine FA-50 and the other a PLAN J-15. From CENTRIX, no parachutes were sighted, and both pilots are presumed KIA. The KD *Jebat* was fired upon with missiles from the Chinese UAV, which the *Jebat* destroyed. Still, shrapnel from the strike killed one Malaysian sailor and wounded four others."

"20MC, give me a sitrep on the Chinese naval ships."

"Sir, the *Liaoning* strike group and the *Nanchang* have changed course to shadow ours. None of their targeting radars has painted any of our ships. The remaining J-15 has returned to the carrier, and the remaining FA-50s are returning to Palawan. The KD *Jebat* is in the area of the downed fighters."

After he keyed his mic off, Jansen wondered how close they had come to shooting at the Chinese and vice-versa. They were strategically outgunned today, and he understood that the PLA could have sunk all three ships. Knowing you could die at twenty-three and never have a life wasn't a pleasant thought.

At that moment, the Dutch kid from Michigan swore that he would do everything in his power to work even harder—to learn, train, and make sure it was the other guy that died—such is war.

# Chapter 38



*THE WHITE HOUSE*
Washington DC


What had been considered a cold war between the US and China had quickly turned into a shooting war, as the world's press proclaimed with large bold headlines.

In Malaysia, with a quarter of the population Chinese, reports said:

CHINA ATTACKS MALAYSIAN SHIP


In the Philippines:

CHINA SHOOTS DOWN FILIPINO FIGHTER—Famed Pilot Killed


In the United States, most reports said:

UNDECLARED WAR IN THE SOUTH CHINA SEA


In China, the state news agency said:

US INSTIGATES ATTACKS ON CHINA


In Europe, most countries' reports said:

CHINA-US NEAR WAR


TV news outlets were also all over the story. Video clips that somehow found their way to social media and were picked up by television stations showed graphic images of a dead sailor and other wounded sailors nearby and blood on the deck of Malaysia's most celebrated ship. Editing together a deceiving video clip of a Chinese destroyer firing missiles from some archived training exercise and then cutting to the blood-soaked bodies of Malaysian sailors made it appear that the media had footage of the Chinese missile firing and the hit aboard the KD *Jebat*.

Early reports got the story wrong and failed to mention that it was a PLA drone that was shot down, causing the casualties, not a missile from a Chinese warship. It didn't matter. Warnings from the news anchors only added to their viewership: "The video you're about to see is disturbing and graphic. Viewer discretion is advised."

In the United States, it was time to extinguish the fire burning with China. Besides, President Taylor wanted more time to move his military assets into place in the Indo-Pacific—just in case. After conferring with his NSC, it was time to act.

"Mary," said the president to his executive assistant, "please get President Zhang on video conference. Let them know it should just be the two of us talking. No aides. He will be expecting the call."

"Yes, Mr. President. I'll put it through to your office."

"Thank you, Mary."

As the president settled behind the massive Resolute Desk, he adjusted his tie. He put his suit coat back on, adorned with the American flag on a lapel. He felt confident, fit, and ready.

"Mr. President," Mary said over the intercom. "President Zhang is on video conference one."

"Thank you, Mary. No interruptions, please."

"Yes, Mr. President."

The president of the United States reached over and hit a button to instantly connect him with President Zhang Wei of the People's Republic of China, who sat behind a nondescript desk 6,921 miles away in Beijing. Taylor noticed the flag of China on the president's lapel. Both world leaders smiled politely as they made small talk before tackling the issues at hand. There was no need for interpreters because Mr. Zhang spoke perfect English with just a hint of an accent.

"President Zhang, I wanted to talk with you in person, with no staff, so we can have a thoughtful discussion about recent events between our countries. While our ideology is diverse, I believe we both desire peace and harmony."

"Yes, I agree. Please continue."

Looking straight into the eyes of the Communist leader, Taylor got to the point. "Mr. Zhang, I want to assure you that the United States had nothing to do with the shooting down of your UAV, even though it was violating Malaysian air space. It was the captain of the KD *Jebat*, who, as I understand, never got over the fact that the PLA recently shot down a Malaysian drone. The captain acted independently and decided to use force against your drone."

"Excuse me, Mr. President, but what you say is wrong. We have information that Malaysia is extending a runway for military use to allow for jet fighters. Our country cannot allow this to take place. Our drone was on the reef, our reef that others falsely claim as theirs, to monitor this escalation of military expansionism.

"Our drone, while only performing routine surveillance, was indiscriminately shot down by the Malaysian Navy. It was only then that the PLA struck back as a matter of national defense. The lone individual killed on that ship was a direct result of the aggression of the Malaysian government against China."

Taylor remained calm as he answered the hot-button question of who owns what in the South China Sea. "President Zhang, I don't want to argue who possesses what in that area. That's been argued for years with no resolution. I just want you to understand that this singular act of force was perpetrated by one individual who refused the requests of a United States Navy captain seeking a peaceful resolution to the incident. We as world leaders can't allow the misdeeds of one to escalate what already happened."

The Chinese president leaned forward in his chair, getting closer to the camera and thus Taylor. "Mr. President, that remains to be seen. We haven't even addressed the shooting down of our naval fighter and the death of a decorated hero of our country. Under the command of the United States, the Philippine Air Force took hostile action against our aircraft flying harmlessly in our territorial waters. The US is complicit in the destruction of our aircraft. As one leader to another, you know and understand we must retaliate in kind. Mr. President, this was an act of war."

As the communist leader spoke—lied—about the incident, Taylor could feel his blood pressure rising as he fought to keep his emotions in check at this deceiving SOB. But as a seasoned politician, he was a master of disguise and control. The president measured his response by leaning toward the camera and the man on the other end. "President Zhang, while I'm disappointed at the outcome of events, we should take a moment to see where the hostilities originated." In anticipation of an interruption, the president held up his hand. "Please let me finish.

"We have a Chinese UAV flying over an island, which the international courts have ruled belongs to Malaysia, and that UAV is spying on their every move. The Malaysian Navy acted alone and shot down the offending drone. We have PLA J-15 advanced fighter aircraft flying toward the Malaysian destroyer targeting it with their missile radar which is the first critical step before launching. As a single jet from the Philippine Air Force approached, a J-15 fired an air-to-air missile, destroying the aircraft that just happened to be flown by the Philippines' most decorated pilot. Only through his training and experience was he prepared to return fire. His missile was launched in self-defense and shot down your fighter. Mr. President, while all this is tragic, I believe we can work this out peaceably and come to a compromise allowing all parties to save face."

In Beijing, as Zhang listened to the lying president, there was an incentive for him to find comprise, to gain more time as he prepared for an attack on the United States in his bold move to reunify Taiwan. "While I have strong objections to your interpretation of what happened in our waters, I'm open to hearing what you have in mind."

"I suggest," said President Taylor, "that the four countries involved make public statements blaming the series of escalating events on one regretful decision by the captain of the KD *Jebat*, who acted without state approval in shooting down what we will say turned out to be a Chinese weather drone. This led to an unfortunate misunderstanding between China and the Philippines, resulting in

146

the death of the two pilots. Each country will agree to reparations for the damage caused. And last, each nation will agree to put this unfortunate incident behind them and to move forward with the desire of peaceful coexistence."

The Chinese president thought for a moment and said, "I can agree to your proposal on the condition that China does not have to admit to any wrongdoing. But I ask you, Mr. President, what about the Philippines and Malaysia? Will they agree to this?"

"I will personally approach each leader and convince them of the importance of our agreement today. I assure you that there will be no problems." And there weren't—especially after the US secretly sold the Philippines and Malaysia advanced weapon systems to complement their expanding inventories. The president reasoned that having a few friends on your block was a good thing. As for Captain Ahmad, he received a medal for his deeds in a hush-hush high-level ceremony. Unbeknownst to each other, the United States and China gained valuable time to prepare for war.

# Chapter 39

*THE GENERAL SECRETARY'S OFFICE*
Beijing, China

Zhang had learned that the key to staying in power was to assemble like-minded people who owed their very existence to you and then, like a ventriloquist, put words into their mouths. The seven members of the Standing Committee of the Politburo, the most powerful men in all of China, waited to hear from Zhang what they were supposed to say. And if any dared to oppose him, the CCDI would handle things.

President Zhang had also learned early on that at meetings such as the one he was about to begin, something as seemingly mundane as a meeting agenda could have dire consequences for his authority. He still had nightmares recalling early challenges to his tenure by men left over from the previous Politburo. Now it was simple to weed out the dissenters. Those who didn't immediately support him put items on the agenda that were simple veils to question his legitimacy. To survive, he had to control the debate by whatever means necessary, which meant the agenda. He saw it wouldn't be discussed if something were not on paper. Today's agenda was brief but would control his destiny. Each attendee had a piece of paper titled, Item for discussion:

**The Reunification of Taiwan**

The ventriloquist was ready. And so were some empty jail cells.

*THE STANDING COMMITTEE MEETING ROOM*
Beijing, China

All seven members who ruled over 1.4 billion souls had assembled: General Wang Yong, commander of the Joint Staff Department of the Central Military and second in command of all military forces after President Zhang; Premier Ye Jiang; Li Shano, the Chairman of the National People's Congress; Executive Vice Premier Wang Qui; Zhao Yong, head of Party Propaganda and Ideology; Vice President Chao Guanting.

President Zhang looked up from the paperwork spread out before him, and the room immediately became quiet for him to speak. "Thank you for attending this crucial meeting as we move forward with our plans to reunify Taiwan and eliminate the Americans from our shores. I want to report that all aspects of Operation Safe Net are ready. We are moving troops and assets into place under the ruse of a war game. Our mobile missile launchers will be redeployed just before zero hour.

"As we've discussed, the date for reunification will begin on the first day of the Chinese New Year. No one will see this coming. The weak Taiwanese Army will be overwhelmed in the first few hours of our attack. Their high command will be on holiday, leaving only inexperienced junior officers on duty.

"While the world shifts their attention to this battle, we'll strike the Americans with such numerical missile superiority that they will have no chance of countering. Their large carriers will be taken out of the war almost immediately, as well as their military bases in the Pacific. This will be a short conflict that the US will take years, if not decades, to recover from. Meanwhile, the Indo-Pacific will belong to us without threats from a peer nation to stop us from reunifying our country with Taiwan."

Zhang then jumped to his feet, startling everyone in the room as he threw up his fist and shouted, "I ask you, who's with me?"

In response, the other men in the room jumped from their seats, clapping, and cheering for their intrepid leader. Premier Ye Jiang applauded the loudest even though he thought the crazy man needed to be stopped before he set China back fifty years. Looking at all the meeting's attendees on closed-circuit television, Zhang's security noted how sincere everyone looked.

# Chapter 40



*MOBILE INTERCONTINENTAL MISSILE BRIGADE*
Jilantai, Inner Mongolia Autonomous Region, China

Leaving the PLA Rocket Force's sprawling 800-mile Jilantai Training Center in his rearview mirror, Staff Sergeant Leung marveled at his country's ingenuity. He was driving—piloting would be a more descriptive word—the split-cab, eight-axle Tai'an HTF5980A1 in a 16x16 off-road configuration, which gave the vehicle complete cross-country mobility. The latest upgrade also allowed the mobile transporter to launch missiles from almost any location, removing the need to position on paved roads or specially designated areas.

His payload was the upgraded Dongfeng DF-31A, a three-stage, solid-fueled ICBM with an enhanced range of 12,000 kilometers, putting much of the United States in its 7,456-mile radius. His sweetheart—Leung always thought of his missiles as his sweethearts—could deliver a heck of a one-megaton kiss. Although he wasn't allowed to talk about it, he relished that his sweetheart was one of the most powerful missiles in the world.

He was so proud to be a part of the PLARF, a high achievement and status for a poor boy from central China. But today, he was sent out with five other launchers, and his sweetheart didn't pack its usual punch. It had a conventional warhead, as did the others. He wasn't told why they switched out, but he didn't care.

While driving through terrain resembling Mars, Leung's company had nine support vehicles, which were necessary even though they created a more significant signature for US spy satellites. One of them was a Dongfeng EQ2050 Humvee, and there were also three cargo trucks and three converted school buses carrying the numerous spools of cabling needed for a launch. Following in the thick dust somewhere in the rear was the brigade command vehicle responsible for coordinating commands for all the launch companies.

They were headed to a predetermined location, and like any practice exercise, they would completely set up for a simulated launch.

Staff Sergeant Leung thought he was the only brigade moving into a launch profile. He had no clue others were doing the same across the entire nation.

# Chapter 41



Sitting at his desk in the Pentagon, Air Force General Robert "Bob" Nierling was reminiscing about his path as the first United States Space Force Chief of Space Operations. He would have to agree with those who said he had done it the hard way. He got his commission not by attending the United States Air Force Academy but by going through ROTC at the University of Michigan. He figured that path probably motivated him like a seventh-round draft pick in pro football. You worked harder than everyone else for every advancement. When Neil Armstrong was the first to walk on the moon, Nierling was in grade school and would never forget the feat.

From then on, he always had a love for the space program and dreamed of someday becoming an astronaut. Although he majored in Mechanical Engineering with a minor in Physics, he didn't enter the Space Shuttle program. However, he still made a military career specializing in anything to do with missile defense. His reward for his dedication and hard work came near Christmas 2019 when he was named the Chief of Space Operations to lead the newest US service branch, the United States Space Force.

As the Air Force grew out of the Army in 1947, the Space Force was evolving from the Air Force, and Nierling was proud to be a big part of the next evolution. Along with some fantastic men and women he recruited as the force's initial cadre, his team soon developed an operational statement. The Space Force was to provide space capabilities and to protect US and allied security interests in space. Further, they would give tactical support to ground combat units using surveillance, communications, and geopositioning data and make the adversaries of the United States comprehend that the Space Force would seek to deter their every move to acquire a military advantage in space.

When Iran fired sixteen ballistic missiles at two US air bases in Iraq, space forces gave the bases an advanced warning to allow troops to take cover and prevent any deaths. Now, General Nierling was waiting for a return call from the Secretary of the Air Force, Margret Riley, regarding a national security issue detected by satellite intelligence.

His secure, direct line lit up, and he answered quickly. "Thank you, Ma'am, for getting right back to me."

"Sorry, general, I had a room full of people to chase off. What do you have for me?"

"I just received information from my staff regarding satellite intelligence. The PLA is moving mobile missile launchers from their base sites to strategic areas in the field. As you know, a major dispersal from their peacetime locations is an extraordinary and dangerous escalation. It's more than anything I've ever seen."

The SECAF immediately asked, "How many and where?"

"We're still compiling that information, but preliminary numbers appear to be at least one hundred spread out all over China."

"Got it. Stay on the line," said SECAF. "I want to get SecDef on the line."

George Mitchell was briefed within minutes, and a couple of moments after that, the president of the United States had another crisis on his hands.

# Chapter 42

*USS MICHIGAN*
South China Sea

"Helm, Conn. Come to bearing two-six-one, speed 5 knots."

"Conn, Helm. Bearing two-six-one, speed 5 knots," came the reply from the twenty-year-old PO3 Justin Richardson, who wasn't even born when the submarine he was guiding was commissioned. Such is the Navy.

One of the rare breeds in high school, Richardson loved history, especially Naval history, so when he found out he was assigned to the USS *Michigan*, he researched everything about the sub. One thing for sure; he would be on one powerful boat.

The Ohio class of submarines was initially designed in 1980 to carry SLBM. After twenty years of service, *Michigan* whipped being decommissioned by taking three years to be reconfigured as a guided-missile submarine as the Cold War ended in 2007. Getting a facelift, the new look for *Michigan* now included its unprecedented strike and unique operation mission capabilities. Its new payload capacity of 154 Tomahawk land-attack cruise missiles made it pretty impressive. The missiles are loaded in seven-shot Multiple-All-Up-Round-Canisters in up to twenty-two missile tubes.

Adding to its beauty was its stealth and survivability using sophisticated, cutting-edge technology, making it hard to detect and track. Its advanced sensor and communication systems enable it to gather critical information and maintain situational awareness while communicating effectively with others.

The USS *Michigan* and several other submarines out of the inventory of sixty-eight operational boats were deployed to the Indo-Pacific to bolster Seventh Fleet's submarine force to twenty-five. Changing the balance of submarine deployment worldwide was not taken lightly—but neither was the escalating aggression of China.

The growing anti-access area denial capabilities of the PLAN were a worrying challenge. However, the ability of submarines to penetrate long-range defenses put attack submarines in the lead. They were the critical component of joint force missions in the US projection of its power and control of the sea. The submarine force gave the US military its most competitive advantage against a peer power like China. If a conflict with PRC were in the cards, America would hold four aces in their underwater battle.

## Chapter 43


*AUGUST 1ST BUILDING*
Beijing, China


As Dr. Dong Liang was ambling back to his office from the cafeteria, he was amazed by the noise and movement. Generals hurried here and there, closely followed by their subordinates. So many leaders giving and taking orders.

But this was to be expected, as the Central Military Commission was the highest military command authority in the nation, and it was always hectic. Anything to do with war, the armed forces, and national defense was controlled by the Communist Party's Politburo, chaired by one man—President Zhang Wei. The only orders that mattered came from that man. In a meeting room, that man was preparing to give the most significant order of his life, one which would impact an entire world.

As Dong walked down the long hallway, it appeared that his feet were trying to catch up with his body. Full of his favorite dish of Lion's Head pork balls covered in a savory brown sauce, he had to hide his smile. Not that anyone would pay a disheveled civilian any attention. But he knew from his handler that big things were about to happen, and he would become the ultimate order-giver.

# Chapter 44



It was cold, minus fifteen Celsius, with just enough wind to make things uncomfortable the day before the start of the Chinese New Year. General Sun Tong was working in the driving wind at 0400 hours, looking after every detail of the aircraft he considered his. He had wondered what to classify it as. Still, nothing did the craft justice, so he had settled on calling it a converted Boeing 747-8 bomber. But from the start, Sun had named the large aircraft "The Brave One" for reasons that would become evident soon enough. He was doing the final walk around the aircraft, preparing for his fourteen-hour flight to San Diego, California, in what appeared like any other China World Airlines Boeing 747-8. But instead of passenger luggage in the hold, his airline carried four YJ-12 anti-ship cruise missiles.

As he climbed the stairs into the plane, thoughts of his last goodbye to his wife haunted him. Of course, she didn't know it was probably the last time she would ever see him, but that was how it had to be. Nothing he had ever done was this classified. He loved her with all his heart, as his two grown kids did, but this was a mission before family. Perhaps if he and his crew of two performed their task flawlessly and if everything went their way, they could make it back home. But probably not.

The plan was to take out two US carriers and hightail it less than one hundred miles south to Ensenada, Mexico, a dual-function civilian airport shared with their Air Force. He was told that there were to be several Chinese MSS officers to whisk them away. Hell, he didn't know what would happen when and if he landed, but he understood that the Chinese government had paid a large sum of money to the powers to allow him to land. Regardless, his focus was on the success of his part of the mission to obliterate two US carriers.

General Sun didn't know everything that was being planned by his country. Still, he had explicit directions to fire his missiles at 1500 hours, Pacific Standard Time. The other Boeing 747-8 had already taken off. It would fire four YJ-12 anti-ship cruise missiles at 1800 hours Eastern Standard Time and in conjunction with Sun. Thoughts of his family crept back, but the general suppressed them. He got behind the pilot's seat to finish his preflight. It was time.

# Chapter 45



To get twelve Bones operational was simply a military miracle, thought Boeing B-1B Lancer pilot Major Thomas "Solo" Kronbach. Designed in the 1970s to replace the aging Boeing B-52 Stratofortress fleet, it looked now like the BUFFs were destined to outlast their replacements. Flying from their home base at Ellsworth AFB in South Dakota, Kronbach's Bone was the last of a trio of bombers off to Wake Island. Considered America's most remote outpost, it was more runway than an island and was in the middle of the enormous Pacific Ocean. If you pictured how far apart Japan and Hawaii were, you could place Wake Island in the middle and get an idea of its location.

Wake was now known as an emergency divert point for aircraft crossing the Pacific and a stopping point for US military aircraft traveling from Asia to the US. The runway could handle any aircraft in the American inventory. The entire airstrip was recently rebuilt, the sizable eastern apron was expanded, and a new secondary apron was added. The Pentagon was pouring money into Wake because of the evolving strategic importance of the remote base. By most accounts, it was the perfect open-air staging area because it was out of range of almost every missile PLARF had. Wake could be the rally point if the United States had to pull back from its close-in bases during a conflict. Being remote has at least one advantage, the major thought.

The strategic importance of Wake Island was not lost on the US Navy of 1941 either. With war raging in different parts of the world and with political rumblings of the United States getting involved, runway construction began on the atoll, an inactive volcano, in January of that year. Later in August, elements of the 1st Marine Defense Battalion occupied the first permanent military garrison. Using the runway they constructed, which still exists today, the Americans parked twelve Grumman F4F-3 Wildcat fighters from Marine Fighting Squadron VMF-211.

The island's strategic importance became quite clear when, just hours after the attack on Pearl Harbor in 1941, thirty-six Japanese Mitsubishi B3M3 medium bombers from bases on the Marshall Islands attacked the Wake garrison, destroying eight of the parked Wildcats. It would have been all twelve, but four were out on patrol and, due to inclement weather, never saw the attacking Japanese planes.

Three days later, a Japanese invasion force of light cruisers and destroyers arrived to capture the island and its prized airstrip. The 450 Marines and 1,100 civilians were in for a fight. In a remarkable feat of bravery, the Marines, with help from the construction workers, used their six 5-inch coastal defense guns that hurled fifty-pound shells at the enemy. The Japanese flagship was struck eleven times, and one destroyer was hit three times, broke apart, and swiftly sunk. The barrage laid near landing craft carrying several Japanese Marines proved too much for the invaders, and they quickly turned back.

Not waiting for an invitation, the four remaining Wildcat fighters flew into the battle. One of the men, Captain Henry Elrod, again proved his prowess in piloting the F4F-3. A few days earlier, he sank the Japanese destroyer *Kisaragi*. When a swarm of twenty-two Japanese aircraft attacked him, he single-handedly assaulted the enemy shooting down two planes, becoming the first Marine to score air-to-air victories in the war.

As other Japanese warships arrived, he strafed them and used his small, one-hundred-pound bombs to wreak havoc on the invaders; he sank one ship when his bomb struck the ship's depth charges. With his plane shot up, he landed, grabbed a rifle, and promptly organized defenses against the invasion headed toward the island.

It wasn't long before the attack, and his men affectionately called the captain "Hammerin' Hank." On December 23, the day the island fell to the Japanese, Hammerin' Hank was killed while covering for Marines resupplying ammunition. Captain Elrod was the first Marine in World War II to be awarded the Medal of Honor. Over eighty years later, forces gathered on Wake Island again but for a different enemy, the Chinese.

# Chapter 46



*THE WHITE HOUSE*
Washington DC


As President Taylor looked around the Situation Room, what he saw was deep concern on the faces of his NSC staff. Since these people made their living on the edge of so many crises, it was somewhat disheartening to see this change. But he was no different. As hard as he tried to convey a sense of calm, he knew his face fit right in with the rest. A war with China seemed more of a reality now than it did a short time ago.

Looking at his Secretary of Defense, the president said, "George, please brief us on the latest about China's military posture."

SecDef Mitchell took a moment, perhaps too long, before he spoke. "Mr. President, the PLA is on the move around the country. Our primary concern is the deployment of their mobile missile launchers from their home base to what appear to be pre-established launching positions. We're talking about the most powerful missiles in their arsenal, the DF-26, DF-31, and DF-41. The complete dispersal of these mobile missiles from their peacetime locations is an extraordinary, dangerous threshold to cross. It's never taken place in any country before. And since 80 percent of their missiles are mobile, locating them is difficult. Even with our best satellites, once the missiles are on the move, the advantage goes to them.

"I've directed all our active carriers to get on the move, especially those in port, the *Roosevelt* and the *Ford*. The *Reagan* is already in the South China Sea along with the *Nimitz*. If a conflict starts, the carriers will be targeted right from the get-go. Our top priority must be the safety of the carriers so we can bring the war to China if that's their intent."

Barely pausing to take a breath, the SecDef continued. "Per INDOPACOM's planning sessions, we have military assets already deployed to the Indo-Pacific. Included are many of our Virginia class attack submarines and our heavy bombers. In a peer war with China, it's imperative to slowly but efficiently degrade China's robust A2/AD bubble so that our less capable and short-range assets can move close enough to be useful. It's a high-stakes process, especially during the early days of the conflict. The bombers will be critical in attacking China's advanced warships that stand between us and targets in and around the Chinese mainland."

Sensing it was time to move on, Taylor said, "Thank you, George. General Matthews, please go over our current strategy for defending Taiwan."

If anyone in the room seemed calm and collected, observed the president, it was the Chairman of the Joint Chiefs of Staff. Right at this moment, Taylor hoped he was right. Perhaps the general's uniform and all the medals made him seem invincible. He was one man I would not hesitate to follow into battle, thought Taylor, because I would be in good hands.

"Mr. President," said the CJCS, "when the Chinese attack Taiwan, and they most certainly will, we'll need to divide our forces in coming to their aid. This will be a joint operation and may include the Japanese Defense Forces. I've stressed to my military counterpart in Taiwan and the INDOPACOM commander that Taiwan's objective would not be to win the war, which they can't, but to take prompt and lethal defensive actions to make China reconsider its objectives. Additionally, we would extend the conflict as long as possible because doing so shifts the advantage to the allies. I won't go into the details, but we have contingency plans for everything we expect to encounter.

"Additionally, Mr. President, we should change the defense readiness of our country. I recommend DEFCON 2, the level just short of when nuclear war is imminent. DEFCON 2 will prepare our armed forces to deploy and engage in less than six hours. We've only been to DEFCON 2 on one occasion, and that was for the 1962 Cuban Missile Crisis. Now should be the second time."

General Matthews sat back in his chair. As the president looked around the room for reactions, he saw that his trusted Director of National Intelligence had a comment. "Yes, Elena."

"Mr. President," said DNI Ramirez, "I agree with General Matthews. The PRC is either attempting to bolster its bargaining position in the Indo-Pacific or they are getting ready for war. I believe the latter, and we should go to DEFCON 2, but with the caveat that we do not go public. Doing so avoids tipping off China. They will eventually find out, but that should take a few days. I want to add that the Chinese New Year is upon us, so what better time for China to strike than on a culturally effective date."

President Taylor had heard enough. "Go to DEFCON 2 but with no public statement. Ladies and gentlemen, if war comes to this country, we didn't ask for it. But by God, we will prevail—we must."

# PART II
# SEA OF RED

# Chapter 47



*CHINA WORLD AIRLINES FLIGHT 25*
Off the coast of San Diego, California

Everything was going smoothly, too smoothly, thought General Sun Tong. The routine communication calls between air traffic controllers and China World Airlines Flight 25 were business as usual for mid-afternoon traffic in February. He hoped it was the same for CWA Flight 35, now nearing Newport News, Virginia, and ostensibly scheduled to land in New York City.

There were no bilateral treaties that governed aviation rights between the US and China like there were for almost every other country in the rest of the world. A regulated number of flights restricted all Chinese airlines, but air travel to and from China was a profitable equation for United States airline businesses. By pressuring the appropriate politicians, the airline executives were able to increase daily nonstop flights between the two countries from ten in 2006 to ninety-eight. Today, each country's airliners were accepted as routine in the skies around the two powerful countries—until there was any deviation from a flight plan.

Conveniently, the real-life China World Airlines flight from Beijing to Las Vegas had been delayed for hours because of mechanical trouble. Unknown to anyone in the China World Airlines organization, a different China World Airlines Boeing 747-8 had taken off from Anquing Tianzhushan Airport and was handled by a designated Chinese air traffic controller. Once airborne, all that flight information and transponder code appeared on the air traffic control radar screens as data from the delayed flight. Sun still couldn't believe how easily the data switch had gone.

Breaking the silence in the Boeing 747-8 airliner-turned-bomber, the weapons officer said over the intercom, "Five hundred kilometers from target."

The three men on board the aircraft understood the following minutes would be crucial to their mission. All knew nothing like what they were attempting—a surprise attack on the US mainland by a foreign government—had ever occurred. The target wasn't Pearl Harbor on an island far from help; it was San Diego, California.

"Make course correction for the target now," ordered General Sun.

The crew knew it was a minor correction, but one that was necessary to close the gap to the target for their YJ-12 missiles, which had a range of four hundred kilometers. Sun wanted to get within two hundred kilometers to launch their missiles, leaving little reaction time for whatever the Americans had defensively on the ground. The crew understood the course correction would send up red flags to the air traffic controllers.

It came sooner than expected.

"CWA 25, SoCal Approach. You have deviated from your assigned flight path. Please correct immediately," said a calm but firm voice.

In preparation for the synchronous bombing mission, they had anticipated contact from US air traffic controllers and had found copilots with the proper credentials. They could speak and understand English perfectly, but they had been trained to use an accent Americans associated with Asian peoples to disrupt the communication flow and buy precious minutes—or so they hoped.

"SoCal Approach," said the copilot in an accent that distorted many consonants and vowel combinations, "CWA 25, say again."

"CWA 25, SoCal Approach," said the air traffic controller slowly and loudly, "You are garbled and unreadable. You are still off course. Put an English-speaking crew member on the radio immediately. Come to a heading of zero-five-four degrees."

Hundreds of miles away, in a darkness illuminated by radar screens, the air traffic controller who had spoken to CWA 25 reached over and pushed a button on his console. His shift supervisor quickly came to his station.

"What have you got for me, Tom." The supervisor plugged his headset into the console to hear the communications.

"I've got—"

"SoCal Approach, CWA 25," said a man with perfect English. "My error. We had unexpected severe turbulence. I took control of the aircraft and drifted off course. Will adjust back to zero-five-four degrees now."

Before responding, Tom told his supervisor, "I don't feel good about this one. Everything about their actions makes me suspicious. First, they went off course, then some guy who can't speak English, and as you can see, no course correction yet."

"What is the flight information?" asked the supervisor.

"CWA to Las Vegas with 408 on board."

The supervisor keyed the comms. "CWA 25, SoCal Approach supervisor. You're violating FAA flight regulations, and I order you to come to heading zero-five-four degrees immediately."

The supervisor and controller waited a few seconds but got no response, and the radar didn't show a course change.

On board CWA 25, the weapons officer said, "General, we're three hundred kilometers from target. Firing solution acquired."

Only a few minutes more, thought Sun.

*FAA Headquarters*
Washington DC

As the young man walked briskly across the room and down the hall to his supervisor's room, he questioned what was happening. Within a few minutes, he received two emergency notices concerning two CWA airliners flying off course, which the FAA called "pilot deviation."

Once in his supervisor's office, he said, "Sir, I've just received two notifications of pilot deviation. One near San Diego and the other on the East Coast approaching Virginia. Both are China World Airlines, and after being ordered to return to their designated courses, the aircraft hasn't responded. Both airliners are each carrying over four hundred passengers."

"Got it, keep me posted as to any changes."

"Yes, sir."

The FAA supervisor immediately called his North American Aerospace Defense Command, NORAD colleague. "General, we have two pilot deviations, both China World Airlines. One is near San Diego, and the other is on the East Coast, flying east near Virginia. Both have ceased communications. We have no explanations."

"Roger that, remain on the line and stand by."

NORAD, headquartered in Colorado Springs, Colorado, was the lead agency to handle unknown, unwanted, and unauthorized air activity in United States airspace. They were tied into a sophisticated worldwide network of satellites, communication nets, and ground and airborne-based radar systems. They had fighters standing by to intercept any threat, if necessary. The lieutenant general immediately got his commanding four-star general, Emit Ginart, in the loop. The general picked up the hotline to the command center.

"This is NORAD command; we have multiple incursions. I want fighters scrambled in Eastern and Western Defense Sectors to intercept China World Airlines aircraft near San Diego and Virginia. Additional information to follow." After hanging up, Ginart turned to his aide, "Get me SecDef. Tell him it's critical, and we may need permission to shoot down two civilian airliners, totaling over eight hundred souls on board."

General Ginart looked at the clock. It was 1600 hours local. He activated comms to listen in on his command and control ops center.

*CHINA WORLD AIRLINES FLIGHT 25*
Off the coast of San Diego, California

General Sun was waiting for his weapons officer to confirm the range to target, and there was still no sign of the Americans.

"Sir," said the weapons officer, "150 kilometers from target. I have a firing solution for all missiles. Rack lowered and locked into position."

General Sun noted the time was 1500 hours local, a perfect time on target. He calmly said, "Fire missiles one, two, three, and four."

The weapons officer pushed four red buttons and proudly announced, "Missiles away!"

At the release of the powerful cruise missiles, the large airliner shook violently as if it were just a toy, not a massive Boeing 747-8.

"Rack up," yelled the general, losing some control of his nerves for the first time on the mission. "Put in the coordinates for Ensenada Airport, Mexico."

Sun pushed his control wheel forward, taking his aircraft into a steep dive. He wanted distance between him and what he knew would come.

As the general flew his aircraft toward the deck, which was the Pacific Ocean, four supersonic YJ-12 anti-ship cruise missiles were traveling at Mach 3 toward the USS *Carl Vinson* and the USS *Abraham Lincoln*. Both carriers were in dry dock at the sprawling Naval Base San Diego, the principal home for the United States Pacific Fleet, which consisted of fifty ships, over twenty-four thousand military personnel, and ten thousand civilians.

*NORAD*
Colorado Springs, Colorado

"General," came the anxious voice over comms, "we have alerts, from both East and West Defense Sectors, of missiles being launched from what appears to be the two Chinese civilian airliners,"

Shit, thought Lieutenant General Ginart. "What is the status of the fighters?" he yelled to the C2 ops center shift commander.

"Sir, we have two F-15s just taking off from Fresno and being directed to the last sighting of CWA Flight 25. Two F-22s from

Langley are already airborne and have the Chinese airliner on their radar. They've requested permission to shoot."

"No, we're not going to kill four hundred passengers until we have the okay from SecDef. Have them track the airliner and stand by," ordered Ginart.

"Sir," said the general's aide, "an emergency call from the SecDef."

As the general picked up the phone, George Mitchell was already talking, no screaming, "What in Jesus's name is going on?"

"Sir, it appears two Chinese civilian airliners, one on each coast, have fired missiles. We have fighters in the air requesting permission to fire on the aircraft."

"Appears? I need solid intelligence before I authorize killing civilians. Now get it!"




Jonathan Carey was a happy young man. Not long out of high school in San Diego, he had already landed a job with a contractor doing a RCOH, a Refueling Complex Overhaul, on the USS *Carl Vinson*. He was told the job could take up to four years, which was fine with him because he made an astounding $27.50 an hour with no college. How cool was that? he thought.

He checked his phone to ensure he wasn't late, and it was nearly three in the afternoon as he boarded the carrier, which looked nothing like it had just a few months ago. Thousands of workers moved around the ship like ants. As it had been for the past two weeks, his job today would be as a painter. He was told he would be going over the carrier's side to remove rust formations. It was hard work but gratifying because he was part of something bigger than himself. He took pride in that achievement, as did his parents.

Nearly at the end of the gangway to the ship, Jonathan heard a loud whooshing sound, a noise he had never heard before. He looked up to see what it was—and that was the last thing he ever did.

The first hypersonic cruise missile hit the USS Carl Vinson forward deck with a speed of 1,200 mph, exploding as it tore through several decks of the mammoth ship and disintegrating everything in its path—metal and humans. A few seconds later, the second missile hit near the stern, exploding in a fireball that reached hundreds of feet in the air in seconds.

The devastation brought on by the two missiles was incomprehensible. Secondary explosions turned the ship into an inferno. What the bombs didn't kill, the raging fire did. Two piers down, the USS *Abraham Lincoln* had met the same fate.

First responders wouldn't be able to approach either ship for hours, while some parts of the vessel took days for them to reach. When they did, they saw horrifying scenes of mass destruction that would follow them for the rest of their lives because no human being should be subjected to such an inhumane act.



For China World Airlines Flight 35, the mission was going smoothly, except they were running a few minutes behind their scheduled weapons release at 1800 hours local.

By chance, the USS *Gravely*, an Arleigh Burke-class guided-missile destroyer, was in Surge Ready configuration, meaning the ship was ready in all aspects for deployment, including being fully armed. But it was tied to a pier just down from the aircraft carriers at the Newport News Shipyard drydock. At 1800 hours local, the ship's CIC received flash comms about aircraft carriers in San Diego being struck by missiles and reported the info to the CO.

Without giving it a second thought, the captain of the *Gravely* went to general quarters as a precautionary move and ordered his AN/SPY-6 radar system to go active instead of remaining in the usual standby mode while in port. Although not as effective because of surrounding buildings, cranes, and heavy equipment, the captain wanted situational awareness.

Just as the system came online, his radar acquired four inbound missiles. They were quickly identified as Chinese YJ-12 anti-ship cruise missiles. Using his Fire Control Directors, they input a solution to the firing crew, and four SM-2 missiles were fired from the ship's MK 41 Vertical Launch System. The fighting equation came down to Chinese versus US technology as the missiles attempted to evade each other but still find their targets.

The danger posed by the YJ-12 came from its four-hundred-kilometer range, the longest for any supersonic anti-ship cruise missile ever designed. Its speed of Mach 3 made it difficult for Aegis Combat Systems and SM-2s to identify and engage the missile since it could be launched beyond their engagement ranges. All of the YJ-12's capabilities reduced reaction time, and it was more difficult to target due to its corkscrew-like turns, which allowed it to evade final defenses.

But its adversary, the SM-2, brought much to the table of missile vs. missile combat. First, it was purposely built for the Aegis Combat System's MK 41 VLS. The predominately used Block III missiles had the addition of the MK 45 MOD 9 target detecting device for improved performance against low altitude targets. The SM-2 also had a dual semiactive and infrared seeker for terminal homing and high electronic countermeasures against targets over the horizon.

But the four YJ-12 missiles weren't over the horizon. They were over Virginia and closing in on their targets, the carriers USS *John C. Stennis* and USS *George Washington*. The USS *Gravely* fired four SM-2s. Two found their mark and destroyed two incoming missiles. The other two SM-2s failed to acquire their targets. The remaining two YJ-12 missiles continued closing in.

The missiles impacted George Washington a moment later, shredding it and killing hundreds of people working on the ship. It could have been even worse, but the day shift had gone home, leaving fewer workers on the ship. Still, it was a bloody scene that the men and women of the *Gravely* would never forget, and they would always regret that two Chinese missiles made it through their best defensive efforts. Grief counselors would later explain to the sailors how they had saved hundreds, if not thousands, of those who worked on the *Stennis*.

But for most, it would always be what they didn't do.



General Ginart told the SecDef on a secure landline, "Sir, I just received confirmation that the missiles fired came from the two Chinese airliners. Request permission to engage."

Without so much as a blink, Secretary of Defense George Mitchell's reply came fast and heated, "Kill the bastards!"



Looking at his watch, Major Carlos "Hog" Garcia noted he had one more hour until his relief would come strolling into the ready room at 1600 hours. Today wasn't just the end of his alert; as they said in the Los Angeles Police Department, it was his end of watch. Not only was he heading home and back to his "day" job as a pilot in the LAPD's Air Support Division, where he flew the Eurocopter AS350 AStar, but today was the official end of his service with the 144th Fighter Wing. He had to admit flying a Boeing F-15C Eagle raised the pucker factor much more than flying his AStar, but chasing bad guys in LA was something he had always wanted to do, and he had loved every minute of his eighteen years on the job.

He noticed that his partner for the day, Captain Amy "Top Dog" Adams, was pacing the floor as usual. She had earned her nickname Top Dog for finishing first in her class at the USAF's prestigious Weapons School. Adams proudly wore the Weapons School patch on her left sleeve.

Top Dog despised sitting behind a desk and not flying—so today, she was pissed. Two F-15Cs were sitting not far away on the tarmac, fully loaded and armed but with no mission. It was like holding a cold, wet beer can in front of a hot, thirsty, alert pilot.

The Klaxon sounded.

"Alpha Alert. Red Shoot. I say again, Red Shoot."

In all his years, Garcia had never heard those words uttered in real life. "Red Shoot" wasn't much different from an "officer needs help" radio call. It meant that some serious shit was going down.

The two pilots sprinted to their aircraft. Maintenance crews were already swarming to do their part in the launch.

Two crew chiefs helped strap the pilots into their fighters and pulled the chocks. The aircraft were airborne within minutes with initial orders to head toward San Diego. Time was critical, and they had a considerable distance to close. Flying at thirty-six thousand feet heading south, the two pilots fought to grasp what they were being told over comms—that a China World Airlines airliner had somehow just bombed the Naval Base San Diego and killed thousands. The pilots had explicit orders from SecDef to locate and destroy the airliner. The last heading of the bandit was south toward Mexico.


*ENSENADA AIRPORT*
Ensenada, Mexico


General Sun rechecked his military-grade radar and couldn't believe American fighters were not hunting them down. Flying just a few hundred feet above the waves of the Pacific Ocean, Sun adjusted course for a landing at the joint military and civilian airport

176

at Ensenada. From secure communications, he knew four Chinese MSS agents would meet him after his aircraft was directed to a remote area on the airfield. Maintaining radio silence as he approached runway three-six-right, a Chinese voice came over his comms telling him he was cleared to land and to follow a truck that would guide him to his parking area.

The other two members of his crew had huge grins on their faces but maintained their professional decorum. Even Sun let out a sigh of relief. He had just accomplished the most successful covert mission in the history of warfare. A quick vision of his homecoming with his wife and family flashed in his mind, but he quickly returned to the task.

Sticking the landing without so much as a bump, Sun saw a large duce and a half on the far end of the runway. He slowed to follow.

*BUREAU OF ALCOHOL, TOBACCO, FIREARMS, AND EXPLOSIVES FIELD UNIT*
Ensenada, Mexico


"Is that it?" asked Agent Sanchez, who looked puzzled.

"Fuck no, stupid. Learn your aircraft," replied element leader Roscoe Blanco. "That's a Boeing 747 from fucking China. We're looking for an unmarked DC-9, which the Wright brothers last flew."

Blanco and his crew from the ATF were on a stakeout with rock-solid intelligence about a large shipment of Fentanyl coming to Ensenada Airport at 1530 hours. He looked at his watch, and the plane would arrive any minute. The mission was a massive undertaking. He had ten of his men backed up by scores of Federales hiding out on the outskirts of the runway—all heavily armed.

Breaking his concentration, his earpiece went off. It was his boss. "Roscoe, we were just contacted through channels that a China World Airlines passenger jet somehow bombed carriers at the naval base in San Diego. Our information is that the airliner just landed at your location. Can you confirm?"

"I sure can. The big mother just landed. I see it at the end of the runway." "Break. Sanchez, keep an eye on the plane you just saw land. Don't let it out of your sight."

"Break. Okay, Tom, we have it under observation. What do you want us to do?"

"Whatever you do, don't let the Mexicans know what we're doing. Give them some excuse to break off the operation, and then you and one other will stay low and follow the aircraft and the people on it. I want constant updates over this secure network. Understand?"

"Yes, sir." His spontaneous reply caught Roscoe off guard because he never called Tom "sir." He felt his heart pounding—this was much bigger than landing a drug haul.

"Sanchez, you're with me. Roberts, we must keep eyes on that Chinese plane, but no one can know it, especially the Mexicans. Think of some excuse to tell them and the rest of our crew that we need to put this operation on hold or cancel. Make it sound real. Got it?"

"Yeah, boss, but what do I tell them?"

"Figure it out, but don't fuck it up. I'll check back with you."

Dressed as Mexican airline workers, the two ATF agents jumped in an official airport pickup truck and headed toward the massive CWA airliner.



Sun applied throttle to keep his 747-8 moving behind the deuce and a half. Four Chinese men dressed in suits approached his aircraft. After making several sweeping turns, they came to the dead end of a runway next to a large dark hanger.

"Copilot, open the hatch. As soon as the stairs are pulled up, let's get going. Do you have the detonator?"

"Yes, general, I do."

After the stairs were pulled up to the aircraft, all three men quickly exited the airliner for the first time in nearly twenty-four hours. They were met on the tarmac by a burly Chinese agent who said, "Follow me."

As they did, someone on the ground opened the hangar doors, revealing a sizable civilian jet with seven round windows and two engines on the aircraft's rear that were already running. The men were pushed into the plane and told to take a seat. The door shut, and the ultra-long-range Gulfstream G500 moved toward the runway.


Ensenada, Mexico

As the Chinese airliner stopped at the end of the tarmac, Roscoe pulled off behind some buildings. The two ATF agents walked inside the structure and then out the back door, giving them eyes on the airliner that was parked next to a large hanger.

"ATF command, Blanco."

"ATF command, what do you have?"

"ATF command, the CWA is parked at the end of a tarmac on the west end of the airport next to a large hanger. We see three crew exiting the jet, met by four Asian men in suits. Wait, okay, now someone just opened the hangar doors, and we see a smaller civilian jet with engines running. The seven men are running and are now boarding the smaller jet. It's on the move. What do we do, over?"

"Don't do anything. Can you get a tail number?"

"Yes, N094523X. It looks like one of those expensive business jets, white with brown trim."

"Okay, return to your unit and play as if nothing happened."

"Roger that, heading out."


Ensenada, Mexico

No one spoke as the Gulfstream taxied toward the active runway with its lights turned off. Finally, the lead Chinese MSS agent spoke up. "Who has the detonator?"

"I do," said Sun's copilot, producing a small handheld device.

"Give it to me," said the agent. The co-pilot looked over at Sun and got a nod. He handed over the device.

The business jet accelerated to take off as the MSS agent grasped the detonator and simultaneously pushed the "Ready Weapon" button with the red "Attack" button.

The sky lit up. What was once CWA Flight 25 blew to pieces. Sun never gave it a second look—he was heading home.

*BOEING F-15C EAGLE FLIGHT*
Near the border of Mexico


"Alpha 11, NORAD Command. Bandit 1 landed at Ensenada Airport, changed aircraft, and went airborne in a Gulfstream G500, bearing two-seven-four, speed 300 knots. Advise when you have radar contact."

"NORAD Command, Alpha 11. Roger."

Looking out from his cockpit, Hog saw Top Dog looking back at him. "Alpha 12, Alpha 11. Let's find these assholes."

"Alpha 11, Alpha 12. Already on that."

Just moments later, both F-15s received information from their pulse-Doppler radar. It was tracking beyond visual range one G500.

"NORAD Command, Alpha 11. Have contact with bandit, seventy miles out." While Gonzales was talking, his radar automatically fed his central computer the coordinates for the kill.

"Alpha 11, NORAD Command. SecDef wants visual ID that this is our bandit. Confirm tail number N094523X."

"NORAD Command, Alpha 11, Roger. Break. Alpha 12, run up there and tell me what you find."

"Roger, on my way." Soon, she was just behind the bogey, looking at the tail number. "Alpha 11, Alpha 12. I have confirmed this is our bogey. Returning now."

When she returned, Alpha 11 had already received permission to engage. "Alpha 12, ready, AMRAAM. At my command, we will each fire one missile for all the American souls lost today. Check. Master-Arm Hot."

Both pilots flipped the master arm switch to the hot position. "Stand by . . . FOX THREE."

The missiles dropped from their pylons. Igniting their solid-fuel rockets, reaching a speed of nearly 3,000 mph as both headed for the G500. Moments later, a fireball illuminated the sky over the Pacific Ocean. Hundreds of small fragments tumbled toward the ocean: one down, one to go.

CHINA WORLD AIRLINES FLIGHT 35
Flying over US Federal Interstate 95

Unlike General Sun, who only had to fly fifty miles to Mexico to escape the wrath of the United States, the pilot of CWA Flight 35 had a different flight profile, with the Atlantic Ocean on one side and the American mainland on the other. As determined by rehearsals, the most advantageous possibility of a successful getaway was maneuvering overpopulated areas of the US so that if they were shot down, the vast debris field would guarantee more dead Americans. With this tactic in mind, the MSS had loaded the Boeing 747-8 with a ton of C4, ensuring that there would be little aircraft left to examine and many dead bodies on the ground. The only hope the captain of CWA 35 had was to make it the 105 miles across the Straits of Florida to Havana, Cuba, where they had permission to land. The pilot understood it was a long shot but so had taking out two US carriers.

LOCKHEED MARTIN F-22 RAPTOR FLIGHT

Captain Andrew "Shooter" Anderson was fighting the urge to release an AMRAAM right up the ass of the Chinese airliner. Instead, he and his wingman, Captain Robbie "Hammer" Matheson, were in constant radio contact with NORAD Command. The bandit was flying just four hundred feet off Interstate 95, the East Coast's major north-to-south roadway.

"Charlie 11, NORAD Command. The North Carolina Highway Patrol has stopped all freeway traffic south of Fayetteville. You have permission to use your cannon on the bogey in the open area just south of Fayetteville."

Looking at their monochrome HUDs, both pilots saw the area marked on their map. Anderson noted they were approximately four minutes out.

"NORAD Command, Charlie 11. roger." Switching frequencies, he said, "Charlie 12, Charlie 11. Maintain current heading. Engage on my command, cannon only, then go full military power to put some distance between the bandit and us."

"Charlie 11, Roger. Fire on your command and get the hell out of Dodge."

The two F-22s followed the bandit at fifteen hundred feet, and their M61A2 Vulcan 20mm rotary cannons embedded in their right wings had a maximum range of two thousand feet. After discharge, both aircraft needed to avoid the fireworks.

Both fighters settled into position.

"Charlie 12, Charlie 11. Fifteen seconds. Retractable door down."

"Retractable door down."

"Five—four—three—two—one—fire."

Both fighters let loose from their M61 Vulcans with a firing rate of six thousand rounds per minute. Instantly, there was a solid streak of red between the enemy aircraft and the F-22s as the tracer rounds found their mark. It sounded like a buzz saw.

The jetliner ripped apart and became a temporary flying ball of fire as the two F-22s went vertical, thundering away from the kill. The airliner crashed just east of the interstate, with the resulting explosions seen for miles away—to mostly farmers. The exception was a young couple from San Francisco who would soon become instant celebrities. Camping out on the roadside, the lovers heard the low-flying jetliner, and both grabbed their smartphones, sensing something cool was about to happen. They were correct and videoed the giant airliner when it disintegrated and showered the area around them with pieces of burning debris. Miraculously, they weren't torched, which added to their story. The videos quickly went viral, becoming the new rallying cry for the US as the modest bit of revenge it showed.

It was only the beginning.

# Chapter 48



*NEAR FORT BRAGG*
Fayetteville, North Carolina

It was getting dark as a bright red 2018 Chevrolet Corvette was pushing the speed limit on Highway 93 near Fayetteville. The fact it was close to nightfall bothered the driver because he had told his family that he would be home before dark. His mom was dying of cancer, and he needed to see her. Deep in his soul, as he drove home from that visit, he knew he wouldn't see her again. It was all too sad.

Pushing that thought out of his crowded mind, he had a vision of his father giving him an ass whipping when he went past his curfew, not wanting to hear his excuse. His dad was a sergeant major in the Army and didn't accept excuses. "Excuses are like assholes. Everyone has one," he would yell at his delinquent son.

Well, Father, thought Captain Nathan Hubbard, if only you could see me now, a company commander assigned to the 1st Brigade Combat Team out of Fort Bragg. Here I am, driving a hot car, the likes of which you never saw, to my beautiful home with a loving family of four waiting for me. There are no ass-whippings in my house. I use reason and logic to teach my children with lots of love thrown in.

Up ahead, he saw a sea of red emergency lights and a line of red brake lights. He wondered what could have happened when suddenly a giant fireball turned dusk into daylight. The distinct sounds of jet fighters going to afterburner roared overhead. If he didn't know better, the traffic stop appeared to be a military operation rather than some police incident.

As he sat in stalled traffic a few moments later, his usually tranquil wife called. "Nathan, Nathan, have you heard? Our country has been invaded. Someone is blowing up Navy carriers in San Diego and Newport News. It's so scary—something terrible is happening. Nathan, please hurry home. The children are upset, and I'm having a hard time keeping it together."

"I just saw a huge explosion near Highway 93 and heard what sounded like military jets storming away. I don't like any of this. Make sure all the doors are locked and that you have access to the forty-five. Understand?"

"Yes, sweetheart, please—" Hubbard's phone beeped for an incoming call. He recognized the number, and it sent a chill down his spine.

"Honey, I've got to go. I'm getting an emergency call from Bragg. Whatever this is, I think I'm about to be part of it."

# Chapter 49


*TASK FORCE-70*
USINDOPACOM Area of Responsibility

Things didn't always move fast in the Navy. Life followed the well-worn adage of "hurry up and wait." But when the military received the alert of DEFCON 2, only the second time in US history, the pace became hurry up and keep hurrying up. No one had to repeat the orders to the USS *Gerald R. Ford* commanders and the USS *Nimitz* carriers, who were both back in their home ports in Singapore and Japan. For the carrier USS *Ronald Reagan*, it was already underway in the East China Sea, accompanied by its strike group. The three carriers were to join forces as Task Force-70 for what many believed was a war with China.

*USS RONALD REAGAN*
East China Sea

Jason Roberts, commanding officer of the USS *Ronald Reagan*, was on the Bridge thoughtfully debating why the Taiwanese celebrated New Year's in February—something he had trouble grasping. Roberts glanced at his watch and noted the time of 0556 hours. Based on his most recent orders from USINDOPACOM, he had stayed outside the Second Island Chain as he maneuvered south to team up with the *Ford*. That order, Roberts thought, was somewhat unusual because, as the commander of the *Reagan*, he usually made those maneuver decisions. He assumed the orders had something to do with the missile capability of the PRC.

Many in the press and some cliquey pundits, mainly those that favored a smaller Navy, praised the PLARF with their stories on China's "carrier killer" ballistic missiles, most notably the DF-21D and the longer-range DF-26. Roberts found it annoying to read press accounts that American carriers were now relics, gone the way of the dinosaurs, because a few days ago, the PRC claimed they made a direct hit on a ship underway and 1,100 miles from where a DF-21 was launched. Of course, there was no independent video to support their claim, just a photo of an old burning Chinese destroyer.

As the "experts" in the media pointed out, the carrier-busting ballistic missiles come as no surprise. How could Earth's most sophisticated missile not hit a carrier over a thousand feet long, with acres of sprawling flight decks, sitting twenty-five stories high, and made of non-stealthy steel with a distinctive optical, infrared radio frequency signature? According to the Chinese, it was a no-brainer. Come within range, Mr. American carrier, and you'll decorate the bottom of the ocean compliments of the People's Liberation Army Rocket Force.

"Captain, CIC." The call broke Roberts' thoughts. "Flash comms. Naval Base San Diego is under missile attack."

"Roger CIC. Sound General Quarters," ordered the captain, "this is no drill."

"Captain, CIC. Guam reports numerous incoming missiles to Anderson—we also have missiles inbound."

"Confirm inbound missiles, CIC. Break. Conn, all ahead flank, change course to zero-nine-seven. Advise escorts."

As the call to General Quarters went out, Roberts knew he had approximately ten to fifteen minutes before the first missiles arrived. At 30 knots in that amount of time, he could be 30 nautical miles in any direction from where the Chinese thought he was. Give him ninety minutes; he could be anywhere within 90 nautical miles. He liked his chances.


*BALLISTIC MISSILE DEFENSE AGENCY, MDA*
Guam


Even in the most elaborate training exercises, Colonel Owens had never seen anything like what he was witnessing. The Missile Defense Agency had layered defense sensors to detect and track missiles through all trajectory phases. The vast system of land- and sea-based radars that provided worldwide coverage to warn of any ballistic missile attack was going berserk. His operators issued missile warnings as quickly as they could detect them—but even then, they couldn't keep up. China had delivered a massive saturation attack against US forces in INDOPACOM. No one and nothing was safe.

Besides ballistic and cruise missiles, China was letting go with their most lethal weapons, the DF-21s and DF-26s, plus the DF-17 hypersonic glide vehicles with 625 and 2,500 miles ranges. Targeted were critical military facilities, command and control systems, communication sites, bases, runways, and, most significantly, three US carrier strike groups. With their revolutionary anti-ship and glide technology, the Chinese missiles were the world's most advanced short- and intermediate-range missiles. For many of these missiles, the US was ill-prepared.


Okinawa, Japan

As sirens blared, klaxons sounded, and orders flashed on computer screens to the untrained eye, it looked like utter confusion in the ready room of the 44th Fighter Squadron as pilots dashed around. But it wasn't. The pilots understood through their training that getting airborne as quickly as possible was critical. Eight alert F-15Cs were armed and parked in the open for a quick getaway. Pilots were driven close to their aircraft and sprinted the last few yards.

Six aircraft made it off the ground, but the last two were struck with submunitions from a Chinese DF-21C as it exploded over the runway. The cluster munitions covered hundreds of feet, also hitting several parked F-15s. Massive explosions threw parts of jets through the air, setting off secondary explosions and striking two buildings near the runway, setting them ablaze.

As the missiles kept coming, the MDA Aegis Ballistic Missile Defense System assigned targets to available Naval units with AN/SPY-6 radar. Under the Treaty of Mutual Cooperation and Security, the United States and Japanese Self-Defense Forces had practiced tactics and responses for such an attack. Today they were living it.

Caught up in the fight were two Aegis-guided missile destroyers from Japan, the JS *Kongo*, the JS *Chokai*, and the USS *Cowpens*. The Aegis ships were armed with the SM-3. The SM-3s, when fired from their vertical launchers, had a hit-to-kill warhead and a kinetic vehicle, and used semiactive radar homing to locate an enemy warhead and collide with it.

It was a numbers game. The PLA was attempting to disrupt air operations by pockmarking the runway and targeting aircraft shelters, fuel supplies, and logistics facilities. The equation was how many missiles the PLARF could throw at Kadena minus how many Japanese and US defenses could launch before their inventory of missiles ran dry. Too many Chinese missiles were getting through.

One of the cruise missiles that evaded all attempts to shoot it down was loaded with a bunker-buster warhead meant to penetrate hardened aircraft shelters, but its targeting computer was defective, and the missile went through the roof of the base's Catholic Church. Inside, thirty-four parishioners and ten children who had gathered for an early church function were instantly killed. The resulting fire burned the church to the ground, leaving not even a hymnal identifiable in the ashes.

Just a few minutes into China's surprise attacks, public opinion was quickly mounting against the communist regime. Photographs of the church in flames appeared on social media and in the press, enraging millions in Japan and around the world. Even in China, thousands, mostly college students, took to the streets to protest what President Zhang and his cronies had wrought on the planet.

For the United States and Japan, the strike was an ominous beginning. Kadena Air Base lay under a sheet of flames as aircraft, fuel tanks, buildings, and command structures were all burning. When those that survived the first onslaught felt it couldn't get any worse, something unexpected occurred—the missiles stopped for a minute, then for five, and then they just stopped.

It was War Fighting 101. To win, one must have the initiative achieved by air superiority. For survival, runways must quickly become operational following enemy attacks. Therefore, quick repair of damaged air bases was critical to bringing the fight back to the enemy. The USAF had the right man for the job at Kadena Air Base.

"I don't give a damn how scared you are," screamed Chief Master Sergeant Horace Washington Smith. "Let's go, RED HORSE; we have some holes to repair." Following right behind the ordnance specialists who were clearing the unexploded bombs, Smith's Rapid Engineer Deployable Heavy Operational Repair Squadron Engineer airmen were doing their thing—supplying critical data to the wing commander so they could direct the repair of the runways. Time was crucial to the four hundred airmen in the engineering unit, many of whom couldn't stop looking skyward, wondering when the next missile would strike.

As one group of airmen extinguished fires and cleared the runways, a larger group began repairs to establish the Minimum Airfield Operating Surface. Chief Smith, his face grimy from his work, looked down the runway. They had to clear at least five thousand feet of concrete, fifty feet wide, just for the fighters. As he scanned the surface, he saw there were more craters than pimples on a teenager's face. The emergency repairs would eventually have to support thousands of sorties. Once that was completed, the airmen would work to achieve Beyond Emergency Repair status with a mission-capable runway long enough to get much-needed refueling aircraft airborne to quench thirsty fighters. It was a lot of work, but the old chief led by example. No one worked harder, whether with a shovel or a bulldozer.

*USS Ronald Reagan*
East China Sea

Supplementing his CAP, Captain Roberts had his air wing launching aircraft as fast and as safely as humanly possible—just in case. Besides, the F-35s gave him additional eyes in the sky to detect and identify incoming missiles. Lieutenant Sarah "Danger" Freeman was already airborne, flying her E-2, built for such a mission. Sitting in the left seat in a fully integrated all-digital glass cockpit featuring three seventeen-inch primary flight displays, she and her crew of five were busy monitoring incoming threats to what she called home, the *Reagan*.

Tied into the Command, Control, Battle Management, and Communications system, she and her crew were inputting data as swiftly and efficiently as possible into C2BMC. This critical information enhanced fleet air defenses by making jamming more difficult and allocating defensive missiles for targets throughout the entire fleet and beyond.

Covering her six was a stealthy sensor platform, the F-35 flown by her buddy, Lieutenant Commander Dick "Mad Dog" Johnson. Acting as a forward observer with his squadron, they could pick up missiles that many others, including ground-based systems, might struggle to acquire—until it was too late. Often called a computer that happens to fly, his F-35 could rapidly maneuver toward new targets and just as quickly change altitude to get precise trajectory information, something his friends on the ground couldn't accomplish—but needed.

Using his secure comms, Mad Dog sounded concerned. "Freedom 21, Boxer 11. Do you have these thirty inbounds headed toward the *Reagan*?"

"Boxer 11, Freedom 21. Roger that, plus five. Fleet has the data."

Thirty-five missiles inbound, all aimed at the *Reagan*—all DF-21Ds, the purported "carrier killers." Besides the carrier's onboard defenses, which included multiple air defense radars, surface-to-air missiles, and electronic warfare systems for deceiving sensors and disrupting command links of incoming threats, the *Reagan* had the layered protection of the strike group. After receiving additional data from nearby satellites, firing solutions were passed to the Aegis ships surrounding the *Reagan*.

The USS *Rafael Peralta* and *John S. McCain* were assigned the targets. Both were prepared. Once engagement coordinates were received from their respective CDSs and their weapon control systems had a lock on the targets, their vertical launch tubes were ready with programmed SM-3s. The CICs got permission to fire. Forty SM-3s roared from their MK 41 vertical launchers toward the thirty-five incoming ballistic missiles.

As the kill missile acquired the enemy's missile, the internal computer constantly processed the data and, using divert thrusters, refined its flightpath, identified its target, and finalized its aim point.

Just as the SM-3s were completing their aim points, the DF-21s launched dozens of balloons made from shiny mylar plastic, surprisingly, not much different from a child's balloon. The warheads and balloons traveled at the same speed since there was no air resistance in space. With each warhead neatly hidden inside its balloon, the dozens of look-alikes traveled along the same path of destruction, all at the same speed and trajectory.

The defense radars couldn't determine which balloons contained the warheads. The shiny coating of the mylar kept the radar from seeing inside each balloon. Small battery-powered heaters in each balloon also countered the SM-3s' abilities to locate the warheads using heat detection. Because the US used kinetic vehicles that didn't use explosive warheads but instead collided with the enemy's warheads, so many balloons released by each missile meant the kill ratio was low. This fact was quickly broadcast, and only four of China's warheads were destroyed. Thirty-one continued on course.


Northern Mariana Islands

Four hundred and fifty miles north of Guam was Tinian, part of the Northern Mariana Islands, a United States commonwealth.

Tinian was chosen for a top-secret project by the US because it had no serious military runway and nowhere to put aircraft if they landed. If the term "low profile" could be used for an island, this was the one, and top-secret folders with Tinian stamped on them were in secure vaults in the Pentagon. Known by only a few, the island was now part of the US antiballistic missile defense system. The latest hardware in the fight to obtain equilibrium in the Pacific was hidden in the island's tropical forest. Patriot missile systems and Terminal High Altitude Area Defense systems, THADD, had prying eyes that could spot incoming hypersonic missiles anywhere. *Reagan* had another protector.

The newly planted THAAD battery consists of one hundred Army specialists controlling six launcher vehicles, each equipped with eight missiles, and two mobile tactical operations centers, each operating AN/TPY-2 ground-based radar. As enemy missiles covered the skies, bedlam was coordinated with constant updates to C2BMC computers. The information came from ships, aircraft, submarines, satellites, and anyone or anything that was tracking the incoming warheads. Every tactical aspect was essential, with thirty-one missiles headed toward *Reagan*. The information flowing in was analyzed by the overall tactical defense authority of the battlegroup: the Composite Warfare Commander, who was continually updated from radio communication and radar. Assisting CWC was the Information Warfare Commander. With thousands of lives on the line, everyone was feeling the pressure.

"COMCARSTRKGRU, THAAD-6. Tracking thirty-one target missiles in their terminal phase of reentry. Break. THAAD-6 to all THAAD units—fire!"

Forty-eight THAAD interceptor missiles, spread out over the remote island, left their launchers. Just as quickly as the tubes went empty, they were reloaded. The unit had prepared for this through countless training exercises. With the intensity of battle firing adrenaline through their bodies, the nearly one hundred soldiers functioned as one in preparing for the next order to fire. No one had to remind them that their brothers and sisters in arms were fighting for survival aboard the *Reagan*.


*USS RONALD REAGAN*
East China Sea


Using speed as an ally, Captain Roberts maneuvered the carrier from the target area. It was a vast sea, and the captain used every inch to look like just another spot on a Dalmatian.

The DF-21D ballistic missiles onboard sensors for target acquisition were insufficient to find a fast-moving carrier in the open sea. Instead, the missile's guidance system needed constant updates from scout platforms, such as aircraft or submarines, combined with data from satellites and radar to strike the carrier. That was made difficult by the carrier battlegroup, which spread out like a mother spider's giant web to protect its ninety-thousand-ton firstborn. Only this silken mesh consisted of the Aegis combat system and Arleigh Burke-class destroyers armed to the hilt with over ninety missiles each, neatly aligned in mainly Mark 41 vertical launchers.

The DF-21 missiles entered the terminal phase and streaked toward the *Reagan*. Piercing the atmosphere at Mach 11 and an altitude of thirty-one miles, the missiles would not slow down to Mach 2 until they reached the lower atmosphere. Ionization buildup would temporarily blind the targeting radar sensors aboard the missiles, but only briefly. US forces had thirty seconds to respond. Now there were no decoys. It was US firepower versus PLA missiles.

The rule in almost any ball sport is to keep your eye on the ball, which could be said when tracking thirty-one incoming ballistic missiles. Any miscalculation could result in devastating results, especially with 7,500 lives in the balance aboard *Reagan*, sailors who were doing everything humanly possible not to be the first carrier sunk since World War II. They had an entire nation and its powerful military using every means possible to keep the mighty supercarrier in the fight.

Radios were squawking as forty THAAD missiles raced toward the Chinese missiles. "We have a hit," echoed from the speakers several times, but so did the misses. Within precious seconds remaining, it was down to five DF-21s surviving the onslaught heading precisely for the *Reagan*.

The US Navy was not stupid—they didn't publish everything about their survival bag of tricks. And nowhere was this more evident than information about their advanced electronic warfare systems that could jam incoming missiles to stop them, destroy their trajectory, or throw the killer missiles off course. Even the SM-6 and ESSM missiles had the latest software and sensor upgrades, which enhanced, distinguished, and allowed for the destruction of approaching targets. None of this, not even a hint, was ever published, remaining America's top secret.

Not needing to be told, the USS *Rafael Peralta* and the USS *John S. McCain* destroyers were prepared. With five missiles closing in on the *Reagan*, both warships fired multiple SM-6s at the ballistic missiles. Streaks of smoke filled the sky as four Chinese missiles went down. The remaining missile exploded harmlessly near where *Reagan* had been when the missiles were first fired. Like a big-city orchestra tuning its instruments to ensure the best performance, the scattered warfighting assets functioned as one integrated network. And it had worked for now.

# Chapter 50



*AUGUST 1ST BUILDING*
Beijing, China

Dr. Dong Liang should have connected all the dots. Here he was on the Chinese New Year, and the entire Central Military Commission was at work, either at their desks or running around, seemingly fearful of something. But he didn't get caught up with this sort of thing. Life was simple for Dong. He followed orders, did his job better than most, and ate.

It was just before 6 a.m., an hour when he usually got up, and a sudden quietness had settled around the compound. Then he noticed it. The command and control network computer, the one computer in all of China that was the gateway for launching missiles, was being inputted for a missile release at precisely six a.m. Dong looked down at his watch. It showed 3:03; then he remembered he had forgotten to wind the stupid thing.

Shit, he thought, President Zhang is starting a war! Looking at the corner of his computer screen, he saw it was 5:58 a.m.

There should be a proverb for men like Dong: Beware the man who knows computer code but does not remember to wind his watch. Dong knew his job as his thoughts darted to his friends who gave their lives in Tiananmen Square so many years ago. His Tiananmen Square was about to begin, and he was prepared.

The key to all this madness was the PAL, or the Permissive Action Links, set up by President Zhang to prevent unauthorized use or control of China's missiles by anyone except himself. No general, politician, or enemy could launch any ballistic missile without inputting the security code—and that singular man with the code was President Zhang. But Dong wrote the codes, which put a smile on his chubby face.

As the clock ticked to six, codes that had been entered for launch kicked in for hundreds of missiles now being fired from across China. Dong cursed himself for being so inattentive to the events leading up to this. He had to make it right—and quickly.

Looking over the data on his monitors, Dong saw that the president had put in a pause, most likely to receive intelligence on the success or failure of the multiple launches giving him some precious time.

During the past few weeks, Dong, between trips to the cafeteria, had been busy writing code for just such a circumstance. His cipher searched for any launch code inputted. Seeing those eight or sixteen digits told the host computer that those missiles had already been launched and that kept launched missiles waiting for further instructions. President Zhang would have no idea some other computer was stopping his launch because Dong's code prevented any representation of what was happening from appearing on any computer screen and blocked out his computer's IP address.

It was time to act. Any delay on his part would allow the president to launch hundreds of additional ballistic missiles. Dong had made his mind up years ago as he watched the PLA slaughter some of his closest friends. He looked down at the large Enter key and smacked his fat finger on it, launching his secret codes. He then casually got up and walked down to the cafeteria to see what was for breakfast.

# Chapter 51



*USS Nimitz*
Yokosuka, Japan

With the USS *Ronald Reagan* out to sea, the USS *Nimitz*, on temporary duty in the Indo-Pacific, was in dock for replenishment. Like a shark who never stops moving to stay alive, the captain of the *Nimitz* was highly uncomfortable being tied up to land, especially considering the state of the world. No, he preferred the open seas where the big carrier was most at home and could use its horsepower to outrun almost any threat. With the *Nimitz* set to be decommissioned in three years, Captain John "Hard Ass" Samson wanted to ensure the ship faded away, not unlike him, at about the same time. But timing was everything, and on this day, the Taiwanese New Year, he was in the wrong place at the wrong time.

"Captain, multiple flash comms," said Samson's XO. "The US has been attacked by China. Report coming in that the *Reagan* is under missile attack." Like a soprano that missed a high note, the XO's voice jumped a pitch. "Sir, we have incoming missiles."

"Emergency departure. Clear the ship for immediate departure. I don't care what has to be done," ordered Samson. He understood time was not his ally.

Patrolling the seas near the *Nimitz* was Destroyer Squadron 9, comprised of the Ticonderoga class guided missile cruiser USS *Princeton* and the Arleigh Burke-class destroyer USS *Sterett*. Alerted to inbound ballistic missiles by soldiers of the 100th Missile Defense Brigade in Colorado Springs, Colorado, the ships fired off a score of SM-6 terminal ballistic missiles. Again, the DF-26 and DF-21 incoming missiles used defensive countermeasures to absorb the brunt of the SM-6s. Hidden in their balloon cocoons, five DF-26s and one DF-21 survived and continued toward the *Nimitz* at Mach 2.

*JAPAN AIR SELF-DEFENSE FORCE PATRIOT MISSILE BATTERY*

Tokyo, Japan

As a participating American antiballistic missile defense program member, the Japan Air Self-Defense Force Patriot missile battery near Tokyo was in the loop about US defenses against the incoming Chinese ballistic missiles. Three Japanese specialists operating the AN/MSQ-104 control station communicated with the M901 launching stations with the surviving six missiles streaking toward the Nimitz.

Using AN/MPQ-53 phased array radar, the unit transmitted target, track, and identification information to the eight Patriot missiles fired from two launchers. As the opposing missiles raced toward each other, the Patriots were fed constant updates to their missile guidance systems. After seconds, proximity fuses detonated the high-explosive warheads, creating a large and spectacular flash.

*USS Nimitz*
Yokosuka, Japan

Working against the American and Japanese allies was the speed and maneuverability of China's missiles. Unlike the *Reagan*, which had an entire ocean to get lost in, the *Nimitz* was tied to a dock with tracking data already being sent to PLARF computers. The lethal missiles required minor correction, only needing to survive the Patriots—and two did.

"Captain, CIC. Two missiles inbound. Impact eight seconds."

"Captain to all hands—brace for missile impact."

The first warhead from the DF-21, confused by the land's proximity, impacted one mile inland, exploding in a large warehouse containing heavy-duty replacement parts for ships. The shrapnel from the impact killed scores of civilians in the area who were driving by and working in nearby buildings. Fortunately, no workers were present in the warehouse.

The second warhead did as programmed, surviving several SM-6s and avoiding eight Patriot missiles. Streaking in at Mach 6, a 1,100-pound warhead hit toward the bow of the ship, between catapults one and two and just in front of the empty weapons elevator, traveling through nearly eight decks and tearing apart the flight and hanger decks with a fireball hot enough to melt steel and everything around it. The result was horrendous. No shipmate should have had to witness such mutilation of fellow sailors.

Watertight doors kept the flooding to a minimum while the men and women of Damage Control fought an expanding fire. Base ambulances, paramedics, and local responders arrived to assist. Personnel from the medical department immediately gave aid to surviving sailors and took the most seriously injured to the ship's hospital.

"CIC, Captain. I need a detailed status report ASAP. I want to know if we're seaworthy."

Captain Samson knew this was the first volley and expected a new attack any minute. While he couldn't launch aircraft, he sure as hell could save his ship by getting out to sea where he liked his chances. It would take more than one missile to stop the *Nimitz*.

# Chapter 52



*USS MUSTIN*
Near Wake Atoll, the Pacific Ocean


Following a briefing from the ship's captain to all officers of the USS *Mustin*, Ensign Jansen better understood why his ship was sent to what seemed to him the remotest place on Earth—Wake Island. In their briefing, they were told the Secretary of Defense had directed the dispersal of military forces in case of a conflict with the PRC. So, USINDOPACOM ordered the *Mustin* to patrol off the shores of Wake to add a layer of protection for B-1Bs and a multitude of other aircraft heading to the island. Located between Japan and Hawaii, fifteen hundred miles from Guam, it was chosen as the fallback center in case of war. Considerable construction was just being completed on the 9,800-foot runway and surrounding parking apron. One of the benefits of being so remote was that Wake was virtually out of the range of every ballistic missile in the PLARF's inventory.

In the opening hours of the battle with the PRC, the war was proving to be incredibly violent and fast-moving, with US bases in Okinawa, Guam, and others in the Indo-Pacific region being struck by missiles fired from the Chinese mainland. Worst of all, the United States had lost five of its eleven carriers, although the USS *Nimitz* was trying to stay in the fight. The *Mustin* was at continuous GQ, expecting incoming missiles at any moment—they just didn't know from where.


*SHANG CLASS TYPE 093 NUCLEAR-POWERED ATTACK SUBMARINE*
West of Wake Atoll, the Pacific Ocean


Captain Li Chang was upset with himself and his crew. His orders were explicit—begin actions at precisely 0600 hours, Beijing time, of the Chinese New Year. His mission was to fire his missiles near Wake Island to demolish the runway and the bombers and further disrupt base operations for as long as possible. Unfortunately for Li, the New Year had begun, and he had yet to empty one launcher.

Despite the setback, Li was honored to have been selected for this mission to command one of the most potent attack submarines in the PLAN submarine force. Not quite the size of the US Navy's Virginia class sub, the Type 093 was not as noisy as other nuclear-powered submarines. It conveniently used its larger size for noise-reducing features, such as acoustic stealth, and had an improved reactor coolant pump design. Its teardrop hull with a wing-shaped cross section provided Li's submarine with enhanced speed and stealth.

For this mission, the submarine was armed with two types of radar-guided YJ-18B cruise missiles, one for anti-ship operations and the other for land attack. The anti-ship version was designed to defeat the American Aegis Combat System. While everything looked good on paper, he could not hide the fact that he had an incompetent crew who couldn't find their asses in a dark room using both hands and who were the reason Li had missed the deadline to launch missiles.

"Captain, radar reports an American Aegis destroyer bearing zero-five-six, 32 kilometers out."

"Slow to eight: set course to zero-nine-three, depth thirty meters. I need missile-firing solutions for the destroyer, the aircraft runway, and the surrounding area. Advise when within range."

This is strange, thought Li. He had received no intelligence reports about an American ship in the area of Wake. But no problem. It was just another target.


Wake Atoll, the Pacific Ocean

LTJG Carlos Martinez was a long way from the hood in East Los Angeles. Still glowing from his encounter with a PLAN submarine tailing an American carrier, he once again found himself in the lonely Pacific Ocean, this time even further from his earlier home at Kadena. His redeployment was part of the American dispersal to Wake before all-out war broke out with the PRC. Martinez now had the privilege of hanging with the big boys who flew stealth bombers and jet fighters, all on Wake for the same reasons. Collectively, the Air Force pilots were all itching for a fight and hated sitting around awaiting orders while hostilities escalated around them. But unlike the other pilots, Martinez had an immediate job. With the USS *Mustin* providing missile defense for Wake, Martinez and his crew would fly their Boeing P-8A Poseidon on ASW missions in support of the *Mustin*.



Operating 250 miles from Wake, the crew of the *Mustin* was still at GQ with one eye to the sky and one to the sea. The Arleigh Burke class destroyer sailors knew the growing number of diesel-electric submarines that boasted exceptional quietness and could operate without surfacing for up to two weeks. The crew was honing their skills at ASW and keeping any potential enemy submarine well out of range of Wake. One of their tools was the AN/SQR-20 three-inch diameter Tactical Towed Array Sonar. TACTAS provided long-range passive detection of enemy submarines. The sonar was towed a mile behind the destroyer to stop noise from radiating back to the ship and overlapping the signature of a possible submarine. Using one of the most extensive computer programs assembled, the sonar operators could determine what ship or submarine was being tracked.

With no sightings of any surface ships or submarines near Wake, Captain Bailey had to make an educated guess about where trouble might appear. He understood the PLAN was essentially a brown water Navy operating close to their littoral waters. But he

203

thought that since they had planned this war, PLAN strategy would also change, perhaps more to blue-water operations.

Since Wake was difficult to hit with missiles from the Chinese mainland, he considered the enemy might bring the missiles closer to the island. Assuming that a submarine would have to travel east from China and get within range of their YJ-18B missile, which he knew to have a range between 136 and 335 miles. Bailey focused his search right in that mix.

On ASW patrol, Jansen couldn't help but notice that he was in the part of the CIC that the CO thought was mission critical. Such responsibility had become his norm. Currently, the ship's fourteen-person sonar division was working port and starboard watch rotations of eight hours on and eight hours off. The destroyer searched for any surface or submarine contact that might have them or Wake in sight.

In the air-conditioned CIC, cooled more for the equipment than for the sailors, seven sonar operators were wearing high-end Bose headphones, listening to the low-volume staticky white noise of the ocean, and trying to detect the elusive sound of an enemy submarine. The eight-hour watches were beginning to seem longer to the crew primarily because of their deep concentration. Each new detection was vigorously scrutinized. Patterns were matched and measured with onscreen tools and cursors. AI algorithms flag potential targets on the computer screen for the sonar operator to verify. Looking over the sailors' backs, the Sonar Supervisor roamed and had the duty of breaking in Jansen to learn the subtleties of the ship's sonar crew.

On the Bridge of the *Mustin*, Captain Bailey decided to take a calculated risk. Since passive sonar had turned up squat, and if an enemy submarine lurked in the vicinity, the Chinese captain had the tactical advantage of knowing the *Mustin*'s location. It was time to level the playing field now that help had arrived.

A P-8 entered their operating area. "21MC, Switchblade. On station."

"Switchblade, 21MC. Roger. Break. 20MC, work directly with Switchblade."

"Switchblade, 20MC. Coordinates sent for sonobuoy grid. Launch at four-second intervals in active mode."

"20MC, Switchblade. Roger. Moving into launch altitude now, two minutes from executing." LTJG Martinez pushed the yoke forward on his large Boeing jet and swiftly descended to two hundred feet. After flying in a broad arc, the aircraft straightened. "20MC, Switchblade. Launching at four-second intervals on active mode."

The plane's L3 Sonobuoy Rotary Launch System began to discharge the buoys. As the instrument reached the water, it deployed an inflatable surface float with a radio transmitter to communicate with the P-8. The transducer descended below the sea surface to two hundred feet, a depth programmed into the buoy. The Directional Command Activated Sonobuoy System went active. It could be programmed to change depth, activate sonar transmissions, or scuttle itself. The echo returns of the active sonar signals provided a range, bearing, and Doppler on any acoustic contact.

The beauty of the P-8 flying just over the whitecaps, dropping scores of sonobuoys with their miniature parachutes swaying down to the ocean, would have received a standing ovation from excited spectators at any airshow. But this was no airshow. This was war, and every sailor understood the life-and-death implications of what they were doing. Get it right—or suffer the consequences.

As the P-8 was flying, the *Mustin*'s captain acted. "Sonar, Conn. Initiate full spectrum active sonar with a burst every ten seconds."

"Conn, Sonar. Initiating full spectrum sonar in ten-second bursts."

The ocean around the active sonar search resonated with acoustic energy from multiple sources. The search grid was covered when there were at least two active sonar sources. It was also much easier on the sonar operators because the return from a ping was much easier to detect than from a passive search. One disadvantage to going active was that the target could hear the sonar ping and could react to minimize detection before the return ping was received by the sender. In the life-and-death encounter between hunter and hunted, the active sonar provided bearing information to the target submarine in just minutes. The advantage to the *Mustin* was that it removed the submarine's primary benefit of concealment. It was a trade-off, not unlike an old western shootout in the middle of town. It was who could get a weapon's bearing so they could shoot first.

"20MC, Switchblade. We have contact on Sonobuoy Sierra niner, range one three miles, bearing zero-three-eight. Hold one." After a few seconds, Switchblade added, "Confirmed submarine. The second sonobuoy has contact. Range eight miles, bearing one-four-two, speed 20 knots. Classified as Alpha 1."

"Switchblade, 21MC," intervened the captain. "Coordinates sent. Set up screen, sonobuoys set in passive mode." Bailey wanted to establish a zone around his warship so that Alpha 1 would have to transverse the area to get within torpedo range.

"21MC, Switchblade. Roger." Martinez flew the P-8 to the designated area and ordered the drop of twenty additional sonobuoys. A third buoy got contact, giving them enough data to classify Alpha 1 as a Shang class Type 093 nuclear-powered attack submarine.

*SHANG CLASS TYPE 093 NUCLEAR-POWERED ATTACK SUBMARINE*
West of Wake Atoll, the Pacific Ocean

As Captain Li Chang maneuvered his submarine through the intensity of electronic pings that got louder with each passing minute, he was driven by his standing orders to destroy the island's runway and aircraft and to cause as much devastation as to render the base useless. Since intelligence didn't mention he would be hounded by an Aegis destroyer, he developed a plan to keep them occupied. At the same time, he got in position to launch missiles.

"Torpedo room, fire control. Target US destroyer. Make tubes one and two ready in all respects and open the outer doors. Use the latest firing solution even if out of range."

"Fire control, torpedo room. Roger. Target out of range by 3.219 kilometers. It will be close, sir. Firing solution entered. Tubes one and two ready."

"Torpedo room, fire control. Fire tubes one and two, five-second interval."

"Fire control, torpedo room. Torpedoes one and two in the water."



"Bridge, sonar. Two torpedoes in the water. Both Type Yu-6, bearing two-eight-seven, distance plus twenty-eight miles, both active." Jansen's delivery was subdued as if it came from a salty veteran rather than from a wide-eyed twenty-three-year-old sailor who never thought he would be on the receiving end of a torpedo that was equivalent to the MK 48.

"Bridge, TAO. We have the AN/SLQ-25B deployed." The Tactical Action Officer referred to the newly installed towed array sensor whose job was to detect incoming active torpedoes by receiving, amplifying, and returning the pings from the Chinese torpedo and present a false target.

The nine-person crew of the P-8, using coordinates from several of their sonobuoys, went to work. "21MC, Switchblade. We have a firing solution for Alpha 1. Prepared to fire Mark fifty-four."

"Switchblade, 21MC. Permission to fire granted."

"TAO, Bridge. Using the coordinates from the P-8, prepare two Mark forty-six torpedoes and advise when ready."

"Bridge, TAO. Roger."

Martinez leveled out his P-8 at twenty thousand feet near the last coordinates of Alpha 1. "WEPS, fire two fifty-fours, five seconds apart, on my command . . . fire one . . . fire two."

A short bomb bay door opened just behind the wing, and the High-Altitude Anti-submarine Warfare Weapon Capability Air

Launch Accessory deployed the two torpedoes. Their GPS-guided parachute kits allowed the drop from twenty thousand feet.

Once in the water, the torpedoes used their internal computers to process algorithms to analyze the information they received. The smart torpedoes were designed to dismiss false targets or countermeasures. The torpedoes began their search for the Shang class Type 093 nuclear-powered attack submarine.

Moments later, the *Mustin* fired two MK 46 torpedoes designed for high-performance submarines. Both were on active acoustic homing.

*SHANG CLASS TYPE 093 NUCLEAR-POWERED ATTACK SUBMARINE*
West of Wake Atoll, the Pacific Ocean

"Captain, sonar reports four transient torpedoes inbound. Classified as two MK 54s and two MK 46s, all approximately two kilometers east of our location and closing."

"Fire decoys. Hard right rudder, come to zero-three-five. Make our level thirty meters and prepare to fire all ten YJ-18Bs at the preprogrammed settings adjusted for our new position."

From intelligence reports, Captain Li knew the exact coordinates of the runway and where several American bombers were parked. He understood he had to hurry since the incoming torpedoes were making everything happen at a faster pace. One or two finely placed, specially converted land-attack missiles would destroy almost all the aircraft. Several warheads were set for land burst just thirty meters off the tarmac. Li had to launch them and dive deep for cover and concealment.

"Captain, sonar reports torpedoes one-and-a-half kilometers, closing quickly. They've acquired us."

"Weapons officer, captain. How much longer until we can fire?"

"Sorry, sir, we're updating the missiles with new coordinates. Any minute now."

"Hurry, you damn fool. We don't have minutes to spare. The homeland expects our success, and we won't fail." Li immediately regretted his comments but had to get the launch off.

"Conn, sonar. Two of the transient torpedoes have exploded on our countermeasures. Two have acquired us, impact in sixty-four seconds."

"Captain, weapons officer. Ready for launch in fifteen seconds. On your command."

"Weapons, officer, launch all missiles one second apart."

At that moment, Captain Li looked around the cramped conn, observing men doing their jobs efficiently even though they knew they might be dead in a few seconds. In the end, he thought, the crew came through.

"Conn, sonar. Thirty seconds until impact."

As the last of the ten cruise missiles left the tubes, Captain Li Chang dropped his head in mental exhaustion, proud of his crew and himself. When he looked up, there were two massive explosions. The American torpedoes did their job, blowing the Shang class Type 093 submarine and crew of one hundred into oblivion.

*USS MUSTIN*
Near Wake Atoll, the Pacific Ocean

"Bridge, sonar. Multiple missiles launched from the area of Alpha 1. Classify missiles as Chinese YJ-18Bs."

"TAO, conn. Fire twelve SM-3s when ready."

"Bridge, TAO. Missiles away."

"Bridge, sonar. Two large explosions in the area of Alpha 1. Sounds of a submarine breaking up. It looks like we got them, sir."

Captain Bailey said when the last missile left the Mustin's vertical launcher, "Helm, ahead flank. Come to zero-three-eight."

As the order was repeated, Bailey thought the chances of the PLAN submarine's torpedoes tracking down the *Mustin* were slim. But there was no need to take chances, and some more distance between them and the submarine was a good thing. What wasn't good was that the ten enemy missiles headed for Wake.

The YJ-18B used a multistage propulsion system, an air-breathing engine for cruising just under Mach 1, and a solid rocket booster to adjust to Mach 3 in a terminal dash to target. Unlike the DF-21, the YJ-18 was not equipped with any countermeasures.

Five missiles were destroyed when SM-3s smashed into them. One missile never reached outer space. Four others continued the journey toward Wake.

"Bridge, TAO. Confirmed kill of six YJ-18s. Three avoided our defenses and are labeled Alphas 2, 3, and 4. Radar indicates that one YJ-18, Alpha 5, is set on a sea-skimming mode."

"TAO, Bridge. Launch four SM-6s at Alphas 2, 3, and 4. Fire two SM-6s at Alpha 5. Fire when ready."

Six SM-6s soared off the ship and used their inertial guidance set up for active radar seeking. Fortunately, these missiles were fitted with the new Block 1B upgrade featuring the twenty-one-inch rocket motor over the previous thirteen-and-a-half-inch motor. This new variant significantly increased the missile's range and speed, enabling a hypersonic anti-surface warfare capability. The SM-6s would need that speed with less than twenty seconds until the YJ-18s impacted Wake.

The *Mustin*'s AN/SPY-6 radar was locked on the YJ-18 missiles, and their coordinates were fed to the Aegis weapon control system, which calculated the solution to the targets for each SM-6 missile. Alphas 2 and 4 were eliminated when the 140-pound warheads of the SM-6s exploded in close proximity to their targeted YJ-18s. Alpha 3 avoided detection by maneuvering away from the SM-6 missiles using data from a Chinese satellite. It struck the center of the runway on Wake, its 660-pound warhead leaving a twenty-foot crater and destroying much of the surrounding area. The Alpha 5 missile approaching Wake made a vertical move to thirty thousand feet before returning to its target of multiple B-1B bombers parked on the apron. If the missile hit one, it would take out a dozen. Unfortunately for the PRC, and fortunate for the Americans, the targeting data was inaccurate. Alpha 5 blew up the chow hall with no casualties since everyone, including the cooks, was staffing defensive positions on the island.

Offshore, the *Mustin* was monitoring the two PLAN torpedoes fired at them. "Bridge, sonar. Both Yu-6 torpedoes have run out of fuel and have sunk. No other contacts detected."

Using the MC-1, Captain Bailey addressed the crew. "This is your captain speaking. For most of us, this is our first time facing the enemy in battle. The Chinese were determined to destroy us and our military brothers and sisters on Wake. You answered the call to duty by performing your responsibilities in an exemplary manner. You should all be extremely proud of what you accomplished today. You have destroyed one of the PLAN's top-level nuclear submarines and have protected Wake from substantial devastation. This war is just beginning, and there will be many more challenges, but I can say this—I would not want to serve on any other ship with any other crew except here on the USS *Mustin*. God bless each of you, and God bless America."

## Chapter 53



*AUGUST 1ST BUILDING*
Beijing, China

"I want a concise report," demanded Chinese President Zhang Wei, of the success or failure of our initial missile attacks against the Americans and their allies. "As we have discussed, I've built a short pause in our campaign to allow for this and to allot time for our missile batteries to reload for phase two."

With no hesitancy, General Wang Yong of the Joint Staff Department of the Central Military Commission and the second in command answered, "Mr. President, your strategy is working to perfection. At precisely 0600 hours, our secret mission to destroy the US carriers in drydock worked flawlessly. We then went after the *Nimitz* and successfully took that carrier out of service in our backyard. The *Reagan* was a different story and was fortunate to fight off our missiles. But we have the carrier on our radar and will attempt to hit it again in phase two."

Taking a breath to see if his news upset Zhang, the general who had a knack for covering his ass, saw only the poker face of his boss. He continued, "Our attacks on allied bases have been remarkably effective. Once again, attacking at 0600 hours, PLARF missiles destroyed hundreds of aircraft located at Kadena Air Base and eliminated the runway for days, if not weeks. The same case was with Anderson on Guam, as well as with Iwakuni and Misawa. While all these bases are reeling from our concentrated attack, it's critical we hit them again, keeping them on the defensive and their aircraft either destroyed or unable to take flight."

Wang took in the room. He had everyone's undivided attention and thought it safe to continue, but only after taking careful note of the president, who seemed to indicate for him to continue.

"With the carriers and bases taken out of the picture, we turn to Taiwan, which has no chance against our forces while the US forces lick their wounds.

"As we've planned, we'll initiate a sustained air attack. With air superiority throughout the region, the PLA-Air Force will devastate Taiwan. We in the military believe that with our aircraft upgrades, air-to-ground sensors, and precision munitions, we can do more damage than by using our ballistic missile inventory, which the allies expect us to do. We can deliver more munitions against targets using hundreds of sorties than the SRBM inventory. Without help from the US, the dependent Taiwanese Air Force will collapse quickly. The key to this scenario is to keep the Americans from digging out of the hole we put them in by using our second wave of ballistic missiles against them. Thank you, Mr. President."

"Thank you, General Wang, for bringing us up to date. Let's get to our workstations, initiate phase two, and remind the Americans who rules now."

Dong Liang, who had microphones planted in two computers in the meeting room, smiled ever so slightly and mumbled, "Good luck with that, Mr. President."

# Chapter 54

*USS Nimitz*
The Pacific Ocean

Captain John Samson, Annapolis class of '92, was not a quitter. As a three-year starter at quarterback—he had proved it. He wasn't large, coming in at what the program said was six feet tall because he was barely five feet ten. He tipped the scales at 198 pounds, somewhat stocky but with powerful, driving legs. He was not exceptionally fast but had an attitude of playing smash-mouth football. The coach recognized his prowess at running and developed a ground-attack football strategy around him. Samson just as soon run through an opponent as around them.

The backwoods boy from the Ozarks in Missouri loved to fish and hunt and was at his best in the outdoors, just like his dad, a St. Louis street cop. He had a shit-eating grin that was contiguous. Even today, his lips seemed to form a perpetual smile, one that was difficult to turn around.

Although the Midshipmen repeated a dismal 1-10 record during his last two years, it was the Army-Navy game of 1992 that went down in Navy lore. Army came in with a five-hundred record while Navy was looking for their first win. Of course, this meant nothing because it was Army-Navy football.

Taking the opening kickoff, the Midshipmen, behind the running of Samson, went the distance and scored quickly. Spotting Army a field goal on their first series, Samson roamed the sidelines, making it clear that would be the final score for the team he called the "Black and Blue Knights."

True to his word, Navy continued to play tough, aggressive football and even threw some passes. On one particular play late in the game, Samson changed the running play to a pass play when he noticed that the left defensive back continued playing up tight in bump-and-run against his tight end, whom he knew could smack that little shit out of his way and get open. Using play action, Samson fell back in the pocket but was quickly dodging a determined pass rush. Glancing over at his tight end, he knew he had called the right play as he knocked the pocket-sized back to the side and ran past him to get open. As Samson threw the ball, his passing hand smashed into the helmet of a rushing lineman and made a sound like breaking a chicken bone. No matter—the ball was in the air to his big tight end, who caught it mid-stride and plowed over the safety as he ran it in for a touchdown. Word spread on the sideline about the tough SOB Samson, which only served to fire up his teammates more. The Midshipmen playing at home went nuts, jumping up and down and slapping each other on their backs while their QB rushed off the field to get his broken pinky taped so he could be ready for the next series.

It was all over by then. Navy held Army to only one first down in the second half. As the gun sounded to end the game, the now 1-10 Midshipmen carried Sampson off the field. A press photographer caught that moment. It soon became a classic image frozen in time of Samson being carried off the field with that shit-eating grin on his face.

Now, thirty years later, Samson still had that grin with the men and women on the Bridge who felt more confident each minute from seeing their captain's conviction as the wounded USS *Nimitz* put water between the ship and land.

"Engineering, Bridge. I want a detailed assessment of what we must do to get back into action. I don't care how impossible it seems. Detail it and pass it along."

The United States was preparing to go on the offensive. With orders from USINDOPACOM, the USS *Nimitz* sailed at its best speed to rendezvous with the USS *Ronald Reagan* carrier group outside the 1,300-mile island chain near Guam. Also heading for the location was America's newest carrier, the USS *Gerald R. Ford*. Together they would form Task Force-70.

# Chapter 55



Beijing, China

As President Zhang settled in behind his master computer, he was ready to begin phase two of his missile campaign against America and its allies. Added to the growing list of targets were the two US air bases in South Korea, Osan and Kunsan. Zhang had already entered the codes to launch the thousands of missiles at his disposal. While he understood his missile supply had limits, he also knew he had a numerical advantage over the enemy. He would cripple the enemy with missiles and finish them with his superior military. With the click of his mouse, Zhang released hundreds of ballistic and cruise missiles.

Watching a six-meter-wide video screen with images from launch sites nationwide, the president waited for missile smoke and fire trails. Shaking his head while staring at the screen, the president saw nothing but clear skies.

With his staff in the room, he yelled to no one in particular, "What's going on here? Why aren't the missiles firing?"

Zhang began smashing the enter key, and still, nothing happened.

No one dared to look at the raging president because they didn't know the answer. Finally, his chief engineer behind the development of the missile launch system spoke up, "Mr. President, our computers are acting as if the missiles have been launched. None of this makes sense. Staff and I should have this fixed right away."

Glaring at his chief engineer with eyes that could kill, Zhang said, "Check to see if the Americans have penetrated our computer infrastructure, especially here at headquarters. In the meantime, I want a computer override to launch the missiles by voice command. Get all our missile field generals on secure comms so I can personally tell them to launch."

Barely looking up, the engineer said, "Sir, I'm afraid that won't be possible. I—"

"Don't give me that, or I'll have you escorted from this room and shot. I want solutions, not excuses. Do you hear me?"

The chief engineer looking like he was about to be shot, replied, "Of course, Mr. President. I'll patch through all the appropriate command staff."

A few minutes later, President Zhang was looking at twenty-one of his top generals, each in charge of a missile division. "We've had technical difficulties here at headquarters for launching the missiles. I've entered the codes to begin phase two of our battle plan, but I see no launches. I'm in the process of sending you new targeting codes for each of your missiles. This will take some time, but I'll give you your launch orders via the link we're currently on. Any questions?"

As if on cue, twenty-one generals looked down, not wanting to make eye contact with their commander. Their training was explicit: no codes, no launch, and no manual override for firing the missiles. It had been drilled into them. Each understood that the coded computer launches were designed, among other things, to defeat any possibility that the president was under duress.

Breaking the silence was General Wang Yong. "Mr. President, the other officers are silent because this is how we trained them. If they don't get the computer-generated launch codes, they have specific instructions not to launch. Sir, I suggest we wait for our chief engineer to repair the glitch in the coding."

"I disagree," said the president, "and it's obvious I don't have a gun pointed at my head. We're losing precious time as the Americans dig themselves out of the hole we put them in. I'll give the engineer one hour. I want action, not people questioning my authority. Understand General Wang?"

Looking bewildered, the general answered respectfully, "Yes, sir."

Two floors down from the president, Dr. Dong Liang was proud of what he had accomplished thus far—buying time for the Americans.

# Chapter 56



*WOODY ISLAND PLA AIR FORCE BASE*
Paracel Islands, South China Sea

Woody Island covered an area of only 2.1 square kilometers, which was less than a square mile. It wasn't all that big—but its strategic importance was. Despite its size, Woody was becoming a trendy and contested piece of real estate—an island that was but a dot in the South China Sea yet had changed hands throughout history. Conflicts between other nations with China over the island had continued for years. In 1956, China established a permanent presence. Vietnam contested China's claim and continued calling for its sovereignty over the island. The Vietnamese made claims to the island after claiming it from the French colonialist regime against whom Vietnam fought a bitter war that ended in 1954. But it was China that settled on the island and made it one of their most significant military outposts in the South China Sea. The PRC would never give it up without a fight.

Woody had been tamed for the 1,400 people living on it. They had FM radio stations. Residents could access mobile communications and were allowed satellite television. There was even a school for the children. And for those nights the inhabitants sought entertainment, there was a state-of-the-art movie theater with 4k resolution on a 3D screen.

The island was but one cog in China's series of small islands. But the reason for the PLA's presence on the island wasn't for tropical luxuries; the island was part of the PRC's long-term defensive strategy of anti-access, area denial. Many places in the island chain had missiles, sensitive radar, advanced aircraft, and differing technologies designed to deny freedom of movement to the United States and its allies. Seven other islands gave China the equivalent of eight aircraft carriers strategically positioned to protect China's homeland.

Woody was a noteworthy example of applying the A2/AD strategy because the island housed deployed J-11 fighters, H-6K long-range strategic bombers, HQ-9B surface-to-air missiles, YJ-62 anti-ship cruise missiles, and other offensive and defensive weapons. The H-6K assets alone could cover nearly all of Southeast Asia, including parts of Myanmar and Indonesia.

With the Chinese military bombing American bases from Kadena to Guam to Wake, including the carriers, the PLARF had rendered the threat of US air superiority a non-issue. The PLAAF, with control of the air, could wreak further havoc on the ability of the US to make war. After the second planned delivery of missiles, the allies would have their hands tied with pock-marked runways and hundreds of aircraft damaged or destroyed.

But the United States didn't become a world power, a leader of the free world, by being foolish or ignorant. One thing Americans did better than most was they created contingency plans using what-if scenarios: If this happens, we do this.

When the possibility of hostilities between China and the US became more of a reality, President Taylor made it abundantly clear to his NSC that he wanted contingency plans set up for nearly every option the Chinese might implement. The loss of all major Air Force bases in the Indo-Pacific region from China's almost unlimited stockpile of cruise missiles was just one example of a scenario and the event most everyone anticipated.

The president went proactive. Besides getting additional American assets to potential war zones and distributing aircraft away from the significant bases, Taylor had as one of his top priorities the capture of one of the islands in China's backyard. The US could then conduct unrefueled missions against critical Chinese targets from this island. Woody Island was the target his military advisers selected. All warned their boss that it would be a costly and hazardous mission, but true to the president's expectations, it would allow American fighters and bombers to surge into the heart of China to take out high-priority targets. President Taylor thought the risk was acceptable and gave the nod to go.

Training for the mission began immediately. Days later, soldiers from the 82nd Airborne Division were flown eight thousand miles from their base in the US to Guam. Part one of the contingency plan was in place.

While the 82nd Airborne was relocated to Guam, the United States Marine Corps was doing what it did best: training for island warfare. In an exercise led by the 3rd Marine Expeditionary Force, MEF, 3rd Marine Division, 4th Marine Regiment, the Marines duplicated a takeover of a peer enemy on a small island in the Pacific.

The Marines were going back to their roots. The new Marine Littoral Regiment was part of a more significant force to challenge enemies in a maritime domain by using amphibious platforms and light amphibious warships.

The refined units could move rapidly within the South and East China Seas Island chains. Gone were most of the tanks and tube artillery batteries, now replaced with long-range anti-ship missiles on Joint Light Tactical Vehicles. With the burden of heavy equipment gone, the Marines looked back at their history of island-hopping missions and focused heavily on naval integration to quickly get them in and out of a conflict.

The recent exercises were about to be tested. If training was preparation for battle, then battle-tested how well one trained. And fighting a peer enemy on their turf would test the limits of everyone's capabilities.

# Chapter 57


*FORT BRAGG*
Fayetteville, North Carolina

As it should, it all happened extremely fast and fast was what soldiers from the 82nd Airborne Division trained for. They were ordered to be able to respond to contingencies anywhere in the world within eighteen hours—about the time it took to walk around the island of Manhattan.

Captain Nathan Hubbard directed his ninety-six troops aboard a USAF Boeing C-17 Globemaster III as the clock ticked to zero hour. In an officer's briefing, Hubbard was told they were headed for the South China Sea, where they would team with Marines to invade Woody Island, one of twenty atolls that made up the Paracel Islands chain. Hubbard felt confident that his men and three women would succeed, having just completed a similar training mission weeks earlier. With all the destruction they had seen on the news, payback would be a welcome change.

After reaching a cruising altitude of forty thousand feet, Hubbard called his junior officers and NCOs to the front of the C-17, where he had worked up a makeshift command post. The captain had to almost yell to overcome the loud hum of the four Pratt & Whitney turbofan engines, but it all worked. Looking into the eyes of his leaders, Hubbard felt even more confident. He would need to, as the mission would be a tough one.

Staff Sergeant Christine Swanson, the only female NCO in the company, was a cutie. Still, she would rip you a new one if you ever referred to anything but her ability to lead—and lead she did. A veteran of Iraq and Afghanistan, she was one of the first women allowed to fight on the front lines with men. Swanson had already brushed death aside, receiving a purple heart early on when a sniper's bullet shaved off part of her left arm. She recovered and was happy to get back to a combat position. Pushing a pen was the last thing on her mind.

Swanson couldn't hold back while the NCOs were forming up. "Cap, tell me we're cruising for a bruising to those PLA assholes."

"Sergeant, do you ever let me go through my piece before chiming in?" said the captain with a smirk on his face.

"Sorry, sir. I'm just so anxious to kick some Chinese ass!"

"We all are," Hubbard said, ending the one-on-one conversation.

As the rest of the leaders gathered around a pallet, Captain Hubbard laid a map of where they were headed. "Here is"—he pointed at a minuscule dot on the map—"Woody Island, owned and operated by the PLA. Our mission is to drop in and work with other assets to secure the island as a forward air base for missions against the Chinese mainland. But here's the kicker. The island is only 2.1 square kilometers, less than one square mile in its entirety. Our LZ is not ideal. In fact, it sucks. But that's war. After talking with the pilots, we all agreed that a drop of twenty at a time at 425 feet should be safe."

The jump altitude left little time to deploy the chute and get feet on the ground safely. That brought on groans and expletives from the veteran paratroopers. But it was a WTF moment of doubt quickly followed by words of encouragement and "we can do this" chatter.

The captain continued, "If we miss the LZ, there's no wiggle room, and we could lose some troops into the sea. Since we have seventeen paratroopers qualified to use the RA-1, I'll lead this group, and we'll go in first from a higher altitude as required by our RAM air wings. We'll take out the tower and secure the area around the runway. Sergeant Swanson, you will accompany me."

After letting the information sink in for a moment, Hubbard said, "This next tidbit is highly classified and still has not been confirmed by the brass, but it appears we'll have the assistance of the USS *Gerald R. Ford* and its complement of aircraft and support ships, including their ability to jam the enemy's highly sophisticated radar." This information raised eyebrows because most knew from the news that *Ford* was just finishing its sea trials. Hubbard continued, "The *Ford*'s support is a must-have because we must protect our asses before, during, and after jump completion. We hope to invite this C-17 to land on our newly acquired runway.

"But listen, we must be prepared for the counterattack we know will come from the PLA Air Force. Understand that they will unleash everything they have to take the island back. They cannot allow the US to set up shop in their garage. The longer we hold the island, the more reinforcements we'll receive. We must hang in there."

Several "hoorahs—Airborne" were shouted in response.

# Chapter 58



As ordered by the commander-in-chief, the dispersal directive issued by the Secretary of Defense had the Amphibious Ready Group on the move south and just outside the nine-dash line, about 1,300 miles from mainland China. Led by the USS *America*, an amphibious assault ship that looked like an aircraft carrier, they were rushing toward a rendezvous with the USS *Gerald R. Ford.* Accompanying *America* were the amphibious transport dock ship USS *New Orleans* and the amphibious landing ship USS *Germantown.*

Optimizing the deployment was the new construct. Consisting of 1,900 Marines and sailors, the 3rd Marine Littoral Regiment had been divided into three elements, down from the standard 3,400 personnel. The Littoral Combat Team was organized around an infantry battalion armed with long-range anti-ship missile batteries. The Littoral Antiair Battalion was focused on training and employing air defense, air surveillance and early warning, air control, and forward rearming and refueling capabilities. The Logistics Battalion supported the whole regiment. The reorganization concept was simple: the MLR was small enough to be survivable, mobile, and lethal. Deployment would tell if the white paper matched the deliverables.

As the *Ford* strike group was sailing north, skirting the nine-dash line near the southernmost island of the Philippines, they were close enough to provide coverage for the *America* ARG, which was turning west toward the northern edge of the Philippines. Guam was slowly returning online with its missile defense and could lend a hand if needed. The following hours would be critical for everyone.

Chapter 59



*WOODY ISLAND PLA AIR FORCE BASE*
Paracel Islands, South China Sea


With the somewhat unexpected war having begun with the Americans, the last few hours had been incredibly hectic for the commander of Woody Island, PLA Colonel Jian Ts'ui. Chinese missiles were flying throughout the China Sea, and the US was reeling from the onslaught.

On high alert, Jian's eight hundred-plus PLA soldiers patrolled the small island, carefully guarding the advanced aircraft parked along the apron. Specialists were staffing the HQ-9 air defense missiles, and J-11 fighter pilots were standing by, ready to respond to any threat. All of this had the colonel worrying that something might go wrong.

Stress affects people in different ways. For Jian, he didn't chew his fingernails. He didn't even clench his jaw. Instead, he burped. He was told he had a form of Eructation. The Colonel was affected by uncontrollable belching. It pissed him off to no end, but under extreme stress, that was what his body did to try and stay calm. Somehow, the burps bypassed his body's defense mechanism to quiet them. But if there was one advantage to his impediment, it warned all those around him to be extra cautious or receive their commanding officer's wrath—between his gastric expulsions.

Different scenarios had been discussed in strategy meetings with commanders from the six militarized island commands. Given the resources at his disposal, the overall commanding general developed strategies for each theater. Every contingency was addressed, and combat plans were developed and continually rehearsed. One assumption became apparent. Should there be a war between China and the US, the Spratly Islands and the Paracel Islands would be attacked in an attempt by the Americans to use the islands as forward military air bases. The commanding general clearly stated that such use would not be acceptable. Orders were to fight using all assets to deny the Americans use of any islands.

Colonel Jian felt confident he would succeed in any attack. He had to.

# Chapter 60



*USS Missouri*

North of the Spratly Islands, South China Sea

Commander Elam Feldner set down the piece of paper with orders from USINDOPACOM for the second time in just a few minutes. They were simple and to the point: seek out and destroy Chinese submarines.

Rules of engagement were changing rapidly. A few days ago, he was playing hide and seek with the PLAN, and now he was listening for any sign of them so he could blow them out of the water. Fair enough, it was what he had trained for over the past two decades, and he felt he was very good at his chosen craft.

His current orders were to proceed within range of Woody Island in the Paracel Island chain in support of the *Ford* carrier group and the *America* amphibious group. The mission to take Woody Island was a bold move, and the crew of the *Missouri* would do everything in their power to aid in that effort. Feldner proceeded north at best speed and knew the PLAN had the same seek-and-destroy orders. His assumption was quickly proven correct.

"Conn, Sonar. Transient sound of torpedo doors flooding, one-three-one degrees."

"Helm, Conn," said Feldner. "Hard left rudder. Come to zero-four-three, ahead flank."

Knowing a Chinese submarine had the *Missouri* in its sights and would be shooting any second, Feldner had to get a bearing on his enemy. "Sonar, Conn. Give two active scanning pings fifteen seconds apart."

After acknowledging the new command, the sonar operator returned with the expected transmission. "Conn, Sonar. Two torpedoes in the water, bearing two-three-zero degrees. Range seventeen miles."

"Weapons, Conn. Prepare torpedo tube one and fire one on the line from the bogey." Feldner thought it was strange that his enemy would fire from such a long distance rather than close the gap. At least that gave him some breathing room to fight back.

"Conn, Sonar. Classify contact as Ming class Type 35 diesel-electric, bearing zero-seven-eight, speed ten knots, depth one hundred feet, distance twenty-six thousand yards. Classify as Sierra One."

"Helm, Conn. Change course to zero-zero-one. Take us to five hundred feet. Maintain flank speed." The helm supervisor repeated the command, and using their four-button, two-axis joystick, the helmsman did as directed. Then it hit Feldner why Sierra One fired from such a long distance—it was a trap.

"Sonar, Conn. Give me two active scanning pings fifteen seconds apart and look for a second bogey."

"Conn, Sonar. Roger, two active scanning pings now," came the reply from Sonar Technician (Submarine) Third Class Jerome Albright, the captain's go-to sonar operator. The answer came too fast, and the captain hoped he was wrong. The sea reverberated with the high-frequency sound of *Missouri*'s active sonar.

In a voice so traumatized that Feldner thought for a moment someone else had taken over the main seat in sonar, Albright said, "Captain, submarine bearing two-one-three, speed negligible, depth three hundred feet, distance thirty-five hundred yards. Classify as Sierra Two."

But before he could finish the transmission, Albright heard the dreadful sound of three torpedoes in the water from Sierra Two. He added, "Captain, three torpedoes in the water. Transients are wire-guided. They've acquired us."

"Helm, Conn. Hard right rudder. Come to zero-niner-three, depth six hundred feet. Weapons, fire off five ADC Mark three decoys."

"Aye aye, sir," repeated the torpedo room.

As *Missouri* made the course and speed changes, the three incoming torpedoes followed as if they were a shadow of the submarine.

"Conn, Sonar. Torpedoes one and two are twelve miles out, and numbers three, four, and five are closing, now seventeen hundred yards. Both have gone active."

"Conn, Helm. Six hundred feet, course one-niner-three, speed twenty-five knots."

"Helm, Conn. Come to one-niner-three, maintain speed and depth. Weapons, fire three Mark threes."

Feldner knew he couldn't outrun the torpedoes and doubted the decoys would stop all three torpedoes, so he made a snap decision. "Conn to all crew. Prepare for emergency blow. Throw the chicken switches and brace yourself."

With the command, the emergency blow's large-handled switches were snapped into position. Injected air was forced into the main ballast tanks in the fore and aft sections of the boat, causing exceedingly positive buoyancy. The sub was now two million pounds lighter, like when you release a ball underwater, and it takes off for the surface.

"Conn, Sonar. Torpedoes three, four, and five are eight hundred yards and closing. Impact in sixty-five seconds."

"Conn, Sonar. Torpedo four has veered off to decoys. Torpedoes three and five are on course to intercept. Impact in fifty-five seconds."

As *Missouri* was rocketing to the surface, anything that wasn't secured flew throughout the ship. The crew held onto whatever they could find, praying that the emergency blow would save them.

"Conn, Sonar. Four and five have changed course and are closing. Impact in thirty seconds."

With ten seconds left until the deadly Yu-6 torpedoes caught up with *Missouri*, the submarine shot through the surface like a breaching whale but just as quickly fell back under the water. As *Missouri* floated towards the surface a second time, both torpedoes smashed into the hull, releasing their combined one thousand pounds of high-energy explosives. Everyone aboard *Missouri* was killed instantly; young men and women with their lives before them were denied any existence of a promised life. As Plato said, only the dead have seen the end of war.

# Chapter 61

*USS MICHIGAN*
South China Sea

When the USS *Missouri* failed to meet its comms deadline, speculation quickly turned to dread since Commander Feldner was not one to miss any deadline, let alone two. The USS *Michigan*, the closest submarine to Woody Island, received orders to participate in the upcoming battle.

In sports, they call it the "next man up" after the star goes down, with an inference the second stringer must step up. But the USS *Michigan* was anything but a benchwarmer. The sub was only one of four and performed some of the Navy's most classified missions. It was the right sub for the right job.

Captain Theodore Cummings II, commander of the USS *Michigan*, was a man of privilege. He grew up surrounded by wealth. His father had invented a new type of ball bearing that was the rage in the 1980s and 1990s. It made him a multi-millionaire, and his empire only grew from there. Young Theodore grew up wanting for nothing but was taught to work for everything he desired because nothing would be given to him. So, for a family with everything, everyone worked hard to gain their footing in life.

Offered an appointment to Annapolis, Cummings said no thank you. Junior had always wanted to attend Harvard. He had no trouble getting accepted into and opted into the ROTC program in partnership with the Massachusetts Institute of Technology. While at the university, Cummings chose not to participate in sports and instead excelled on the Harvard debate team. His second love was the International and Multicultural Club, who explored over fifty cultural, ethnic, and international organizations. Cummings participated in those activities while learning to become an officer in the United States Navy. He graduated top of his class, being voted by his peers as the cadet with the highest leadership skills. Two decades later, he was leading his sailors into battle against a culture he had studied. Captain Theodore Cummings II was ready and prepared for what lay ahead, like his sub and crew.

Looking around the wardroom at twelve of his fourteen officers, Cummings liked what he saw. When all eyes were on him, he began.

"As some of you heard through the grapevine, we've received orders to assist in taking Woody Island, part of the Paracel Islands in the South China Sea." He hit a button on his computer remote, and a PowerPoint slide was displayed on a screen. "As you can see, this is smack in the middle of China's exclusion zone and is one of five militarized islands with fighter aircraft. To succeed in this upcoming battle for the island, we'll have to be mindful that we'll have company in the area, folks who don't know the words to pledge allegiance. Once we fire our missiles, we'll have an $X$ on our back and likely have to fight our way out of trouble.

"Need I remind you, there's no larger Navy in the Indo-Pacific region than the PLAN. The Chinese have over three hundred ships, along with numerous submarines. These include four nuclear-powered ballistic subs, two nuclear attack, and sixteen diesel-powered submarines. The XO will now go over specific targets." All eyes shifted to the XO, who had the crew's undivided attention for the upcoming battle that would be a first for nearly everyone aboard.

# Chapter 62


Beijing, China

"General Wang, your time is up. Are we ready to launch missiles?" asked President Zhang.

"Sir, the chief engineer tested and retested the system. Everything is in order and as it should be. He and his staff have no explanation, and there's no override to bypass this step. The only other possibility is that the code somehow got corrupted or was not entered in the proper sequence."

"Wrong," said President Zhang. "I entered the final codes for the first launch the same as I did for the second. For the first, it worked to perfection, and the second, well, the second, is faulty. Now, get me, Dr. Dong. He headed the code-writing team. Let's see what he thinks."

A few minutes later, Dong Liang ambled into the missile command center. All eyes shifted to the unkept, soiled, and out-of-sorts man. As he moved slowly across the floor towards the president, it appeared his feet did not want to follow him as they dragged along the floor, making a weird screeching sound.

"Dr. Dong," said the president, keeping his temper under control for the last time, "as you have heard, I entered the launch codes for our missiles, but nothing happened on launch two. Why?"

Slowly looking in the direction of one of the most authoritative men his country had ever put in power, Dong acted like he was seeing him for the first time. He said matter-of-factly, "I don't know what happened."

"I see," came back the president. "Before I shoot you and the other incompetents, I'll give you one chance to explain why. Then you fix it quickly, or you will die. Your choice—the clock is ticking."

Dong never changed his expression. "Of course, I'd like to help, but no one asked me. Now that you have, I'll sit down with the mainframe computer, run some tests, and see what I can do. I should have a solution in three hours.”

Zhang’s jaw tightened, and his eyes bulged as he looked at the sorry excuse for a man. Still, he had to admit that Dong was one of the most intelligent people he had ever met—when it came to computers. Talking slowly to avoid losing it, Zhang said, “Dr. Dong, you have exactly two hours. Now, please get with it.”

Dong looked at Zhang with doubt written all over his face. He was a precise man and knew it would take three hours to run his checks. Well, at least that was what he thought was an appropriate time to delay Zhang and keep the missiles from launching. Dong slowly shuffled over to where Zhang was waiting for him, unaware that he was scratching his bulging mid-section. As he mostly fell into the president’s seat, he mumbled okay and immediately began running his phony checks.

## Chapter 63



*USS Nimitz*
East China Sea

Navy doctrine made it clear: "The effectiveness of an aircraft carrier depends upon the speed of its launching operations. Therefore, a compact and efficient device for quickly getting all airplanes into the air is critical to operations. The modern carrier catapult meets this requirement."

Catapults one and two were seriously damaged, and number three was partially damaged, leaving catapult four operational. Samson's goal was to repair all the catapults along with the flight deck and to resume operations quickly. Meeting with his XO, chief engineer, and air boss, Captain "Hard Ass," Samson was looking for answers to questions that could easily cast doubt on his sanity.

"Sir, said his chief engineer, Lieutenant Commander Tom Ringwald, "even in drydock, what you're proposing would take at least a year."

"That's if you go by the book," said Samson. "We're at war. We've got a damaged ship, and our country needs us now—like never before. I don't want to hear excuses for not getting the Nimitz up and running. I want to hear how we can get it done. We must think not only outside the box but outside the universe. Understand?"

"Yes, sir," everyone answered in unison.

"Good. We can launch aircraft off catapult four, but we can't recover any of our birds until we repair the hole in our flight deck. Call it a patch job or whatever—we just need to fix it. I've sent photographs and a detailed list of damage to Newport News. I plan to see what our ship needs and then have it transported to us at sea. In the interim, I want crews working around the clock to prepare for this contingency so we're ready to go when we get our new flight deck."

# Chapter 64



For special ops, the night is your friend. As the sixteen-man platoon from SEAL Team 10 gathered around two H-60K Black Hawk helicopters, it was pitch-black with no moon as they traveled on the USS *New Orleans* flight deck. The two stealthy helicopters were prepped by members of the 160th Special Operations Aviation Regiment (Airborne), a unit that transported operators and had aviators who were the best of the best. Nearly every soldier in the SOAR was a highly qualified volunteer for their exceptionally dangerous missions.

The last time the Night Stalkers of the SOAR had an operation this significant was in 2011 when they flew in SEAL Team to purge a terrorist by the name of Osama bin Laden. As fate would have it, today's mission to Woody Island in the middle of the South China Sea involved one from that mission, Ronald "Rocky" Skalbeck, who was the junior officer at the time.

The plan for this assignment had many "what ifs." From top to bottom, it would be a seat-of-your-pants mission with a detailed plan only coming together while the platoon assembled intel as they swept the island. Detailed tactical photographs were hard to come by. Intel was weak since the US had no infiltrators on the island.

The basic plan was to land on the island's north end, away from populated areas and on a grassy knoll sticking out in the sea, about four hundred meters from the end of the extended runway. From here, the team would work southwest down the runway and eliminate any hostiles they encountered. The platoon would look for the launching areas for HQ-9 surface-to-air missiles and YJ-12B anti-ship cruise missiles. The latest satellite intel indicated several fighters were parked on the apron; those targets would also be a high priority. Once the SEALs felt confident it was safe to call in support troops, they would signal the 82nd Airborne and 3rd MLR to implement their landing plans. All of it would be accomplished under cover of darkness.

When the *New Orleans* arrived two hundred miles from Woody Island, just outside YJ-12B anti-ship missile range, the sailors immediately released two Landing Craft Air Cushions.

LCAC-1 was deployed with a company of the newly constructed 3rd MLR, which was now a leaner and swifter Marine assault unit, and which used the highly effective shoulder-fired M3E1 Multi-Role Antiarmor Antipersonnel Weapon System, or MAAWS. Loaded on LCAC-2 were two new eight-wheel tactical vehicles, ACV-30s, armed with twin turret 30mm cannons. Also loaded on LCAC-2 was one Joint Light Tactical Vehicle specially armed with Naval Strike Missiles, NSM, to be used as anti-ship and land-attack missiles. It was a long haul to Woody Island, but necessary considering the YJ-12Bs were ready to take out any ships without a red star on them. On board, the LCACs had specially designed auxiliary fuel tanks to get them to their target.

Finally, the call went out: "Saddle up and move out." Already split into two landing squads of eight, the SEALs boarded the two helicopters. Making a helicopter stealthy had been a goal of developers for years. The extremely loud rotor blades had been painstakingly redesigned to incorporate a top-secret system to reduce noise output significantly. Engineers used profiled fuselages and distinctive, classified materials throughout the aircraft to lessen the helo's radar signature. Named after the famous Native American war leader Black Hawk, it's most fitting that the helicopter got a new quill for the quiver.

The lead pilot checked in with his support team on secure comms as the two Black Hawk helicopters flew ahead just feet above the sea. "Moose 12, Stalker 11 Fifteen miles out. Will contact you when safe."

"Stalker 11, Moose 12. Roger. Nearing station now."

"Stalker11 to Moose 12. Weapons ready. Twelve miles out."

As zero hour approached, the SEALs checked that their weapons were ready, locked, and loaded. Weapons ready wasn't a command that needed repeating. Each SEAL carried a SIG-Sauer P226 MK 25 pistol and a Colt M7 rifle, and others in each squad had M136 AT4 rocket launchers and FGM-148 Javelins. Additionally, a SEAL in each squad was armed with the new M3E1 MAAWS.

As Stalker 11 arrived on station, Moose 12 hung back to provide backup. When Stalker 11 reached the edge of the grassy knoll on the island's north end, eight SEALS rappelled from the helicopter and assumed defensive positions as the crew chief tossed them their remaining gear. The helo silently peeled off to allow Moose 12 to replicate the maneuver.

It was 0300—right on time. With their night vision goggles providing clear peeks into the pitch-black night, Alpha squad's point man noticed movement out of the corner of his eye. What the fuck was that? he thought. Then he saw it again—two uniformed Chinese soldiers sprinting toward their location, 75 yards out with rifles in the firing position. Fortunately, it appeared they were not on the radio. Not yet, anyway.

Using his AN/PRC-126 radio, Alpha Squad's point man said, "Five. On point. Two hostiles, my nine, sprinting in from 75 yards. Engaging." Taking the safety off his suppressed M7 and leading the first soldier, Five let loose with one round aimed at center mass. He couldn't hear the hit but watched the lead hostile go down while the second tripped and fell over the prone body. As the lead soldier moved to get up, Five let loose with one more round, striking hostile one in the head, which splattered his skull into small fragments. Five used his scope to sweep the area, saw no other movement, and reported, "Five. Two hostiles down. Five clear."

"One. Moose squad has landed and is position," said platoon leader, Lieutenant Commander Rocky Skalbeck. "Full platoon, move out toward the runway. Eyes open, move fast."

Spread out along the knoll, the sixteen SEALs ran in a combat crouch with weapons ready. Five took a slight detour to ensure his hostiles were dead. They were. He grabbed one of their radios as he sprinted by, barely missing a stride.

Besides taking control of the runway, the SEALs' other objective was to destroy the infrastructure that launched missiles. Once that was accomplished, they could get reinforcements in somewhat safely. But they had limited intelligence about where the headquarters was located.

"One. Spread out and move southwest on either side of the runway. Nine, take your detail and check out the three buildings coming up in two hundred meters."

Using their night vision goggles, the platoon moved slowly and cautiously.

"Ten, movement on the roof of the first building. Three hostiles, all armed. One of three behind a machine gun placement."

"One. Everyone make yourselves invisible. Sixteen, do you have eyes on the three hostiles?"

"Sixteen. I can take out the machine gunner."

"One. Who has eyes on the other two?"

"Eight does."

"Twelve does."

"Thirteen does."

"One. Call out your targets. All be ready for any misses."

"Eight has the center hostile."

"Twelve has the hostile furthest south."

"Thirteen picking up the leftovers."

"Sixteen has the machine gunner."

"One. Take charge, Eight. Call out when all three are in sight."

"Eight. Roger. Stand by twelve, thirteen, and sixteen. Only have two in sight."

As the seconds turned into minutes, only two targets were visible. "One to eight. Wait another minute, then take out the two."

"Eight. Roger. On my command, sixteen take out the machine gunner. I'll take out the other."

As sixty seconds ticked by, each of which allowed the possibility that the hostiles might glimpse a bunch of soldiers lying near the runway—fingers were inching towards the trigger.

"Eight. On my command. Countdown—three—two—one—fire."

Like a precision military funeral, four shots went off almost in unison. And then instantly, two more.

"One. Status?"

"Eight. Three hostiles down. The third jumped up when his friends probably landed on his lap. Three down, unknown condition."

"One. Bravo squad, confirm."

Eight men jumped to their feet and scrambled toward the building. Alpha squad also moved forward to provide cover. Someone had their mic keyed and could be heard breathing hard as he ran.

Quickly, the open mic was clicked off.

"One. Watch the open mic."

"Nine. Hostile coming out the front door of building one."

Eight SEALs of Bravo squad hit the ground without moving so much as a loose rock. It appeared that the Chinese sentry had just come out to get a breath of fresh air as he casually looked around—bad timing. Making a quick decision, Nine aimed and hit the walking man in the back of his head, splattering blood onto the walls of the building.

"Nine. Get into the building now. Go, Go, Go!"

Bravo squad swiftly closed the distance to the building. Nine and Fourteen arrived first. Unable to see through the dark glass, they entered the building, each moving to one side as they did. Both sets of eyes went to movement on the right side to a bank of computers, and each man instinctively fired and hit their target, throwing a Chinese soldier back against a bank of panels. Just as fast, Nine and Fourteen kept moving, attempting to clear the building, which was one large room. Two more SEALs entered the room and assisted. As they moved through the open area, their calls of "clear" echoed through the room.

"Nine. I've located the stairs. Going up with Fourteen."

Quickly and efficiently, a third SEAL covered the two. Nine led, each with their carbines at the ready. Slowly, they went up the stairs, every cell in their bodies prepped to respond to the slightest movement, all masters at keeping their adrenaline in check. Nine saw the ladder to the roof and immediately started to climb. The upper floor was partially built out and appeared to contain surplus equipment. While moving, he slung his rifle and pulled out his MK25. At the ladder, the top cover was set to one side, and Nine could see the stars in the black sky. Whispering on his comms, he said, "Nine. Going to the roof now."

Nine slowly peeked around at the roofline in all directions, passing his eyes over the three prone Chinese soldiers as he searched for additional targets. None seen, he carefully climbed to the roof as Fourteen covered. Nine moved to the three bodies and confirmed each was dead. More importantly, their radios were quiet. "Nine. Roof clear."

So far, so good.

"Nine to One. Good to move to the next building."

"One, Roger that. Alpha squad, approach the next building and make entry. Bravo squad, take the furthest building."

Nine and Fourteen rapidly exited the roof to join their squad. Since the next two buildings were close together, the two teams entered each one simultaneously. Five members from Bravo squad exited the smaller building to assist Alpha squad. Nine was one of them, leaving three SEALs behind to decide what they had and to rig explosives around the building, regardless of the answer.

Rapidly going through unlocked doors, it was apparent that the buildings were vacant but stocked to the ceilings with computers and gadgets the men knew nothing about. Finished clearing, the SEALs quickly rigged all three buildings with explosives and remote-control detonators, the primary carried by One and Nine having the backup. One decided to complete the runway sweep before calling in the 82nd.

As they all took up positions, still moving south, the PLA radios remained quiet, no doubt like their sleeping operators. The SEALs moved down the runway using their night vision goggles and observed six hulking PLAAF J-11 fighter jets. Orders went out with no movement in the area and no nearby buildings.

"One. Rig each fighter with explosives. Two and Three, to cover. Move out."

The men removed C-4 from their packs and planted the heavy-duty explosive on each plane.

"Three. Military transport truck coming down the runway with lights on. Six hostiles."

"One. Wait as long as you can, and then use your MAAWS. Okay, boys, things are about to get interesting. Finish planting your explosives. Meet up in the area behind building three."

Switching frequencies to secure comms to command and control, One said, "Jaguar 21 net, SEAL platoon. Commence operations. I say again, commence operations. We will be lighting this place up any second."

"SEAL platoon, Jaguar 21 roger. Nearly in position. Expect the first load in ten. Good luck."

The MLR, hearing the comms report, responded, "MLR five-zero minutes out, approaching at best speed."

Squad Alpha's leader heard the captured Chinese radio come to life. The enemy had begun to notice inconsistencies in their working routines. Soldiers were not checking in, and missile headquarters was not answering radio calls. Chinese marines had been sent to investigate, riding out in a Dongfeng EQ245 military transport truck.

What seemed suspicious to the Chinese soon became a reality. Four aimed at the fast-approaching transport, putting the crosshairs of his recoilless rocket system on the front of the truck. He fired one round. The missile broke the silence on the island as the explosive warhead slammed through the radiator into the engine bay, tearing the truck into thousands of pieces along with the crew and the marines riding in the bed. A vast fire announced to everyone on the island that war for them had just arrived.

"One. Detonating explosives in three buildings now."

With the push of a button, all three buildings went up in a vast explosion, peppering debris over a sizable portion of the runway and showering the SEALs with burning fragments.

"One to all units. Pull back to the line of buildings west of the blown ones. Find some high ground."

The sixteen-man platoon moved past the burning structures and across a grassy area to three more nondescript small facilities with no windows. As they were moving, an unexpected comm came in.

"SEAL platoon, Growler 41. We're on station. Electronic jamming commenced. We have four F-18s to assist."

"Growler 41, SEAL platoon. Roger. Good news. We're moving to the northernmost grassy area at the island's center. Expecting contact anytime."

*C-17*
Over Woody Island

Captain Nathan Hubbard of the 82nd Airborne was first at the aircraft jump door while waiting for the command to go. His second in command, Sergeant Swanson, would be last. The group of seventeen was specially trained with the RA-1 parachute that allowed speeds up to 30 mph and precise maneuverability to nail their LZ. With RAM air wing canopies, there had to be at least a second or two between each trooper to avoid collisions. Still, today, the spacing would barely be one second. Given the ten-second sign, Hubbard was ready. Ten seconds later, he jumped, followed by the next trooper, until Swanson was last.

Swanson loved the shock between the warmth of the aircraft and the cold air that smacked you hard when you hit the wash from the plane. As she always did, she issued her not-so-famous scream that didn't matter as no one could hear it, "Yee ha! Let's go. You better watch out, you stupid mother fuckers." Flipping her night goggles down, Swanson saw that, sure as shit, she was over water, not terra firma. Adjusting her air wing canopies to gain maximum speed, she circled back toward land and was greeted with a laser marker telling her where the LZ was. Beating out one of her brother paratroopers, Swanson nailed a perfect upright landing smack dab next to her boss, Captain Hubbard, who hardly gave her a second look. He was getting used to it. After the rest of the paratroopers maneuvered into the LZ, they teamed up with the SEAL platoon.



Networking together, the EA-18G flight isolated real-time targeting tracks from Chinese radio frequency sources using their EW pods to locate signal sources. Not having to use detectable radar emissions, their targeting data was fed into the computer that programmed three AGM-88 HARMs and high-speed antiradiation missiles. The HARMs would do all the work finding radar antennae and transmissions. The weapons officer simply had to launch them. Once released, the seekers inside the missiles' noses would direct them to the target as they reached Mach 2.



Colonel Jian Ts'ui couldn't comprehend—but should have—that the Americans were attacking his island and had already blown apart his missile headquarters and who knew what else. *Burp. Burp.* For the last five minutes, since he was awakened from a sound sleep, he was having an attack of his own. "Get control," he yelled, "get control!" *Burp.*

The radio blasted, "Sir, radar indicates four F-18s approaching."

"Captain," Jian screamed between belches, "get our fighters in the air and handle this problem. You understand?" *Burp*.

A frightened captain, fearful of his own people much more than the four F-18s circling the base, answered decisively, "Yes sir, on my way now."

The captain was out of sorts on this piece-of-a-shit island because he was accustomed to the superior quarters on the mainland. Here, he had little backing and little flight line help from these Navy fools. Hell, most didn't know the difference between JET-A fuel and drinking water. Fortunately, he had had his squadron of six-armed J-11s fueled and parked on the flight line, ready to go.

As requested, a jeep pulled up to drive him to his aircraft. He had alerted his other five pilots, who should already be with their planes. As the jeep neared the fighters, he noticed the runway littered with burning debris. At first, he doubted the planes could get airborne until he saw numerous soldiers rapidly cleaning the runway. All while being shot at.

When he arrived at his plane, he heard shots and saw several soldiers struck. As two truckloads of reinforcements arrived around the jets, he saw a brilliant flash around his fighters, and then everything went black, black as the night sky he would never see again.



Platoon leader Ronald "Rocky" Skalbeck, call sign One, the veteran from the bin Laden raid, had his finger on the detonator button that would ignite one hell of an explosion as soon as his hoped-for PLA reinforcements arrived. He thought how weird it was that he was cheering for hundreds of soldiers to come to kill him. No, he thought, I want lots of them—as long as they park where the others did, on the apron next to those pretty Chinese fighters. Come on, come on.

And come they did, seemingly led by a small jeep carrying two soldiers.

"Come to me, boys," whispered Rocky. Sensing this was the moment, he was on his comms. "One to all forces. Fire in the hole, J-11s, fire in the hole."

As a row of Dongfeng transports pulled up by the fighters, Skalbeck pushed the detonator button. Having never blown up a fourth-generation fighter, or any fighter for that matter, he had no idea of the immense fireball it could generate. Shit, he thought, I might even get thrown in the mix.

The Americans positioned near the flight line became as small as they could, disappearing deeper into the grass as fireballs erupted around them. Bullets and parts of missiles flew in every direction, leaving trails of smoke behind. The massive explosions disintegrated everything within a few meters.

Skalbeck would never forget that moment, and the intense heat he felt penetrate his uniform. It made the Osama bin Laden raid seem like a high school outing. And when it was quiet momentarily, he swore he heard someone burping.

3RD MARINE LITTORAL REGIMENT
Woody Island, South China Sea


LCAC-1 and LCAC-2 drove ashore on Woody Island, and the Marines of the 3rd MLR took up positions with the 82nd and the SEALs. With their arrival, Captain Hubbard ordered the SEALs back to the USS *New Orleans* since only light resistance was being experienced. They had done their job, saving them for upcoming missions was better. Amazingly, the SEAL platoon had only two wounded, and both were expected to recover quickly.

The *America* Amphibious Ready Group, including the USS *America* and the USS *Germantown*, joined up with the USS *New Orleans* for a final push on Woody Island. The USS *Gerald R. Ford* headed outside the nine-dash line to rendezvous with the USS *Ronald Reagan* and the USS *Nimitz*, which was limping alone. All involved understood Woody Island was too important an asset and expected air and missile strikes soon. Defenses were being set up, and contingency plans were made. The battle to hold Woody Island was beginning.

Chapter 65



On station in the South China Sea, the USS *Michigan* expected to back up American forces landing on Woody Island. But with the initial success, their services were not needed. New orders came in during the last comms download. Now, they were directed to be within range of the Spratly Islands and were given targets for seven Chinese-inhabited military islands. Their mission would indirectly support the troops on Woody Island and the allied ships in the South China Sea.

*Michigan* was to target PLA air and surface radar installations—twenty-seven large radomes housed radars that could detect any movement in the area. Two of the radar sites were reported to be able to see America's stealth aircraft. Intelligence reports indicated that the outposts used a diverse, redundant, overlapping frequency coverage that controlled the battlespace. Some radomes were as high as thirty-five meters and could send target tracking data straight to missiles.

Captain Cummings directed his weapons officer to program twenty-five Tomahawk cruise missiles for specific targets on multiple locations in the Spratly Island chain, including Fiery Cross Reef, Subi Reef, Mischief Reef, Cuarteron Reef, Gaven Reef, Hughes Reef, Johnson Reef, and a smaller reef with no name that was referred to as Target 8.

Since there were twenty-seven individual radar sites, some of the programmed Tomahawks were TLAM-Ds that carried 166 submunitions in twenty-four canisters, ideal for targets that were in close proximity.

Skirting the coast of Vietnam near Nha Trang, five hundred miles from the Spratly Islands, *Michigan* released twenty-five

Tomahawk missiles and quickly disappeared. No PLAN submarines were able to locate the source of the missiles.



At nearly the same time the USS *Michigan* was preparing to launch missiles, a single Boeing B-52 Stratofortress armed with one AGM-183 Air-Launched Rapid Response Weapon was airborne over the Pacific, heading toward South Korea. The AGM-183 was a hypersonic weapon with a range of one thousand miles and flight speeds over 4,000 mph or eight times the speed of sound. The weapons officer joked that the missile was so new that the paint was still wet while it was chipping off his antique bomber.

The advantages of hypersonic glide vehicles were that they were fast, nearly indestructible, and could maneuver and change course after being released from their rocket boosters. While the PLARF had had the technology for some time, the United States was playing catch-up, and with this mission, they would see how far they had come in closing the gap.

On the books for over a year in case of war with China, and in conjunction with the developing technology, the US had prearranged high-value targets for those "just in case" moments. This was one of them.

The Central Military Commission housed the command and control infrastructure for the PLA. It was supervised by the Standing Committee of the National People's Congress. The CMC was the home of supreme military policy, and the chairman was Chinese President Zhang. US Intelligence suggested that if there were a war with the US, it would be headquartered out of the CMC's August 1st Building, located in Beijing. The CMC's nondescript ten-story concrete structure was the high-value target for the B-52's lone AGM-183.

On board the B-52, none of the five-person crew were even born, or, for that matter, neither were their parents, when the first B-

52 was produced in 1952. The youngsters who piloted the massive aircraft today followed the long-standing tradition of calling the plane the "BUFF," short for Big Ugly Fat Fucker, or Fella for tamer souls. Call it what you want, but this crew was flying BUFF in the most important mission of their careers—a direct strike on the leadership of the PLA.

"Major," said the navigator, "we're now entering South Korean airspace." Both pilots noticed they had some company, two American F-22s, and two Republic of Korea Air Force FA-50s. Always nice to have the fast guys around just in case, thought the aircraft commander. Strangely, the two massive US air bases in South Korea, bases closest to China, had not been attacked.

"Sir," said his weapons officer, "we're 514 miles from target."

"Roger, WEPS. Begin firing sequence."

As the weapons officer smacked at some computer keys, the crew was anxious about the anticipated launch of the AGM-183.

"Sir, ready to fire," said WEPS.

"Fire," said the aircraft commander.

"Fox-Fox," warned WEPS.

After the AGM-183 dropped from under the aircraft's wing, the crew heard a powerful rocket blast as the missile began its faster-than-sound journey. Unless the Chinese got lucky, they would have a colossal wake-up call in about seven minutes.



*PEOPLE'S LIBERATION ARMY ROCKET FORCE*
Qinghe, Haidian District of Beijing, China

The first sign of trouble came when Chinese radar picked up a launch from an altitude of fifty thousand feet and classified it as a hypersonic missile over South Korea. Projections put the rocket on course for Beijing with an estimated impact in less than seven minutes. Immediately, all missile defense batteries were notified. An HQ-9 portable launcher near Yantai fired two active radar-homing surface-to-air missiles using their HT-233 PESA radar system. Both missed.

In Dalian, China, an HQ-16A firing vehicle let loose with four semiactive radar-homing surface-to-air missiles. The missiles could hit targets as low as fifteen meters, and the Chinese manufacturer claimed a single shoot-to-kill probability of 60 percent against cruise missiles. But this was no cruise missile as it stormed toward its target at close to 5,000 mph. It was almost like the American cartoon Road Runner, which went *beep-beep* and was gone in a flash.



The internal PA system blurted out a message that President Zhang had thought he would never hear in his lifetime. "Attention, Attention. Incoming ballistic missile. All personnel report to their designated protection area. This is not drill."

It was organized chaos, as everyone from generals to privates made for the exits and ran down hallways to a designated area that was heavily fortified. President Zhang initially refused to go but was forced to by his security officers.

Dr. Dong left behind in the chaos, couldn't believe how bold the Americans were by going after such an important objective. Deep in his soul, he hoped he had something to do with it. All his actions were for his dear friends he loved so much but were gone at such young ages thanks to the murdering Chinese government. Dong hoped he had enough time to finish entering the code to disable the entire conventional ballistic missile launch system—he was sorry he didn't have time for the nukes. Dong had to thank the Americans again for giving him this precious time; with no one looking over his shoulder, he could do his thing with his fingers flying around the keyboard like a virtuoso pianist.

Outside, in front of the August 1st Building, were the newest items in China's defense against incoming missiles, the HQ-17 all-weather low-to-medium-altitude short-range surface-to-air missiles. They were housed in a specially designed wheeled launch vehicle that could fire while moving, even in populated areas. When the launch order came, all eight HQ-17 missiles flew from the truck in a spectacular show of fire, flames, and whooshing sounds. As the last line of defense, either these missiles were successful or bad things would soon happen—and they did.

While the HQ-17 missiles were fast, the AGM-183 Air-Launched Rapid Response Weapon was much faster and easily maneuvered from the enemy's defensive missiles to home in on its target.

Dong had a fleeting image as his fingers worked the keyboard in a frantic attempt to complete his work before the missile struck. It was like some Saturday matinee movie he watched as a kid when the main character had just seconds to stop a catastrophe, except now Dong was playing the leading role. The computer whiz worked frantically to enter the final sequence of codes that would prevent such madness from happening again. As he inputted the last string of codes, the powerful missile penetrated the building and released its Lethality Enhanced Ordnance from its blast fragmentation warhead.

The shock from the powerful weapon killed hundreds even before chucks of shrapnel and the firebomb killed many more. Even the reinforced missile launch room was devastated. As the room exploded around Dong, he was hit multiple times with flying debris that failed to remove the smirk on his face. Dong died knowing he had just hit the enter key to begin a chain of events preventing the PLARF from launching their powerful, conventional hypersonic missiles from anywhere in China. He only wished the Americans knew they had some precious time to bring the battle to the PLA.

The last thought Dong would ever have was how content he was to be joining his friends from Tiananmen Square. He was finally at peace.

# Chapter 66


*SUBI REEF*

The Spratly Islands, South China Sea


Located in a building that served many purposes, Colonel Yen Ming-wai was the commanding officer of what seemed like everything on the island of Subi. He had to monitor all radar installations and check the weather. Still, primarily he was responsible for the large military runway and accompanying aircraft. His HF arrays, located at his building, were used for early warning and detection of incoming missiles. He was also in charge of numerous HQ-9 batteries, most of which were mobile and hidden throughout the small island reef. The vertical launch and medium- and long-range surface-to-air missile defense systems were designed to intercept airborne targets 250 km/h away.

On this day, Yen was preparing for a field exercise to break in several new HQ-9 batteries. The kids—they were kids to him—didn't seem to have a clue about their mission or how to use deception as a survival tool.

As he was communicating with one of his batteries about concealment, every alarm in his headquarters building went off.

One of his kids, a lieutenant, screamed into his mic, "Colonel, what are you doing? I have alarms going off indicating incoming missiles. You didn't mention this would be part of our assessment today."

"Shut up, stupid; this is not a test. Those are incoming American missiles. Jam them and launch your countered defenses as soon as you get a lock—do it now!"

Joining the cacophony were blaring phones, no doubt calls from his utterly confused, untested troops. Over it all came a booming voice, "All batteries, this is not a test. This is an American missile attack. Stop the exercise and launch your missiles. We have little time."

As targets were being identified and called out, the sky was soon full of streaking lines of smoke. The HQ-9s raced to intercept American Tomahawk missiles.

To counter the latest Chinese radar, the new Block V upgraded Tomahawk used its improved communication and navigation systems to make detecting it much more challenging. The missile could now work through jamming more effectively.

The Chinese delay in engaging the US missiles allowed the Tomahawks to close on their objectives. Quickly, many of the twenty-five missiles struck their targets spread out over eight islands. Six of the Tomahawks were shot down. One of the missiles that got through had used its capability of loitering over a target, in this case, Colonel Yen's building. The Tomahawk was reprogrammed to strike the radar installation by sending back images with its onboard camera to Okinawa.

Colonel Yen Ming-wai was in mid-sentence, ordering the reloading of missiles, when the one-thousand-pound fragmentary warhead exploded, turning the radar site and building into a raging inferno and leaving no evidence that Yen had ever existed.

Several of the surviving nineteen TLAM-D Tomahawks had submunitions dispensers containing eighteen bomblets that exploded over areas where the radars were located. By all standards, USINDOPACOM was pleased with the outcome. But leaving nothing to chance, part two of the attack was about to begin.



Flying at fifty-thousand feet in supercruise mode near Mach 1.5, a squadron of F-22 Raptors from the 199th Fighter Squadron, based in Hawaii but flying from their temporary location in the Northern Mariana Islands, was heading west to the Spratly Islands.

The 199th was composed of primarily National Guard jocks, with a sprinkling of regular Air Force pilots.

"Okay, people," said Mytai 11, the squadron commander to the fifteen other F-22s, "fifteen minutes out. Prepare to break into flights."

The mission called for eight flights of two to follow up on the missile attacks on eight islands of concern to American strategic war planners. Targeted were any remaining HQ-9 batteries, surviving radar sites, runways, and aircraft on the Fiery Cross, Subi, and Mischief reefs. The F-22s needed every bit of their stealth for this mission, so all the fighters were using only their limited internal weapons bays to carry two AIM-120D air-to-air missiles and four five-hundred-pound JDAMs. After completing the task, the squadron would land on the US-held Woody Island, where Chinese-hardened aircraft shelters would protect the planes and their delicate stealth coatings.

Flying wingman for Mytai 11 was Mytai 12, Captain Isaiah "Cheetah" Azikiwe, one of the few pilots who took their call sign from life before joining the military. Azikiwe was from Namibia, an African country of two-and-a-half million people, where cheetahs were somehow surviving humanity in growing numbers. He considered himself a rarity, being from Africa and flying one of the United States' most advanced fighters—he'd come a long way from the dirt streets of his childhood village.

Cheetah recalled how his dad moved the family from Namibia when he was ten. They relocated to Hawaii when friends found work at then Hickman Air Force Base and had told his dad to join them since there was a need for aircraft mechanics.

Isaiah grew up around the early models of the F-15. Many friends, although they changed often, were kids of pilots. For them, life was spent dreaming of someday flying. While Isaiah was sure now most of them never did, he had known in his heart that he would. Becoming a US citizen in his early teens, he was fortunate to attend the United States Air Force Academy, where he graduated fifth in his class. Years later, he was flying into battle with aviators for whom he would give his life.

"Mytai squadron, Mytai 11. Commence attacks in five—four—three—two—one—execute."

On the word execute, fourteen F-22 fighters broke from their formation into flights of two. Each flight headed for its assigned island.

"Mytai 12, Mytai 11. You ready, Cheetah?"

"Yes, sir."

Both pilots, using their hands-on throttle and stick controls, called HOTAS, rolled in unison toward Fiery Cross, rocketing down to just three hundred feet above the South China Sea. Both had agreed to take the most formidable island to attack. US intelligence confirmed it was the most advanced Chinese base in the Spratly Islands chain. The two elite pilots would use their stealth to attack what might have survived the earlier missile strike. They would get anything left in the twelve hardened shelters, and their other targets were twenty-four hangars that accommodated Chinese combat aircraft. Finally, they would have to avoid the close-in weapon systems set up for taking out enemy aircraft that might have slipped through the attack. But both men felt confident with their Raptors and their abilities.

Flying at 900 mph, Cheetah's AN/APG-77 radar picked up two bandits and bleeped an audio warning.

"Mytai 11, Mytai 12. Two bandits, bearing two-one-three, twenty miles out."

"Mytai 12, Mytai 11. The bandits are blind to us. Bat-turn to one-five thousand on their six. Engage with cannons."

Cheetah acknowledged and maneuvered his F-22 as directed. Sweeping in from a 180-degree turn to within fifteen hundred feet behind the two unsuspecting bandits, both pilots coordinated their fire from their M61A2 Vulcan cannons, lining up the two targets using their eight-by-eight-inch tactical screen that had crosshairs on the two Chinese Xian JH-7 fighters. Using the F-22's linear linkless ammunition feed system, the two pilots let loose bursts from their six-barrel 20mm Gatling guns. Instantly, two hundred rounds slammed into the bandits, tearing them to shreds with little left that identified them as two Chinese fighters: elapsed time—three seconds.

As soon as the triggers were depressed on their HOTASs, the two F-22s maneuvered away from the aircraft, climbing to fifteen thousand feet.

"Holy shit," said Cheetah, "it's been a while since I've seen anything like that—they just disintegrated."

"Focus Mytai 12," said the commander, "we're five minutes out."

Controlling the adrenaline piercing through his veins, Cheetah did just that. Taking deep breaths and exhaling slowly, he was soon prepared for whatever targets appeared on his HUD and the three other displays dedicated to tracking air and ground threats. Bring it on, he thought; this is just what I've trained for.

Part of his training was to learn the habits of his enemy. From intel briefs, he knew that the PLARF was ratcheting up the use of mobile SAM sites, including the HQ-9. The concealment and mobility of the HQ-9 made life difficult for the hunters flying F-22s. Rather than leaving their radar active, the Chinese only used it intermittently, sniffing out the attacking aircraft and shutting it down just as quickly. This tactic left little wiggle room for the F-22s to find the missile trucks.

As they approached the island, Cheetah continually monitored his ALR-94 radar, searching for targets that could hopefully return enough information for a radar lock that would automatically feed to the computers on the JDAM.

"Mytai 12, do you have the return from your ninety-four?"

"Roger, Mytai 11. I have a fix. One HQ-9 missile battery just activated its radar. No other radar emissions spotted. Information programmed to JDAM."

"Mytai 12, take your shot. I will maintain course and speed, looking for others as you make your run."

Going into a slight dive, Cheetah quickly checked his systems and let loose one of his four JDAM smart bombs. He felt the aircraft shake a little as the bomb released from the internal rail of his Raptor. The JDAM autonomously navigated to the coordinates Cheetah had fed the computer. Guidance for the bomb was through a tail control system aided with GPS, which would put it within fifteen feet of the target—half a car's length. In this instance, the JDAM directly hit the truck loaded with four HQ-9 missiles. The secondary explosion took out two other launchers in the immediate area. Both pilots saw the flashes proliferate as they moved in unison, looking for additional targets. The wait was short.

Both fighters got a return on their radar from several hardened shelters the HQ-9s were protecting and whose occupants were now aware of the enemy's presence. Using their Synthetic Aperture Radar, the return from their pings gave them an exact rendering of the terrain where the hardened shelters were located.

"Mytai 12, take targets one and two on your radar. I have the other two."

Both F-22s separated enough to make their bomb runs. As they released two JDAMs each, they received a radar warning of two HQ-9 missiles being fired. Both pilots unconsciously quickened their breathing, knowing they would have their hands full if the killer missiles got a lock. But to get a lock, the smart missiles had to find their target; they didn't and continued off into the wild blue yonder.

Simultaneously, the F-22s' integrated radar warning receivers indicated two bandits taking off from the island. Both RWRs rapidly provided firing solutions for both PLAAF fighters, fulfilling the adage of Lockheed Martin, "first look, first shot, first kill."

"Mytai 12, take target one," said Mytai 11. "I have target two. Execute."

Using their right-hand control sticks while looking through their heads-up displays directly in front of them, both pilots fired one AMRAAM. Cheetah guessed that the two fighters neither saw nor had a warning of the stealthy F-22 Raptors. It would have only been when their missile warning alarms went off that they would have known they were dead men.

Both Americans watched the smoke trails from their missiles chase after the bandits, who released countermeasures. Still, the home-on-jamming capabilities of the AMRAAMs quickly overcame these, and the missiles slammed into the two JH-7 fighters, tearing apart the aircraft in flashes of explosions.

After ten minutes on station with no other signs of activity, the F-22 pilots dropped several JDAMs on the runway for good measure. They rendezvoused with several additional F-22s returning from their missions. They were off to Woody Island, which was just being prepared for them.

# Chapter 67

*WOODY ISLAND US BASE*
Paracel Islands, South China Sea

With the remainder of the 3rd Marine Littoral Regiment on shore, troops quickly began to secure the rest of the island. Almost immediately, white flags of surrender came out of homes and businesses from citizens who didn't want to be taken prisoner or shot. Although there were some skirmishes with PLA ground troops, they, too, saw the futility and surrendered. A makeshift prisoner-of-war compound was set up in the local park. Marines laid out concertina wire to confine 324 PLA soldiers, including one burping Colonel Jian Ts'ui, who was most cooperative and soon had his ailment under control.

Colonel Henry "Hank" Winston, USMC, commanded all US forces on the island. As he told his command staff, the first order of business was to employ air defenses, air surveillance/early warning, air control, and forward rearming and refueling capabilities. Everyone understood the counter-offensive from China was just a matter of time. The MLR was ordered to set up crucial long-range anti-ship missile batteries quickly. The Marines and not the Navy would take the lead in this new twenty-first-century island-hopping campaign. Marines would no longer just assault and capture enemy-held islands but would turn them into fortresses of powerful American firepower. The Marines would deny access to all submarines and surface ships using the latest technology. Winston told his troops they were small enough to be survivable while remaining mobile and lethal.

As US forces stormed the island, USINDOPACOM ordered the shipment of twenty-five Naval Strike Missiles combined with Tomahawk missiles. With this order were Oshkosh-built Remotely Operated Ground Unit trucks for the unmanned launching of Navy missiles. Also sent were ten Long Range Anti-Ship missiles known as LRASMs. The United States Marine Corps would send a clear message to the PRC: We are back doing what we do best, island-hopping while protecting our turf in the Pacific.

# Chapter 68



*AUGUST 1ST BUILDING*
Beijing, China

Like their enemy, the PRC were no fools. Chinese leaders thoroughly understood that the August 1st Building would be a prime target on the bucket list for the US. What they didn't expect was the use of a hypersonic weapon that could so easily defeat PLARF defenses.

President Zhang Wei, by design, was well protected. He survived the blast from his secure location deep inside the August 1st Building's specially built protection area. After a short hibernation, he exited and immediately headed to the missile control room. Since the door was blown off, Zhang walked into what had been a massive working chamber full of his command staff a few hours ago, but what was now almost unrecognizable.

The president looked over to his master computer area and could just make out the torched corpse of the last man sitting in his chair, Dr. Dong Liang. He was amazed that Dong never gave up on his duties to solve the incorrect codes. Not even the threat of a missile barreling down on him had deterred him. What a brave man, thought the president. He then silently scolded himself for being so harsh on the perennially disheveled man. He would make it up to China's newest war hero.

Zhang's aids, nervous about seeing their president around the devastation, whisked him to the PLARF headquarters at Qinghe, in the Haidian District of Beijing. The president quickly convened a meeting of his most trusted political subordinates and advisers.

Looking around the room slowly, Zhang wanted to ensure everyone in the room was focused on him before he began. He stood up to face those gathered in the large room, which was uncharacteristic for the president, but today was not a typical day.

"I have witnessed Dr. Dong's brave attempt to correct the codes, an attempt cut short by a lucky missile strike from the US. From this point on, all launch orders will work like this. As we did earlier, we will use our separate command and control structure that begins when I give the orders to launch missiles; it won't go through a computer but through our secure comms to the headquarters here at the PLARF. From here, the orders go to the seven artillery bases and each Brigade. My order to fire missiles from the Brigade goes out to the launch companies, who will fire the missiles at previously programmed targets. Any change to those orders must come from me or my designee. All missiles are programmed to accept this order directly from the launch companies and will bypass the previous codes inputted from me. Any comments? Questions?"

"Sir, if I may," said General Wang Yong, always speaking for the rest because the frightened staff members were perpetually silent. They concerned themselves more about not uttering the wrong comment—the wrong anything; consequently, not much got done that was spontaneous or forward-thinking.

The general continued after the president nodded. "In anticipation of this order, I've contacted our commanding generals at each base. We ran a simulated launch that didn't work because of a conflict with differing codes. We estimate it will take no more than twenty-four hours to remedy this." Continuing quickly to avoid being interrupted by the president, he added, "We did run a test at one launch company using just one missile where we performed a code elimination, and it succeeded with a simulated launch. Mr. President, this will work, but it will take some time. Success is just a day away."

"Really, general? One day?" questioned the president, who was sick of delays and could shoot the whole lot of them and not give it a second thought. "If you go over by one second in your time estimate—well, you can complete the sentence yourself."

Pausing a bit to let his comment sink in for all to ponder, Zhang said, "Now for Taiwan—the reason for all of this—as you recall, we planned to gain air superiority, which we have, and then we planned to commence our air campaign against predetermined strategic targets." He saw one of his generals start to raise his hand to interrupt, but he gave him a glance that said not now, stupid. The hand quickly lowered. Zhang continued, "To safeguard our success in the air, we will use our missiles for select targets as soon as we can get the missiles online."

Now for his key point. After taking his time to peer into the faces of the men around him, as if to warn them resistance was a death sentence, he announced, "With the combination of the air campaign and the devastating attack of our ballistic missiles, we'll seek the surrender of Taiwan, and the reunification can begin immediately. Therefore, today at 1600 hours, I want the air campaign to commence. All commands have their targeting data. Is there any reason we cannot meet this deadline?" Seeing no objection, Zhang walked from the room, leaving the powerful men feeling less powerful.

# Chapter 69


South and East China Sea

On orders from President Taylor, issued before hostilities with the PRC, twenty-five of the fifty submarines stationed outside the Indo-Pacific were redeployed to supplement the twenty submarines already in the USINDOPACOM AOR. These forty-five-attack submarines represented one of America's superior military strengths against a peer enemy.

When compared, the two navies were as different as a football was to a golf ball, except the golf ball was beginning to morph into a football. With more than a century of experience, the US Navy was a blue-water navy with submarines that roamed the entire world and remained underwater indefinitely due to their nuclear-powered propulsion.

On the other hand, China had only thirteen or fourteen nuclear-powered submarines. Still, they did have seventy much cheaper and quieter diesel submarines that used air-independent propulsion. The diesel subs operated almost entirely in the littoral waters off China's coast. Since 1996, the PLAN has been steadily closing the gap with the US Navy and could no longer be taken lightly. The upcoming battles would determine who had been doing their homework.

When orders were sent out to the forty-five US submarines, each was given precise targets and secondary objectives. Thirty percent of the targets were directed toward suppressing enemy air defenses, an activity called SEAD. The remainder of the submarine force would lessen China's air superiority over its coastal waters. To accomplish this, the US would strike PLAAF bases in all six Chinese geographic theaters.

Fortunately for the United States, five of the Virginia class attack submarines were now armed with the latest Block V upgrade to the VLS, adding twenty-eight more slots to triple the number of missiles that could be carried. In those slots went an upgraded Block V Tomahawk missile. In this era of peer competition, particularly regarding distance and accuracy, the Tomahawk's range was increased to more than one thousand miles. The integration of a new seeker and a new warhead complemented it. The Block V improvement also covered communication and navigation systems, making the missile tougher to counter and detect electronically and helping the missile to counter jamming attempts. Although subsonic, playing the part of the turtle in the race against the Chinese hare, the Tomahawk was more fuel-efficient and traveled a thousand miles while still maintaining a small signature. And another positive, it was affordable, meaning the US could buy lots of them.

In the South China Sea, one Virginia class attack submarine was carrying newly installed Long Range Hypersonic Weapons based on the Air Force's AGM-183 Air-Launched Rapid Response Weapon. The same missile destroyed the August 1st Building in Beijing. To guarantee that the headquarters of the PLA would not be operational anytime soon, one more missile was targeted for the building. The other three missiles were for the Zhongnanhai compound, serving as the Chinese Communist Party's central headquarters and State Council. Anyone who was somebody worked in that area.

With the availability of so many attack submarines in the region, a top-secret directive from the Department of Defense was sent to USINDOPACOM. Each submarine would team with a second, receiving exact details of where to take station, from the Yellow Sea in the north to the South China Sea. The objective was to send in the first submarines to reconnoiter their assigned areas and wait as the second submarines came in. If any PLAN submarines came sniffing around after detecting the active submarine, the stationary sub would handle it.

After the first strike was completed, the active submarine would take evasive actions while heading toward the next predetermined launching point. It would then assume the duties of the submarine lying in wait while the second submarine released its ordnance. When completed, both submarines would travel to another predetermined location to replenish their weapons. The attack was scheduled for 2400 hours. All involved had to be in a position ready to launch.

# Chapter 70



Being married to the daughter of the Chinese president came with unwanted pressure—pressure to continually prove he was worthy or to simply play the part of an obedient husband, especially at state-sponsored functions. As Major Chang Huang looked around the ready room at the scores of other PLAAF pilots, all identically dressed except for differing patches on their uniform shoulders, he knew he was at his best. At his home base at Quzhou, he was one of the guys, a pilot respected for his outright skill and one of their best at flying the most sophisticated aircraft in their Air Force, the J-20 fifth-generation fighter. At a war game exercise just before his accident, Chang received several commendations when he and his wingman took down seventeen opposing fighters with no damage to themselves, despite the numerical disadvantage.

Completely recovered from the injured shoulder suffered when he was forced to punch out of his J-20, Chang was ready for real action against the Americans he despised even more now that he had experienced them while a detainee aboard the *Reagan*. Chang listened as the flight brief seemed to go on too long.

"I want to emphasize," said the PLAAF general for the fifth time, "that our goal here is air superiority throughout the region. We need to maintain it. Whatever your mission, always make that your priority. If you should encounter an American aircraft, but your target is something else, stop that run, go after the US aircraft, and eliminate one more pest from our skies. Any questions?"

There wasn't a sound in the room because, to the man, the pilots just wanted to get airborne. For most of them, the looming battles would be their first and, for others, their last—no more training but the real deal, a chance to demonstrate why they were elite fighter pilots. As Chang and his wingman walked out of the briefing, both were elated because their target seemed most appropriate—the Office of the President of Taiwan.

# Chapter 71


Philippine Sea

Rear Admiral Robert "Bobby" Wisniewski, the son of Polish immigrants, leaned his chair back to the stops. He was feeling the pressure that comes from those that command. He thought deeply about the burdens of a new war as the commander of Task Force-70, comprised of three Carrier Strike Groups. Under his leadership, they would now work as one entity. He alone was responsible for three of the US's remaining seven operating carriers, a force of more than eighteen thousand personnel and 180 aircraft, which was numerically larger than most countries' entire Air Forces, along with a score of escort cruisers and destroyers.

By tripling his assets with three carriers, Wisniewski understood that his ability to hit inland targets, boost target-searching dwell time, and enable coordinated multi-platform strikes was significantly increased. With three times the number of destroyers and cruisers, launched missile attacks and the defense of the immense task force would become more effective.

Despite this, what bothered him the most and kept him from getting his much-needed sleep was the knowledge that the entire task force was within range of PLARF land-based missiles—even a thousand miles from mainland China. It was a calculated risk. Unlike the numerous US bases already devastated by the Chinese, Wisniewski had several advantages going for himself and his task force. They fell under two words: kill chain. The enemy had tried several times to strike the fleet and succeeded only once with a single hit on the *Nimitz* while it was tied up dockside for replenishment. Despite this setback, Captain Samson of the *Nimitz*, through pure determination, had his carrier right back in the mix, although admittedly with his hands tied behind his back.

Wisniewski knew the PRC must complete a complex sequence of events to strike his fleet of ships. That was where the kill chain came in. First, they must locate a task force that was always on the move, not unlike a shark in the ocean. At a speed of thirty-plus knots, his ships could cover a lot of sea in a short time. Even if located using such things as over-the-horizon radar, the PLA needed a precise continual fix to update their targeting information. If that all came together, their missiles had to make it through a sophisticated layered defense, measures from both land and sea and locate the fast-moving carriers again. It was like a row of dominoes lined up in a straight line and ready to tumble once started; remove even one, and the domino effect ceased. As he looked down at his watch, the admiral noted that it was near the time that one of the Chinese dominoes was about to be eliminated.



Adjusting his ever-expanding ass in the left seat of the love of his life, Major Dakota "Cowboy" Remy, a US Air Force aircraft commander and pilot of the Northrop Grumman B-2 Spirit, was settling in behind the controls of one of America's long-range heavy bombers. It was no wonder his ass was getting as big as his gut, he thought. It was his "darling's" fault since the aircraft could travel six thousand miles unrefueled and ten thousand miles with just one fill-up; he spent much time on his bottom. As Dakota squirmed in his seat to get comfortable, he fondly recalled it wasn't always like this.

Growing up in Waco, Texas, Dakota could ride a horse before he could walk. He lived on a sprawling cattle ranch and loved to ride his horse and tend to the cattle. There were days Dakota would come home so dusty his dad hardly recognized him. It was his dad because he lost his mom to cancer when he was just ten. The young man kept her picture beside his bed so he would never forget her.

Dakota worked hard on the ranch because he loved it, and his dad demanded it. He recalled riding into a swollen river to snag a bellowing calf as the current swept it away. His dad was along that day and leaned back in his saddle while his only child almost drowned, rescuing the calf. When asked about it later, his dad told Dakota without so much as a smirk, "In life, kid, you can either sink or swim. It was God giving you a test, and you passed it." Dakota became accustomed to such life lessons and begrudgingly respected his dad for them.

One evening when his father was late for supper, Dakota became concerned and rode out where he had last seen him. In the dimming light, he spotted a riderless horse standing over a man sprawled on the ground. As he rode up to the figure, Dakota saw it was his dad. He wasn't moving. It appeared the horse had been spooked because he'd never seen his dad thrown before. Yet there he was, with his head split open on a rock and the surrounding dirt turning into dark red mud from the blood of the man he respected most in the world. At seventeen, he didn't know how he would go on. He felt so alone.

As he was going about the details for the funeral, Dakota recalled that his dad had made it abundantly clear how important it was for him to graduate from high school, hang up his spurs, and go to college. Working a cattle ranch had supported several generations of the family, but Dakota had seen how it had been increasingly difficult for his dad to earn a living. His dad had always said times were changing, and he wanted Dakota to change with them.

Dakota, as he always did, took his father's advice, and enrolled at Texas A&M. Taking guidance from an uncle who had been a pilot in the Air Force, he decided the structure of the military sounded just right for him and enrolled in the largest Air Force ROTC detachment in the nation. Now, years later, he was about to pilot a B-2 right into the heart of China—God willing.

# Chapter 72


Mount Lu Chang, Taiwan

Sitting at the lead position of the Precision Acquisition Vehicle Entry Phased Array Warning System, called PAVE PAWS for short, Albert Chang was contemplating, like so many other Taiwanese, why missiles were not raining down on them like a summer monsoon. But he knew the rain was coming, and he and his staff would be the first to know when the storm clouds opened.

The radar the civilian was supervising was the most vital radar site in Taiwan—primarily because it was extremely effective. The PAVE PAWS had a three-thousand-mile range, covering most of mainland China and surrounding areas well into the South China Sea. His role was to alert his superiors if any ballistic or cruise missiles, aircraft, or surface vessels hinted at attacking his country or violated their airspace.

For the past six months, he had been very busy with PLAAF aircraft approaching Taiwan and only turning back when they were lit up by targeting radar. It appeared to him that that practice runs against his country would not be much different in war. Time would prove him correct.

*NORTHROP GRUMMAN B-2 SPIRIT*
Over the Sea of Japan

Leveling out at fifty thousand feet but not traveling much faster than a modern airliner, Major Dakota "Cowboy" Remy's thoughts were on his plane. The only other person in the B-2 was his mission commander and co-pilot, Major Richard "Go To" Sullivan, riding shotgun in the right seat. Sullivan had earned a reputation as the "Go-To guy" for anything concerning the aging B-2. Let's face it, Cowboy thought; as much as he loved his darling, the darn thing constantly broke down. He blamed it on too many gadgets. Like his daddy always said, "The more gadgets, the more things that can go wrong." Cowboy always liked to have Go To on board to help figure out what different warning lights meant—even if he was a city dude.

Today's mission was why his darling was developed in the first place. Built in the late 1980s during the Cold War, the Pentagon wanted a long-range, multipurpose bomber to penetrate integrated Soviet air defense networks and deliver ordnances to high-priority targets. The only way to accomplish that was to develop a stealthy bomber with a minimal radar cross-section, allowing it to sneak in, do its thing, and get out undetected.

Flying out of Wake as the morning sun peeked over the horizon were three other B-2s, all traveling different westerly routes toward their newly branded enemy, China. The targets were the PLA's over-the-horizon and sky-wave radars, which reportedly could locate and target US aircraft carriers cruising the South China Sea. The coordinates of the carriers could be instantly transmitted, if acquired, to the PLARF, who could then program their long-range missiles, such as the DF-21, to destroy America's largest and most feared ships. The PLARF had already demonstrated their capabilities with a strike on the USS *Nimitz*, now hobbling along in the South China Sea like a wounded duck on a lake. Destroying these radar sites and others along the Chinese coast would go a long way in protecting US carriers and helping US forces gain air superiority.

Cowboy had the nose of his aircraft pointed toward Darhan Muminggan United Banner in the province of Inner Mongolia, a radar base located four hundred miles northwest of Beijing. The weapon of choice for the mission was the AGM-158 Joint Air-to-Surface Standoff Missile. The JASSM had a range of over 1,200 miles, so the mission was for Cowboy to launch it from South Korea, giving them additional security from being detected by Chinese long-range radar.

Since their first target was deep within China and heavily defended, Cowboy liked that the AGM-158 had the proven tactical effectiveness of a cruise missile with the added benefit of stealth technology. Their plan relied on AGMs being difficult to detect when launched in quantities, resulting in a virtually impossible missile to identify on radar. Their B-2 was loaded with twelve.

Piloting his aircraft west over Japan and nearing South Korea, Cowboy went into full stealth mode. As he had done on countless missions, he retracted antennae, cut select communication links, and restricted the use of flaps. Glancing down at his Low Probability of Intercept Radar, Go To noticed the APR-63 Defensive Measures Suite altered the plane's course slightly to lessen the possibility of being detected by China's densest radar.

"Approaching launch point, Cowboy. The latest coordinates are relayed to weapons computers. Nothing on the APR-63."

"Okay, prepare to fire," Cowboy replied. "Fire four—now."

"Firing four 158s."

The large B-2 momentary shuddered as the four turbofan-powered cruise missiles dropped from their internal racks. As the AGM-158s blasted toward their target some one thousand miles distant, they were constantly updating using their internal navigation and terrain contour matching radar that was enhanced by highly accurate speed updates from their laser Doppler velocimeter. After the four missiles streaked from the B-2 at 500 mph, Cowboy's mind was on the next target.

"Go To, prepare for our next target."

"Roger, coordinates are in."



Military police officer Sang Sen-fan was enjoying a perfect life. He was married with two adorable six-year-old twins, a loving wife, and a job, so he couldn't wait to get to each day. His father was a successful banker, and his mother taught first grade at a local school. Sang had graduated number one in his Academy class and was having an exemplary career. After several years in the field, Sang was promoted to lieutenant and transferred to the elite Special

Service Command Center, Presidential Security and Protection Detail, which meant he was tasked with guarding Taiwan's president, Chen Guang.

After another uneventful day, meaning the president was safe, Sang, who parked in the employee parking lot, was surprised when his car failed to start. Strange, he thought, his car was only a few months old.

Deciding to look after it tomorrow, Sang headed for the bus station just outside the high-security zone that housed many of Taiwan's most significant offices. The area contained the Ministry of National Defense, the Ministry of the Interior, and most importantly, the Presidential Office Building, where he was assigned.

Sang walked down a dark side street to shave off time to the bus stop. He noticed a van approach him with its bright lights pointed directly at him. His cop senses told him something wasn't right. As his hand slid toward his Smith & Wesson M&P semi-automatic pistol on his hip, someone with a vice-like grip grabbed him from behind, pinned his arms, and threw him into the black van just as the door slid open. The van was off in less than five seconds.

When Sang was thrown to the floor of the darkened interior, someone forced a black hood over his head while someone else cuffed his hands behind his back and took his gun. A warning came from the front of the van: "Don't say a word or make any attempt to escape, or you will be killed. Do you understand?"

"What's going on here," Sang asked, more in shock than anything else.

"Yes or no, do you understand? Make any other comment again, and I will put a bullet in your head."

"Yes," replied Sang, quickly computing what was happening to him. As he tried to slow down his adrenaline flow, the lieutenant quickly changed to survival mode and started using his senses to help diagnose the situation.

As Sang Sen-fan was dragged down a flight of stairs and thrown onto a cold metal chair, he vainly tried to see through his black hood, which had taken him captive. But Sang couldn't see the five-person PLA Special Operations Force crew specially trained for this mission. To the man, they were the best of a very elite force.

Sitting in the chair, Sang was listening for anything that might help him develop an escape plan. Abruptly, his hood was ripped off, stinging his ears. After his vision adjusted to the lights, he saw his captors for the first time. Sang's heart skipped a beat. None of them were protecting their identity, which could only mean one thing for him—he wouldn't see the morning sun.

Sitting directly before him was a small muscular man with piercing brown eyes. He was dressed in black and looked like he would just as soon kill him as talk. "Listen carefully," he said. "I don't like to repeat myself, which is not good for you if you interrupt me. We have a favor to ask, and it is quite simple. We ask that you give us precise information about the whereabouts of President Chen Guang and where he will be tomorrow afternoon. Now—"

"Why in the fuck—" Sang was thrown back in his chair after the small man jolted him with a Vipertek stun gun. The pain was excruciating.

Speaking in a slow, controlled voice, the small man leaned closer to Sang, "If you interrupt me again, I will put a bullet right between your eyes. You're not the only show going on right now."

Still reeling from the pain, Sang nodded, thinking rapidly about how to escape this mess.

The small man continued, "Oh, I'm sorry, I forgot to mention that your wife and beautiful twins have guns pointed at their heads as we talk. If you don't comply with my demands and tell me where your president will be tomorrow, you will all be dead."

At that moment, a video image appeared on a monitor above the small man's head. It showed Sang's wife and children curled up on the couch in his home. Both girls were crying hysterically. His wife had her arms around their children, bravely attempting to shield them from whatever was about to happen. Then the TV went black.

"Please don't hurt them," cried out Sang. "I will do whatever you want, but please don't harm them."

"Okay," said the small man. "Here is what is going to happen." One of the other Chinese men came from behind Sang and handed the small man an ordinary looking cell phone. "When we're finished here, you will place this phone in your uniform pocket and leave it there. It's not a cell phone you can make calls on, but it does contain a highly sophisticated GPS tracking device. We know that you will be in the motorcade with the president tomorrow. If that should change, you need to contact us immediately and tell us where the president is by using this phone and simply pressing the green button here." He pointed to a large button. "Failure to comply in any way will end in the death of your family. Do you understand?"

"Yes, I understand. Please don't kill my family—I'll do as you ask." Sang sank into his chair, defeated.

*PRESIDENTIAL MOTORCADE*
Taipei, Taiwan

Riding in the back seat of his armored Audi A8 L, the president of Taiwan was busy reviewing his notes for his upcoming phone call with the president of the United States. President Chen Guang knew his country needed American help with the PRC. It was a mystery why it had not happened yet, but like his countrymen, he knew it was just a matter of time.

Riding in one of the nine Audi A8s in the presidential motorcade was Lieutenant Sang Sen-fan, whom his partner noticed seemed extremely edgy, not a usual trait for his boss. The vehicles in their security convoy all appeared precisely like the one carrying the president or, for that matter, any other Audi A8 on the road. The reasoning was simple: to confuse any possible attackers about which black sedan contained the president. The convoy also had the additional assistance of Taipei City Police Department motor officers, who blocked each intersection as the string of cars approached. Several black and whites were leading and following the procession of vehicles. Nothing was left to chance.



Major Chang Huang was flying his fifth-generation stealth fighter toward the heart of Taipei with his wingman, Jaeger 2 when his radio came to life. "Jaeger 1, Air Ops. Update to target. Data sent to your weapons computer. Do you copy?"

"Air Ops, Jaeger 1. Message received. Targeting data confirmed updated. Time to target, eleven minutes."

Over intra-flight comms, Chang said, "Jaeger 2, did you copy?"

"Roger. Good to go with the new coordinates."

On board each aircraft, besides air-to-air and air-to-ground missiles, were twelve YL-12 laser-guided bombs in the internal bays to keep the aircraft stealthy. The YL-12 would be the ideal method to destroy the president's convoy before it arrived at the Presidential Office Building. With satellite positioning correction after bomb release and photoelectric terminal guidance technology, the ordnance was designed for moving targets such as high-speed tanks. But against cars in traffic, it would be no contest since the bomb's accuracy was measured in meters, not city blocks.

The two fighters received continual location data from a Chinese GPS device planted in the procession. Chang noted they were ten minutes out.

*PRESIDENTIAL MOTORCADE*
Taipei, Taiwan

Even with all the intersections blocked off by the motor cops, the motorcade was slowed because of rush hour traffic. It was just a fact of life. Sensing an opportunity to see what was eating at his boss, the second in command of security blurted out, "Hey, lieutenant, I've known you for years, and I can see that something is up. What did you have, a fight with the misses? We've all been there."

"Sergeant let's concentrate on our mission and not speculate on someone's mood. Got it?"

"Yes, sir, my bad."

Just then, traffic opened up, and they were on the move again, giving Sang a chance to figure out what to do. In his heart, he knew he could do nothing without jeopardizing his wife's and children's lives. He conceded that his family was dead if he went off the grid or tried to tip off his superiors. No, he would have to keep carrying the GPS-emitting phone and look for an opportunity to make something happen. The only overt thing he had done thus far was to leave a note in his locker explaining what happened should he not return.

"Ten minutes out, sir," exclaimed the sergeant. Sang nodded as strategies for survival and redemption crowded his every thought.

*PLAAF Chengdu J-20*
Taipei, Taiwan


"Jaeger 2, Jaeger 1. Target motorcade is now heading west on Section 1, Guiyang Street. Targeting data updated—good luck, brother."

Both pilots dove their stealth fighters sharply from twenty thousand feet straight for their target, passing Jeshou Park just blocks from the Presidential Office Building.

*Presidential Motorcade*
Taipei, Taiwan

As the motorcade approached the Taipei First Girls High School near the southeast corner of the Presidential Office Building, several students hanging around for a ride home waved as the first security car passed. Sang saw the kid waving just as the brightest light he had ever seen blinded him. It was the last thing he would ever see as it was replaced with total blackness as he and the entire motorcade was wiped from the face of the earth in a series of continual explosions, disintegrating everything in the area.

## Chapter 73



Mount Lu Chang, Taiwan

Looking like an oversized speaker casually set in a forest, the sophisticated radar sent data alerts to veteran radar supervisor Albert Chang. The signals were anything but music to his ears. In his thirty-three years of witnessing every drill and every real-life encounter with the PLA, his screens had never registered such massive penetration. It sent a cold chill down his spine.

Taiwan's $1.4 billion PAVE PAWS radar was doing just what it was designed to do, providing an early warning of Chinese aircraft about to enter Taiwanese airspace. Not just in the north toward Taipei—the entire island was being overwhelmed from every direction as if being entombed by tentacles from some giant squid.

Chang immediately sent flash comms notifying his military, national leaders, and USINDOPACOM. Things happened very quickly when separated by only ninety miles from the mainland. But this wasn't the ROC's first ball game; they had continually rehearsed this scenario since 1949. It was time to put those plans into action.

*PLA FORCES*
Taiwan Strait

They came from everywhere starting at 1600 hours, from scores of bases spread over the entire expanse of China. Like a swarm of angry bees, PLAAF fighters, bombers, early warning and control, and support aircraft took to the air in droves. PLAN ships began surrounding the island and firing missiles. In their sights was the island of Taiwan, a country of twenty-three million people that was not much larger than the state of Maryland. They were an independent population, a constant thorn that dug into the hard skin of the PRC.

It was now over seventy years since the Communist Party seized control of mainland China through a bloody war. The overwhelmed Nationalist government escaped to Taiwan and developed into a self-governing democracy reflecting the ideals the US embraced. Like a gambler in a high-stakes poker game, the PRC was now going all in to reunite the two. And why not? With control of Taiwan, President Zhang's esteem within his country would support his quest to control all of the first island chains, from the Kuril Islands to the Japanese archipelago to Taiwan, the Philippines, and Borneo, all of which enclosed China's coastal seas. As President Zhang had imprinted on his Army, success against Taiwan, and thus against the US and its allies, would undermine Japan, India, Australia, and South Korea. China would be able to project its military muscle deep into the Pacific.

With the PLARF's horde of ballistic missiles temporarily unable to launch—thanks to the clandestine sabotage by Dr. Dong, who, ironically, was quickly becoming a national hero in his home country—it was up to the rest of the military to make the initial strike on Taiwan. Hopefully, for the PLARF, the missiles would soon follow.

The ingress routes to targets within Taiwan had been refined to near perfection. For decades, but much more in the past year, PLAAF fighters and bombers had flown routes to test the response of the ROC's armed forces. Detailed logs were kept of those responses, including what type of aircraft scrambled from what specific bases and which missile batteries activated. The logs provided an exact blueprint for the pathways PLAAF aircraft were now flying. Win the battle of Taiwan and the United States would be supplanted by the PRC as the dominant power in Asia, if not the world.

The targets for the first wave of attack had been on the books for years, and their exact locations were refined in detail during the last month. Select high-value targets, such as early warning radar sites, air defense batteries, critical command and control centers, and infrastructure, were topping the list. The PLAAF would brush aside the ROC Air Force like a piece of lint off a jacket.



*OVER-THE-HORIZON RADAR SITE*

Darhan Muminggan United Banner, Inner Mongolia, China

Looking more like a gigantic fence to trap dinosaurs than like a highly sophisticated over-the-horizon radar, it was one of the PRC's prized sites. Its ability to track American aircraft carriers in the South China Sea was integral to the PLARF's tools. Location information could be input into their long-range ballistic missiles to strike at the heart of the US Navy's ability to bring the war to China. But unfortunately for the PLARF, someone had input codes to block the launch of those missiles, at least for the present time. But that wasn't their only problem.

As civilian technicians and PLA security forces did their business at the remote site in Inner Mongolia, they had just seconds to live. Unknown to them, four AGM-158s were heading their way. The JASSMs locked onto their targets, and the air-to-surface cruise missiles, each carrying a one-thousand-pound warhead, struck the radar site, obliterating everything. The JASSMs launched from three other B-2 bombers were repeating this scenario at other radar sites. Thousands of miles away, it just became a little safer for the three carriers because China had one eye smashed by the brute force of the United States Air Force.

# Chapter 74



*KINMEN ISLAND*
Taiwan

Since the Ming Dynasty, the island sitting just over a mile from China was called Kinmen, meaning strong gates made of gold; so named because the island was like a gateway to the sea around it. The problem was that a gate was also a doorway—which goes both ways.

The strategic island of Kinmen had seen its share of battles. Still, the one in 1950 where First Lieutenant Hu Ying, a tank commander, led the island's defenses against a concentrated PLA attack and defeated the communist forces stood out the most. President Zhang Wei understood all too well that bypassing Kinmen Island in his invasion of Taiwan would be simple. He could return later to clean up the mess on that troublesome atoll. But no, he wanted to even the score and destroy the island that had been so crucial to the nationalists who created the Republic of China—call it a historical payback.

The grandson of the great hero Lieutenant Hu Ying, Captain Liu Ying, cursed under his breath at all the tourists. Even the posted sign of "No Trespassing - Military Security Zone" didn't deter the pricks from being on the beach, tourists who were mainly from the Chinese mainland. They came to see the old fortifications and the anti-amphibious emplacements. That was fine, but when they laid eyes on Taiwan's newest tank, his American-made Abrams M1A2T, they went bonkers. If Liu and his tank crew didn't stay on the move, the dummies would jump in front of the massive tank to get a selfie or to pose with their family. It was crazy. As he always did, Liu called in the military police so they could chase them off. Hell, a war was going on—and those tourists were the enemy.

The United States had recently sold the Taiwanese Army 106 M1A2T Abrams tanks, with the odd six assigned to Liu's 10th Tank

Company on Kinmen. It was a huge technological step, and Liu's tankers were learning on the go. With the war between the PRC and the US, intelligence suggested that their little island would again be in the sights of the enemy, the same as in the 1949–1950 war. He would be fighting the same enemy as his grandfather had fought and beat—the Communists.

After an hour of dodging picture-taking civilians, the military police dispersed them. Once again, his tank company could begin training against a simulated landing by the PLAN. Along with the 10th were the 7th, 8th, and 9th platoons, consisting of five tanks each, sixteen aging CM-11 Brave Tiger Tanks, the mainstay of the force for over twenty years.

As the twenty-two tanks lined up on the beach facing toward China, a radio transmission stopped everything. "All tank platoons, take cover immediately. Missiles inbound from the mainland."

Liu figured they had just minutes to hightail it to cover. "TC10 to all platoons. Get off the beach and take cover." On his internal coms to his driver, he said, "Henry, head for that underpass, due east at top speed."

As the tanks scattered, they could see and hear missiles overhead. Within minutes, they could tell their base was under attack because vast plumes of fire, smoke, and debris filled the air. Liu understood all too well that this was the first salvo of an invasion.

The PLA was unleashing an air, artillery, and missile barrage against Kinmen's ROC Army infrastructure on the island. The tank platoons had no idea just how big the onslaught would be. If it was related to the island's defense, it had to of been targeted with exact coordinates gleaned from spies acting as tourists over the years. The only ones with a chance for survival were those who could move and understood where to go.

The tankers hunkered down and witnessed hundreds of munitions smashing down on troop barracks, headquarters buildings, and defensive positions around the island. Locals knew to hideout in the old underground bunkers and tunnels that crisscrossed the island. Hundreds of tourists were not so lucky. Unknowingly, they were being slaughtered in the open all over the island by their country's missiles.

As the aerial bombardment eased, the skies filled with PLAAF fighters and bombers. With exact targeting information for their smart bombs and missiles, the raids were highly successful, and the entire island quickly appeared as one giant inferno. One of the primary targets was Shang Yi Airport. Having been turned over by the military for civilian use years earlier, there was little military presence to protect it. The bombers were careful not to strike the ten-thousand-foot runway, but all other structures and the few remaining missile batteries were destroyed.

"TC10 to all platoons," hollered Liu over comms, "radar reports no enemy amphibious or naval activity on our shores—believe the airport to be the staging area for the invasion. Platoons 7 and 8, stay under cover near the beach and report any activity. I want Platoon 9 to accompany me to the airport. Execute."

As platoons 9 and 10 moved out, they now consisted of ten CM-11s and six Abrams—sixteen tanks to take on whatever the Chinese were about to throw at them. Liu was back on the radio. "I want all elements to find cover around the airport but seek concealment so we can hit the enemy's aircraft when they land. Any questions?" With no replies, the tanks spread out, speeding toward the airport. For the Abrams, that meant at up to 45 mph when they could find a stretch of road where destroyed civilian cars weren't blocking their path.

As in years past, Kinmen was considered a critical island to defend as the gateway to Taiwan. However, over the years, the military presence went from nearly one hundred thousand personnel to less than three thousand troops with little air cover or heavy weapons to support them. Moving as quickly as possible to the airport, the tanks at times had to push wrecked vehicles off the streets, but for the most part, the tanks went through fields and found areas with less damage to maneuver the three miles.

"TC10, Raider 20 with 21. Sir, we are all that is left of our air unit, standing by to assist."

Like most things in the ROC military, most weapons—whether they flew, sailed, went underwater, or were driven—were castoffs and ancient relics of the past. Liu knew that his Air Force consisted of two aging 1980s Bell OH-58 Kiowas, aircraft based on the long-produced Bell Ranger helicopter. They had been put out to pasture on Kinmen from the big island when the newer Boeing AH-64 Apaches were purchased from the US. The Kiowa's primary role was supporting ground troops—so they had no air-to-air missiles.

"Raider 20, TC10, roger. Appreciate the help. Is this Richard?"

"Roger that, Liu," came back the reply from Raider 20.

Liu knew he could count on this man, no matter the situation. He and Richard went back to high school when they were both on the wrestling team. As a wrestler, Liu was good, but Richard was one tough son of a bitch who fought harder than anyone else he had ever competed against. The man could never accept a loss, so he wrestled like his life was at stake. Staying in touch through the years, they renewed their friendship when both were assigned to Kinmen.

On secure comms, Liu gave his friend a sitrep and issued orders. "Raider two-zero, stay close but go covert. Enemy landings imminent. The troop transporters will no doubt have air support. Do what you do best—kick ass. Good luck."

With most of the buildings around the airport burning or shot up, Liu, with one other Abrams, could conceal their tanks among the rubble. The rest of the platoon was set up inside the bordering tree line. Liu didn't like their chances, but he was sure his grandfather hadn't either all those years ago.

His thoughts were abruptly wiped away when several Chengdu J-10 fighters roared over the airport, made a tight turn, and came back just feet over the runway. The roar of the engines as they echoed in the tight confines of his tank caused drops of sweat to drip down his back.

As the jets flew from view, six Chinese CAIC Z-10 tank-killing helicopters came in hot, pulled their noses up to slow down, and then spread out to reconnoiter the airport. Liu instinctively knew they were the advanced units for whatever planes were to follow. Those with a view from their tanks didn't miss the Z-10s, crammed with a full complement of sixteen missiles manufactured for killing tanks and anything that flew near them that didn't have a red star painted on the side. Breaking off abruptly, one of the helicopters made an aggressive turn, pointed the nose downward, and fired two deadly Hongjian HJ-10 laser-homing antitank missiles. The resulting fireball threw up debris and pieces of what had been a CM-11 tank— one of Liu's.

"TC10 to all elements," yelled Liu, "don't leave your position. Stay in position. Don't be drawn out. We have a mission to complete."

Richard's voice rang in Liu's earpiece. "I'm going after that bastard."

Before Liu could stop him, seemingly out of nowhere appeared Richard's Kiowa flying right toward the Z-10 that had just fired the missiles and was turning away. The little single-engine, single-rotor helicopter looked quite small compared to its target. The Kiowa was armed with LAU-68 70mm rockets for attacking ground troops, which were useless for this mission, but the disadvantage didn't stop its pilot. Richard used his only available weapon and fired his fifty-caliber M3P side-mounted machine gun. Before the Z-10 could react, the large caliber rounds destroyed the rear rotor and damaged the main rotor, resulting in a fire. The Chinese pilot fought to gain control but ran out of altitude. The helicopter slammed into an already burning hanger, adding to the inferno.

A second Z-10 quickly took up the battle using its superior electro-optical fire control system; the helicopter fired two TY-90 Sky Swallow air-to-air missiles specifically developed for helicopter dogfights. Richard quickly threw his Kiowa into a steep turn and dove just above tree level as he fought to outmaneuver his pursuers. He knew others would be on the way. It was no match.

Within seconds Liu's best friend was blown from the sky as both missiles obliterated the Kiowa. Fortunately for Liu, he only saw a glimpse of smoke in the distance, not Richard being blown apart.

Trying to raise Raider 20 on silent comms told him what he expected; Richard and his copilot gave it up for their country. And Liu would make the Chinese bastards pay.

For the next hour, there was little activity around the airport, either on the ground or in the air. The tankers were getting restless, and Liu wondered if he had guessed wrong about the PLA attempting to take the island from the air versus an amphibious landing from the sea. He decided to stick with his gut feelings. He thought they would perhaps bypass Kinmen as many pundits suggested—the Chinese version of island-hopping.

"TC10, control. You have incoming bandits, you're twenty. One Shaanxi Y-9 transport accompanied by three J-10s and four helicopters. ETA three minutes."

This surprised Liu. He had assumed paratroopers would parachute in to secure the airport first. Then the aircraft would land, but for whatever reason, the PLA was flying them in, or so it sounded. Perhaps they were satisfied with the recon accomplished by the helicopters since the entire airport was destroyed and burning. This was the war's opening salvo, and events were moving quickly.

"TC10 all platoons. Wait until the transports unload and direct your fire to the enemy troops debarking. Raider 21, when you hear our fire, do what you can with the enemy helicopters. Good luck."

Liu understood there was little hope for them, but theirs was a mission that had to be done. Any delays thrown at the PLA would give the US time to react and get into the battle, which Liu was sure would happen.

The PLAAF fighters flew low over the runway in less than a minute, making their presence known. They were followed immediately by four Z-10s, which hovered at all four corners of the runway. Moments later, a Y-9 turboprop transport, able to haul up to thirty tons of personnel and machinery, landed effortlessly. Throwing the brakes on at the end of the runway, the rear cargo door opened. As it did, paratroopers quickly jumped onto the runway and began to spread out to secure the area. It was weird for Liu to see

PLA troops running around on his island in full battle gear. He would quickly fix that.

With no radio formalities, Liu yelled over his mic, "FIRE!"

Already loaded into their 120mm smoothbore was the new M1028 antipersonnel canister cartridge containing 1,098 three-eighths-inch diameter tungsten balls. As the round was fired, a PLA ZBD-03 airborne infantry fighting vehicle began moving down the ramp. The lethal tungsten balls spread out from the muzzle of Liu's Abrams, much like a shotgun, inflicting heavy damage to the dismounted paratroopers just as they were deploying. Liu's tactic worked to perfection, immediately stopping the forward progress of the PLA as rounds from the other tanks slammed into the aircraft. Almost instantly, secondary explosions caused a major explosion, turning the Chinese Y-9 transport into an enormous blazing fireball and tossing the massive eight-ton fighting vehicle through the top of the disintegrating aircraft. As the other tanks fired, there were explosions everywhere.

"Quick," screamed Liu over the noise of the battle, "load an antitank shell with the proximity fuse set at fifty feet."

They had trained for this event numerous times, and the possibility of shooting down an enemy helicopter using an M830A1 round with a proximity fuse was proven to work. As the first Z-10 got his nose down to fire, Liu's crew fired their round just as the helicopter crew fired one AKD-10 antitank missile. In a nanosecond, the missile from the tank passed the inbound missile.

The Chinese AKD-10 missile immediately identified its target using its automatic guidance system. With an accuracy of within nine meters, the missile gave Liu and his crew little chance. The tank killer struck with such impact that the Abrams M1A2T disintegrated in flames, and parts of the tank were thrown twenty feet in the air. The fire was so intense that it showered the area with molten steel. Like his grandfather decades earlier, Captain Liu Ying, commander of the 1st Platoon of the 10th Tank Company of the Chinese Nationalist Army, and his crew perished. Outgunned, outnumbered, and knowing they stood little chance, the remaining tankers fought to their death with a simple ideal of doing their duty to keep Taiwan a shining example of democracy and freedom.

Liu and his crew didn't see how their extensive training to kill an attacking helicopter worked to perfection. A second after their tank exploded, their M830A1 round found its target, and just as designed, the proximity fuse detonated the large warhead mere feet from the Z-10. Both pilots died instantly as the attack helicopter exploded midair, showering the runway with debris.

Within minutes, the PLAAF fighters were given coordinates from the Z-10s and the surviving Chinese paratroopers. The fighters carpet-bombed the forested area where the remaining tanks were attacking, causing numerous secondary explosions after the remaining tanks were hit. As the J-10s flew from the area, the Z-10 attack helicopters fired at the blazing tanks to finish off whatever was left.

The remaining tanks near the beach and the few others spread out over the Island were located and destroyed without further casualties to the Chinese. The battle for Kinmen was over; the PRC stood victorious this time. President Zhang Wei would celebrate the loudest—a small Island but a bit of revenge.

# Chapter 75



*NEAR THE PRESIDENTIAL OFFICE BUILDING*

Taipei, Taiwan


In just the first few minutes of the battle for Taiwan, the PLA had struck—and struck hard. The bombs had rained in, decimating the entire presidential motorcade. No one survived—every sedan, every police car, every motor officer, and every human anywhere near the strike zone was disintegrated. The Taipei First Girls High School was included in the destruction, which was leveled by multiple thousand-pound warheads. Body parts were strewn for blocks. Taiwanese citizens just going about their lives were gone in a heartbeat. Social media instantly spread the word and the gruesome pictures to an anxious public who heard for the first time that their president was so dead that not even a part of his body would ever be found. Then before the stunned citizens could even begin to grieve, all hell broke loose.


*LESHAN RADAR STATION*

Mount Lu Chang, Taiwan


Albert Chang noticed he had a front-row seat to the action that was about to take place. As he scanned his monitors, it seemed like the PAVE PAWS radar was going wacky because it displayed hundreds of fighters and bombers headed directly to their exact position atop an eight-thousand-foot mountain with a radar view of over three thousand miles, a place which he likened to standing in Taipei and seeing things happening in Beijing.

With thirty-nine bases all within eight hundred kilometers or five hundred miles, most of the 2,250 PLAAF combat aircraft were within unrefueled striking radius of targets anywhere in Taiwan. At that moment, Albert would have bet his next paycheck, if there would even be one, that all of the PLAAF aircraft had gone airborne at the exact moment. But being prepared for such a calamity helped one's psyche. Through continually updated intelligence, the ROC military was as ready for the attack as humanly possible. It had always been anticipated that the enemy would come in droves, just minutes apart. Chang's radar installation sent coordinates all over Taiwan and beyond to fight back against the giant.



Scrambling to the airspace around Mount Lu Chang, Captain Jimmy Chen, a pilot in Squadron 5 of the 21st Tactical Fighter Group, was responding to the imminent attack on Taiwan and the country's most valuable radar site.

His squadron of ten fighters flew the F-16V, the world's most advanced version of the Fighting Falcon.

Jimmy had graduated from the ROC Air Force Academy near the bottom of his class. He blamed it on his lack of interest in technical courses, most of which were required but, as he thought, didn't make him fly faster or better. Giving him a class on anything to do with flying was different. The proof was in his flight training group, where he was constantly one of the top pilots in his class. One instructor commented, "This boy can straight out fly like few others I have ever trained."

Always a ladies' man, at over six feet tall with six-pack abs, Jimmy looked like a movie star with his long mop of black hair. When not breaking the sound barrier, Jimmy was breaking the heart of one of his many girlfriends, always sure the next one he found— usually at a bar—was his true love. But none of that mattered now because Captain Jimmy Chen was about to experience war as he had never thought possible.

*CNS LHASA*
South China Sea

Cutting through the water at 25 knots was the *Lhasa*, one of China's new Type 055 guided missile destroyers, which used stealth technology. Its crew was at general quarters. With the homeland still unable to launch ballistic missiles, their singular mission was to support the aerial invasion of Taiwan. Their primary target in the initial phase of the attack was the Leshan Radar Station in the mountains south of Taipei. The large ship was heavily armed with missiles in its 112 vertical launch tubes, including an assortment of HQ-9 surface-to-air missiles, YJ-18 anti-ship missiles, and Yu-8 rocket-propelled anti-submarine torpedoes. But there were also forty navy versions of the land-based DH-10 cruise missile for this critical mission. The missile had a range between 930 to 1,240 miles. The powerful missile was outfitted with multiple guidance systems, including inertial navigation, GPS, and terrain-matching radar. The Taiwanese knew the missile's capability because the Chinese had based the DH-10 on the US Tomahawk cruise missile, a technology the ROC military had used in the past.

As the *Lhasa* was approaching its launch point, using a precise route gathered from years of intelligence gathering of Taiwanese mine-laying operations, the captain had already enabled the ship's electronic warfare capabilities that could disrupt or deceive the sensors and detonation mechanisms of the hundreds if not thousands of mines planted by the ROC Navy. Employing his Mine Detection and Avoidance Systems using the ship's sonar and state-of-the-art underwater sensors to detect and avoid mines in real time, the ship of war was ready to launch.

As the captain of the *Lhasa* received ready reports from the combat operations center, he gave the order to fire. Instantly, VLS cell covers flew open as twenty DH-10 cruise missiles began blasting from their tubes. As the missiles soared upward, they left behind bright streaks of light. The initial stage of the flight was a simple vertical liftoff until the missile was well clear of the ship. Then the DH-10 fired its main engines and turned effortlessly toward Leshan Radar Station.

It was a beautiful site for crew members of the *Lhasa* of so many missiles being fired in succession; the visual experience brought smiles of confidence to the sailors. Some took a moment to ponder what it would be like to be on the receiving end of that onslaught bringing even bigger smiles.



Throughout the history of aerial warfare, the side that could detect and engage threats first was typically the one still flying at the end. While that looked good as a prophecy, pilots of Squadron 5 were receiving numerous warnings simultaneously about incoming threats. They silently wondered if they would be on the wrong end of the prediction.

The first notice came from an E-2 aircraft. "Hummer Alpha, Squadron 5, you have numerous bandits closing from one-two-four at twenty-five thousand feet. Range five-zero miles."

Following this was a transmission from the same radar site they were protecting. "We have numerous missiles inbound, classified as DH-10s, launched from a PLA ship. Eight minutes until impact."

"Roger, Leshan," came the reply from an excited Victor 31, the leader of Squadron 5. "We copy but are protecting your flank with bandits inbound your location." For now, the squadron must address the incoming hostile aircraft and hope the missile defense at Leshan Radar Station could stop the incoming DH-10s.

Operating with their updated Link-16 and AN/APG-83 SABR computer-controlled fire radar, derived from the F-22 and F-35, ten F-16s directed their radar toward the incoming threats. Viewed on the large Center Pedestal Display, the six-by-eight-inch high-resolution monitor with its color maps, Captain Jimmy Chen couldn't help but compare the picture to a video game, except in this game, if you screwed up, you would be dead—there was no reboot.

"Victor units, Victor 31. Come to intercept course two-four-zero. Identify targets using Link-16."

Jimmy, call sign Victor 31, adjusted his radar scope, set the altitude to eighteen thousand feet and above, and went through his mental checklist to ensure his Viper was ready for combat.

Thundering in from the west were two squadrons of PLAAF fighters heading straight toward Leshan. Out front were two PLAAF J-16s armed with electronic warfare pods and antiradiation missiles. The squadron of ten ROC F-16s took a defensive position in their path. In the battle for control of electronic supremacy in the skies, both combatants used their fully digital, modular systems with ultra-wideband digital receivers to detect the enemy, fix them, and defeat their sensors and weapons. With that accomplished, hopefully, they could stick an AARAM up their asses.

In support of the PLAAF's electronic wizards were several J-16 fighters, accompanied by J-10s flying escort for two long-range H-6 bombers. The PLA strategy was straightforward: attack Taiwan's military infrastructure, including land, air, and sea radar sites, to produce maximum confusion and pressure while maintaining aerial superiority, and after poking out their eyes, everything else would fall into place.

Abruptly, warnings sounded from the RWRs in all of the Taiwanese jets of Squadron 5, with numerous spikes popping up on the azimuth with symbols 16, 10, and 6, several with diamonds around them indicating the most serious threats. The Viper's sophisticated radar had analyzed the enemy's incoming radar and identified each threat with a number of the type of aircraft.

"Victor 31 to all Victor units. Identify targets and engage."

Using his AESA radar, Jimmy identified the leading edge of the attack was over fifty miles out but closing quickly. Jimmy sent out false radar targets that surrounded his Viper using his electronic warfare suite of countermeasures, both noise and barrage jamming. The object was to confuse a Chinese fighter's radar receiver, which hopefully couldn't identify the false reflected signals from the actual ones.

With his fingers and eyes moving around his cockpit at lightning speed, Jimmy set up the digital radar warning memory jamming system, which manipulated the incoming radar signals trying to lock on to him. He knew from his training that if he executed this correctly, his chance of survival would significantly increase.

Suddenly, but not unexpectedly, missile warning sounds filled his cockpit; it was time to go on the offensive—precisely why the Viper was made. His F-16V was equipped with new triple-rail launchers to carry his nine AIM-120D. Pilots worldwide knew that the guy with the larger number of pointiest sticks had the advantage. It was time to play that forward.

Jimmy communicated with his wingman, Victor 35. "Going into S cycle, Angel 36. I will take the lead," which told his partner he was using BVR tactics and for him to stay a few kilometers behind. Both fighters went to afterburner, allowing them to quickly get to the thinner atmosphere to launch their AMRAAMs from a thirty-degree nose angle. Approaching the bandits nose-on and getting a lock from his AESA radar, Jimmy launched six AIM-120Ds and made a complicated split-S turn to go back and defend against the PLAAF's BVR incoming missiles. As they had practiced countless times, Victor 32 flew toward the enemy, launched six of his AMRAAMs, and made his split-S turn. As the Chinese pilots maneuvered from Victor 31's missiles, Victor's 32's AMRAAMs would come streaking in on the evading bandits.

With his RWR sounding the alarm for incoming missiles, Jimmy's used an energy equation to fight back. He wanted to bleed as much energy from the fast-approaching missiles as possible. Already in the split-S maneuver and considering the distance from the missile, Jimmy attempted to put space between him and the PL-12 approaching him at a blistering 3,000 mph. Grunting in short breaths, Jimmy pulled 7-g's as he shot toward the sea, quickly picking up speed. To him, it felt like his entire body was being smothered by a gym full of weights. Firing chaff as he fought to maintain consciousness, he saw the water of the South China Sea fill his canopy just before pulling out of the dive at one hundred feet.

The PL-12 missile trying to kill him used active radar-guided BVR and made a sharp turn to follow the radar signature of the F-16. Jimmy had calculated that it lost energy from the turn and slowed down due to the lower altitude's thicker air. The fast-paced chirping blasting in his ears told Jimmy he was losing the battle to evade. His finger went to the button to release more chaff. In survival mode, Jimmy made several zigzag turns, knowing that the PL-12 was constantly trying to lead his fighter to calculate the impact point given the speed and course of the Viper. To counter his turns, the missile repeatedly made sharp turns to keep the equation valid, losing more energy it couldn't understand—but Jimmy did.

Like a hunter who knew the woods like the back of his hand, Captain Jimmy Chen knew every valley of the mountainous terrain of Taiwan, having run hundreds of training missions through all of them. He also knew the beeping in his ears might be the last thing he ever heard. As his evasive tactics took him over Taiwan, Jimmy had seconds to decide his next move as the PL-12 closed. Throwing his side stick over to the stops, his Viper, already near ground level, responded. He flew into a tightly enclosed valley, flying close to Mach speed.

The PL-12 needed a continuous, line-of-sight signal from its prey. As Jimmy dove into the valley, the missile momentarily lost the signal and, before correcting, crashed into the side of the mountain, exploding into a conflagration of fire and metal. Jimmy felt the shock wave of the explosion reverberate through his entire body. But he had no time to celebrate. Seeing he was bingo fuel, he headed to the nearest base for tactical refueling to get back in the fight. As he radioed Victor 32, he heard the dreaded news that his wingman had been shot down. Tears blurred his vision as he flew on.

Of the fourteen Vipers that stood between China and the Mount Lu Chang radar site, three F-16s were lost, while the PLAAF lost four J-16 fighters and five J-10s. One J-10 and both H-6 bombers continued eastward, hell-bent for Taiwan's largest and most treasured radar site.



### *PATRIOT PAC-3 COASTAL DEFENSE SYSTEM*

Undisclosed location, Taiwan

Scattered around the hills of Taiwan were several Patriot PAC-3 mobile launch batteries. With each launcher packed with sixteen interceptor missiles, the US made Patriot system was a force to be dealt with. Deployed just before hostilities broke out with the PRC, the PAC-3 Fire Control Team was monitoring the action in the skies near the Leshan Radar Station. The ROC team was prepared to fire if any PLAAF aircraft survived Squadron 5s attack. As the F-16s broke from the battle to refuel, the PAC-3 commander ordered ten missiles skyward when he confirmed that one J-10 and both H-6 bombers survived the attack. As the Patriot missiles flew skyward at Mach 3, they used their own onboard guidance mode while constantly using a combination of radar homing and command guidance to locate the three targets. Immediately, the enemy aircraft began using countermeasures in conjunction with drastic course changes. The PAC-3s had the latest enhanced resistance to these countermeasures, and both H-6 bombers were blown from the sky. Using evasive tactics, the J-10 continued and realigned for a strike on the radar base.

As an escort aircraft for the now destroyed H-6s, the pilot of the J-10 fighter, with nothing to protect, quickly set his sights on the radar installation. Efficiently, the pilot selected his LS-500KG satellite-guided bomb. Knowing he was being targeted, he rapidly began his approach, diving from thirty thousand feet. As his fighter's nose pointed toward the Earth, the Leshan Radar Station's air defenses fired two MIM-23 Hawk missiles from close range, catching the J-10 just as the pilot reached the bomb's release point. Almost immediately, the Chinese fighter was struck by both missiles. Debris rained down parts of the missiles and what was left of the aircraft all over the base. A wing from the J-10 crashed through the dining hall, killing three cooks preparing for the next meal.

Through all of this, Albert Chang hardly noticed as he had more important things on his plate as twenty DH-10 missiles were streaking his way to destroy him and the radar installation.

*LESHAN RADAR STATION*

Mount Lu Chang, Taiwan

In the world of missiles, events moved almost as fast as the threat. Albert Chang knew, as did his country's leaders, that Taiwan continually confronted the most challenging land-attack cruise missile threat of any nation in the world. Consequently, you devise ways to stay alive when you are the perennial ant and anticipate being stepped on. For ants, you find a crack in the sidewalk; for Taiwan, you invested heavily in a layered missile defense system. You must spot the enemy missile launch, identify the target, calculate the exact trajectory, and fire an interceptor. On its way, the missile has to be guided to the threat for the meeting in midair, and for warfighters like Chang, every second counts to protect his country and the Leshan Radar Station. In such critical moments, there was no room for error. A wrong calculation or response could signal the end for everyone, including the twenty-three million souls of Taiwan who counted on you to get it right.

Deep in the bowels of the island, men and women like Albert Chang, all integral parts of the island nation's Missile Defense System, were connected and working together to employ their integrated, layered C2BMC architecture. Commanders at all levels had to be able to see the battlefield and manage weapons systems to keep Taiwan in the "sidewalk cracks" for survivability.

*AIR DEFENSE PLATOON*
Northwest of Taipei, Taiwan

Secluded in the mountains of Taiwan was one of six land-based TC-2 batteries, which altogether were armed with a total of 246 missiles. Major Roger Huang was in command of forty missiles and was in his Engagement Control Station. He constantly received critical data from C2BMC and his target acquisition radar, a CS/MPQ-90 Bee Eye AESA. Mounted on a high-mobility, cross-country chassis were forty TC-2 surface-to-air missiles in container launcher tubes waiting for final mission coordinates. Their assignment was to destroy the twenty incoming DH-10 cruise missiles heading steadfastly for the Leshan Radar Station.

Huang's operation was highly challenging. With the radar clutter of the sea, his target acquisition radar was having trouble acquiring the missiles. The incoming DH-10s used terrain-matching radar, skimming the ocean at just a few feet while achieving a speed of over 1,200 mph.

In a voice Huang thought was way too calm for the circumstances, someone said, "TC units, this is E-2 Hummer Alpha tracking the incoming DH-10 missiles. Tally twenty, zero-seven-six degrees, skimming. Two-point-five miles until impact."

As the missiles were acquired not only by the E-2 but also by coastal defenses around the radar site, satellites continuously sent out jamming and spoofing signals to disrupt the internal GPSs in the DH-10s. But the missiles used a compass satellite navigation system using five Geostationary Earth Orbit satellites to counter the threat and stay on track. All the defenders heard their internal clocks ticking—two minutes until impact.

With the incoming missiles screaming toward the Leshan Radar Station, the orders came to the air defense platoon to fire. At eight thousand feet, the DH-10s apexed and made a wide arc downward toward their preselected targets. The score of incoming missiles went feet dry and abruptly shot upward, allowing their infrared homing guidance system to locate and verify the target data.

After the order to fire, forty TC-2 missiles were in the battle to save Taiwan's most prized and indispensable radar installation. Using their midcourse inertial guidance with data link and terminal active radar guidance schemes, the aerial combat of missile versus missile looked like hunting dogs chasing a group of crazed runaway cats. Several missiles fired from the large ROC truck located and destroyed some of the incoming DH-10 missiles just as they went feet dry. Others were blown up as they raced skyward. One DH-10 missile never made the turn and kept heading skyward, eventually running out of fuel and crashing a mile from its target. But three DH-10 missiles penetrated all defenses and were on target to strike the radar installation. Everyone clearly understood the results would devastate Taiwan's early war effort.

Standing in the way of the highly sophisticated DH-10 cruise missiles was the fictionalized last soldier, standing tall and ready to swipe the missiles from the sky. This phantom soldier, not unlike the R2-D2 droid from *Star Wars*, was the Phalanx Close-In Weapon System, designed to be the last line of defense against just such an attack. At lightning speed, the system used one of its two targeting radar antennae to search out the targets, providing the system's computer with bearing, range, velocity, heading, and altitude. This information was passed on in nanoseconds to the tracking antenna, which was extremely precise. The computer analyzed all the info, maximized the probability of a hit, and fired automatically. Shooting 4,500 rounds per minute, the system tracked the outgoing armor-piercing tungsten rounds and "walked" them into the incoming missiles.

Sounding like a buzz saw as it was fired, the Phalanx's 20mm rounds were engineered to destroy a missile's airframe and its aerodynamic design, keeping the exploding shrapnel to a minimum. All three DH-10 missiles were demolished in seconds. Spontaneous high-fives happened all around the radar compound. They all knew there would be more attacks, but like in sports, momentum made all the difference. For this moment, the "mo" was on the side of the Republic of China.

# Chapter 76



*USS OREGON*
East China Sea

Standing with her most senior officers in the newly enlarged control room of one of the Navy's newest attack submarines, the USS *Oregon*, Captain Colleen Panchak was waiting for confirmation from Nav on the latest incoming comms. The captain knew that the two-photonics mast with multiple sensors could simultaneously receive vital orders via satellite.

Word came quickly. "Conn, Nav. GPS fix received."

"Helm, Conn. Make your depth three hundred feet, heading zero-one-five. Speed 10 knots."

Giving orders to a predominately male crew was nothing new for Panchak, who had graduated from Annapolis in the class of '08. As the first female captain of a nuclear-powered attack submarine, she was responsible for the crew of 132, including fourteen officers and 118 enlisted, six of whom were also women. But she didn't differentiate between male and female, as they were all simply submariners in her eyes.

Her journey to captain a submarine preparing for battle in the East China Sea was not easy to put into words. No one from her family had ever been in the military, and she wasn't even sure why she chose to join. But if she had to narrow it down to what had inspired her, it was the day she tagged along with her best friend to a Navy recruiting office in her hometown of Des Moines, Iowa, a place hardly noted for anything to do with the ocean. She was hooked when she heard of all the opportunities in the Navy, including traveling the world. Being a three-sport star in high school and a perennial on the top of the honor roll, she planned to attend a division one school with an academic and tennis scholarship. After researching different opportunities, she pursued Annapolis instead and let Uncle Sam pay for her education.

In 2010, two years after graduating with a degree in Nuclear Engineering, the Navy, under Secretary of Defense James Gates, lifted the ban on female officers serving aboard submarines. She told her commanding officer that she wanted to volunteer for submarine duty. There was just something about prowling the seas in defense of your country that was appealing to her. She definitely had the leadership skill set, and the thought of serving in an enclosed environment with no sunlight and in close quarters was no big deal. As one submariner had told her, "You're a different sailor than most others in the Navy. It takes a unique mindset to be isolated from people, the sun, and fresh air for weeks, but if you're ready, I think it's the best job in the world." Colleen went on to earn her Dolphins; years later, she was in command of the USS *Oregon* attack submarine.

Turning to her XO, Panchak said, "Call a meeting in the wardroom in five minutes. Besides yourself, I want all department heads."

"Roger, ma'am," said her XO. "On it now."

Four minutes later, the captain addressed those whose job was to keep the boat afloat. Present were her XO, the engineer officer called the Eng, her Nav, the weapons officer or WSO, and the supply officer. The remaining nine first-tour junior officers were crewing the boat.

Looking around the wardroom, Captain Panchak was confident. "The time has come. The PRC is in the process of a surge strike on the entirety of Taiwan. They're attacking from the sea and the air using surface-to-air missiles. We just received our mission orders, and as you would expect for our country's newest attack submarine, we're going after high-value targets." The return looks from her senior officers indicated they were as ready as she was to deliver a solid blow to the Chinese.

She continued, "For the past two years, the PLA has been boosting its airpower capabilities by constructing and upgrading close-in bases at Longtian, Huian, and Zhangzhou—all of which are only one to two hundred miles from Taiwan."

She pushed a button on her computer remote. A PowerPoint slide illuminated the room and showed the location of the three tactical bases. "These are the bases the PLAAF have used for their tactical flights through Taiwan's ADIZ. One of our targets will be the newly created munition bunkers at Longtian. We'll also hit the new hardened aircraft structures."

Corresponding slides displayed the exact targets. The pictures weren't all that important to a crew located four hundred feet underwater. Still, Panchak showed them so each officer could visualize what they would accomplish to complement the war effort.

"At the other two bases"—she went to another slide—"similar construction has occurred. Additionally, all the bases have expanded their apron parking areas, indicating the potential for additional aircraft deployment." As she displayed each target, the captain couldn't help but notice the WSO taking notes even though the targeting information was predetermined and would be inputted into each missile. Great attitude, she thought.

Panchak continued the slides to the last location. "At Zhangzhou, there is evidence of new surface-to-air missile defense emplacements and the completed construction of a substantial heliport. All the sites I've shown you will expand the surge capability of the enemy. *Oregon* and thirty-nine other boats will do something about that. For our mission, we will be accompanied by the USS *Jefferson City*, which will have our six going in and whose back we'll have when it's their turn. Questions?"

The room remained silent, but a determined spark charged the air.

"Okay," she said. "Let's make this happen."

# Chapter 77

*ARMED FORCES OF THE REPUBLIC OF CHINA*
*Taiwan*

Electronic warfare was not unlike certain sports that employed both offense and defense in the game. As missiles fell across Taiwan, the PLA attacked the island using EW. As the PLA took the offensive attacking Taiwan, they were doing their best to disrupt the electronic spectrum. The ROC military did everything possible to counter this attack by employing defensive electronic countermeasures. The EW attacks could come from manned and unmanned systems and anywhere: space, land, air, and sea.

For decades, Taiwan had rehearsed for a preemptive strike by the PRC. ROC forces had countermeasures ready, waiting only for a launch command. One of these advanced weapons was concealed in the forest of the mountains to avoid the lenses of enemy satellites. The just-acquired American-made AN/TPS-59 radar, with its cutting-edge, 360-degree coverage, detected incoming tactical missiles and noted where the launches occurred. The advanced radar system tied into the ROC's Advanced Tactical Data Link System could identify numerous targets and relay targeting information so Taiwan's cued-up missiles could strike back.

With hundreds of aircraft attacking Taiwan, targeting commands were sent to the ROC's Antelope air defense systems for low-flying PLA helicopters, bombers, and fighters. The systems engaged the enemy using TC-1 Sky Sword surface-to-air missiles. Taiwan turned to its Chaparral and Skyguard air and missile defenses for the high-flying invading aircraft. ROC forces targeted the aircraft deep in China with Hsiung Feng and Tomahawk long-range cruise missiles. Many of these missiles were preprogrammed and aimed at PLA surveillance and reconnaissance assets, radar sites, airfields, missile sites, and command and control emplacements. With a goal of destroying as many incoming aircraft and missiles as possible,

Taiwan would force the PLA to allocate more missiles per salvo, chipping away at their vast inventory.

For the past several years, President Chen Guang had insisted on a military-style "Porcupine Strategy" to be used against the PRC that, in its simplest terms, meant the ROC had numerous small things that used the country's geographic and technological advantages. They were directed toward the PLA's vulnerabilities in coming to Taiwan to displace the free democratic people. Each porcupine spine was developed to be affordable, survivable, stealthy, mobile, hard to detect, and distributed throughout the island. The asymmetric defenses dovetailed nicely with Taiwan's natural defensive geographic advantages, and ROC forces had decades to prepare. In their bid to reunify Taiwan, the PLA needed boots on the ground, and that was when the porcupine would swing its tail and smack the enemy with a face of quills. Missiles could destroy many porcupines, but not all of them.



If Taiwan needed a reason to improve the president's security, China had given them all the warnings that an enemy could in the past few weeks. It had come in the form of a video of PLA specially trained troops entering streets that looked eerily just like the Bo'ai Special Zone in Taipei and attacking a full-scale replica of the Presidential Office Building. When it was over, the building lay smoking in ruins, and the video ended with a life-size mannequin of President Chen Guang being drug through the streets behind a PLA jeep.

Presidential Security and Protection Military Police Officer Second Class Master Sergeant Randy Sha remembered the details of the video all too well. A graduate of the National Security Bureau, Randy switched his career path as a spy in China to protect the most important man in Taiwan. He was the lead agent in the Presidential Security and Protective Service. The images of that Chinese propaganda piece reminded him each day that the mannequin being dragged around China could never be replaced with the actual president of Taiwan as long as he was sucking air on this planet.

The news media now played an endless loop of graphic video footage of what used to be the presidential motorcade being ripped apart by several one-thousand-pound bombs dropped by PLAAF stealth fighters. There were no survivors. Those not in the motorcade last saw the president and his driver, with Randy sitting in his customary right front seat, as they drove from a meeting with a group of citizens. The string of black armored vehicles stretched for nearly a block.

But that was then, and this was now.

Randy yelled to his protection detail, "We have more incoming aircraft and missiles. Get POROC to Alpha Tower now."

Four agents worked in unison to grab President Chen Guang and rush him to a secure elevator reserved for such an emergency. As they ran by a startled woman in the hallway, she couldn't believe what she saw. Scurrying past her was the president of Taiwan. She couldn't help crying, "Mr. President—you're alive!"

Not breaking stride, the very best of the presidential protection detail got their charge in the elevator and quickly shot down several hundred feet. They stopped in Alpha Tower, a heavily reinforced bunker deep underground of the Presidential Office Building.

Once in Alpha Tower, a sprawling, well-lit room brimming with secure, advanced communications equipment, the president could maintain command and control of his forces anywhere on the island, in the air, or on the sea. His vice president and most immediate staff and advisers were already nestled there. Except for his security detail, everyone was in shock as they looked into the eyes of a man they never expected to see again. Yet there he was.

"That's right," Chen said in as strong a voice as anyone had ever heard the president use. "I'm not dead. Now continue what you're doing. We are at war, and every second counts to countering this all-out surge from the PRC." His poise was like a slap in the face, and everyone immediately resumed their duties, cheering under their breath that their beloved leader was alive.

Although there was no time to discuss how the president came to be in Alpha Tower at that moment, Randy knew because he alone had made the call. As the motorcade left the citizens' meeting, his instincts told him not to follow the route. After going just a block, he had the driver make a sudden turn, shooting down an alleyway away from the protection that a convoy brought to the table. Randy advised the rest of the motorcade on secure comms to continue on their predetermined route. Chen had hardly noticed the change in course as he prepared for his talk with the US president. For Randy, to break from protocol was his call; if anything went wrong, he understood it would be his last detail. When the large motorcade came under fire, the car containing the president was driving down the service entrance ramp to the Presidential Office Building. With the push of a button that opened a secure hidden door, the lone wolf was glad he had followed his instincts. The President of the Republic of China could defend his country against the People's Republic of China.

# Chapter 78



Undisclosed location, Taiwan

Early warning radar systems dispersed around Taiwan proved their worth early in the conflict by identifying the litany of incoming threats. One was the attack on the Leshan Radar Station by the CNS *Lhasa* stealth-guided missile destroyer. The ship had plenty of missiles but was in a holding pattern. At the same time, the captain awaited a battlefield assessment of what survived his twenty-missile onslaught. He wanted exact coordinates to fire another volley of DH-10 cruise missiles at anything that had survived. When word finally came back, he was stunned to learn that the site was still functioning.

Albert Chang, the lead specialist at the Leshan Radar Station, was also busy. His radar specialists were preparing to fight back with their weapon of choice, the PAVE PAWS radar that could spot a flea on an elephant's ass from three thousand miles. Albert was communicating with the ROC Harpoon Coastal Defense System commander, who would oversee the delivery of a counterblow from his location.

Speaking in a confident voice despite nearly being wiped from the face of the Earth by cruise missiles, Albert carefully gave the precise coordinates of the *Lhasa* to the CO of HCDS. With each Block II RGM-84L-4 costing $1.5 million, the CO decided to let go with just five over-the-horizon anti-ship cruise missiles. There would be plenty of other targets for their inventory, which were now 495 missiles.

Coordinates were sent to the targeting computers of a skillfully camouflaged road-mobile launcher strategically located at the base of a mountain. At the command to fire, the missiles left on their flight to *Lhasa*. Set for a low-level sea-skimming cruise trajectory, the missiles' active radar guidance systems were being constantly updated.

As the captain of the *Lhasa*, one of the fleet's mightiest ships gave orders to his weapons officer for another launch on the Leshan radar site, a call from his action information center stopped everything. "Captain, we have five missiles inbound. Four minutes out, sea-skimming, course zero-eight-five."

The captain's first thought was why he didn't have protection and support from the mainland, just twenty miles away. He directed, "Ready Block 15 and fire."

A point defense missile system, Block 15 was fifteen HQ-10 short-range surface-to-air missiles that could be launched within ten to twenty seconds. With a range of just under six miles, the computers waited until targets were within range and fired from their vertical launchers.

With the missiles airborne, the captain prepared for any misses. "Quickly ready the HPJ," he said, referring to the ship's eleven-barrel Type 1130 30mm Gatling gun. Whatever was going to happen next could be measured in seconds.

As the missiles screamed toward each other at high subsonic speeds, two Harpoon missiles used pop-up maneuvers to go from just five feet above the sea to six thousand feet. All the Harpoon missiles were continually updated with final targeting data for the *Lhasa* through their GPS-aided inertial navigation systems. The guidance of the Chinese missiles used advanced matrix imaging infrared seekers. With the use of superior numbers, two of the Harpoon missiles were struck by several HQ-10 missiles, exploding within eyesight of the *Lhasa*. Three Harpoons made it through the maze of Chinese missiles and continued toward the ship.

One of the three missiles shot skyward and was destroyed as it reached its zenith and maneuvered to arch back toward the *Lhasa*. On the tip of the surviving Harpoon missiles was a 221-kilogram penetration blast warhead ready to tear apart the Chinese destroyer.

As the two remaining missiles closed on the *Lhasa*, the 11-barrelled Type 1130 30mm Gatling gun, using an electro-optical tracking system, calculated the exact speed, course, and trajectory of the inbound missiles. When they got within three kilometers, the gun's computer activated firing, spitting nearly two hundred 30mm rounds per second. The HPJ locked onto the closest missile, skimming the South China Sea at just five feet. As the computer identified a sure kill after a six-second burst, the gun's automated turret swept skyward in milliseconds to aim at the remaining threat. Just as rounds were fired, the Harpoon struck within two feet of the Bridge, shredding it and everyone in it. The resulting blast shook the *Lhasa* from bow to stern, causing a loss of power throughout the ship. Immediately, the large ship glided to a halt.

None of this was lost on the Harpoon Coastal Defense System commander, who let loose five more Harpoon missiles after seeing the ship dead in the water. The CO knew doing so was dangerous because it again exposed his position to Chinese radar. As the missiles left their launchers, he quickly gave the order to his squadron to pack and run so they could relocate to a new location. Unfortunately, his instincts and training were correct—his radar detected a PLAAF Shenyang J-15 lighting up his area with its targeting radar. Seconds later, two YJ-83KH land-attack missiles came in at Mach 2, killing and destroying everyone and everything that had been Squadron 10.

Despite losing the brave crew, the five Harpoon missiles raced toward the now defenseless destroyer in sea-skimming mode, directed in by GPS and their internal radar. But while the *Lhasa* couldn't fight back, the ship was close to the Chinese mainland where an air defense battery of HQ-16 missiles, with four launch vehicles and their two radar vehicles, quickly obtained a firing solution from their computers. With their vertical launchers upright behind a 6x6 high-mobility truck, the crew was prepared and fired six missiles. The HQ-16 was well-designed and could destroy both high-flying targets and sea-skimming missiles.

One advantage the Harpoon missiles had was their ability to evade defenses and get lost in the clutter of the ocean by flying as low as four feet above sea level. Using inertial guidance and semiactive radar homing at the terminal phase, the surface-to-air missiles went to Mach 2.5 toward the much slower Harpoon missiles, which did have a head start. As the five missiles closed on the destroyer, the HQ-16 missiles struck two Harpoons. But three evaded detection and slammed into the stationary ship, lifting it out of the water and breaking it in half. As it crashed back into the sea, the ship quickly sank, taking all but twenty-six of the crew of 311 to the bottom of the South China Sea.

"Thou shalt give life for life, eye for eye, tooth for tooth, hand for hand, foot for foot," says the scripture in the Book of Exodus. War knows no civility.

# Chapter 79

*USS OREGON*
East China Sea

"Helm, Conn," said Captain Colleen Panchak. "Come to bearing one-eight-six, speed 5 knots. Make your depth one-five-zero."

At the same time, Oregon took up an attack position. As her order was repeated like a long-drawn-out echo, she took the sub to a spot in the East China Sea labeled Sierra 2-6. It was a block of water on a map that the CO of the USS Jefferson knew would contain one friendly submarine, just as Panchak understood that the Jefferson was in Block Sierra 4-5 with them right now. Any contact outside the two blocks would be considered hostile. *Jefferson* had reconnoitered the area and was lying in wait, as quiet as a church mouse, using passive sonar to look for any nearby PLAN submarines that might want to crash the party.

"WSO, Conn. Prepare all VLS tubes for launch."

*Oregon* had a vertical launch system payload of twelve BGM-109 Tomahawk missiles. Working with her weapons officer, Panchak ensured that the appropriate number of Tomahawks were armed with one thousand-pound warheads, guaranteeing a roughly twenty-foot-wide crater while destroying everything in the area. Several more missiles were armed with a package of 166 cluster bombs, and others had new enhanced penetration warheads with blast fragmentation. The two additional configurations would enable the Tomahawks to attack soft targets such as parked aircraft and vehicles, plus hardened targets like the newly built munition bunkers and the hardened aircraft structures at Longtian.

"WSO, Conn, fire when ready."

After four seconds, "Conn, WSO. Weapons away,"

As soon as all the missiles were fired, the captain didn't waste any time. "Helm, Conn. Flank speed, course two-four-eight, depth four hundred."

With the flick of a button on his four-button, two-axis joystick, the sub-pilot executed the captain's command.



During World War II, targets were primarily destroyed by high-flying bombers, but the devastation in Taiwan was initially carried out by missiles. While ROC forces saved Leshan Radar Station, the remainder of the country suffered through one of the most significant bombardments of a nation in history, including Ukraine. The PLA had decades of intelligence and comprehensive targeting coordinates to program their missiles to shoot from the ground or a fighter against the military infrastructure of Taiwan.

The first wave of attacks were cruise missiles used by the PLARF for SEAD to take out critical radar and air defense systems, communication facilities, vital fuel and weapons depots, Air Force bases, and runways. Simultaneously, China used high-powered microwave and laser weapons to destroy computer hardware and electronic systems, weakening Taiwan's information domination and situational awareness.

Leading the aerial assault were the PLAAF's new J-16 electronic attack fighters alongside J-20 and J-10 jets. All three types of aircraft were outfitted with computer-controlled AESA radars. The systems allowed the pilots to improve communications and detect enemy fighters and other threats sooner.

The flight lead for another critical mission was Major Chang Huang in a freshly refueled and rearmed J-20, who was fresh off the destruction of the ROC presidential convey and the president of Taiwan. Once again, he and his squadron would target Taiwanese government entities in the Zhongzheng District. According to Chinese spies working inside the building, some of the mission's fourteen aircraft flew toward the Executive Yuan, where the ROC's premier was reported. Some of the PLAAF pilots had the Legislative Yuan and its 113 legislators in their sights, along with the Ministry of Foreign Affairs and the Ministry of Economic Planning. The mission makeup was four J-16 fighters, six J-20s, and four J-10s.

"Jaeger 1, Max 10," said a young Chinese pilot flying his J-16 in harm's way for the first time. "Initiating jamming and electronic suppression."

"Max 10, Jaeger 1. Roger." Hopefully, thought Major Chang, the ROC's air-defense missile bases and radar systems situated around the government buildings would be impacted. The fighters' electromagnetic systems created many indistinguishable, confusing signals for radar operators to decipher. To them, it would appear that there were more incoming aircraft than existed. With so many apparent threats, the ROC commanders would hesitate to assign defensive missiles to so many fighters—they would be confused about which ones to shoot at and how many missiles to use.

The missiles were equipped with passive radar seekers and two-hundred-pound blasting warheads. While the squadron of fighters approached Taipei, electromagnetic systems mounted on each wing tip of the J-16s efficiently analyzed the radar frequencies that ROC search radars emitted. As the computers on board the J-16s analyzed this information, firing coordinates were programmed to each aircraft's six YJ-91 antiradiation warheads.

The Taiwanese radar operators protecting the Zhongzheng District were in a Catch-22 situation. Their SAMs needed radar to identify, track, and attack incoming air threats. But by lighting up the sky with their emitting radar, they provided missile coordinates for the enemy. The survivability of the critical radar sites was consequently short-lived. But the ROC Army, having years to refine and strategize counter-missile tactics, their answer was numbers. With scores of radar and missile sites spread out around the country, Taiwan used many sites to counter the incoming threats while preserving other concealed locations by keeping those radars turned off—the porcupine effect. Taiwan authorities understood that the longer they could survive the first surge from the PRC, the better the chances the United States would have time to respond.



*LONGTIAN AIR BASE*
Fujian Province, China

Lieutenant General Xuan Chun, the Eastern Theater Commander of the PLAAF, felt the stress of a war still in its infancy. It didn't help that he had the president's son-in-law on another risky mission to the heart of Taiwan. This worried him. He knew all too well if you failed in your duties with the current regime, you didn't get a second chance. Instead, you would be accused of corruption and, without a trial, find yourself in prison or with a bullet to the head.

Xuan was proud of the hundreds of sorties in Taiwan's ADIZ. Over the past year, his pilots had flown brazen flights to test Taiwan's response. The data collected provided the PLAAF with the information they needed for the actual combat missions they had been flying since the war started.

The general was in his usual seat in the administration building overlooking the runway where his aircraft were coming and going like so many bees to a hive. He was elated; everything was going according to plan. As a smile formed on his lips, an excited voice reverberated through the room, changing everything in his life, "missiles inbound! Sir, fifty-one Tomahawks. Defensive fire implemented, sixty HQ-9s."

Xuan was quick to respond. "I want all aircraft airborne immediately. Radar, find me the source of these missiles."

"Yes, general. Radar indicates inbound missiles were fired from a submarine."

The battle of technology was a gigantic aerial battle of numbers and situational awareness. The Tomahawk cruise missiles were multi-tasking, searching out their targets and attempting to jam and evade the Chinese HQ-9 missiles that were intent on destroying them. There were always winners and losers in this tit-for-tat confrontation. It was ultimately a simple equation. One side would eventually prevail, and the losing side could only hope to eliminate as many missiles as possible.

With the sky over Longtian illuminated by multiple explosions of losers, a winner began to emerge. Numerous US missiles penetrated the umbrella of defensive missiles. Two Tomahawks with bunker-penetrating warheads struck two of the five concrete munitions storage shelters. A massive secondary explosion took out a third bunker. The resulting shock wave knocked General Xuan from his chair as he smacked his head on his desk on the way to the floor. As he got up, bloodied but alive, Tomahawk missiles, each armed with 166 cluster bombs, hit the runways. One of the missiles penetrated the Administration Building, killing most inside, including Lieutenant General Xuan Chun.

Also struck was one of the four hardened aircraft shelters, destroying several planes. With the large runway filled with craters from the cluster bombs, no aircraft would be taking off or landing anytime soon.


*ZHONGZHENG DISTRICT*
Taipei, Taiwan

People in Taiwan were not accustomed to seeing or hearing jet fighters scrambling around their skies. No, if it wasn't a parade or some important holiday, strolling citizens listened to the sound of horns, not afterburners. Today was different. They were under attack and had been since their beloved president was killed by Chinese fighter jets.

For the casual observer, it was strange, perhaps surreal, to see town folk stop what they were doing and reach in their pockets for a government-issued thirty-page handbook with QR codes to direct them to bomb shelters and water or food if things got out of hand. The small pamphlet also told valuable military reservists where to report. With the sounds of explosions all around them, now was the time for a country to take cover.

Hidden multiple stories deep inside the earth, in Alpha Tower of the Heng Shan Military Command Center, was the president of Taiwan, Chen Guang, who was thought to be a dead man but was receiving and giving orders as quickly as they came flooding in. His safety in the reinforced bunker was the only certainty during the war.

Designed to withstand a twenty-kiloton nuclear blast, the bunker had state-of-the-art tactical systems, fiber optics, emergency power generators, and a water supply. Despite this, even hundreds of feet underground, the bunker protecting the president and his staff shook from the bombs falling on the Zhongzheng District.

Flying twenty-five thousand feet above the president of Taiwan were twelve of the PLAAF's most elite fighters doing everything in their power to kill every single government official in the sprawling government building complex.

"All units, Jaeger 1. Missiles away," directed Major Chang.

Guided missiles attempting to strike his fighter had to aim ahead while anticipating where he would be when they caught up to the plane. Pilots like Chang were experts in exploiting this fact by continually maneuvering. Hitting the countermeasures trigger while making an extreme turn, he sent out twin streamers of brightly burning flares to confuse any heat-seeking warheads that might be taking to the sky. The missiles did the same but with one caveat. With only so much fuel, it didn't take long before the tanks went empty, forcing the missiles to go on pure momentum, quickly burning off speed and distance.

"Jaeger 1, Jaeger 2. I got a missile lock on me. Evading."

In the background of that transmission, Chang could hear the sound all pilots dreaded, the *beep* of a missile lock blasted through the cockpit. There was nothing Chang could do but sneak a peek, and he saw Jaeger 2 race down toward the mountains, exchanging the danger of the ground with that of an ever-closing missile. It didn't work. Chang caught a glimpse of his friend and wingman for the past year blown apart by a missile. In seconds what was left of a J-20 fifth-generation fighter disintegrated as it struck the side of a mountain. It would be one fireball Chang would never forget.

While inflicting severe damage to the collection of government buildings and, hopefully, their leaders, the PLAAF pilots saw numerous smoke trails emerging through the fog of battle, missiles aimed at them. Like a heavy-weight boxing match, the ROC forces took blow after blow to their chins while holding back their rights. With eleven fighters preparing for another run, Taiwan's right fist exploded in the form of ROC missiles, which had been silent to preserve their stealth. It pounded the enemy with scores of Hawk and Sky Bow surface-to-air missiles. The small island was trying hard for a knockout blow against its much larger, heavy-weight opponent.

Busy with their targeting radars, Major Chang and his squadron quickly switched to survival mode as a fresh onslaught of missiles headed their way. Never had any of the fighter pilots, the best in China, witnessed so many missiles rising from the Earth on a singular mission to destroy them. Like Jaeger 2, all the fighters were spiked hard. The *beep—beep—beep* warnings filled their eardrums, telling them they were about to die if they didn't do everything right in the next few seconds. It was a confrontation between missiles and fighters. Killer missiles screamed in at Mach 2, leaving no room for pilot error.

With over 250 buttons and controls in their cockpits, choices had to be made as fast as reflexes could respond. For some, they were too slow. In most cases, how quickly a pilot made decisions meant the difference between life and death. Chang was extremely fast.

As the jets made evasive maneuvers, most pilots hit their countermeasures switches, releasing flares and chaff. The bursts created a large infrared heat signature for heat-seeking missiles. At the same time, the chaff bloomed into a large radar signature to hopefully hide the aircraft within the disguise. But it was hard to hide with so many missiles filling the sky. Pulling high g's as Chang evaded the missiles, his vision started graying out as blood was being forced from his brain, even while his G-suit squeezed tightly against his body's muscles. He took short, forceful breaths, almost like a cough. Glancing down at his Vertical Situation Display, Chang saw his squadron mates were overwhelmed. The screen had letters and number codes indicating too many missiles to continue the mission. Punching up his comm net, he said, "Squad 11, abort, abort, abort. Evade back to base."

Looking past his right wing, Chang glimpsed two J-20s get hit almost simultaneously. What was left of the two fighters drifted in a fiery ball back to Earth. When it was over, only five of the twelve aircraft of Squadron 11 survived. Such numbers were unacceptable to Chang, no matter how much damage they had inflicted on the Zhongzheng District.

*USS RONALD REAGAN, USS NIMITZ, USS GERALD R. FORD Task Force-70*
Philippine Sea

Anyone who set eyes on the deck and catapults of the USS *Nimitz* wouldn't hesitate to write it off as a casualty of war. But given five minutes with the ship's Captain, "Hard Ass" Samson, that same individual would be frantically searching for a wrench to lend a hand, another person convinced the carrier could be brought back online.

With the smoke still smoldering from the Chinese ballistic missile hit, Samson had received a battle damage assessment report from his chief engineer, Tom Ringwald, whom he ordered to "throw the damn peacetime repair book overboard" and "give me something that can be done to the gaping hole in the flight deck in twenty-four hours." Within hours of the missile hitting his ship, Samson sent a repair order to Naval Sea Systems Command.

Fortunately, on orders from the Secretary of Defense, the US Pacific Fleet had just completed setting up an Expeditionary At-Sea Repair program with specialists and repair equipment in fifteen field offices throughout the Pacific. As part of the program's delivery system, two specially modified C-130s, with smaller nose-landing gear and improved anti-skid braking systems, could do carrier landings. The aircraft could transport 12.5 tons of cargo, travel 2,500 miles, and then land on and take off from a carrier.

Less than twenty-four hours after the missile struck the *Nimitz*, the first of two C-130s was unloading valuable cargo aboard the USS *Gerald R. Ford*. Just as quickly, helicopters were scurrying between the carriers delivering Captain Samson's "special order." As soon as the cargo hit the deck of the *Nimitz*, Chief Engineer Ringwald had his work party begin patching the gigantic hole. Overlooking everything was Samson with his signature shit-eating grin spread across his face.



After the four American B-2 bombers completed their missions against mainland China, they flew to the Navy Support Facility on the British-owned island of Diego Garcia in the middle of the Indian Ocean. The crews were thrilled after destroying several of China's over-the-horizon radar installations.

The aircraft commander, Major Dakota "Cowboy" Remy, was squirming in his seat as he always did. His cowboy ass was getting too old and rickety for this crap. While he loved to fly his beloved B-2, he sure as hell didn't like sitting for nearly twenty hours. "I must say, Go To, I sure love being above snakes."

"What's that supposed to mean?"

"Come on, boy, above the snakes is what my daddy told me many times late in his life. It means it's great being above ground. You city boys crack me up. By the way, how long before we reach our home away from home?"

Go To looked at the only other person on the bomber, shrugged his shoulders, and said, "Ten minutes out to Diego, Cowboy. But you already knew that."

Returning his glance, Cowboy said, "Okay, tell me something I don't know. Like, why the shit are we landing there instead of at Wake, where we left a day ago?"

"I swear you're getting senile. Again, in case you forgot, we're at war with China. Capisce? The dudes with more stars than you will ever wear have decided it makes sense to spread out our bombers all over the Pacific. We drew a straw for Diego, and here we come. By the way, five minutes out. Turning over control. You have the aircraft."


Paracel Islands, South China Sea

Only seven hundred miles from Taiwan but much closer to mainland China, Woody Island was, after a hard-fought battle, quite literally a strategic centerpiece for the United States. Consequently, USINDOPACOM made it a high priority to reinforce the tiny island immediately. With the runway still operable, the only question was how to get the critical supplies past the nose of the PLA.

An informed President, Mark Taylor, understood the importance of a supply spearhead in the Indo-Pacific region when relations with China were deteriorating. Behind the scenes, the president, working with the Philippine government under the 2014 Enhanced Defense Cooperation Agreement, put some teeth into a slow-moving process by sending his Secretary of State, Brad Kelly, to prod select influential government officials. What could be achieved by asking "What do you need to make this work" in person was incredible. With orders from Taylor to grant the Philippine officials almost anything they needed; bureaucratic roadblocks were quickly swept aside. And the United States secretly built up the Antonio Bautista Air Base in Puerto Princesa, Province of Palawan. Hidden from view in newly built warehouses and existing buildings that were suddenly made available to the US, most everything needed for Woody Island and the rest of the Pacific was stored at the massive new complex.

A load of twenty-five Naval Strike Missiles, Tomahawk missiles, and their Oshkosh Ground Unit transports were quickly flown to Woody by a fleet of C-17s shadowed by fighter escorts from

Antonio Bautista. Added to the flights were goodies for the sixteen F-22s that we're now calling Woody Island home. All combined, the Americans on the island would have a chance of survival despite being just a few hundred miles from China.



The 12,100-foot runway at Kadena Air Base was far from perfect. Chief Master Sergeant Horace Washington Smith was exhausted—as were his much younger RED HORSE airmen. Looking down the runway, Smith shoved the brim of his hat up to better take it all in. Compared to what it was just a day earlier, with more craters than he cared to remember, he was incredibly proud of his 401 men and women. They had answered the call to get America's aircraft back in the air—from his runway. Their training and exercises had paid off.

"Tower, Red Horse 1," Smith's black forearm glistened with sweat. "The runway is ready for whatever you want to throw at it. Give us a minute to clear our gear and get out of the way."

"Red Horse 1, Woody 1," replied the base commander instead. "I can't believe the job you and your crew just completed. This will go down in the annals of Air Force history as one of the best base recoveries—ever. What you all just did is something I will never forget. Thank you, Chief Smith, and RED HORSE!"

It was a matter of deception and sabotage that helped keep the PLARF from launching additional missiles at Kadena. Weeks before hostilities, the base commander had assigned select personnel to form a MILDEC or military deception unit. The task for the team was to develop a believable story that was simply a deception. The specialists ensured that mission information was leaked. Suppose there was a war between China and the US. In that case, USINDOPACOM planned to disperse several squadrons of B-2 bombers, F-35 fighters, and ten KC-135 and KC-130J refueling tankers from other bases in the Indo-Pacific region to Kadena. Detailed maps were drawn and "accidentally" left on an unsecured server, plans that indicated where the planes would be hidden on the base and how they would be camouflaged.

Part of the plot involved four aircraft flown to Kadena for enemy verification purposes. All four planes were being cycled out of inventory or had significant problems yet could still fly. Around these actual jets would be a score of hidden planes, props with enough of the fake aircraft revealed so that they could be identified. The story was leaked using available intelligence channels, and sources thought to be used by China.

Next, the members of RED HORSE constructed portable fuel "bombs" and dispersed them around the base to ignite them by remote control. The entire base would appear under fire if set ablaze, and all the aircraft would be struck and destroyed. Many of the fake bombs were set among the decoys. Strict security was put in place to ensure the deception remained secret.

As the ruse was being constructed, mostly at night to avoid satellite detection, the fighters and refueling tankers were dispersed to bases in Korea, Japan, and other areas, leaving a skeleton crew on Kadena.

When the missiles started to strike Kadena in the first minutes of the war, RED HORSE airmen ignited the fuel bombs, blowing up all the phony planes and starting massive fires. Base command felt confident that intelligence experts in the PLA would quickly believe their eyes and their apparent success.

With the emergency repairs completed on the runway, Kadena could use the massive base to begin a counter-offensive, at least for the immediate future.

*ZHONGNANHAI, CENTRAL HEADQUARTERS OF THE COMMUNIST PARTY*
Beijing, China

Built around two ancient lakes adjacent to the Forbidden City were the scores of buildings that comprised the Central Headquarters of the Chinese Communist Party. State leaders, including the president, who was also the general secretary, conducted day-to-day duties there to keep their massive country functioning. Many lived in the area. With the war escalating by the hour and China's attack on the infrastructure of Taiwan, the US took off the wraps on the targeting coordinates for Zhongnanhai.

With hostilities escalating, many Chinese state workers failed to show up for work, defying their president's orders to return. Fortunately for the United States, most bureaucratic bosses did return as they were told, although hidden away in underground bunkers.

With sirens blaring in ear-piercing intensity, workers scrambled for cover as two US AGM-183 hypersonic missiles made it through a maze of defensive fire. One missile incinerated the Central Headquarters, and the second struck the State Council of China's building as programmed. The resulting two-hundred-foot-high fireballs spread quickly to adjoining buildings, setting them ablaze too. Soon, the resulting fires generated their own fierce storm of damaging winds and intense heat, keeping responders at bay. The firestorm ripped through a substantial portion of the Zhongnanhai district. Within minutes of the strike, day turned to night from the blanket of smoke.

# Chapter 80



*USS Ronald Reagan, USS Nimitz, USS Gerald R. Ford Task Force-70*

Philippine Sea

Rear Admiral Robert "Bobby" Wisniewski was sitting in his chair on the Bridge of the USS *Ronald Reagan*, which sailed eight hundred miles east of China's coast. His thoughts were on his ships' crews as Task Force-70 prepared to launch 150 aircraft. It was always hard for him to get his head around the fact that he was the one giving the orders that affected the lives of over eighteen thousand men and women, many of whom were just teenagers.

But he understood that the sailors and Marines were as ready to defend their country as he was to order them into battle. Every individual answered the call to arms, as countless others had done throughout eternity.

One advantage now working for the task force was the destruction of most of China's over-the-horizon radar sites. With a three-thousand-mile detection range, the PLA could no longer supply targeting data for any enemy ship in the coverage area. This data could be programmed into "carrier killer" ballistic missiles, such as the DF-21, which had nearly sunk the *Nimitz* and had just missed the *Reagan*.

"Admiral?" A familiar voice interrupted his thoughts.

"Yes, captain?"

"Ready to launch aircraft. Waiting for your order."

The admiral looked around the Bridge and saw nothing but eager faces. "Launch aircraft."

As the last syllable drifted from his mouth, the reply from Captain Jason Roberts was an enthusiastic, "Yes, sir!"

Already airborne in the CAP protecting the task force was Lieutenant Sarah "Danger" Freeman, who had gained fame as the pilot who saved her crew after an encounter with an over-exuberant J-20 PLAAF pilot. She and her team of four were concentrating on the hundreds of targets illuminating their screens, and they couldn't wait to get into the fight along with the aircraft launching from the carriers.

Along with two other E-2s, their mission was to supply the fighters with C4ISR data to defend Taiwan. Instead of "dogfights," aircraft-to-aircraft aerial combat made popular by movies such as *Top Gun*, today's focus was situational awareness and BVR tactics so that the enemy fighters would be busy avoiding US missiles rather than the aircraft that fired them.

Freeman would not only do CAP duties but also be responsible for northern Taiwan, while the other E-2s were assigned to central and southern Taiwan. In this counterstrike by allies of Taiwan—the United States, Japan, and Korea—all their efforts were focused on engaging the surge of PLAAF fighters swarming all over Taiwan and denying the enemy air superiority.

Key to the Allied mission was the ability to keep so many jets from going bingo on fuel. Fortunately for the allies, Australia had allowed the United States to build a massive base called the East Arm Fuel Storage Facility near Darwin on the very northern tip of the country. The new base had over seventy-nine million gallons stored, allowing plenty of fuel to go around.

The US had four hundred tanker aircraft, making it the largest aerial refueler fleet on the planet. The rest of the world had two hundred and fifty tankers, with the PLAAF having around thirty. Staying behind the line of battle, the string of US tankers would significantly increase the ranges of the attacking fighters and support aircraft.

Having completed hooking up with a Boeing KC-130 to top off his fuel, flight lead Lieutenant Commander Dick "Mad Dog" Johnson flew his F-35 along with seven others from the *Ford*, America's newest aircraft carrier and the namesake of its class.

Accompanying Mad Dog's flight were ten Gladiators from VFA-106 flying the F/A-18E/F Super Hornet. Lieutenant Jessie

Hampton was bringing up the rear of the Gladiators' formation, fresh out of advanced flight school and participating in his first combat mission.

Throughout his life, it was rare that Hampton was ever last; on the contrary, the five-foot-eight jock was blessed with unshakable determination and an undeniable resolve to be the best at his craft. No one who had flown with him in flight school would disagree—he was a generational pilot. His lightning-fast reactions and critical thinking skills put him in a league of his own, and his only glitch was that he knew it and had difficulty disguising that fact. He even walked like he was the best pilot in the Navy.

As the three flights approached northern Taiwan, Mad Dog's RWR system detected radar emissions from scores of enemy fighters, including J-11 and J-20 stealth fighters. Anticipating such an encounter, Johnson had already turned down the system's volume to save his brain from being distracted by warning alarms.

"Strike flights, Freedom 21," came Freeman's voice over secure comms from her circling E-2. "Twenty-four bandits, grid zone designation 5Q-FJ three-two-four-niner. Heading zero-six-three, speed 500, flight level three-five-zero.

"Freedom 21, Boxer 11. Roger," replied Mad Dog. The surge from PLAAF bases in mainland China was expected, but it was much more than the ROC Air Force could handle using its four hundred, primarily outdated, fighters. The halt of ballistic missile launches for nearly two days had allowed US forces, especially the task force, to move just a little closer to Taiwan to launch aircraft.

As discussed in their mission briefings, Mad Dog's flight, made up of eight F-35s, was the vanguard that would penetrate the combat radius of the enemy. They would identify the aircraft through Cooperative Engagement Ability, allowing real-time sensor nets to enable high-quality situational awareness so the F/A-18s could employ BVR tactics and fire missiles to their advantage. The F-35's excellent sensors and data links made it the perfect clandestine fighter.

As Mad Dog's flight flew within the combat radius of the Chinese, they provided ISTAR—intelligence, surveillance, target acquisition, and reconnaissance—to all involved in the mission. Mad Dog began to feel an internal warning growl in his stomach, a sense earned from countless hours of training for this situation. It was time to switch from ISTAR to combat mode.

"Boxer 11 to flight. Switch to EOTS and prepare to engage." Positioned on the F-35 fuselage looking through a sapphire window and linked to the aircraft's integrated central computer by high-speed fiber optics, the Electro-Optical Targeting System's forward-looking infrared search and track functionality allowed all the pilots to identify targets for their GPS-guided and laser-guided weapons. The eight F-35 fighters each had four internal AIM-260 BVRAAMs that would target two missiles per bandit. The F/A-18s would have to target the remaining sixteen enemy fighters.



Breaking away from missions in Taiwan, Major Chang Huang and his friends had a surprise for the Americans. His flight of four J-20s was heading for an area in the Philippine Sea where their radar had spotted numerous American KC-130s refueling aircraft. If they could take out the flying gas stations, the US would have little choice but to park their expensive jets in the ocean—a one-way trip, Chang thought.

Skimming the sea at 700 mph, the four stealth J-20 fighters raced to get within ninety miles of the tankers. In each of their jets' bellies were four PL-15Es, some of China's most potent air-to-air missiles.

"Jaeger 1, to all. Target selection identified. Use three missiles, one for each tanker. Keep one for combat if needed." This is going to be one challenging mission, thought Chang.

The American tankers were a high-priority target. Consequently, they were well protected. Using their stealth, the four pilots hoped to get within range, fire their ordnance, and use their covertness to escape. Chang had confidence in his flight and their J-20s, now fitted with new powerful, redesigned Chinese engines.

In the US E-2's most forward seat in the fuselage tunnel, RO Billy Ottenberg was occupied with many targets flying every which way. But he caught a glimpse of something on his low-bandwidth VHF and UHF radar, which was the ideal tool to identify low-observable aircraft. On internal comms, he said, "L-T, I have a tentative lock on four Chinese stealth aircraft flying one-three-two, approximately ninety-five miles out, close to the surface."

Freeman understood the limits of the radar Ottenberg was using and didn't push him for specific information she knew he wouldn't have. "Following their direction of travel, are there targets in the area?"

"Yes, ma'am. I show multiple US tankers and our CAP in their direction of travel."

Freeman hurriedly spoke on a radio channel for emergencies like this: "Freedom 21 to all Tankers and CAP. You have four low-flying stealth bandits approximately ninety-five miles due west of your location. The closest friendlies to intercept are Victor 29 and Victor 30."

On the E-2's internal comms, Freeman said, "Good job Ottenberg. Stay on it."

For the first time in his young career, the RO felt a tinge of pride that he was catching on to all this craziness.


Philippine Sea

"Victor 29, Victor 21. You and your wingman break from formation and engage bandits heading for the tankers. Break. All others in the flight, prepare to engage the enemy."

Hampton's wingman slammed his stick over, pulling a 9G turn. Hampton did the same. The only things keeping the two pilots conscious were their G-suits.

As Hampton made his turn, he couldn't believe his good fortune. He was about to engage four J-20 stealth fighters—the best of the PLAAF against the new Block III F/A-18E Super Hornet. He felt confident about his role and his aircraft.

Working in their favor, the Hawkeye had given them a place to look as they pointed their new centerline tank-mounted infrared search track systems in the last known direction of the bandits. IRST was a stealth equalizer capable of locating the enemy from one hundred miles out. It was a passive system that didn't alert the enemy and enabled offensive air engagements when radar was not an option. In the process, IRST balanced the spreadsheet between fourth-generation and fifth-generation fighters in the battlespace.

As they flew west at thirty thousand feet, both Super Hornet pilots heard a sound in their headsets that indicated target locks. Efficiently, as only computers could be, targeting solutions from the AN/ASQ-228 Advanced Targeting Forward-Looking Infrared Radars were instantly sent to AIM-120Ds with the F3R upgrade for improved guidance circuitry and software.

"Victor 30, target bandit one and two. I have three and four. Fire two missiles at fifteen-second separation."

"Roger, Victor 29. On your command."

"Fire one," said Victor 29.

Pushing the buttons on their sticks, both F/A-18 pilots fired their missiles. The missiles were released with a reduced thrust, and then they pulled a sharp turn to point down at the targets and increase propulsion to intercept.

Fifteen seconds later, Victor 29 said, "Fire two."

As the four missiles closed to self-homing distance, their onboard active radars guided them toward four fleeing J-20s.

*PLAAF CHENGDU J-20 FLIGHT*
Philippine Sea

All four PLAAF pilots simultaneously heard the dreaded *beep* indicating a missile lock on them. Immediately, they released chaff while using defensive maneuvers to evade the incoming AMRAAMs.

With the beeping in the background, Major Chang quickly broadcasted, "Evade and fire missiles."

As he eluded the AMRAAMs, Chang checked his AESA radar, infrared search, and track system to see who was trying to kill him. Flying almost vertically to fifty thousand feet, Chang got an ID from his RWR—two F-18 fighters had separated and were fleeing.

Chang released more chaff and activated his jamming system. His objective was to bleed off the speed of the perusing missile. He knew it was a trade-off, painting him and sending data that might confuse the inbound missile. Expertly, he rolled his J-20 on its back and dove for the sea's surface using a snaking maneuver.

As Chang fought to stay alive, two other J-20 fighters were struck by the AIM-120Ds. Flaming wreckage scattered all over the Philippine Sea. The fourth fighter, Jaeger 3, watched the missiles chasing him run out of fuel and crash into the sea. Jaeger 3 went to twenty thousand feet and fired three PL-15E missiles at the tankers and, just as quickly, turned back toward the mainland, happy to have survived but failing to remain to support Jaeger 1.

Having outlasted the AMRAAMs, Chang made visual contact with the American F-18s maneuvering outside the kill zone of Chang's brothers, who had just been shot down. In a split second, he decided the tankers could wait. First up was the pilot of the F-18 that had killed two of his comrades. Chang went vertical with no other threat warning on his RWR, flying above his enemy, who was making a sweeping high-g turn. Chang wanted to get inside the American's turn to put his nose on him and fire his PL-10 short-range missile.

*TWO BOEING F/A-18E SUPER HORNETS*
Philippine Sea

Both Super Hornet pilots caught a glimpse of two J-20 fighters bursting apart and crashing into the sea.

"Victor 30, stay with bandit one. I'm after Bandit 3. Good luck."

"Same to you, brother."

Watching the J-20 dodge one of America's best-designed air-to-air missiles, Lieutenant Jessie Hampton wasted no time and went into attack mode—just like his enemy did at that exact moment. Both fighters were now at fifty thousand feet, performing a two-circle flow, each attempting to gain an angular advantage over their opponent. Hampton felt confident his Super Hornet had a higher turn rate at its corner speed. Both aircraft were rolling their fighters in a direction below the horizon, pulling max g's, continuing in a spiral toward the ocean. Each was trying to take advantage of exchanging altitude for speed and compute the ideal speed to get a nose on his adversary.

Hampton was snapping his head around in the cockpit to keep his eyes on the J-20 while pulling high g's. He knew that losing sight of his enemy would prove fatal. From his dogfighting days in flight school, Hampton understood his specific optimal cornering velocity would give him the greatest rate of turn to maximize his F-18's maneuverability. To him, it was second nature; he had refined getting his enemy into his missile no-escape zone. But he thought this is one hell of a pilot I'm trying to kill. As they spiraled toward the ocean, Hampton's instincts told him he was close to his most advantageous shooting position.

He slammed his fighter to the right, released infrared countermeasures, and hit the switch on his stick, letting loose with one AIM-9 Sidewinder, a supersonic, heat-seeking missile. After the missile jumped off the rack, Hampton went to afterburners to get out of his no-escape zone. His threat warning radar went off as he did so, telling him he had a PL-10 short-range infrared homing missile searching him out. Hampton hit his IR countermeasures switch again, letting out numerous flares as he started evasive maneuvers.

Having just defeated one of America's most deadly missiles, Chang was thrown into a dogfight with an F-18. He was maneuvering his fighter downward, trying to get inside the circle he was making with the F-18 to get a kill shot. Dogfighting hailed from the days of World War I, but while most countries trained less and less for the encounters, Chang had never stopped. In today's world, it comes down to using countermeasures and tactics. Countermeasures were equalizers; tactics were all about a pilot's skill. Chang was sure of one thing. Whoever was flying the Hornet was good—but he knew he was better if only his fighter could hold up.

Chang was keen on his situational awareness, continuously slamming high G turns to gain an advantage, his head on a swivel. When he saw an opportunity, he fired one of his PL-10 missiles. He heard a loud whoosh as the short-range infrared-homing air-to-air missile left his internal rack. He used the missile's high off-boresight capability and kept his nose constantly on the target so the warhead could lock on. The PL-10 had the latest IR sensor that targeted an aircraft based on its shape, a method impervious to flares or chaff.

Chang's MAWS alerted, telling him an AIM-9 was targeting him.

He changed tactics and went to his J-20's new Thrust-Vector Controls, which tilted the exhaust nozzles of his twin jet engines and allowed him to perform a very high angle of attack maneuver to get his nose at an angle that greatly exceeded the plane's current vector. Pulling his nose up vertically, his J-20 came to a sudden mid-air "stop," and the missile flew past him. Jamming the stick forward, Chang went for the deck, got just feet off the sea, then quickly turned and went vertical, pulling the same stunt again. It worked as the AIM-9 flew past him again, using up all its energy and fuel.

Just then, Chang saw a massive fireball as the F-18 went up in flames. Sorry, kid, he thought, you messed with the wrong pilot. His second thought was to get back to the mainland as he was bingo on fuel.



Hampton was making several high-g turns, attempting to evade the PL-10 missile and praying it would use up its fuel. Suddenly, his MAWS told him the deadly missile had a lock. Beating a PL-10 when locked on was nearly impossible since technology now trumped a pilot's defensive skills. Looking at his helmet-mounted HUD, Hampton saw he had seconds until the missile blew him out of the sky. Quickly, he reached over and, with his adrenaline pumping through his body, pulled the looped yellow and black ejection seat handle. An electrical pulse traveled to twin thrusters under his seat, blasting him at 18 g's like a human rocket into the air at sixteen thousand feet, where he met a wall of air from his flying speed of 650 mph. Immediately, Hampton felt restraining straps wrap around his arms and legs as an emergency oxygen supply was released. When he hit the force of the atmosphere, it felt like twenty huge men were stomping on his chest in unison. He couldn't breathe for a second and thought he was about to die.

Hampton fought blacking out by biting his tongue and immediately tasted blood. A parachute opened in less than three seconds, triggering a bell crank that pulled the ends off his seat belts to allow the seat to fall away. Hampton couldn't believe how quiet it got as the parachute stopped his fall. Thinking he might make it, he saw his jet—the same jet he was flying just seconds ago—turn into a gigantic fireball. The heat and flames reached out for him, but only by God's will did Hampton survive.

As he saw the Philippine Sea below him, a twenty-five-foot line with his survival kit dropped below him. When the line hit the water, the kit's raft automatically inflated. Silently, Hampton thanked the Almighty for still being conscious and not missing any extremities. Then he noticed his right boot was missing. As he looked down, expecting to see only a stump, Hampton was elated to see his bare foot, which had to be as white as his face.



The KC-130 refuelers were making sure to stay out of PLAAF missile range after topping off the aircraft involved in the mission. The tanker pilots were leery of more PL-15s like the one fired at them in their refueling track, but they were out of range: one thing the crews noticed was there were fewer aircraft to fill.

The reason was straightforward—war. This battle had been BVR combat between the PLAAF, the US Navy, the ROC Air Force, and a sprinkling of Korean and Japanese fighters—all clashing from a distance, some up close and personal, to obliterate each other and gain air superiority, the golden grail of winning. As pilots liked to say, let the other bastard die for their country.

*Reagan* had a boatload of pilots that went by that motto. One of those was Lieutenant Lucy Wu, lead pilot of the MH-60R Sea Hawk helicopter; Lucy and her crew consisted of her copilot, ATO Greg "Wild Dog" Giesen, and her SAR, Naval Aircrewman (Helicopter) Third Class Liam Javernick. To his credit, Javernick was a nugget with one confirmed rescue of a downed pilot. He took a lot of jeering because his recovery was a Chinese fighter pilot.

Wu and her crew were monitoring comms at the edge of their westernmost deployment zone. Set up for search and rescue; they expected to be called in at any time to rescue a downed pilot. They were correct.

"Ramrod, Starlight. PLB transmission just received. Coordinates sent. Proceed at best speed—it's one of our F-18 pilots."

"Starlight, Ramrod. Roger."

Lucy knew that at a max speed of 180 knots and a distance of four hundred miles, the flight would be nearly two hours plus another air refuel. She would attempt to shave off minutes wherever she could because she visualized an American pilot being tossed around in a small raft by an unforgiving sea.

The PLAAF was closing rapidly on the mainland of Taiwan as Mad Dog Johnson confirmed that the range of his radar was set at sixty-five miles and that the search altitude was above twenty-five thousand feet. He verified that his electronic countermeasures pod was activated and that his flares and chaff were armed. Check, check, check, and check. The entirety of his flight had adjusted their pattern to avoid certain angles of the enemy's search radars. Avoiding those zones made them less likely to be detected.

During their mission brief aboard the *Ford*, it was decided to launch their AIM-260s from fifty-five miles. The pilots agreed they would launch flying at just over Mach 1 to give the missiles the best chance kinetically to fly their most extended range at a fifteen-degree angle and provide the deadly missiles with some loft. Two missiles would be fired ten miles apart to take advantage of the enemy using up a great deal of force to avoid the first AIM-260s heading for them at Mach 5, making them more vulnerable to the second missiles.

Using collaborative data, both networked and third-party sensors plus the radar on the E-2, the F-35s didn't have to have a radar lock on the enemy, allowing them a measure of safety. After singling out Chinese targets, the eight F-35s knew their exact objectives.

"Boxer 11 to flight. Standby to launch… Launch." Mad Dog ordered. Being fire-and-forget missiles, the AIM-260s began their journeys using inputted coordinates, and they quickly sought out their targets using their onboard radars. Knowing that the enemy would immediately return fire with their missiles, the eight fighters turned to distance themselves from any possible inbound missiles, many of which would likely be the PL-15.

Almost immediately, pilots were calling out inbound missiles. Mad Dog and the flight made evasive ninety-degree turns, forcing the missiles to maneuver against them. The pilots dove to the deck and then accelerated to fifty thousand feet, all the time making high-g turns. The air quickly filled with chaff as the F-35s employed electronic countermeasures.

The PL-15 missiles closed at supersonic speeds using improved detection ranges and double-pulse solid rocket motors. Utilizing their anti-jamming data links, the Chinese BVR air-to-air missiles made it a formidable survival task for the F-35s.

The missiles from both sides used their two-way data links, constantly receiving information from the fighters and early warning aircraft.

Meanwhile, the E-2 radar continuously tracked the targets and updated the fighters by data link. Quickly, the advantage shifted to the Americans, who had fired their missiles first. As the Chinese fighters fought to defeat the AIM-260 missiles, much of the information they received could not be used while they fought to stay in the sky.

Surviving air-to-air missile attacks has much to do with a pilot's skill, regardless of their country. Technology plays an enormous part, but it's a pilot's competence to use the technology that separates the aces from a gravestone. On the battlefield of the heavens, skill was of paramount importance. Of the twenty-four bandits, eighteen of the PLAAF fighters were shot from the sky. Three of the eight F-35s were shot down, and five of the ten F/A-18s were obliterated. Such numbers were enormous losses for both air forces.

As the Chinese survivors returned to their home bases, the US fighters turned around and hooked up with the tankers before proceeding on the long flight back to the *Ford*. For Mad Dog Johnson, the mission had been mentally exhausting. The major was saddened at losing his wingman when a PL-15 found him skimming the sea. The vision of his buddy's F-35 tumbling in a fireball over the ocean was a sight he would never blot out.

With most of her assigned aircraft heading back to their ships, Lieutenant Sarah "Danger" Freeman made a wide arching turn to do the same. Two other E-2s would stay on station to assist the aircraft still in the fight. As she went through the steps of returning to the *Reagan*, Freeman, like everyone else on the plane, was disheartened by the loss of life. Each sailor aboard felt they could have done better. With so many missiles fired by hundreds of aircraft, it was nearly impossible to identify and call out each target—no matter how hard they tried. None of them had ever experienced the depths of war or the horror, at least not like this.

Lost in her thoughts, everything she was doing was muscle memory. Coming to twenty thousand feet, she leveled the aircraft and was about to put it on autopilot when alarms began sounding in the cockpit. She quickly identified a red blinking light, telling her she had a fire on engine number one. As she peered out her left window, she saw smoke and flames, seemingly growing by the second. It didn't look good.

"Rogers," she said to the copilot, "initiate the controls for the fire extinguisher."

Quickly, Rogers hit the switch for engine one's fire extinguisher. Freeman looked out the window, nothing. If anything, the fire was expanding and appeared to be impacting the left wing.

Reducing power and fighting for control, Freeman dialed the emergency channel and announced, "Mayday, Mayday, Mayday. This is Freedom 21. I have a fire on engine one that is spreading. I'm at eighteen thousand feet and descending for a possible ditch. We are transmitting our GPS location now."

"Freedom 21, Ranger," responded *Reagan*. "We copy. Computing ETA. We have one asset in your vicinity, a Sea Hawk, call sign Ramrod, on a rescue mission for a downed pilot. Stand by."

"Ranger, Freedom 21. Copy. We are descending through thirteen thousand feet. Fire is intensifying. Control becoming more difficult." Freeman clicked the mic for internal comms and said, "CICO, prepare for ditching. Begin your checklist and implement."

"Roger that, L-T."

As she looked out the cockpit window, Freeman saw it would be close. Either she got the aircraft down now, or they would be forced to evacuate the plane. She knew from experience that bailing wasn't a good choice. No, she thought, I'm going to land this puppy on the sea, and we'll take our chances there.

"Okay, guys," she said. "Hang on. I must get this plane down on the surface now, or bad things will happen."

She pushed the yoke forward, increasing their rate of descent from controlled panic to oh shit mode. She watched as the sea rose to meet her, and the altimeter, spinning and spinning toward zero, confirmed what her eyes told her was true.

Fortunately for them, the seas were relatively calm, with only occasional swells. Freeman marveled at how things looked so different a few feet above the sea.

"Prepare for ditch," she ordered. "CICO, open aft hatch. After we stop, everyone grab a life vest and get your asses out of this plane. Okay, standby . . . hang on, here we go."

With her speed just above stall, she flashed back to flight school, where the instructor hammered away with the essential axiom for a water landing, "AVOID THE FACE OF A SWELL." As she was taught, Freeman cut power, aimed for the top of a slight swell, and gently lowered the E-2 to the surface. When the plane struck the water, everyone was amazed at how mild it felt. After the first impact, they glided along the surface with spray covering the windshield. She could feel the aircraft begin to settle down into the water once they skidded five hundred feet. Then they stopped.

Freeman yelled, "CICO, get the raft out. Everyone get their vest and exit through the escape hatch—move, move, move."

As she scrambled from her seat to follow her copilot and crew, Freeman slipped on some water, flying forward, striking her head hard on the pointy edge of some equipment. As she crumpled to the metal floor, Freeman saw everything fading to black. As she began losing consciousness, she glimpsed Rogers grabbing her. and dragging her toward the escape hatch. She could feel cold water rushing in all around her but couldn't manage to stand up. Rogers was saying something, but she couldn't understand him. With blood running into her eyes, Freeman tried to get up again but found she didn't have the strength. Then she heard yelling: but couldn't make out the words: " . . . need . . . L - T . . . help."

She could feel the warm sun on her now. Rogers kept talking, but she couldn't understand him. She felt someone's arms pulling her up and saw the light coming from the hatch. She saw an outline of what appeared to be Ottenberg, who was leaning down from the hatch, grabbing at her arms.

What was he doing?

She felt the water rushing in, lifting her toward the hatch. "On three," she managed to hear. Suddenly, she felt her body being lifted toward the blue sky and saw the look of determination on Rogers's face as he lifted her up—struggling the whole time as he lifted her body toward the hatch.

Sarah felt herself being lifted, then realized air was blowing on her face. She was no longer in the plane. Fuck, where's the plane? With that single thought echoing in her head, where's the plane, she was engulfed by blackness.

# Chapter 81



*SIKORSKY MH-60R SEA HAWK*
Philippine Sea

"Lieutenant, we just got flash comms to divert from pilot down to a Hawkeye ditching just three miles west from here."

Lieutenant Lucy Wu twisted the throttle on the collective to maximum and turned hard to the coordinates on her screen. "SAR, are you ready?"

"Yes, ma'am, suited up and ready to deploy," replied Javernick.

As the Sea Hawk came screaming to the coordinates east of Taiwan, they made visual contact with a raft. Dropping to five hundred feet, they could see three sailors waving frantically at them as the turbulence from the helo's blades rippled the sea. One of the occupants was lying at the bottom of the raft with blood smeared all over them. Offset from the raft, Wu lowered the helicopter to thirty feet as Javernick hurried over to the side door and jumped.

As quickly as he hit the sea, Javernick was swimming over to the raft. With the helo hovering overhead, he had to scream to be heard. "Tell me what we have here."

Ottenberg answered first. "We just ditched our E-2. Our pilot is unconscious and bleeding pretty good. But we're missing our co-pilot. He was helping me get the Lieutenant out of the plane when it suddenly sank with him still in it. We can't find him."

Javernick quickly gave hand signals to his crew, informing them of the missing sailor in the area and asking for the rescue basket. Soon, the four members of Freedom 21 were on board the Sikorsky. After a brief search for Rogers, the helo had to depart the area to rescue the downed pilot. Meanwhile, Javernick began rendering first aid to Freeman, who was still unconscious.

*VICTOR 30*

As Hampton gently bobbed up and down in his raft in the relatively calm Philippine Sea, he had plenty of time to relive his encounter with the J-20. Like a video recording, he played it back, reversed it, and paused it. But each time he did a review, the result was the same; he was shot down, losing out, he had to admit to a very talented Chinese fighter pilot. While most pilots would have thanked the Almighty for still being alive, Hampton was pissed that he was beaten in his first real-life dogfight. But for a man who was always at the top of everything he ever set his mind to, he swore he would learn from his mistakes.

Finally pausing his playback of the encounter, Hampton took in his surroundings. They weren't too exciting, just water, no matter what direction he looked. He had been floating for nearly three hours and was praying for a rescue and the opportunity to get back for the fight. He figured since he wasn't seriously injured, although he was a little sore all over, nothing would keep him out of his F-18.

As he was about to play his mental video again to look for the glaring error he had made, Hampton thought he heard the thumping of helicopter blades against the still ocean air. It was faint over the weighty silence of the sea. Taking his mind off the play button, he listened intently.

Yep, it was the distinct sound of a helo hauling ass, getting louder by the second. Before he could see it, Hampton waved his arms like one of those advertising windsocks at a business. Fucking A! He was getting rescued.

As the MH-60 hovered near him, Hampton thought he was about to be blown out of his tiny roofless home. Then he breathed easy when someone jumped out of the copter, landing about fifty yards away. In what seemed an instant, Hampton was looking into the eyes of the SAR, who was smiling despite the snorkel in his mouth. It was contagious. Hampton smiled back and thought, Yeah, back in the saddle soon.

Lifted skyward by a strap under his arms, Hampton slowly ascended to the aircraft. As his eyes peered into the safety of the helicopter, he was stunned to see it full of people—all in flight gear. Well, he thought, I'm not the only one who fucked up.

As he removed his rescue rig, Hampton glanced over to the corner of the aircraft and saw what appeared to be a pilot with blood all over his—no, her—uniform. He sat in the last open seat near the wounded woman. The copilot fired questions at him like a 20mm Gatling gun, and when the interrogator ran out of ammo, Hampton heard a moan. Looking over, he saw the woman stir and open her eyes.

As Lieutenant Sarah "Danger" Freeman was coming out of the blackness, the first thing she saw was something that made no sense—someone's huge white foot.

# Chapter 82

*USS NIMITZ,* Task Force-70
Philippine Sea

With his uniform soaked in sweat and dirt creeping into every crevice of his body, Captain John "Hard Ass" Samson was not supervising so much as he was adding another set of hands to his personal battle to get the USS *Nimitz* operational. Helping a sailor prop a large metal support beam into position, he heard a voice call for him.

"Captain?" echoed the voice from somewhere.

"Down here," he hesitantly replied, not wanting to be removed from the vital work. Besides, he had his XO handling the Bridge and keeping them nine hundred miles off the east coast of China. He had complete confidence in him.

Looking over his shoulder, he saw his chief engineer approaching. A sailor Samson had displaced earlier saw the captain could use some help, and he quickly moved into position to relieve his boss.

"Here, take this sailor," said Samson. With that, the sailor returned to what he was doing before the captain of the USS *Nimitz* took over his job.

"Yes, Ringwald," said Samson. "What do you have for me?"

"Sorry to bother you, sir," said Ringwald in a somewhat sheepish tone. "It's USINDOPACOM inquiring about our status with the repairs. They wanted to hear it from you, not me." He wanted to add, "Even though I'm the only one aboard this ship who understands the impossible task we're faced with," but like all good sailors, he thought better of it.

"What's your best estimate right now?" said the captain.

"Sir, if we keep the same pace that we've been maintaining, we can launch from catapult three and recover the aircraft within the next eight hours. We can continue working around the clock and maybe get catapult two up within forty-eight hours." Looking the captain square in his eyes, Ringwald said, "What our sailors are doing is nothing short of a miracle. What they've done, and will do, will go down in Naval history. Sir, I say this with all seriousness—you are the reason. Your planning and perseverance are why the *Nimitz* will go after the assholes who did this." That made the shit-eating grin grow even more on the captain's face.



Lying in the same bed in sick bay as the man who shot him down once occupied, Lieutenant Jessie Hampton was anything but the ideal patient. From the moment he entered sick bay, he made it clear to anyone who entered the room that he was fine and needed to return to the *Ford*. He questioned every poke and instrument used to test his ability to fly. But less than ideal patients weren't tolerated in the Navy, and Hampton earned a visit from the carrier's XO. It wasn't a "how you doing" visit, but a warning that he better behave, or the only thing he would be flying was a desk. The Navy had a way of doing things, and no young, arrogant fighter pilot was going to change that.

"Listen, Lieutenant Hampton," said the stern-faced second in command of the *Reagan*, "you'll spend the next twenty-four hours here for observation. You don't have a choice in the matter. Ejecting from an F-18 can cause more damage to you than you can comprehend. That's why we have doctors aboard this ship. You understand, sailor?"

"But sir—"

"Don't give me that 'but sir' crap, do you understand?"

With the XO about to explode in his face, Hampton nodded his head up and down, not wanting to actually say 'yes' to any attempt to keep him from the war.

"Excuse me, lieutenant. Was that a yes, sir?"

Timidly and without looking up, Hampton replied, "Yes, sir. Twenty-four hours, sir."

"Good, now carry on with your recovery." The XO made an about-face and was gone before Hampton realized it.

"Such bullshit," Hampton mumbled, quickly looking up to see if the XO might have somehow heard him.

In an adjoining room was another anxious sailor, Lieutenant Sarah "Danger" Freeman, who was already responding to the treatment by the best doctors *Reagan* had to offer. She reflected on the conversation she had earlier with the chief surgeon.

"Look, Lieutenant, you had one nasty fall and have what I classify as a Grade 3 concussion." His seriousness was getting her attention. "You've been in and out of consciousness. You've complained of a headache, which is to be expected. You show signs of dizziness. And you've suffered some memory loss. Your concentration isn't good, and you're a bit confused. All of this is to be expected with the type of fall you suffered, but it's something that we will have to monitor for up to forty-eight hours."

Freeman just lay there and took it all in. She watched his lips move but had difficulty concentrating on each word.

"To put it in flight terms," the surgeon added, "you won't be flying for at least two to four weeks, and then you'll gradually return to your normal activities."

She felt a tear well up and roll down her cheek, then another. It was devastating news. She was needed more than ever in a war, especially with her experience. Two to four weeks—bullshit, she thought. She would get over it sooner than that. Whatever it would take, she would be back flying in no time.

The surgeon looked down at her with an "I understand how you feel" look, touching her shoulder while telling her to rest. As his back faded from the room, she started crying, then sobbing. Giant gushes of tears flowed from the corner of her eyes. She couldn't believe it—she was being denied the one thing she lived for, flying.

Hearing a commotion from the next bay, Hampton, wearing his regulation hospital attire, headed for the sound. Peaking around the corner, he barely recognized the woman from the helicopter. She sounded like he felt, but being a tough son of a bitch, he surely wouldn't cry.

Freeman sensed someone's presence, looked up, and saw a man in pajamas. Quickly, like a faucet that was just turned off, the tears stopped, and she immediately regained her composure. She hated it when she cried. It was a sign of weakness, which she didn't have or would ever admit to.

She was pissed, and the words that followed exposed those feelings. "What the hell do you want?" she asked, followed quickly by, "And who the fuck are you anyway, standing there in pajamas in my room?"

That caught the fighter jock by surprise, which was not easy to do. "Shit, sorry, lieutenant. I heard something and wanted to make sure you were okay. You and I haven't formally met, but I was in the same rescue helicopter after my F-18 was shot down."

She let that soak in and instantly felt compassion for the man. "Sorry, lieutenant, my bad. I'm a little . . . no, I am incredibly pissed. Some doctor just told me I can't fly for two to four weeks." She caught her breath and yelled, "No way is that going to happen—not with a war going on."

"I'm sorry to hear that," he said with true conviction coming from one pilot to another, someone who completely understood the need to fly was a compulsion not many comprehended. "I was told I can't fly for a while too." Hampton didn't want to say it was just twenty-four hours for him because he liked the girl's spunk and wanted more than anything to figure out how to calm her down—to help her with the same pain he was feeling.

"Shit," Freeman replied, "there's a war going on, and they're grounding people? This sucks. I'm sorry for you too," she said with an equal amount of empathy for the same reasons. Just then, shooting pain ran through her head, more pain than she had ever experienced.

Hampton saw the anguish on her face as she closed her eyes and moaned loudly. He was out the door in a second, yelling for a

medic and feeling more emotion for that girl than he had experienced
in a long time for anything—it surprised him.

# Chapter 83

*NORTHROP GRUMMAN B-2 SPIRIT*
South China Sea

One thing you learned quickly about flying a B-2 bomber was always to be prepared for a long flight. Major Dakota "Cowboy" Remy was a believer. For flying what he considered the best bomber ever built, most flights were up to twenty hours long, some longer. He had undergone a rigorous selection procedure where personality and compatibility were paramount, among other things. With only a two-person crew, you had to have that inner strength to handle mission stress with your partner, no matter how long the flight was.

As mission commander, Captain Richard "Go To" Sullivan constantly scanned the gauges for signs of trouble. Cowboy liked his MC because he gave a shit about his darling. It was cool how much they both loved the aircraft.

Leaving Go To with his gauges, Cowboy, the aircraft commander, went over their mission in his head. A high-value target, the PLARF headquarters, had so far fought off all incoming missiles and stood intact. Intelligence indicated that the August 1st Building was destroyed. There was a good chance, President Zhang Wei, if he weren't already dead, would be holed up in the PLARF HQ building in Qinghe, in the Haidian District of Beijing. With over 120,000 personnel assigned to six missile brigades, many top dogs would no doubt be posted at the headquarters too.

With the onset of the war, China had let loose hundreds of missiles from its arsenal, considered the world's largest. The PLARF had inflicted heavy damage across the Indo-Pacific, taking out bases like Kadena and Anderson. Then, inexplicably, the missiles stopped. No explanation existed, but most felt it was only a matter of time until the missiles started flying again. Well, not if I can help it, Cowboy thought.

"Cowboy," said the MC, "approaching our target release point, six hundred miles out. Over Seoul."

He knew the answer, but Cowboy asked, "Did you verify we're in stealth mode?"

"Roger that," said Go To in his easy-going drawl. Both glanced down at the " PEN " button to ensure it was active. The penetrate enemy defenses button did a lot automatically for the pilots to make their B-2 less observable—an excellent thing since they had no escort or defensive weapons.

An alarm sounded in the aircraft, not the raise-the-hair-on-the-back-of-your-neck kind, but one that was nearly as important. Both men immediately saw what it was—the contrail warning alarm, meaning they were leaving a very noticeable contrail that was unsuitable for a stealthy B-2. Cowboy quickly adjusted their altitude, and the light went off. Always something to keep you on the edge of your seat thought Cowboy.

Once again, their B-2 was armed with twelve AGM-158 JASSM low-observable standoff cruise missiles, each with a 450-kilogram armor-piercing warhead. All twelve were targeted for the sprawling headquarters complex covering several miles around Qinghe. When both men were satisfied they had reached the point for the best probability of success, they launched the AGM-158s. As the twelve missiles dropped from the belly of the B-2, their turbofan engines ignited, and they flew away so rapidly that you couldn't have blinked, or you might have missed the beautiful sight. GPS/INS guided each with an IR seeker for terminal guidance, the three-dimensional targeting software with targeting models of all the intended targets. The highly technical missiles had a three-meter circular error probability, meaning you didn't want to be on the receiving end.


*PLARF HEADQUARTERS*
Qinghe, Haidian District of Beijing, China

About to be on the receiving end was the president of China, Zhang Wei, who had barely survived an earlier attack by an American cruise missile. A second one had hit the August 1st Building later, but he had already been whisked away to Qinghe, where the PLARF Headquarters was located. Once again, Zhang was surrounded by his command staff and was demanding answers.

"General Wang, you are several hours past a deadline you set for yourself, and I sure as hell don't see any confirmation we have our ballistic missiles launching. Before I demote you to private and put you in front of a firing squad of people that all outrank you, you have thirty seconds to explain." After a deep breath, Zhang stared through the man and yelled, "Begin—your clock is running."

You didn't become second in command of the PLA by not having contingency plans or, in this case, a survival plan. General Wang was always prepared for such harassment. He replied, "Mr. President, I share the same wants and desires for our country, to rid ourselves of the Americans, rule the Indo-Pacific region, and take back Taiwan."

After composing himself for one of his precious seconds, Wang continued, "Sir, half of our missile force is ready to launch. You may give the order at any time. Still, due to extremely technical details that I'm sure even the eminent Doctor Dong would have had trouble with, the other half of the missile force is delayed by stubborn computer code conflicts. We will have this rectified shortly."

"What do you mean half the missile force is ready to launch? How would I know that and which companies are ready?"

"Mr. President, on your computer screen, you will see a list of missile companies prepared to launch, their locations, and their targeting information—all tied into our secure comms. If you click on any one of them, the commander in the field will be automatically connected through video comms for your orders to fire missiles. All codes have been cleared from these missiles."

Zhang took a moment to study the missile-ready companies and precisely what they were preprogrammed to target. As he was about to test the system and launch, sirens began to scream, indicating incoming missiles. Alarms within the building flashed, and out of the corner of his eye, the president saw his security staff come rushing at him. What the fuck, he thought, not this bullshit again.

With that thought in mind, the largest man in his detail snatched up Zhang and ran him outside the room to the secure "President Only" elevator. They got in, and in seconds, they were shooting downward into the depths of an underground bunker made for this occasion.

Everything that was topside was also in the bunker. Duplicates of all the computers, comms, you name it, were there. Once inside the bunker, Zhang made a beeline to his computer workstation. Finally, he could launch his much-feared hypersonic cruise missiles. With his fingers hovering over his keyboard, Zhang scanned the targeting information on the screen.

Outside his enclosed world, it was again a battle of technology. Cruise missile computers fought to do the job they were programmed to complete. Chinese HQ-9 two-stage missiles with thrust vector control were fired from fixed and mobile-based units. They used their inertial guidance systems, constantly making midcourse corrections using active radar-homing. Missiles versus missiles, the projectiles were changing the face of battle.

Attempting to terminate the president and stop the onslaught of missiles were the American AGM-158s. The high-tech weapons of low-observable design primarily aimed to destroy high-value targets, such as the PLARF headquarters. Using automatic target recognition with autonomous guidance, the missiles were doing as programmed, with ten of the twelve penetrating the air defenses surrounding the area. Several JASSM missiles were outfitted with Hard Target Smart Fuses, accelerometer-based electronic fuses controlling the detonation point by layer counting. The accelerometer sensed g-loads on the bomb due to deceleration as it penetrated through defenses to the target. Able to distinguish between earth, concrete, and rock, one of the ten missiles hit the building where President Zhang was holed up.

But officials were prepared for such a strike and any missiles that might penetrate their air defenses. The bunker housing the president was built using high-stress concrete—the toughest in the business— and the bunker had earned the nickname "the Underground Great Wall." Like at the August 1st Building, special tunneling equipment had also constructed safe areas for personnel and equipment.

The American's earth-penetrating weapon could only burrow a few meters before it exploded. Mother Earth slowed the warhead down quickly. But just those few meters made a difference.

As the AGM-158 plunged through the building and the earth it was built on, a significant fraction of energy from the explosion was transmitted to the ground, creating a strong seismic shock wave that propagated downward. The energy shock wave hit the bunker room housing the president and his elite staff, who had followed him through the tunnels, knocking some people to the ground while sending debris flying like confetti and injuring several people. A large storage cabinet was torn from the wall and crushed a PLA general. Not unlike in the movies, the lights of the immense underground headquarters blinked and then went dark before the emergency generators, large enough to power a large city, turned them back on.

President Zhang Wei never stopped punching the keys on his keyboard while attempting to launch missiles through a video link. As each command was met with a black screen, Zhang smashed his fingers harder and harder on the keys until, thoroughly disgruntled, he picked up the wireless keyboard and threw it in the direction of General Wang.

With the dust so thick you could cut it with a knife, the rumbling finally ceased, the ground stopped shaking, and some form of order quickly took over from the panic. Most were alive and anxious for a reply to the Americans—none more so than President Zhang.

# Chapter 84



*USS Ronald Reagan,* Task Force-70
Philippine Sea


Lieutenant Jessie Hampton was confused while he sat in his sick bay room. He knew it was about time to catch a ride back to the *Ford* to resume his duties as an F-18 fighter pilot, but he was having second thoughts. Second thoughts—what the fuck am I thinking? Hours earlier, he had been ready to get in the face of anyone who would keep him from climbing the ladder into his fighter, including *Reagan*'s XO, whom he was expecting any minute.

Hampton had no time for women in his pursuit to be the best of the best in flying, or in life, for that matter. He had always had a one-track mind to succeed. But he was now beginning to get it—and "it" had something to do with the woman in the next room. Since Freeman had come, no crashed, into his life, and during their ride together in the rescue helicopter back to the *Reagan*, Hampton had taken every opportunity he could find to visit her. After a rough beginning, which he blamed on her concussion, the two now chatted like canaries singing to one another.

He admired her spunk, her intellect, and even how she tugged at her unruly hair while they talked. He could find no wrong with this strong, type-A pilot. He was smitten.

A knock on his door interrupted his thoughts. The XO didn't wait for an answer and briskly entered the room, leaving the door open. "Lieutenant Hampton, time to pack your things. The docs have cleared you back to the *Ford*."

"Yes, sir," said Hampton, who immediately noticed his tone lacked its usual conviction. It wasn't lost on the XO, either.

"What is it, Hampton? You sound like you lost your best friend, not like a guy chewing my ass twenty-four hours ago because I wouldn't allow him to jump back in a fighter."

"My bad, sir. I forget how lucky I am to return to flying while the lieutenant next door was told it would be a while for her. That girl loves to fly. I was feeling it for her."

The XO couldn't help but smile. "My, my, listen to you, mister homebody, now. That's so sweet," said the XO sarcastically. "But your helicopter leaves in one hour. I need you on deck in forty-five minutes. Any questions, lieutenant?"

"No, sir. It's time I get strapped in and go after the son-of-a-bitch that blew me out of the sky. Gotta return the favor. Thank you for the hospitality, sir."

The young lieutenant jumped from his sick bed to salute the XO, who was out the door as fast as a carrier launch of an F-18. Immediately, he heard a voice from the next room.

"Jessie, what was that all about?"

Just hearing her voice gave him shivers up and down his spine. What the hell was going on? And as fast as the XO had left his room, he was in hers.

"Hi, Sarah. That was the XO telling me I'm out of here in forty-five minutes." He hid his emotions as skillfully as if he was flying air-to-air combat.

"Well, shit," said Freeman, showing too much emotion and not caring. "It figures. I just get to know you, and off you go. You fighter guys never stick around too long, do you?"

Looking into her deep blue eyes, Hampton confessed, "Sarah, I thought I would never say this, but for the first time in my life, I don't want to go." He took her hand in his and moved closer to her. "I . . . care about you and will miss you a ton, but we both know I've got to get back in the war like you hopefully will soon too. It's what we do."

Freeman squeezed his hand and put it behind his head, pulling him close to her. She kissed him, a kiss that left no doubt about what her feelings were for him.

A tear ran down her cheek as she said, "I'll miss you too. You've been such an inspiration to me through all this bullshit, and I'll never forget our time together—never. Let's promise each other we'll stay in touch and hope that sometime in the future, we get together."

Feeling stronger and happier than he had in a long time, he said, "I'll be counting the days until we can do just that. I'll miss you too. And I can guarantee that when I'm shooting down Chinese assholes, I'll think of you." He bent down and kissed her again, showing there was a lot of meaning to what he had just said. "Take care, Sarah."

He was out of the room before she could see the tears forming in his eyes and was gone.

## Chapter 85



*USS Mustin,* Task Force-70
Philippine Sea

The men and women of the USS *Mustin* were still pumped after sinking one of China's most advanced submarines, the Shang class Type 093G nuclear-powered attack submarine. Being relieved from their temporary assignment to protect Wake Island, the *Mustin* was back helping to protect the USS *Ronald Reagan* as a part of Task Force-70.

Orders had just redeployed the three-carrier task force closer to Woody Island, near Luzon of the Philippine Islands chain but still within supporting distance of Taiwan. American intelligence had received increased communications indicating the Chinese were preparing to take back Woody.

Ensign Brett Jansen shifted in his chair as his commanding officer reviewed their new deployment's finer points with the gathered officers. The CO was feeling the stress of the war, but who wasn't?

No matter the pressure, Captain Tod Bailey was an even-keeled guy, even as he talked about the dangers of the Chinese missile threat. A PowerPoint map of China and the surrounding area was up on a screen. Radiating 2,800 miles were nine uneven circles indicating the range of all PLARF missiles. Jansen noted that their ship and other ships of the task force were within range of almost every one of the missiles.

"Being this close to the mainland of China," Bailey went on, "puts in play hundreds of aircraft that can fly unrefueled to Woody Island and even close to our current location. Throw in the PLAN's Southern Theater forces, which, if you need reminding, includes an aircraft carrier, submarines, destroyers, and other accompanying ships; we'll have our hands full protecting our ship and the *Reagan.*"

The CO paused to let his words sink in. "I want each officer to instill in their sailors the need for preparation and readiness for any contingency. As time permits, train, train, train. Any questions?"

Jansen raised his hand. "Sir, I've heard scuttlebutt regarding our rules of engagement changing now that we are at war."

"Ensign, it's quite simple now. See a threat, kill the threat. Okay, let's get to our assigned areas and prepare."



On Woody, preparations and briefings were underway as the small strategic island found itself in the crosshairs of one of the most powerful nations in the world—China. Isolated but supplied for battle, the Americans on the remote outpost felt relieved, knowing three carriers would be there to have their back.

Sitting in the Raptor squadron's briefing room with fifteen others dressed like him, Captain Isaiah "Cheetah" Azikiwe had his pen and pocket notebook out, but he mostly memorized everything the commanding officer said. He thought it was interesting how much a person's attention span increased when their life was on the line. The training was one thing, but the war changed the equation entirely.

His squadron of sixteen F-22s would fly CAP around the island, favoring the northwest where a PLAAF strike was anticipated. The pilots were briefed that the *Reagan* would be on station to assist along with the carrier's assets. Adding fuel to the growing fire, the Raptors would be easily within range of almost the entire inventory of Chinese land-to-air missiles. Assisting on their mission would be E-2s to pinpoint the mobile launching sites of the PLARF and to direct fighters to the precise locations.

On Woody were one thousand Marines from the 3rd MLR. They were hustling to finish deploying Oshkosh-built Remotely Operated Ground Unit trucks for unmanned launching of the Naval Strike Missiles. Elsewhere on the island, they were setting up

Tomahawk cruise missiles and ten Long Range Naval Anti-Ship Missiles. Along with their powerful radar, the Marines were preparing for any attack, whether from the sea or the air.



*BOEING B-1B LANCER FLIGHT*
South China Sea

The president of the United States viewed the newly acquired Woody Island as a strategic gem that should be protected at all costs. Major Thomas "Solo" Kronbach was excited that four aging B-1B bombers from his squadron were assigned to do their part. Flying from Wake Island, the long-range aircraft were known to be able to carry the largest conventional payloads of both guided and unguided weapons in the Air Force. The four Lancers were tasked with destroying missile launch sites, both mobile and fixed, on mainland China.

Solo earned his nickname early on while attending the United States Air Force Academy. A brilliant man, Kronbach was a loner who preferred studying to going out. Walking to classes, he preferred his self-imposed solitude to grab-assing with what few friends he had. Everyone accepted him for that but also respected him for his intellect and the help he gave each of them before a big test. Solo had a way of making everything seem much simpler than it was.

As today's mission commander, the other three aircraft pilots knew it would be important if they heard anything from Solo. They all agreed that the loner knew his shit, especially when keeping them alive, so they all paid attention to his every word—when there were some.

*PLAN AMPHIBIOUS READY GROUP 1*
South China Sea

The CNS *Hainan* was constructed for just this occasion, observed Rear Admiral Jia Xiao as he looked out from the Bridge of the massive Type 075 amphibious assault support ship. Unfortunately, the Americans had gained control of Yongxing Island, which they called Woody Island, but Jia was about to change that. It was a hasty plan, but in the early stages of war, you must adapt and react to your enemy. The concept was to act swiftly before a massive force of US troops made taking back the island impossible. He understood the risk, but allowing the enemy a strategic base so close to the Chinese mainland could not be tolerated.

Jia was the ideal officer to lead Amphibious Ready Group 1. Growing up in Guangzhou, seventy-five miles northwest of Hong Kong, as the only child of middle-class parents who taught at the university, young Jia had everything needed to succeed in life. In high school, he enjoyed Radio Exercises but especially fencing. Listening to the rich stories about fencing in his country, he was inspired. It turned him from a timid child to a young adult who found confidence in himself and developed an intense fighting spirit to serve him through his adult life.

His love for his country won him a position in the People's Liberation Army Dalian Naval Academy, where he finished number one in his class. Through the years, Jia worked his way up the chain of command with assignments on all types of ships. After being stuck behind a desk, he rattled enough doors to be assigned to China's newest amphibious ship, second only in size to his country's two aircraft carriers. At his age, he knew this mission would probably be his last hoorah, and he was determined to parry his way to success.

# Chapter 86



Intelligence was critical to war planning. Throughout the history of warfare, those with the most information about their enemy would likely succeed. The United States had always been a force to reckon with because of its warfighting ethos, an endless determination to get in the heads of the enemy, and to know what they planned as they planned it. Grouping assets at the right time would be vital to the battle for Woody Island, just as it was for Taiwan. Time on station for aircraft flying from longer distances benefited from this calculation.

One sailor who appreciated this importance was Lieutenant Commander Dick "Mad Dog" Johnson, call sign Boxer 11. Piloting his F-35, Mad Dog was the flight leader of five other F-35s flying west off Woody and waiting for targets to appear. Also in the area were sixteen F-22s maxed out with air-to-air missiles. In addition, four B-1B bombers were positioned to destroy Chinese missile launch sites at the first sign of trouble.

That first sign came when a US satellite detected several missile launches. The data was instantly sent via Link 16 to the command and control network's radar sites, the E-2, the airborne B-1Bs, and Aegis destroyers. The USS *Mustin* was one of the ships assigned to destroy incoming DF-21s.

Supervising his weapons specialists in the CIC, Ensign Brett Jansen was leaning over the mostly nineteen-year-olds, ensuring orders from the CO were being carried out correctly. Using the Aegis passive electronically scanned array radar, the *Mustin* was tracking ten DF-21 ballistic missiles as they headed toward Woody Island.

The order came through their headsets: "Launch fifteen SM-3s using system data track from C2BMC. You have permission to fire."

"Roger, control," said Jansen, glancing down at the monitors to verify all systems were locked on the targets traveling at Mach 10 through the atmosphere. He told his specialists, "Fire missiles six through twenty-one." Sixteen missile doors flew open at his command, and the powerful SM-3s roared skyward for destiny with their programmed enemy.

As the *Mustin* fired its missiles to thirty thousand feet, Major Thomas "Solo" Kronbach used the B-1s upgraded ultra-high-resolution radar with automatic target recognition to track and target the Chinese mobile trucks that had fired the deadly DF-21s. Solo ordered fire by calling out specific targets for the other three bombers.

Before the subsonic missiles dropped from the Bone's racks, they were programmed with automatic target recognition and autonomous and precision guidance. The smart missiles knew precisely what they were looking for. Even though the DF-21 batteries' massive mobile launchers would be on the move after letting loose with the missiles, the seeing eyes of the AGM-158s would track them down and, when found, shred them to pieces.

PLAN Amphibious Ready Group 1
South China Sea

Rear Admiral Jia Xiao sighed noticeably as he sat in the captain's chair aboard the *Hainan*. None of the sailors near him dared to look at the man, obviously deep in thought. Jia knew all too well that the amphibious landing of troops on a beachhead was one of the most complex maneuvers executed by any military. All aspects of the plan left no room for error. Air power, naval gunfire, transport, logistics, specialized equipment, and land warfare must be integrated into one cohesive fighting unit. The failure of one could lead to disaster for all.

His Amphibious Ready Group was prepared mentally, but they had had no time to rehearse any aspect of the landing, which was quite unfortunate. But Jia felt confident with his force of ships and planes. Along with his flagship, the *Hainan*, was the amphibious warfare ship, the CNS *Changbaishan*. The Type 071 ship was transporting five hundred marines, two Harbin Z-8 transport helicopters, and in the well deck, four Type 726 LCACs, plus all the required support equipment. The CNS *Shenzhen*, a Luhai class Type 051B destroyer, supported the Amphibious Ready Group.

The high-speed LCACs were critical to his planned landing on the east end of Woody Island, the same place the Americans had used for their surprise attack. He could not only land seventy armed marines but armored vehicles and supplies as well.

On the deck of his flagship, a look-a-like carrier, was pennant number 31, which labeled the ship in the same class as PLAN carriers. The uninterrupted flight deck contained seven deck points and was carrying thirty helicopters, consisting of Harbin Z-8 transports, Harbin Z-9 gunships, CAIC Z-10 gunships, and some Harbin Z-20 multi-mission helos used for transportation. The Hainan didn't have VTOL fighters, unlike the American's amphibious assault ship, the USS *Wasp*.

In the hold of his ship were an additional nine hundred marines. The Hainan didn't have independent watertight compartments like most warships so it could carry extra supplies and troops. Jia knew too well that it wouldn't take much to sink the mammoth ship, which worried him.

3RD MARINE LITTORAL REGIMENT
Woody Island, South China Sea


Putting the final touches on the Marine Corps' newest Naval Strike Missile Defense System, Gunnery Sergeant Harley "Snake Eyes" Jennings was blaring out orders as he always did. But it just wasn't the same for the veteran. Life was different for him when the Corps did away with his M1A1 Abrams tank. Snake Eyes found himself constantly adjusting to the "new" Corps, which he had to admit he was not a fan of. He would much rather be blowing the shit out of things than expending effort about where to park a fucking radar truck—give me a break, he thought.

For eighteen years, Snake Eyes had been a proud member of the famed United States Marine Corps 3rd Division that, overnight, it seemed, was now called the 3rd Marine Littoral Regiment. Hell, he didn't even know what littoral meant. And now, the Corps was doing work for the squids. Him, in charge of an anti-ship missile battery—"Holly Mother of Jesus," he mumbled.

Interrupting his thoughts was a snot-nosed kid of nineteen. "Hey, Gunny, where do you want the Radar Equipment truck positioned?" Snake Eyes casually waved his arm in the direction facing east and wondered if this shit could get any worse.

Out of the corner of his eye, he saw another snot-nosed kid, this one not much older but wearing the butter bars of a second lieutenant.

"Gunny, I thought we discussed this. I want the Radar Equipment truck pointing northeast. Got it?"

Snake Eyes replied, not showing the slightest bit of annoyance, "Yes, sir, my bad." He turned to the nearest person and said, "Private, face that RE truck northeast, on the double."

As the RE truck was about to be moved, sirens began screaming. A voice-over on Snake Eye's radio was shouting about incoming missiles.

"Take cover away from the equipment," Snake Eyes ordered over the comms and for those within hearing distance. Not one to do as he ordered, he made a beeline to the last radar truck, now empty, and maneuvered it to place it in the most strategic position. Through Link-16, defenses on Woody were receiving targeting information for an amphibious group approaching the island. Having control over the radar and the long-range anti-ship missiles they were programmed to support, Snake Eyes quickly but efficiently put the battery online.

Surging from the mainland of China's Southern Theater were fourteen PLAAF J-16s and twelve J-10 fighters, spreading out over the South China Sea to assault American-held Woody Island. Six of the J-16 fourth-generation fighters provided air cover for the amphibious force approaching the island from the northeast. Joining the attack were two H-6 bombers with a mission to destroy the single runway and any aircraft parked in the open. Additional fighters would have been deployed, but the PLAAF was stretched thin with their ongoing attacks on Taiwan.

But the force wasn't invisible. The US had eyes on them with satellites, an E-2 playing digital quarterback, F-35s with advanced AN/APG-81 radars, and F-22s with their 77-series radar.

"Boxer 11, Starlight 92," came the call from the circling E-2. "Enemy amphibious force of four ships and six J-16 bandits, heading two-four-six. GPS coordinates on Link 16."

"Starlight 92, Boxer 11. Roger," replied Mad Dog. He switched to internal comms. "Boxer 15 and Boxer 16 stay on station. All others on me."

Dipping his right wing toward the sea below, Mad Dog made a 5-g turn to approach the oncoming bandits head-on, and three F-35s followed him. Using their newly upgraded Advanced EOTS, they aimed at the Chinese pilots. After the automatic tracking lasers locked onto the six enemy aircraft, high-resolution imagery flashed onto their screens. It flashed the returns onto each pilot's HUD. With the directional information from the laser tracker, Mad Dog put his crosshairs on two illuminated targets. The other three pilots did the same; all six J-16 aircraft were targeted.

"Don't fire until within range," said Mad Dog. "Fire your 260s when 180 miles out." Using stealth and a 180-mile range for the new missile, Mad Dog liked his odds with the BVR shoot-and-forget missile.

In war, one learned to expect the unexpected. During recent briefs aboard the *Reagan*, it was revealed that the PLAAF had armed their J-16s and J-20s with PL-21 ultra-long-range air-to-air missiles.

More conventional rocket motor-powered missiles relied upon an initial boost phase to achieve the high speed needed for the coasting stage to intercept the target. This new generation missile relied on maneuverability and used an air-breathing motor that provided sustained power following the initial boost to run down and destroy the target. The range was almost precisely that of the US AIM-260—180 miles. Locating the enemy first came with rewards, namely shooting down the assholes. Both high-tech missiles provided the largest no-escape zone of any air-to-air weapon out there. Mad Dog still liked his odds in his F-35—you gotta see me to kill me.

While the F-35s were tracking the J-16s coming into range of the AIM-260s, a flight of sixteen F-22s received contact information from the E-2 about incoming bandits, although they had seen them before the E-2's alert.

"Mytai 11, Starlight 92. Thirty-four bandits at two-eight-four, flight level 350, 850 knots, traveling due east. Force of J-16s and J-10s."

"Starlight 92, Mytai 11. Roger." On internal comms, the F-22 mission commander said, "All aircraft, use Link 16, communicate all target sorting. We will use a bracket maneuver."

The pilots called out their targets, knowing they would attack from the flank. In BVR warfare, the battle was more about total information awareness. Sharing targeting data allowed each fighter to see the same battlefield picture as everyone else—a huge advantage. As quickly as the order was given, targeting data was shared with all American assets.

In the battle for Woody Island, the US relied on hit-and-run tactics, using their stealth technology to secure air superiority against the mostly third and fourth-generation enemy fighters.

As they closed the distance to the six J-16s flying cover for the amphibious group, Mad Dog's flight was preparing to let loose with their missiles. Meanwhile, "Cheetah" Azikiwe awaited orders to fire five AMRAAMs from his internal weapons bay. Staying with BVR tactics, the outnumbered Americans needed to deny the enemy their first-shot capability.

Making the turn for the enemy flank, the F-22s had increased their speed to 1,200 mph as the order came to fire their AIM-120s. Cheetah launched quickly after ensuring he had a lock on his targets. Stealth was one thing, but once you fired your missiles, you had to assume there would be incoming missiles from where you had fired.

*Beep, beep, beep.* The alarm rang in Cheetah's cockpit, confirming his prediction. The sound raised the hairs on his arms.

Although the enemy was firing blind, the missiles they fired were not. Instantly, the sky was full of maneuvering fighters and streaks of vapor as missiles raced toward their intended victims. Cheetah released chaff and flares and made a 180-degree turn followed by several 90-degree turns. He was forcing the incoming missiles to maneuver against him and burn off their fuel and kinetic energy. He also continued to use his electronic jamming.

Stealth worked to the American's advantage as the F-22s' AIM-120Ds raced close to Mach 4 toward their targets, giving the J-16s and J-10s little time to react. As the Chinese pilots fought off one missile, they were locked on by one of the other eighty missiles filling the space around them. The sky was soon filled with explosions, burning debris, and a scattering of parachutes.

Not immune to the destruction were the American pilots. Five F-22s went down.

Surviving pilots from both sides quickly altered tactics from BVR to WVR. What was just an electronic blip on a radar screen a few moments ago was a shrieking fighter aircraft with a pilot seeking revenge within visual range.

Cheetah's senses were already on high alert because his high-resolution radar warning receiver indicated a J-16 was on him.

"Mytai 11, Mytai 12. Radar contact, bandit turning on me. Spiked." Cheetah jammed the throttle forward to throw his F-22 into a deep dive and to keep the J-16 defensive and distracted. At the same time, his flight leader positioned himself to fire one of his sidewinders.

"Mytai 12, Mytai 11. I'm outside the circle taking the shot now." With the bandit in his sights, the flight leader let loose with one Block III AIM-9 missile.

Distracted from his attack on the F-22, about the time the Chinese pilot heard his missile alarm, he was torn apart by the impact from the ten-foot missile. The shredded J-16 plunged into the South China Sea. The Chinese pilot had no idea who killed him.

Attacking the CAP flying cover for the PLAN Amphibious Ready Group, Mad Dog fired two AIM-260s from 180 miles out. The range was achieved by the top-secret air-breathing ramjet technology replacing the traditional, solid-fuel rocket motor, giving the AIM-260 an impressive range. With superior radar, the four F-35s avoided random missile shots and concentrated on firing their second missiles. Knowing that as soon as the J-16s understood there were incoming missiles, they would fire down the trajectory line back at their enemy, the jets took immediate evasive action.

Using their EOTS gave the American pilots the situational awareness to quickly and efficiently identify, analyze, and respond to threats. Two Chinese J-16s were swiftly obliterated, while the secondary missiles demolished the other four fighters that evaded the original missiles—so much for the Chinese CAP.

"All Boxers, Boxer 11. Bingo fuel. Meet altitude block Alpha-niner."

As the four F-35s flew to the rendezvous point, Lieutenant Wilson "Steady" Sanderson was piloting his KC-130 precisely on the tanker track specified in the air-tasking order. While his next customers entered the track and lined up for service, Sanderson, from Portsmouth, New Hampshire, couldn't help his eastern accent as he communicated the fighters' arrival with boom operator CPO Shirley Sansong.

"Are you kidding me, Steady? If I hadn't flown with you for the past year, I wouldn't know the altitude you just gave me. Receiver at one thousand feet on track."

"Roger, Boom." Sanderson smiled to himself. Sansong constantly teased him about his accent even though she was from Texas, and he almost needed an interpreter to understand her.

Talking her receiver into position, Sansong called out the distance to the F-35, "Forty—thirty—twenty—"

"BREAK, BREAK," yelled Mad Dog. "Inbound missile."

When his RWR blared a warning, adrenaline surged through Mad Dog's body. Throwing his stick over, he went to afterburner and dove for the ocean to put as much distance between him and the KC-130. As he dove, he released chaff, hoping to trick the missile. With a million details going through his head, he heard excited chatter as the other three F-35s took defensive maneuvers.

It was a sight Mad Dog would never forget. Suddenly, it seemed as if the entire sky was on fire with multiple explosions, enormous fireballs, and debris raining down like molten lava from a volcano. The first to get struck was Sanderson's KC-130, followed by two more refuelers and one F-35, which couldn't break away fast enough. There was little warning. Whoever did it got past the CAP flying cover for the refuelers and past the F-35s' radars.

Mad Dog and the surviving F-35s formed up, conserving fuel as best they could as additional KC-130s were at maximum military power to meet up and fuel their thirsty brethren. Feeling grief over the loss of life, Mad Dog promised himself a day of reckoning would come, and he wouldn't be on the losing end.

Chinese fighter pilot Major Chang Huang couldn't help cheering so loud that he almost blew off his oxygen mask. Having attempted the same mission earlier and nearly gotten shot down, he and his wingman changed tactics to fly just a few feet above the sea and only pop up to let loose long-range missiles. Now they were both repeating the operation in reverse, escaping back to the mainland just a few feet above the South China Sea. Tankers destroyed—mission accomplished.

*PLAN AMPHIBIOUS READY GROUP 1*

With the loss of his air cover, Read Admiral Jia Xiao was feeling vulnerable. Eighty miles from Yongxing Island, Jia decided to launch his four type 726 LCACs, three loaded with seventy marines and a fourth loaded with two ZTD-05 light amphibious tanks and the marines to operate the tanks. The *Changbaishan* was assigned to provide combat helicopter support and to transport an additional five hundred troops to retake the island the Americans called Woody.

"XO, launch the LCACs and supporting helicopters."

The amphibious group slowed to discharge the landing craft. Three Z-9 and Z-10 gunship helicopters took to the air to lead the formation to the LZ.

As the LCACs hit the water, two of the ten Chinese DF-21 missiles struck the small town on Woody Island, defeating all attempts to shoot them down. One missile destroyed two blocks of businesses and left behind a burning inferno of structures. The second missile hit near the runway, demolishing a portion of the east end and several outbuildings. When the all-clear was broadcast, a small RED HORSE detachment began to repair the damage.

Further inland on Woody, Gunnery Sergeant Harley "Snake Eyes" Jennings had moved his marines away from the radar emplacement and the ROGUE anti-ship missile launcher. Like in his tank days, he knew that once a missile battery fired, you could bet return fire was coming. Consequently, the unit launched remotely.

"Alpha One, Alpha Charlie. Amphibious unit identified, eight-one miles east. Four LCACs breaking away speed 80 knots. Have coordinates on three supporting ships, identified as PLAN amphibious detachment."

"Alpha Charlie, Alpha One. Roger that," replied Second Lieutenant Ronald Otis. A few moments passed, with Otis remaining silent.

"Sir," said Snake Eyes, working the battery command vehicle with the twenty-four-year-old lieutenant, "we need to jump on this. They'll be on us quickly. Suggest we fire at the supporting ships and LCACs now."

"Slow down, Gunny. Let's think this through. We've barely set up our battery and haven't run any tests to ensure we're good too—"

"Sir, this shit will work. Trust me, we must act now, or we'll have a thousand Chinese marines all over our asses." Snake Eyes was trying hard to show patience with the boot lieutenant on his first real assignment, but in war, there was no time to fuck around. You had to get it right the first time or pay the price for the second try.

Just then, the battalion commander was on comms. "Lieutenant, what's your status? We need to get those missiles in the air now; what's the problem?"

After a second to ponder, Otis answered, "No problem, sir, just going over our options with Gunny."

"Lieutenant, there are no options, get those missiles in the air now. Do you understand?"

Without hesitating, Otis replied, "Yes, sir. Plugging in coordinates now." The young boot was beginning to see the big picture.

At their disposal were three missile launcher vehicles each armed with four NSMs. Using their TRS-15C radar and the shared targeting data from Link 16, the Marines launched twelve missiles, which roared skyward toward the PLAN amphibious force.

The Norwegian-designed NSM had composite materials to give the missile stealth capabilities. It combined a high-strength titanium alloy and a blast fragmentation warhead with insensitive high explosives.

As Snake Eyes held back a smirk, he complimented the lieutenant on his quick thinking; the NSMs were traveling at supersonic speeds, skimming the sea just feet off the surface, and performing random bank-to-turn flight adjustments to make it difficult for the Chinese to shoot them down.

Aboard the *Hainan*, Admiral Jia Xiao received comms about a missile attack. Before he could order countermeasures, the *Shenzhen* began tracking the missiles using its E/F-band Doppler search radar, which was stretched thin, tracking its max-allowable targets at a time. The *Shenzhen* fired eight HQ-7s from the cell launcher that was quickly reloaded. Using IR-tracking cameras while flying at Mach 2.3, the missiles were playing catch up to the much faster NSMs.

The first casualty from an NSM was the lead LCAC with seventy Chinese marines aboard. It was no contest, as the powerful missile designed for destroyers obliterated the landing craft. There were no survivors. The three other LCACs roared on at 80 mph carrying two light amphibious tanks and 180 Chinese marines hellbent on revenge for their fallen comrades.

Two NSMs used their video-enhanced radar to search out the Type 051B destroyer that had fired the retaliatory missiles. Based on their onboard computer's list of Chinese destroyers, the programmed missiles knew precisely what they were looking for. As the two missiles came in at supersonic speed, *Shenzhen* fired thousands of rounds from its Type 730 seven-barreled rotary 30mm Gatling gun. The gun's OFC-3 fire control used color video radar of its own in conjunction with a laser range finder. As the two missiles came in visual range, one of the two NSMs exploded from a direct hit.

The second missile escaped the same fate, and the 276-pound warhead struck the *Shenzhen* amidships, blasting through the outer armor and detonating inside just at the waterline. The explosion broke the beam of the mighty warship and caused *Shenzhen* to split in two. Both halves sank to the bottom of the sea in less than three minutes. Thirteen sailors were blown from the ship and survived, but the rest of the crew of 248 found the sea as their eternal resting place. Beat up but not down, the remainder of PLAN Amphibious Ready Group 1 plowed on with a mission to retake Yongxing Island.

# Chapter 87

*PLARF HEADQUARTERS*
Qinghe, Haidian District of Beijing, China

As the dust settled around the underground bunker, President Zhang Wei was not surprised he had survived another ballistic missile strike. He expected it. Not pausing for a moment, Zhang shrieked at anyone within earshot to get his ballistic missile brigades back online as he tried to find another keyboard to smack around.

"Mr. President," said his second in command, General Wang, "we are attempting to get back online using every means possible. Much of our infrastructure has been damaged here and elsewhere by the Americans. This will take some time to work through."

"Time is a commodity in short supply, general," said the president. "I have a very proficient firing squad standing by for my command to shoot you and your incompetent staff. I don't need excuses. I need results—now."

Taking out the sidearm he had been wearing since the beginning of hostilities, the president of China pointed it directly between the eyes of Wang. Then quickly pointed his 9mm at the ceiling and fired. It was surprising how loud a pistol shot could be after the blast they had just experienced—many in the room dove for cover.

"I swear, General Wang," the president calmly said, "I will shoot you myself if I don't get results in minutes. Not hours, not days, but minutes. Do you understand?"

Picking himself up from behind a large wooden desk, General Wang sheepishly replied, "Yes, sir. Minutes, not hours." He then rushed out of the room to the bathroom.

*WOODY ISLAND*
Paracel Islands, South China Sea

With the limited success of the missile strike on the PLAN amphibious group, Gunnery Sergeant Harley "Snake Eyes," Jennings knew shit was going to happen fast, and he was getting prepared. Bouncing along in a purpose-built 4x4 Marine Air Defense Integrated System, MADIS, Snake Eyes was positioning his Mk1 vehicle to get a shot at an incoming flight of Chinese attack helicopters. In his deployment area was an Mk2 outfitted with the unique RPS-42 that can detect the extremely small radar cross-sections of commercial, off-the-shelf drones and pinpoint low-flying high-speed fixed-winged aircraft, and most importantly for this mission, helicopters.

Two additional Mk1 and Mk2 radar units were also preparing to defend the island. They were positioned at the eastern end, near a sandy beach that the amphibious force was sure to use, just as the US had.

Leading the Chinese attack were several Z-10 helicopters, the same type of helos that had blown the shit out of a battalion of ROC tanks on Kinmen Island just a few days ago. The MADIS were Joint Light Tactical Vehicles, not tanks, armed with one four-turret launcher for their Stinger missiles.

This was like a homecoming for Snake Eyes, who sorely missed his tank. Speeding along at 50 mph with his crew inside the armored vehicle, they were busy inputting targeting data from their 360-degree aerial surveillance radar.

Five miles from the eastern shore of Yongxing Island, the lead Z-10 attack helicopter, with the pilot and gunner comfortable in their stepped tandem cockpit and using their HUDs, was gathering target data against the six MADIAS vehicles. The information was sent to eight HJ-12 antitank missile computers. The crew was flying at 186 mph toward their targets to get within range of 2.2 miles. The gunner noted that one of the targets was zigzagging and never stopped. The gunner thought, play your games, you dumb ass American, but my heat-seeking missile will find you no matter where you go and blow you apart.

"Rainbow 1, Rainbow 2, Gunny, we have a targeting solution for three incoming PLA helicopters. Missiles programmed and ready to fire."

Still maneuvering around the island's east end, Gunny gave the command to fire. Just as quickly, four Stinger missiles ignited and raced toward their targets, leaving a trail of thick smoke.

The two other units, stationary in the tree line just back of the sandy beach area, fired four missiles each at the incoming helicopters. Almost simultaneously, the three Z-10 attack helicopters fired their HJ-12 fire-and-forget missiles set in top-attack mode. When the Stingers cleared the launchers, Bravo's Multifunctional Self-protection System passive sensor heads automatically began jamming the incoming missiles to disrupt the guidance software. The MUSS worked perfectly on one missile, sending it fifty meters from their vehicle. Still, a second HJ-12 smashed into the Mk1 from above. As it hit, the missile released a high-explosive, anti-tank warhead using a precursor charge to defeat the Explosive Reactive Armor and allow the primary warhead to penetrate the base armor and explode inside the vehicle. The crew was killed instantly, leaving little that resembled an Mk1.

While Bravo lost its battle against the HJ-12, Gunny's Alpha unit fought to survive. When the MUSS indicated incoming missiles, Snake Eyes yelled, "All stop."

The Mk1 tires locked up, throwing the crew forward and stopping the vehicle almost in its tracks. The MUSS computer, taking into account every conceivable piece of data, including the direction and speed of the vehicle and the incoming missiles, automatically initiated all necessary countermeasures. Jamming forced one missile to fly by the crew as if they were invisible. The computer also deployed a specially designed smoke grenade, concealing the vehicle in a massive cloud of black smoke and disrupting the sensors on the HJ-12 missile. As the second missile flew by, the third struck the sand near the vehicle, blasting it two feet into the air, and just as quickly, it slammed back to Mother Earth in one piece.

"Fuck me." Gunny's ragged voice echoed through the crew compartment. He would mourn for the crew of Bravo at the appropriate time—if he was still alive. But he marveled that they were still in the fight along with Charlie.

While the MADIS vehicles fought for survival, the three Chinese attack helicopters did the same. Their battle to survive was like an old West gunfight in the streets of Tombstone, where the gunslingers faced off in the middle of the street both fired their six shooters at the other, each hoping to kill their adversary. Bullets flew then; missiles flew now.

The lead Z-10 reacted first to the incoming Stinger missiles by using its infrared jammer, firing off chaff and flare, and banking steeply down to the ocean floor. It didn't matter. One missile penetrated the front cockpit, exploding and instantly killing both men. The second blew up in the already growing fireball. Meanwhile, the two other Z-10 attack helicopters suffered the same fate. The pilot didn't know it, but the one Mk1 vehicle he had made fun of was the one that had sent the missiles that blew his Z-10 into oblivion.

Colonel Henry "Hank" Winston, who joined the Marine Corps twenty-one years ago as an eighteen-year-old private, was a Mustang. As an enlisted Marine, it hadn't taken long for his superiors to recognize Winston's leadership abilities and attitude to get the job done no matter what. He was sent to Officer Candidates School, worked up to a full-bird Colonel, and was now in charge of all American forces on Woody Island. The razor-thin officer looked like he was chiseled from granite. Every morning since he could remember, he did his pull-ups, sit-ups, and push-ups before he even had a sip of coffee. Even today with a Chinese amphibious assault force bearing down on "his" island, he had done his morning routine.

Attacking America's newest territory was a PLAN amphibious force that would be the first test of his newly formed

MLR. Winston wasn't going to screw it up. With a grunt's thirst to be on the front lines, the Colonel and his aides jumped into one of two ACV-30s on the island and took up a place of advantage and concealment should the amphibious units somehow make it to the beach. This spot was now his headquarters.

"Stargazer, Rainbow 1," radioed Snake Eyes. "Enemy LCACs are 1.5 miles east, traveling at 75 knots. Four miles east is one Yuzhao class landing ship. We are low on Stingers and are reloading. Suggest you take the three LCACs. Radar indicates several additional attack helicopters inbound. Good luck, sir."

"Rainbow 1, Stargazer. "Roger and good hunting," replied Colonel Winston.

Using targeting data from its onboard radar, sublimated from island radar and sent via Link 16, Winston ordered both his ACV-30s to target the Chinese landing craft using 30mm high-explosive rounds.

While this was occurring, the Z-10 attack helicopters flew over the island. The first thing the Marines on the ground noticed was how quiet they were. There wasn't the usual roar from blades pounding the air but more of an acoustic stealthiness. With eyes on their targets, Stinger elements pointed their air defense missiles skyward, ready to fire in less than five seconds of contact. As the attack helicopters fired missiles and guns at the dug-in Marines, the shooters were sighting in their targets to put crosshairs on the enemy. As the Marine specialist squeezed the triggers, the missiles quickly reached a speed of Mach 2, giving the enemy little time to react. All around the beach, helicopters were blown from the sky, with fire and debris raining down over the island.

Moving along the east end, the ACV-30 carrying Colonel Winston slammed on its brakes to avoid debris that smashed down just in front of them. Winston flew from the back into the driver. "Sorry, sir," echoed through the cabin as the armored vehicle took off again. Fitted on top of the ACV was a remotely operated 30mm cannon. With their valuable payload, the ACV's crew of three was reading the targeting coordinates from their sensor suite and fire control software. Doing so allowed them to keep moving to get in position for a first-burst target engagement of the Chinese landing craft approaching Woody.

Coordinating with Starlight-2, the other ACV-30, the firing commenced. With the ability to fire up to 200 rounds per minute, a steady thump, thump, thump filled the air as the two vehicles fired and maneuvered. The guns targeting computers began walking the rounds into the path of the PLAN's LCACs.



Rear Admiral Jia Xiao was discouraged by the results of his attempted landing on Yongxing Island. He had lost one LCAC, a destroyer, and supporting fighter escorts. Now he was told of renewed attacks on his three remaining LCACs and the *Changbaishan*. In such challenging times, Jia sought out the past to calm himself and regain the confidence that had made him who he was.

For a brief moment, his thoughts drifted back to the Olympic Games when he was losing the fencing match for a gold medal to a competitor who was genuinely gifted and amazingly fast. But Jia had one attribute that had always served him well—endurance. As the match continued, he could feel his challenger slow down. Countering, Jia committed to a burst of energy to overcome his faster opponent and heard "halt" as he scored his fifteenth point to win gold. But now, he was not fighting for gold but for his country's security.

"Weapons, Bridge," Jia called out. "Prepare and fire twenty-four HHQ-10 missiles at beach emplacements and the guns firing on our LCACs."

"Weapons to Bridge, Roger, sir." After a pause, the voice said, "Bridge, missiles away."

"Helm," Jia said, "make for new course zero-five-eight, ahead flank."

As the *Hainan* changed course, the *Changbaishan* was maneuvering in defense against several incoming NSM missiles. With no support, the warship was on its own.

"Weapons, Bridge," the *Changbaishan*'s captain said, "six incoming missiles. Fire decoys and employ the AK-176 at optimal range, rate 120." The Soviet-built naval gun, mounted in an enclosed turret, was a good choice against the sea-skimming Stingers. The crew also employed their 30mm AK-630 fully automatic rotary cannon close-in weapons system, feeding in 152 ready-to-fire rounds. Every round would be critical in the next few seconds since the crew understood it took an average of twenty-five rounds to obtain a kill.

For a few seconds, it appeared the strong defensive weapons of the sizable amphibious transport with 653 Chinese Marines aboard would survive the six incoming missiles. As the first four were destroyed within sight of the ship, two other NSMs continued their deadly journey at 700 mph. Because of a slight programming error, one missile elevated at the last moment and took out the mast of the ship, causing little other damage. The second missile struck the front hull and blew a gaping hole near the water line. Anyone in that area was instantly killed. Despite the near-fatal strike, the ship stayed afloat.

A mile and a half ahead of the *Changbaishan*, the three LCACs carrying specialized Chinese Marines and two amphibious tanks were met with heavy gunfire from the American armored vehicles on Woody Island. As designed, the 30mm rounds made large waterspouts as they "walked" toward the approaching LCACs, even while the craft was making radical course changes to avoid the deadly rounds. But in war, sometimes it's better to zig than zag, and the lead LCAC turned into five projectiles. One of the 30mm shells struck the engine compartment and ignited a secondary explosion that killed several crew and marines; ten jumped overboard to escape the scorching flames.

A second LCAC was hit with one round, suffering slight damage, and the transport with the two tanks was unscathed. Both

LCACs stopped long enough to pick up survivors and in minutes, they were closing on the island again at max speed of 80 knots.

On Woody Island, all hell was breaking loose. Twenty-four Chinese HHQ-10 missiles were raining down all over the island, just over half the size of Manhattan's Central Park. Several landed in the small village, starting fires and killing civilians. Two missiles struck the runway and support buildings, killing several airmen from the RED HORSE Squadron. Another HHQ-10 hit a hardened structure housing an F-22, destroying the stealth aircraft.

Alpha-2, one of the two ACV-30s, was sprayed with shrapnel from a near miss, blowing out all four tires on the right side, nearly causing the armored vehicle to roll over. Only through the skillful driving of a young lance corporal was the ACV kept in service.

After the terror from the sky stopped and, with it, the deafening sounds of bombs exploding, the eerie quiet was surreal. But even that momentary stoppage lasted but a few minutes. All over the island, Marine comms were hearing the same thing.

"Starlight to all detachments," said the poised voice of Colonel Winston. "Reinitiate all mission directives. Two enemy LCACs one mile out, approaching from the east at zero-niner-zero at 70 knots. Fire when within range."

"Weapons, Bridge," Jia said. "Ready three Z-18s and load each with twenty-seven Marines. Prepare for immediate—"

"Captain, four torpedoes bearing two-four-zero, distance 3,200 meters, speed 96 km/h."

Without their destroyer escort to shield the amphibious group against submarines, the *Hainan* had little defense against the deadly torpedoes.

Dismissing all formalities, Jia fired off orders. "Right full rudder, come to one-eight-three, ahead flank." With his mission at the forefront of all decisions he made, Jia ordered, "I want those helicopters airborne immediately. Get the troops on and go. Weapons, fire on torpedoes."

"Captain, four torpedoes have a lock. Two minutes until impact."

The three massive Z-18 transport helicopters were prepped on the deck and ready to go. The last of the marines scrambled to get on board.

"This is the captain," Jia screamed over the radio. "Get those units in the air now!"

"Captain, forty-five seconds until impact."

"Left full rudder, come to two-six-zero, ahead flank."

"Sir, weapons report they have no visible targets."

"Fire anyway."

As the ship changed course, three Z-18 helicopters took off, with several Marines staring in disbelief as the side doors slammed shut.

"Fifteen seconds until impact."

In those last seconds, Jia couldn't help but notice how the crew on the Bridge stared at him, perhaps hoping he would somehow save them because he was the man they entrusted with their lives. And now he had let them down.

After the powerful torpedoes adjusted their course to come under the ship's keel, they exploded, tossing the *Hainan* into the air like a bathtub toy. The resulting fireball engulfed one of the three helicopters and blew it from the sky. As the ship fell back to the sea, the force from the torpedoes destroyed the little structural integrity left in the keel, breaking it into two pieces. It sunk quickly. There were nine survivors, but the captain was not one of them.

A few miles away and one hundred and fifty feet below the surface, Captain Colleen Panchak, commanding officer of the Virginia class attack submarine USS *Oregon*, was changing course. "Helm, Conn. Come to bearing one-six-eight, speed 10 knots. Make your depth four hundred feet."

Moments earlier, her crew had flawlessly come into position to launch four MK 48 torpedoes at the unsuspecting *Hainan*. Now it was time to sneak away silently and prepare to finish the crippled *Changbaishan.*

As the two LCACs approached the beach, they laid down heavy ground fire as eighty Chinese Marines made their presence felt by the US Marines who defended what days ago had belonged to the PLA.

The firefight between the two nations' Marines was pandemonium. As bullets whizzed around the beach, sand slammed into the air, while cries of agony were heard above the sound of automatic gunfire as both sides were being hit hard. Planted on the beach, both LCACs continued to lay down thousands of rounds from four Type 2 heavy 14.5mm machine guns. Also in the fight were their four 7.62mm light machine guns.

As the LCACs kept the pressure on the Marines, the operators of two Chinese ZTD-05 light amphibious tanks fired up their engines and plunged off the LCAC, immediately heading inland with their 30mm guns blazing away. Using their battle management command and control system with a digital map interface, the four-person crew of one tank identified a stationary American ACV and fired one HJ-73C missile. Using an infrared tracking system, the missile operator kept the target in sight for the short time it took for the missile to impact the ACV. It ripped apart in one spectacular explosion. Fortunately for the ACV's crew, who had four tires shredded from an earlier near hit, were a safe distance away taking cover.

When the Chinese ZTD-05 fired its missile, a lance corporal concealed behind cover used his Javelin's command launch unit and quickly located the amphibious tank. Ensuring he had missile alignment and lock, he fired. Thundering away at over 600 miles per hour, the tandem warhead penetrated the armor, tearing it apart in one giant flash as the tank fragmented into hundreds of molten pieces of flaming metal.

Events on the island were getting dicey. With marines fighting it out on the beachhead, two Z-18 transport helicopters from the *Hainan* appeared on radar, flying nearly fifteen thousand feet at over 200 mph. Avoiding the battlefield, both enemy helicopters were headed to the island's west end, which was isolated from the fighting providing a safer LZ.

Waiting on the outskirts was Corporal Randy Steketee, fresh out of Low Altitude Air Defense Gunner's Course, where he had trained to shoot the Stinger air defense missile. Throughout his instruction, Steketee couldn't figure out why he was chosen as a shooter because he never volunteered for anything. But here he was, preparing to shoot down two Chinese Z-18 helicopters descending to an open area loaded with Chinese marines. He could feel beads of sweat run down his forehead as he rehashed everything he needed to do. Shit, it wasn't like he shot missiles every day—he'd fired only a few live rounds during his training.

Steketee pushed his eye against the optic sight with his assistant beside him. Over his radio warning network, he received orders to take out both enemy helicopters. As the first helicopter reached the far edge of his launch radius, in just seconds, Steketee got in the proper firing position with a clear line of sight to the first helicopter. He quickly attached the battery assembly to the launcher. Next, Steketee armed and enabled the Stinger guidance system. He acquired the Chinese Z-18 using the thermal sight and put the crosshairs smack in the middle. He pushed the launcher securely against his shoulder and pulled the trigger. As the missile shot from the launcher, he kept the crosshairs on the target until there was a massive ball of flames from what was once a Z-18 Chinese helicopter.

As he glanced at pieces of the aircraft drift to the ground, his assistant helped Steketee load another missile. A moment later, he fired another Stinger that raced toward the second helicopter. Although the second Z-18 made a radical course change and dove for the deck, it was too late. The second missile found its mark, turning the sky into two bright flashes of fire and smoke.

As his loader slapped Steketee on the back, the marine felt pride because he had done as he was trained. Later, he couldn't help but ponder the enormity of what he did.

As the two Chinese helicopters were shot from the sky, Snake Eyes, and his crew were redeploying at top speed, aware that the ZTD-05 tank would want to stick a missile up their tailpipe.

"Hurry it up, Marines," said Snake Eyes. "We sure as hell can't dilly-dally around here. Find the tank and prepare the 30s with armor-piercing rounds."

His gunner quickly replied, "Gunny, we have a lock."

"Fire!"

With a thunderous roar, the cannon unleashed a hailstorm of 30 mm rounds, two of which impacted the heavily armored hull of the amphibious tank, causing a brilliant flash of light and sending shards of metal flying through the air. Inside the tank, the crew was thrown around violently. Smoke poured from damaged electronics obscuring the crew's vision. As the tank commander shouted orders, several additional 30 mm rounds struck the tank, killing everyone inside. Instantly, secondary explosions ripped the tank completely apart.

As the last rounds were fired, the driver turned the Mk1 so sharply that Snake Eyes thought they would roll, which would have been a big pisser. He could feel the four massive tires fight to gain traction. Gunny felt the left side of the vehicle lift from the ground, then just as quickly settle back down as the tires dug in, helping the combat vehicle take off in a new direction. As they did so, a gigantic explosion shook the entire armored vehicle but wasn't close enough to cause any damage.

As the battle for Woody Island diminished, the Marines began mop-up operations against little resistance as Chinese Marines threw their weapons down and held up their arms to surrender. These men would soon join their brethren from the initial takeover in the makeshift prison camp erected in the island town's park.

But out at sea, one more detail had to be attended to.

Sitting tight, Captain Colleen Panchak wanted to make sure their destruction of what, in essence, was a PLAN carrier didn't draw in any nearby Chinese submarines. She checked with Sonar.

"Conn, Sonar. Still have no contacts other than the sounds of the *Hainan* breaking up and settling on the sea floor and the *Changbaishan* dead in the water."

"Weapons, Conn," said *Oregon*'s captain, "Input your firing solutions for two fish for the *Changbaishan* and fire when ready."

A moment passed. "Conn, Weapons. Two torpedoes away."

Everyone was silent for a few seconds.

"Conn, Weapons. Confirm both torpedoes have acquired the target, and both have a lock. Three minutes until impact."

"Good job, Weapons," said Panchak. "Helm, new course one-eight-zero. Set depth six hundred feet ahead flank. Secure from GQ, except radar. Let's get out of here."

On the surface of the South China Sea, the Chinese amphibious ship *Changbaishan* was dead in the water, and the firing solution had been a simple math equation for the weapons officers aboard the *Oregon*. As programmed, both MK 48 torpedoes detonated directly underneath the *Changbaishan*. The massive pressure bubble from the gigantic explosion sliced through the ship's bulk, snapping the keel. With just minutes to evacuate, the ship's crew had little chance. Only fourteen survivors were left bobbing in the sea.

The PLAN sent rescue helicopters and a Y-8 anti-submarine aircraft, but the USS *Oregon* escaped outside their search radius. The second battle for Woody Island was a significant success, and the United States planned to exploit it. Reinforcements, resupply, and additional air assets were en route as the last bullet was fired.

# Chapter 88



*PLARF HEADQUARTERS*
Qinghe, Haidian District of Beijing, China


General Li Jung was a conspirator in overthrowing the president of China. Still, he worked best in the background behind his only boss, General Wang Yong, who President Zhang had almost shot.

After the president's demonstrative gunshot, Li carefully followed Wang into the bathroom and promptly locked the door. Getting inches from his boss's pale face, Li exclaimed, "Do we do something now, or do we wait for this crazy man to set our country back decades? He has gone off the rails, Wang. We have to act now before it is too late."

Still visibly shaking from the encounter with the president, Wang, who had learned of the conspiracy but kept it from Li and everyone else to keep his options open, said, "Yes, I've had enough. I'm only moments away from being hauled to who knows where. Tell me where we stand quickly—I must get back in there." He motioned with his head in the direction of the door.

"With the loss of Woody Island and key radar installations," Li said, "and with evidence that Taiwan will not give up anytime soon, we must act. But we also have no choice but to put the entire inventory of ballistic missiles back online, or Zhang will kill us all.

"Premier Ye and former president Wan Jun have used their immense influence and pressure to line up all the necessary party elites to step forward once they are sure our plan can work. By neutralizing our ballistic missile stockpile by inserting bogus codes into the software, we have successfully tied the hands of the missile force and, thus, the president. But we can't stall anymore. We must act now."

General Wang thought long enough to visualize himself before a firing squad and said, "Do we have the kitchen staff on board?"

"Yes, of course," Li said, "they will do anything I tell them. They understand their lives depend on following my orders."

Without hesitation, General Wang Yong agreed to move forward, removing the last hurdle the conspirators believed they needed. "Make it happen."

In the kitchen, the head chef for the past year and a half, Bingwen Lai, was preparing for the president's 3:00 p.m. snack of unfermented green tea served in a bowl. Along with the tea were exactly two plums, each 5 cm long. For the past generation, most Chinese had preferred their tea in a mug with lids and handles. President Zhang was old school and took his tea from a bowl like his father had.

Seeing Li approaching, Bingwen didn't like the look on Li's face. Bingwen knew longevity depended on perfection, and he was a master. The chef also understood that the previous one overcooked a meal and was never heard from again. He would not suffer the same fate; he would play whatever game was necessary to keep his head on his shoulders.

Not even bothering to look around the kitchen, Li approached Bingwen with a small bottle. Everyone within sight looked the other way so they could later say they had seen nothing unusual between the chef and the general.

"Listen, chef," said an intense Li, "the time has come to stop this madman. I want you to put this"—he handed the chef the tiny bottle—"in Zhang's bowl of tea and make sure he suspects nothing. Do you understand?" Bingwen nodded his head in the affirmative.

"No, do you understand? You can't screw this up. I want the man out cold right away."

"Yes, general, I understand. I'm very adept at what you ask, having used drugs several times in the past—part of the job, you could say."

"Use the entire bottle. The proper dose has been measured out carefully." Lin turned away, walked a few steps, stopped, and looked around the kitchen, staring at each set of eyes in the room to ensure he saw no one he couldn't trust. No one in the kitchen dared to look back at such a powerful man.

Bingwen carefully poured the contents of the small bottle of GHB, gamma-Hydroxybutyric acid, into the tea he would serve the president of China in five minutes. The dose was enough to incapacitate Zhang but not kill him.

At precisely 3:00 p.m., Bingwen entered the control center and climbed the four steps up to the large desk where President Zhang was sitting. As always, he set the tea and plums on the top right corner of the desk and quickly faded from sight.

True to form, the president picked up one of the plums and devoured it in one bite. When he reached for the bowl of tea, he stopped and used both hands to smack away again at a keyboard that didn't seem to cooperate. He mumbled something, but the people around him pretended to hear nothing.

Ordering out loud to no one in particular, Zhang said, "Get me, Wang. Right now." Someone yelled yes, sir, and disappeared through the same door Wang had walked through minutes ago.

Picking up his bowl of tea that was cooling off, Zhang took a big gulp just as Wang walked toward his perch that towered above everyone else in the room.

"Well, general, I almost saved the cost of a firing squad, which is still awaiting my order. Tell me what you are going to do for your country right now." Zhang took another big gulp of his favorite tea, which he swore tasted slightly salty. Strange, he thought, he would talk about this with his chef.

Wang noticed the president's hands were not as steady as usual when he took his second drink. "Mr. President, you have given me only a few minutes, but I did consult with our engineers, and I have a solution."

"Finally," said the president. "Tell me . . . no . . . tell . . . me . . . what's . . . wrong . . . with m . . . ." The president tried to jump up from his chair, but while doing so, lost consciousness and fell off the side of the raised platform. He plunged five meters, snapping his neck when his head hit the concrete floor, making a loud audible thud.

At first, no one moved or spoke. Everything seemed to have happened in slow motion except the dreadful smack of Zhang's head that split open leaving a growing pool of blood. Wang acted first, rushing over to the president and gently picking up his head to cradle it in his lap.

"Get a doctor, get a doctor," Wang screamed. Immediately, several men crashed together at a door as they rushed out to find one. The scene would have been comical if the situation wasn't so dire.

As blood soaked into the uniform pants of the second in command of the PLA, Wang rocked back and forth ever so slightly, repeating the president's name. He had to congratulate himself on this scenario and was already preparing to take overall command of the PLA now that it appeared the president had had a stroke from all the stress and fell off the platform. He would have his staff remove the president's uneaten snack and tea at the appropriate time.

In the background, General Li looked on, trying his best to hide a smile that kept wanting to creep upon his lips. He was a professional; he would manage.

After the president's doctor arrived, he felt for a pulse, mainly to look like he was trying to do something for a man who was obviously dead. The doctor slowly shook his head back and forth, indicating that China's president was dead. He then gently held the deceased president's head so General Wang could remove himself. Someone brought a blanket and carefully placed it over former president Zhang.

Covered in blood, General Wang appeared as if he had been seriously wounded. He climbed the steps to the top of the platform overlooking the vast room and addressed his troops.

"I don't think anyone in this room worked more closely with our dear president than me. While we had our disagreements, my respect and love for the man were everlasting. As the second in command only to the president, I now command all aspects of our beloved People's Liberation Army. I need each of you to follow my orders as if they came from the mouth of the president—this is how he would have wanted it. We must continue our mission and our war against the United States. Please return to work, and may the president look after us all. General Li, in my office."

As the two generals exited, Bingwen entered the room and removed the unfinished snack and tea. It was taken care of in a blink.

With the support of the conspirators, Premier Ye Jiang, Li Zhang from the State Council, General Li Jung, and the commander of all PLA forces, General Wang Yong, former president Wan Jun served as interim president of China. The combined power of these men ensured there were no challengers who dared step forward. To the world, the PRC demonstrated that more level heads were guiding the country toward a peaceful existence and returning to the status quo with Taiwan.

A day after the unfortunate death of President Zhang Wei from what appeared to be a stroke (confirmed a month later in an official medical report listing the cause of death as an ischemic stroke), President Wan Jun phoned the president of the United States, Mark Taylor. In a conciliatory phone call, Wan explained that he had ordered all PLA forces to stand down immediately. All hostilities against the United States and its allies would cease immediately.

The interim president clarified that no further action would be taken against Taiwan and that China would stop all reunification attempts. But he did ask that the US respect the One-China principle.

"But Mr. President," said Taylor, "the most salient problem facing my countrymen and I is that you invaded our nation without warning or provocation and bombed two of our cities, killing thousands of Americans, not to mention destroying three of our aircraft carriers and a fourth at sea. I have senators who want to nuke you for what your country did."

"President Taylor, we had a rogue president that got it all wrong. He wanted reunification with Taiwan and never understood the cost to our country. Wiser heads eventually prevailed, and with his unfortunate death, we can step forward with plans to put this country on a peaceful path with the world. My record as president demonstrated this, as will my replacement. You have my word on this."

After three months of Congressional hearings and heated discussions on the Hill, TV talk shows, social media editorials in every newspaper in the country, and at every dinner table, a consensus was finally reached on the Chinese bombing of the United States. It was written that:

- The People's Republic of China will compensate the families of each American killed in the bombings at Newport News Shipyard and Naval Base San Diego $500,000 for each American killed.
- The PRC will make reparations of $52 billion for the destruction of three US aircraft carriers and the damage to the USS *Nimitz*.
- PRC will concede Yongxing Island, known in the West as Woody Island to the United States.
- The PRC will sign a proclamation agreeing that Taiwan retains its democracy as it is today, and that the PRC has a nonintervention policy for fifty years. After fifty years, the issue of reunification can be addressed if both parties agree.

Although there was a call to restrict the PRC's annual military spending from 5 percent to 2 percent (as a percent of GDP) for five years, the majority in Congress felt the measure was too restrictive and would be difficult to enforce. It was clear to Washington that Americans generally wanted to return to peaceful coexistence with China, a country that had now sworn off war as a means of national policy, not unlike what Japan did at the end of World War II.

Behind the scenes, the Chinese are patient people who have watched the sands of time slowly flow as they contemplated when they might be reunited with their brothers and sisters in Taiwan. Like the unpredictable winds of autumn, the people could blow the PRC back to a more aggressive policy of reunification with Taiwan. But for now, most agreed and supported the proclamation signed by the new president of China, who promised cooperation and peaceful consistence with the world, especially the United States.

As the snow slowly drifted down from dreary skies, the white flakes settled on the newest bronze statue of those surrounding Tiananmen Square in the heart of Beijing. As statues went, it was somewhat unusual in that it showed a man bent over a computer keyboard staring up with a look of impending death. On the base of the granite stand was a simple proverb:

THE PATH OF DUTY LIES IN WHAT IS NEAR AT HAND IN
PROTECTING AND SERVING YOUR COUNTRY
DR. DONG LIAN